The Geomagician

The Geomagician

Jennifer Mandula

DEL REY

UK | USA | Canada | Ireland | Australia
India | New Zealand | South Africa

Del Rey is part of the Penguin Random House group of companies
whose addresses can be found at global.penguinrandomhouse.com

Penguin Random House UK,
One Embassy Gardens, 8 Viaduct Gardens, London SW11 7BW

penguin.co.uk

First published in the US by Del Rey, an imprint of Random House,
a division of Penguin Random House LLC, 2026
First published in the UK by Del Rey 2026
001

Copyright © Jennifer Mandula, 2026

The moral right of the author has been asserted

Penguin Random House values and supports copyright. Copyright fuels creativity, encourages diverse voices, promotes freedom of expression and supports a vibrant culture. Thank you for purchasing an authorised edition of this book and for respecting intellectual property laws by not reproducing, scanning or distributing any part of it by any means without permission. You are supporting authors and enabling Penguin Random House to continue to publish books for everyone. No part of this book may be used or reproduced in any manner for the purpose of training artificial intelligence technologies or systems. In accordance with Article 4(3) of the DSM Directive 2019/790, Penguin Random House expressly reserves this work from the text and data mining exception.

Adobe Stock Illustrations: Art used on chapter openers:
OlgaKorneeva (plants), lynea (spiral seashell), Morphart (trilobites),
Renee (trilobite), ruskpp (dinosaur skeleton), aliakseizykau (pterodactyl);
space break ornament: Natalia (vintage flourish)

Book design by Sara Bereta

Printed and bound in Great Britain by Clays Ltd, Elcograf S.p.A.

The authorised representative in the EEA is Penguin Random House Ireland,
Morrison Chambers, 32 Nassau Street, Dublin D02 YH68

A CIP catalogue record for this book is available from the British Library

ISBN: 978–1–529–95400–5 (hardback)
ISBN: 978–1–529–95401–2 (trade paperback)

Penguin Random House is committed to a sustainable future
for our business, our readers and our planet. This book is made
from Forest Stewardship Council® certified paper.

For my daughters

The Geomagician

Chapter 1

Every fossil is a miracle. All living things—*regno animalium et vegetabilium*—eventually die, and the vast majority of these, swallowed by earth or exposed to the elements, fall, in the end, to dust. That's a rather romantic summary of the messy business of decomposition, but the point is, few organisms escape that fate. Any that do are one in a million.

That's what I wanted to say to the tourist with the yellow dress, when she muttered to her husband, "But they're just *seashells.*"

I bit my tongue. My rent was two months overdue, and these were the first customers in almost as long.

So instead of giving a lecture about death and decay as I wanted, I set down the crinoid fossil I was cleaning and came round the counter.

"The disks in the case to your left are actually ichthyosaur vertebrae."

I tried to smile; Lucy always said I was too surly with customers. "Ichthyosaurs looked something like ugly, fat dolphins, we think, but with the jaws of a crocodile."

Even I heard the pride in my voice as I gestured to the plaster cast of an ichthyosaur skeleton, framed and mounted on the wall behind my counter.

That was my first great find. I was twelve years old the summer I found the skull, half-buried. It took me another year to find the rest: the curving spine, the strange flippers, the humped back. Over my mother's protests, I arranged it on our dining room table, piecing the monster back together with skill guided by instinct. I sold the specimen for twenty-three pounds to my mentor, William Buckland.

That ichthyosaur was the very first found in England. The discovery, and the furious scholarship in its wake, had made the careers of half the geomagicians in England.

It always cut like a knife to think of the gentlemen scholars in their wood-paneled studies, surrounded by shelves of books I could never afford, drafting society papers by lamplight—writing about *my* finds. Only Buckland ever even mentioned my name.

And Henry.

The reminder was a betrayal, and I scowled at the traitorous thought.

Fine. And Henry.

Henry Stanton, for all his many, many flaws, did cite my name when he discussed my discoveries. Though that certainly didn't outweigh his other transgressions.

The tourist husband picked up one of the round, concave stone disks, weighing it in his palm.

"They make excellent reliqs," I said quickly. "Good storage capacity in one that size."

The wife frowned. "They're awfully plain-looking. Do you have any of the swirling ones?" She traced a spiral in the air.

"Ammonites. Yes."

I walked her to the case. Ammonites were my bestseller with women. Men tended to prefer bones from ichthyosaurs or plesiosaurs. Belemnites—long, bullet-shaped shells that once housed ancient squids—could go either way. They always looked nice on a chain.

My ammonites were arranged in rows, from smallest to largest, on a bed of felted wool. I couldn't afford the velvet that geomagicians preferred for their personal collections.

"I do have several larger ones, if you're interested." I pointed across the shop, to the cabinet where I kept rarer finds—partial skeletons, or, say, ammonites too large to wear as a reliq, but that would look lovely on display in a rich woman's home.

The woman looked at me properly for the first time, her eyebrows climbing.

I flushed, seeing myself as she must: plain-faced and beak-nosed, my brown skirts mud-streaked and my hair in a black tangle of a crooked bun. She touched her cheek, and I mirrored the gesture. I'd wiped my face after hunting this morning, but clearly not well enough.

I scrubbed with the heel of my hand.

"Other side," she said gently, and I scowled, turning back to my counter.

"Let me know if I can help you with anything else."

As the wife browsed, I worked furiously at the crinoid stem, chipping dried mud from the grooves, then brushing and blowing it loose.

I'd hunted more than three hours this morning, wading through clay-thick mud and searching the slippery limestone cliffs for any sign of fossils. But all I found were the usual little ones—belemnites and small ammonites, mollusk and bivalve shells. The seashells, as she called them. They *were* miracles. Really, they were. But miracles couldn't pay Mr. Bolington when he came tomorrow and demanded the rent I owed.

If it were summer, and not dreary, dawdling April, Lyme Regis would be crawling with tourists eager to take the sea air. I would set up my table out front, and sell at a markup most tourists wouldn't question. But locals know better. You could stub your toe on an ichthyosaur vertebra—*verteberries,* we called them as children—and hardly bother to stop. Lyme Regis is probably the only place in England where even the poor have fossil reliqs to collect their magic.

What I needed was a skull. I could sell a good skull to a collector and cover the March and April rent on the store and flat, plus part of May's. I would have to go out hunting again, after I closed the shop.

"Ahem."

I jumped. The husband was leaning against my work-counter, his elbow slung casually over the lip.

"I studied with Buckland, you know. At Oxford."

I set down my pick.

I'd known William Buckland most of my life. My father came early to fossil hunting; some reliquemist discovered fossils held magic even better than gold or gems, and soon educated men arrived in Lyme Regis in search of fossils to sell to the slickers. The Geomagical Society of London was founded soon after, dually chartered to study the emerging field of geomagic, and to supply reliquemists with fossils for enchantment.

Father closed his carpentry business—which was never much of a success anyway—and devoted himself full time to fossil hunting. He sold to Buckland many times, and after he died, the professor bought from me instead.

Buckland still came to Lyme Regis several times a year so that we could hunt fossils together. He was a capable searcher, with good instincts and a sharp eye, and he never complained about the cold rain or his muddied boots the way some of the other geomagicians did.

I adored and admired William Buckland in equal measure, but right now, I was furious with him.

"Did he send you, then?" I narrowed my eyes as I shuffled through my stack of papers. I waved the letter before his face. "It wasn't enough to write it? Buckland thought he had to send some lackey to try and soothe my pride? You're not even an actual geomagician, are you? You didn't recognize the plesiosaur fin over there; I saw you walk right past it without a glance. And yet Buckland sent *you*?"

The man stammered. He'd backed up during my tirade, and his wife rushed over to take his hand.

"Miss Anning," the man said stiffly, frowning, "I haven't spoken to William Buckland in three years."

I dropped my waving arm. "Oh. Oh, dear."

"You are correct. I am not a geomagician. I am a barrister. And I only meant to tell you that I learned of your shop from the professor. Buckland told all his students that if we wanted to buy the best fossils in England, we ought to visit Anning's Fossil Depot, in Lyme Regis. Come, darling. We can buy you that ammonite somewhere else."

His wife sniffed, nose up, and looped her arm through his.

"Wait, please, I'm sorry—"

The bells on the door jangled merrily as it slammed shut behind them.

Chapter 2

After you survive a lightning strike, everyone will say you were saved for a reason. Why else would God have stayed His hand? The burden of those expectations—of greatness, of brilliance, of success—is a heavy weight to bear.

I know this from experience.

Just before my father died, he called me to his bed. I could hardly see his face through my tears. His cheeks were sunken, and his hand was boned and paled like an old man's.

"My little Mary," Father said to me, with the rasp of death already in his throat. "God Himself has blessed you. You are bound for great things, my girl. Great, great things."

I wished it were a fluke of fate instead. An accident of chance. Easier that than to believe I'd been chosen by God, and to know that I had failed.

On the day of the storm, my mother was having one of her spells. What if she had been well? The neighbor girl, Elizabeth, offered to watch me. What if she hadn't? When the rain rolled in, heavy clouds and rumbling thunder, Elizabeth took shelter under an elm. What if she'd chosen the oak instead?

I imagine, sometimes, how Elizabeth would've held me close. I was scarcely one year old; small and sickly, I've been told. I might have trembled. Might have cried. Maybe she whispered into my ear, softly. *It's only a storm. It will be all right.*

I wish, sometimes, that I could remember it. Usually I'm glad I can't.

When the lightning came, the current ripped through the trunk. Elizabeth died instantly, along with two others.

I was the only survivor under the elm.

I carry that with me. How could I not? I lived, and they died. I had to be great, for them. From my earliest memories, I knew I was meant to mark this world, this earth, this *life*, because those three women never had the chance.

Which is why every failure burned; every bill and debt and back-owed rent and walk to the slicks when there was nothing left. *God Himself has blessed you, and this is the best you can do with it?*

I slumped at my desk, head in my hands.

The letter from Buckland was already worn soft from rereading, but I picked it up again, now skimming to the final blow.

. . . these things take time, Mary. There are delicate questions at play, and difficult to address quickly . . .

The questions weren't delicate. Only my sex was. I was a woman. According to the Geomagical Society's Charter, candidates had to be proposed by an existing member, and no woman had ever even been nominated, let alone elected by majority vote.

I didn't resent that truth. What I resented was that Buckland wouldn't even *try*. Why not put my name forth, explain my accomplishments, and see how the votes fell out?

Well, I knew why: the current Society president had announced plans to step down at the annual meeting in June, and Buckland—currently vice president—was actively campaigning to replace him. Which meant Buckland was even more concerned about his reputation than usual.

There were a few other geomagicians to whom I often sold fossils. But no one I knew well enough to ask for nomination. Buckland was my only hope.

It is my sincerest hope that we will see you named a geomagician within the decade, he wrote. *I know this will be a disappointment, but I can only urge you to give the matter time.*

Except I didn't have time to give. Besides the rent I owed for my shop and the flat upstairs, my Aunt Patricia had written three times this month, begging funds to pay for Mother's medical care. My purse was dry.

Even before Father's death, we were poor, and after came grim, lean years of grief, where only the slicks and Parish charity kept us fed. Mother was useless, but my skill with fossils had been our salvation. With Buckland's help and connections, I made a name for myself. Collectors, geomagicians, and artisanal reliq-makers all flocked to Lyme Regis to buy the things I unearthed. For a few years, I thought I was finally free. Safe. That's when I signed the lease for the shop and the flat above.

Oh, I'd been a fool. I could only sell what the earth and sea unveiled, and I'd made no more great discoveries—the kind that could fill my coffers—in years.

But Society members received an annuity. It was a modest salary, but more than I'd ever dreamed in my life. I thought I might be able to plead a bit more time from my landlord if I knew I would be named a geomagician in three months, with the income to match.

And I deserved it. Buckland knew that, too. It wasn't arrogance to call myself the most accomplished fossilist in England, and possibly the whole of Europe: I'd uncovered nearly all the best ichthyosaur and plesiosaur specimens. Apparently, one of my plesiosaur skeletons was even displayed in the atrium of the Geomagical Society's Palmanaeus House.

So, I had gathered all my courage, set aside my pride, and written the letter. I had asked him, point-blank, to put my name forward in nomination at the annual meeting.

I'd tried not to let my desperation show, but I now feared it had seeped onto the page with the ink.

There was only one option left. The one option always available to those of us desperate and poor enough to take it.

It's a terrible thing, to sell one's magic. To take a bit of yourself, a piece of your very soul, and hand it over for coin.

But as long as there has been magic—or as long as there have been reliquaries, I suppose—magic has been bought and sold. Bought by the richest; sold by the poorest.

Because what use was a little magic—only enough for fire-starting or scrape-healing, if you managed to store enough—when a little coin could buy bread? No reliq could hold enough magic to build a shelter or summon a meal. Not even a fossil.

I touched the reliq hanging round my own neck. A delicate, perfect ammonite—yes; I might be a plain and unfashionable one, but I *was* still a woman, and ammonites *are* lovely—strung on a leather thong.

I didn't use much magic, day to day. Once in a while, I might tap a reliq to dust the top of the cabinets, or sharpen my knives, but mostly I held my magic in reserve, too scarred by those dark years. I'd last tapped my reliquary six weeks ago, mending my boots when the sole fell off and I couldn't afford the cobbler's fee. And a good thing, too, because that meant the reliq around my neck was full again. I'd get a decent price for it in the slicks.

My stomach was sour, my mouth dry. I could already hear Lucy's tutting disapproval about how "participation grants legitimacy," or something similarly idealistic pulled straight from her Promethean pamphlets. But I wasn't the daughter of a viscount, even a disinherited one like Lucy Murray, witch of Lyme Regis. If Lucy were ever on the verge of eviction and skipping meals to save the coin, she could just write to her brother, Edgar, and ask for a loan.

Yes, yes, *fine*, I could, too. We'd all been dear friends, once, that summer I was fifteen. That brightest year of my life, now half a lifetime past. But I could never ask Edgar for money. Just as I would never ask Lucy.

She'd insisted, once, and I wallowed in shame for weeks, trying to repay her. Eventually I wrote to a Swiss geomagician and agreed to sell the precious collection of ichthyosaur eye-rings he wanted.

I had hoped to write my first real, scholarly paper about those eye-rings. Most geomagicians assumed the ichthyosaur would have hunted in shallows, or near the surface, like the crocodile and dolphin it resembled. But from my analysis of the sclerotic rings of their eyes—like a bony, cored round of pineapple—I suspected the creatures were actually deep-water hunters.

The Swiss geomagician came to the same conclusion. His paper, *On the Optical Structures of the Ichthyosaur and Its Hunting*

Patterns, was published the following year. Buckland sent me a translated copy.

I should have just gone to the slicks. It might be terrible, but it was honest. And the shame, at least, was private.

My shop was on the main promenade, behind the seawall. On stormy days I could see the waves crashing, white froth and spray, and on pleasant ones I watched couples with parasols walking along the sand. Today the sky was ominous, bruised with roiling clouds, and the street out front was nearly empty. If I was going to go, I might as well get on with it. Storm be damned.

I carefully wiped and stored my tools, then tidied the display counters a bit, dawdling while I arranged a tray of shining belemnites. I tucked the paper I was reading, *Observations on the Dietary Habits of the Marine 'Plesiosaurus'* by Archibald Taylor, into my satchel. It was one of my plesiosaurs Mr. Taylor had observed, and it would cheer me up to add my own annotated corrections.

I put on my black top hat and quilted coat, then locked up the shop. I'd come back afterward to grab my supplies for an evening hunt.

I had to hold my hat as the wind tried to snatch it, sputtering and spitting the loose strands of hair that whipped into my mouth. My tongue tasted iron, and gooseflesh rose on my arms. There was a sensation of the air pulled taut.

Lightning.

I squared my shoulders and set off toward Broad Street. I was never afraid of lightning.

Lyme Regis sloped to the sea, the main road splitting the town. Off this trunk branched lanes and alleyways, some with houses or flats, others with shops, like Butcher's Row and Baker's Alley. The rich of Lyme Regis, and the businesses they frequented, clustered here in the upper western quarter off the main road. A view of the sea but little risk of flooding. That's where Edgar and Lucy stayed, the summer they spent in Lyme Regis.

And Henry's mother still lived nearby, actually, in that very whitewashed house with a turret, next to a haberdasher. Reliqlamps glowed in the window, illuminating the grand, empty library.

The ache of my longing surprised me. It was almost fifteen years since I'd sprawled on that red-and-gold rug, pulling books from those shelves in stacks tall as my nose, greedy for everything—Latin and Greek, the science magics and philosophy, history and theomagic—that Henry and Edgar had to teach.

I turned away before the memory could burrow too deep. The streets were almost empty. I could smell rain on the wind, and it felt like twilight, even though sunset should be hours away.

It would be an awful storm. That put a spring in my step. Storms meant fossils. The hunting would be good. *Maybe I should wait*, I thought. *Go straight to the beach and see if the storm shakes anything out of the cliffs—*

No. I'd already made up my mind. I couldn't keep hoping.

<hr />

They're called the slicks because of the serum. Shining, black, and viscous. Slippery and staining. Lucy says larger towns often have more than one slicker. In London, she says, there are even multiple reliquemical quarters in different areas of the city, with slickers competing for business. I asked once if that meant the rates were different, so people would use one slicker over another. *You would think so,* she'd said darkly. She explained the government set the rate-of-pay, and the Reliquemical Guild frowned on anyone who strayed.

But slickers had other tactics, Lucy said, to ensure repeat business. Unenforceable contracts given to the illiterate, requiring exclusivity. Pallet beds for the homeless, to lure them in. A hunk of bread and butter when the transactions were complete.

There was only one slicker in Lyme Regis, so she didn't have to resort to any tactics. The desperate would come to her anyway.

I sat on a wooden bench in the cramped waiting room, reading the Taylor paper. I muttered to myself as I made notes in the margins, and the man across from me—a fisherman, by the smell—avoided eye contact.

The black door, marked with the guild's silver crest, opened. A hooded figure hurried out. The slicker called the fisherman back—not by name; we didn't give names here—and he disappeared. The black door closed again.

Plesiosaurs have thin, pointed teeth. Good for catching small fish and cephalopods, true, but Taylor was wrong to say these comprised the whole of their diet. I'd once seen remnants of gastropod shell in the stomach region of a partial plesiosaur skeleton. I wasn't sure how they managed it, given their teeth and jaw structure, but it was clear their diet was more varied than Taylor suggested.

"I'm ready for you." The slicker beckoned. I stuffed away the paper.

It was always cool behind the black door, as if the air temperature dropped several degrees. The room smelled oily and acrid, a little like sulfur. Two reliq-lamps gave off a warm yellow glow, despite the black-painted walls. The slicker leaned against her stool.

Her name was Arabella Greene, but I couldn't remember how I learned it. People only ever called her "the slicker"—or, if she was within earshot, the *reliquemist*. She'd been the town's slicker long before I was born, but her face was hardly lined, and her hair only dusted gray. Lucy theorized there was something in the serum that did it. "*Why is it every slicker is the most beautiful person you've ever met?*" she'd whispered once, when we passed Arabella in town. I'd shrugged; I'd only ever met the one.

The slicker never made small talk. I appreciated that.

"Consignment, enchantment, or sale?" Her tone was clipped.

I'd never worked consignment. You had to put down some kind of collateral, and the slicker provided the base reliq, probably bone or shell or metal. You wore it for a week or so—long enough to fill—and then returned it for your payment and collateral. The reliq you filled could then be resold.

I had brought my own objects to be enchanted, though. I'd brought this same ammonite to her a few years ago and paid the fee to have it turned into a reliq capable of collecting and storing my magic.

"Sale."

I reached into my collar and slipped off the ammonite. I knew it was coming, but the overwhelming sensation of *wrongness* still caught me off guard as the fossil's warmth left my skin. I swallowed, nostrils flaring. That sensation, a curdling in my stomach, would linger a few days. Best just to ignore it.

I saw the flash of nails as her palm turned over, the skin around them black from the serum.

She took my ammonite and turned to her desk, where serum

and other chemicals bubbled away in tubes of glass. She worked quickly, dropping my ammonite into something clear that might have been vinegar, and measuring it against the tick marks on the side and jotting down notes. Then she weighed it on a set of scales.

Slickers paid out the set-rate based on the quantity of magic stored in the object.

Any object could be turned into a reliq, but not everything was a good choice. Fabric, for example, was a very poor vessel for reliqs. Any magic leaches immediately through the strands. The same for wood. Stone was better, though not by much, but shells and bone were fair, and affordable. Those are common reliqs among the poor. For the rich, metal is a reliable holder, and gems, too, but obviously expensive. But of all the substances tried and tested, fossils, we know now, are the best.

There was no magic in reliquemistry, any more than there was in geomagic. The magic was metaphorical here; it was careful science that made everyday objects capable of holding magic. I had some begrudging respect for that.

The precise chemical composition of the serum was known only to practitioners. But it was an open secret that bitumen—pitch, or tar—was one of the main ingredients in the formula. That much was obvious from the smell.

"I can give you six shillings, three pence."

I winced. My rent was almost two pounds a month. But at least it was something I could hand to Mr. Bolington tomorrow. I just had to hope that would buy me more time.

I would write more letters, try to sell off more of my collection. Maybe I could take on some housecleaning work, too. It would cut into time for fossil hunting, but at least that would be cash, and not hope. I swallowed.

"Yes. All right."

She nodded and took out the wooden payment box.

The black door burst open. Coins clattered as the slicker and I both jumped.

Lucy Murray panted in the doorway, her amber eyes huge.

My face flushed hot—shame that Lucy would catch me here, tainted coin nearly in my palm—but annoyance followed close behind. I had no patience for a lecture. I couldn't afford her ideals today. Not with rent due tomorrow.

"*Why*," I half hissed, half groaned, "can't you ever mind your own business?"

Lucy ignored my seething. Her eyes sparked as she said, "Fishermen are reporting a landslide near Black Ven. Big one."

My anger turned to a thrill of hope, probably just as she'd anticipated.

Not all landslides revealed treasures. But nearly every wondrous discovery—the first ichthyosaur, my best plesiosaur—had followed one. And Black Ven . . .

I looked between the indifferent slicker and Lucy, at war with myself. The slicker would soon close for the night, and Bolington expected rent first thing in the morning. But if I sold my reliq now, I would have no magic for the search.

"I'm sorry," I said finally. "May I have my reliq back, please?"

The slicker shrugged, the barest hint of amusement on her lips as she set the coin box on the counter and returned my ammonite. "As you wish."

Lucy grabbed my hand, and we hurried out into the storm. The cold wind stung my lips, but my reliq was warm against my chest, and my blood thrummed with the thrill of the hunt.

Chapter 3

"I TOLD YOU," LUCY SAID, RAISING HER VOICE TO BE HEARD over the wind as we tried not to slip on the cobblestones, wet with the mist. "If you ever need money, I can help. I *want* to help. You don't have to go to the slicks!"

"And I told you"—I stumbled, and she caught me by the elbow—"not to track me with magic like that. It's unsettling."

"All right, next time I hear about a huge landslide, I'll keep it to myself."

I scowled, and she grinned.

Lucy was a witch. Witches didn't need reliquaries. Somehow, they were able to store and access power without an object to harness it, and those reserves ran much, much deeper than any reliquary could, and refilled far faster.

That meant Lucy had almost limitless magic. She once even managed to breathe underwater, though afterward she was stuck in bed for three days recovering.

But she could easily do things—like track me through town—

that even the wealthiest, with their troves of reliqs, would be hard-pressed to manage.

Theomagicians and philosophers posed a range of explanations for the phenomenon of witchery. Why could some people—one in ten thousand, maybe fewer—use magic without a reliq?

In the old days, people thought witches used other people as their reliqs, draining their magic and life force at once. *Vampyrism de l'âme,* they'd called it. Vampyrism of the soul.

I shivered, watching Lucy's honey-colored braid bounce across her back, thinking of all the witches who burned back then, before the Witch Queen split England from the Catholic Church. Some people might cross to the other side of the street when a witch passed, but at least we didn't tie them to stakes and light them aflame anymore.

The glow of the streetlamps reflected in the glassy pools we splashed through. We stopped at my shop, and I grabbed my tools, hooking my belt and swinging a canvas bag over my shoulder.

"I won't be long," I said, but Lucy shook her head.

"I'm coming with you."

"What? But why?"

Lucy was a good friend, so she listened patiently when I recounted my fossil hunts or summarized some inane paper from an underqualified geomagician. But she didn't care a whit about fossils beyond that. Her passions were far more political.

"Well. It is a landslide on Black Ven," was all she said.

I nodded, throat tight. We locked up again, walking east, first over the promenade, then across the sand, until the lights and sounds of town faded.

I walked these beaches every day, my eye sweeping over the cliffs and surf. I knew when the tide was low, and when it would be high. I knew when stone had shifted. I knew where the gulls liked to roost, and where they hunted scuttling crabs. These were my lands.

Our footsteps slapped at damp sand and stone as we dodged the bubbling surf. The sound of the waves was rhythmic and urgent as they washed in and out and nipped our heels: *hurry, hurry—hurry!*

We came into the curve of the cliff and saw the landslide at the same moment.

Lucy swore softly.

The cliffs here were lime and shale, laid in a pattern of sheets that can look almost brick-like with their jutting, sharp edges. This one had been sheared away, sliced like cake. And the fallen stone had unrolled itself, unfurled down to the sea like a staircase of blue-gray stone, now slick with rain.

Waves crashed against it, thin white rivulets running down the steps.

The stone would be wet and treacherous to climb; with no time to settle, any section could slip farther to the sea or crumble away. My heart pinched with fear.

"Mary?" Lucy said, and I heard my own thoughts echoed in my friend's questioning voice.

My father had died after a landslide like this, in this same place.

The ground, too loose, slid away faster than he could catch his balance, and Father had fallen. Whatever had broken in his spine had broken then.

I was there. I'd thrown aside the wicker basket—I remembered the shattering, rattling, of my shells and fossils breaking on stone as I ran to his side.

I remembered the sharp stubble of his jaw under my fingers as I begged him to hold on, just a minute more, both small hands pressed to his face. "Please," I wept, kneeling on wet-slicked stone just like this. "Please, Father."

My reliq, a small ammonite, warmed against my chest.

I hadn't used magic in weeks; I'd been saving it up to use for my next turn scrubbing the chamber pot, and my reliq was full. I pressed all my magic into my father, willing him to heal, but it was too little.

It was always too little.

If we'd been richer, we could have bought reliqs for the physiomagicians to use. Mother and I sold what we could. Everything of value. But it wasn't enough. It was never enough.

Father lingered a week in agony. I remembered those days perhaps too well, the smell of sweat and unwashed bedding, and the sound of his rattled breath. Mother sitting in the chair by his bed and worrying her hands like yarn. I was nine years old, and my father was my world, and then he was gone.

"Mary," Lucy said again. "Perhaps this was a bad idea. Maybe you should wait until tomorrow."

I shook my head. Lucy nodded and pressed her lips together, accepting my decision.

My gaze roved over the newly exposed rock, searching. Fossils could be found in a range of shades, from pale white to coppery brown to black. The color was determined by the mineral composition of the surrounding stone and what had leached into the bone. Even from here, I could tell I would find plenty of little fossils when we stepped close.

But because I knew these hills, these cliffs, these stones—I felt sure there would be something more. Not just ammonites or belemnites worth a few shillings, though I knew those were scattered all across these rocks. No. I wanted skeletons. The giants.

You are bound for great things, my girl, my father said.

I always felt him, here, on the beach, between rock and sea.

"I'm going to get closer," I said. "Stay back. Where it's safe."

Lucy laughed, her eyes sparkling. "Did you really think that would work?"

We scrambled over the sliding gravel and stone, catching ourselves and each other when we started to slip.

We reached the sheared-off cliff with only a few stumbles, necks craning back to see the top. It was a curiously sacred thing to look at a piece of earth that hadn't seen sunlight or air for millions of years.

I shivered, then chided myself. *Don't get excited. You've been lucky before, but it was only that.*

Well. A little skill, too.

There were tiny, broken bits of fossil shell embedded in the layers of striation, both whole—body fossils, the bone or shell replaced with mineral—and imprints where something had dissolved over time.

I reached out, ran my palm across the brick-like rectangles protruding from the sloped wall. I kept my fingertips on the stone as I began to walk, my eyes scanning up and down, searching for anomalies.

The wind whipped, and my lips tasted like salt. Despite my best efforts to keep a cool, rational head, hope fluttered in my breast. I felt somehow sure that something special was waiting in these rocks, even as my mind struggled to stay rational. To think like a geomagician.

Black Ven was a Blue Lias geomagical formation of the Jura limestone type, part of the Secondary Series. More ancient than chalk but younger than variegated sandstone, the Lias's layers of clay shale and limestone—and the marine life entombed within—were formed by sediment settling to the ocean floor, layer upon a thousand layers, year over a thousand years.

"That one's pretty, isn't it?" Lucy said, and I turned to see her pointing at a nicely preserved bivalve shell in some fallen stone.

"Hmm." I turned back to the cliff.

"Well, if I knew what you were searching for—"

"Lucy." I thrust out a hand as I caught my breath. The hair at the back of my neck rose. "Look."

She squinted as I pointed upward, about twenty feet overhead. Slender, brown, and fragile, it looked almost like a broken stick embedded in the rock.

"What is it?"

"Bone." The smile stretched across my face. "Fossilized bone."

Chapter 4

It was only a sliver, but bone meant skeleton. A vertebrate this low in the Blue Lias was likely an ichthyosaur or plesiosaur. Well. Or a fish.

I tried not to let my hope dim; fish weren't necessarily exciting, but a quality skeleton could pay the rent through to tourist season. And on the off chance it was something spectacular ...

"I'm going to climb up. Take a closer look," I said, tying my skirts into a knot above my knees. "Hold my hat."

Lucy wrinkled her nose. "Are you sure it's safe?"

I studied the sloping cliff, already destabilized from the earlier rockslide. I remembered my father's face, drawn and white after his fall. *No.* I wasn't sure. But I needed to see that bone.

"Why, Lucy Murray, I didn't think you even knew the word," I dodged the question, wiggling my foot into a foothold as I began the ascent.

Lucy gasped in mock offense, and I chuckled. Once, that summer I was fifteen, Lucy declared that she wanted to climb to the top of the village clocktower. Henry, Edgar, and I tried to talk her out of it. She was only thirteen, younger than the three of us, but she couldn't be deterred. And with her witch magic, she couldn't be stopped. In the end, we stood at the base of the tower and watched her climb.

I was never so fearless. Even now my mouth was dry. But the need to see—to find, to *know*—overrode the fear.

"And besides," I added, over my shoulder, "I know you'll catch me if I fall."

Thus assuaged, Lucy shouted out guidance, recommending outcropped holds for my fingers and feet. My boots were old and worn; I hadn't bought new ones in two years. But their threadbare quality proved a boon now, my toes and the leather working together to provide a firm grip on the crumbly rock face.

My pulse beat faster in my aching fingertips. I shimmied to the right, toward the bone, and briefly pulled my hand from the wall to brush away the top layer of dirt.

It was an unfamiliar shape. Bowed, almost. And chipped at one end—enough that I could tell the interior was . . .

Hollow. My heart leapt in my chest.

I checked that my feet were solidly anchored and then pulled a chisel from my belt to pry some of the stone loose.

I'd spent plenty of time with bird skeletons—pigeons or seagulls I found dead and used beetles and boiling to pick clean—and I was reminded at once of those bones. But that made no sense. This geomagical strata was older than birds.

I had the sense that I was on the edge, on the verge, of learning something *new*.

My left foot slipped.

I gasped and flung my body into the rock. The chisel fell with a clatter as I clung to the wall.

"Mary!" Lucy exclaimed.

I inhaled, the cold salt air helping to ground me.

"I'm fine." I exhaled. "I'm perfectly fine."

"I really think you should come down now." Her voice was thin and high. In all the years I'd known Lucy, I could count on one hand the times she'd expressed something close to *caution*. If Lucy thought this a bad idea, it probably was.

But I had to get that bone. I had to see if there were any others. I looked around, quickly assessing.

There was no time to build a scaffold. No time for a careful excavation. My reliq was full, but that wouldn't be anywhere close to enough magic for such a large working.

I want to help, Lucy told me when we left the slicker, and I knew it was true. I didn't want her money. But I would gladly use her magic.

"Actually, Luce," I called down, over my shoulder, "do you think you could carve out a cave?" I met her eyes and raised a brow. "Now, we both know precision isn't always your strength—"

"Oh, hush." Lucy laughed, but her cheeks reddened, likely remembering last week when she'd tried to magically stoke the fire and nearly burned down her cottage. "Are you sure that won't weaken the cliff?"

"It'll be safer than continuing to dangle here like a monkey in petticoats. If you make a little tunnel, I can climb in and extract the rest of the bone. Just be sure not to cut down into this layer. See where the stone changes?" I tapped at the rock just above my head. "I'll do that myself."

"And shall I fetch you some tea while I'm at it?" But Lucy was smiling as she moved her hands.

With a grinding, crunching rumble, the stone above my brow began to *swirl*. I squeezed my eyes shut as fine black dust fell across my nose and cheeks. I tried not to think what other fossils might be caught in the vortex, crushed to nothing. I opened one eye to peek as the hole deepened and darkened into a small, yawning mouth.

"Precise enough?" Lucy sniffed when she was done.

"Luce, you're a marvel—"

My praise twisted to a scream as part of the wall to my right peeled itself from the cliff and tumbled, striking and splitting as it fell with a sound like cracking thunder.

"Run!" I shouted down to her, as more cracks pinged across the cliff. "Get back! Go!"

Something hard struck my eyebrow, and I looked up, terror in my throat. More small stones fell, shrapnel-sharp, over my shoulders and arms. The cliff was going to slide again.

Lucy shrieked, but I didn't catch the words. I could only hope she'd run back toward the sea.

I heaved myself up into the cave mouth, tumbling into the darkness. I held my breath, counting the heartbeats in my ear—one, two, three—until the roar of the earth went still. Silence—horrible silence—stretched too long. Only crashing waves and howling wind.

"Mary! Mary!"

Oh, thank God. The cords of fear in my neck slackened, and my jaw unclenched.

I grunted as I tried to turn around. I have never been a dainty woman; my hips pressed at the sides of the cave, and the ceiling rock scraped painfully at my shoulder blades as I twisted back toward the opening. Perhaps I should have been more specific about the required cave dimensions.

I poked out my head. "Luce! I'm alive!"

She burst into relieved tears. "Right—well—you come down

from there at once, Mary Anning, or God help me I'll bring the whole cliff down on purpose this time!"

"In a minute," I said, starting to scoot backward on hands and knees. "I'm going to take a look around first."

She called me several awful names in response as I wiggled myself around again to properly study my surroundings.

I'd expected the cave to be shallow, but the tunnel stretched deep into the darkness of the cliff itself.

I cursed my lack of a lantern and pulled the ammonite reliq from my blouse. *Light,* I willed it, and the reliq began to glow, bouncing like a little star on my chest.

The light was dim, but my eyes adjusted, even as I crawled farther into the dark.

I'd only traveled a few feet when my fingers touched *something*, and I knew at once by the texture it was bone.

I worked furiously with a chisel and brush, hands shaking. Embedded in the stone were more fossilized bones like the one under the lip of the cliff: brown, long, thin, and *hollow.*

I wished again for a better light. And a notebook. But as I had neither, I did my best to memorize the exact layout: the bisecting spine, the skull, the triangular arch of the wings—for now I was sure they were wings.

I cleared the last of the dust and gravel, and the whole shape of it lay before me in the stone.

My skin pricked with goosebumps. I had read accounts of flying creatures out of Germany, but none had ever been found in England. Yet the sketches had looked like this. *Pterodactyl,* they called the creatures, kin to both bird and lizard.

There was an odd thing, though. An oval shape near what I guessed to be the creature's foot. I hadn't seen anything like that in the German sketches.

It took me a moment to make sense of what I was seeing, because it was so unexpected. I pulled the smallest chisel from my belt pouch and began to loosen the rock, careful not to disturb the main skeleton. The stone came free easily, gray and cool to my touch.

It was—somehow, remarkably, incredibly—an egg, which fit perfectly between my two cupped palms.

This alone was a second miracle find. Most geomagicians agreed that the ancient beasts likely laid eggs like birds or reptiles, but there was flimsy evidence. This was clear, though. An egg. Whole, and unbroken. Perfect.

I twisted to sit, hunched and cross-legged, and cradled the egg, staring with naked delight. It hardly seemed possible. *Shouldn't* be possible.

The pterodactyl was female. She'd died, here, with her clutch of eggs. Now that I knew what I was seeing, I recognized the rounded remnants of the other eggs.

I pictured the mother crouched over a nest, her wings spread protectively as she died. Her neck bent, her eyes closed.

Had she made her nest in a cave much like this? Had the mud or water risen to fill it? Or maybe she died in a landslide, like the one I'd just survived? Whatever killed her, the mother had died protecting her young. Protecting this egg.

I knew better than to assign such a creature human motives. But my thumbs nevertheless ran across the stone surface of the fossilized shell, an awe thrumming through me. The egg felt almost warm in my hands.

It *twitched*.

I cursed and dropped it, then cursed again as I failed to catch it. Thankfully the egg landed on the soft pillow of bundled skirts around my legs.

I touched it tentatively. And it gave way to my finger. I'd imagined that, right? Surely I'd imagined it.

A small spiderweb crack had appeared near the top. I picked it up again. A queasy feeling roiled in my stomach, because the egg was now soft and pliable, like a snake's. And the color was no longer smooth gray, but mottled cream and brown.

And it was this realization that finally made me exclaim, in a breathless rush, "Oh. Oh my. It's about to hatch."

Chapter

5

THE FIRST BIT OF SHELL BROKE AWAY, AND I SAW SOFT down.

The drop in my heart was sudden and fierce. I'd been a fool letting silly fancies get hold of my head.

This was a bird's egg, and no more. A large, odd bird. But a bird nonetheless.

I knew baby birds gained strength from their struggle to hatch, so I schooled my thoughts, narrowing them to a sharp and scientific point, and watched the egg as it rocked and warped, with a clinical eye.

There must have been a natural cave here, before Lucy's working. A bird must have laid her egg near the fossil. It was only coincidence. And I soothed my wounded ego by reminding myself that even without a hatched pterodactyl—God, what a foolish thought—I'd still found the only extant pterodactyl fossil in Britain.

I've done it, I thought, and the relief that poured over me was like warm water, washing away the fear that had taken root in my chest.

I would sell the pterodactyl skeleton and pay the rent on the house and store. I could buy meat again, and bread that wasn't so stale I had to soften it with precious magic. Aunt Patricia would have what she needed for Mother's physiomagician visits. This find would buy me years of stability.

A loopy, giddy grin spread across my face. I settled back to watch the egg, fantasizing about the letter I would write to Buckland, telling him about the pterodactyl skeleton. It couldn't hurt to remind him how valuable I was.

Maybe—I could dream, couldn't I?—maybe this would even change his mind about my nomination.

Small claws scraped against the shell's inside, and soon the shell fell away in larger and larger chunks.

Here was the head, a long orange bill and the crest upon it. And now—now the animal stood upon the mess of its shell, shaking loose the sticky fluid and slime from its winged front legs, and making a dear little infant *squawk*.

It was not a bird.

It *was* a pterodactyl.

I did not suffer false modesty. In the course of my career, I had already discovered two—now three!—of the most significant geomagical artifacts known to science.

This creature, though ...

This creature was the single most important find in—*my God*—not just geomagical history, but human history. *All* of human history.

My thoughts went blank. My heart was a drum. Fingers trembled as I reached out to touch the creature's translucent wings.

This couldn't be real. I was imagining things. Maybe there was some noxious gas in the cave, and I was hallucinating.

But no. I touched flesh. The leathery skin was a light reddish brown, the shade of a roe deer's hide, and its wings were like a bat's. What I'd thought was down were really soft hairlike filaments, closer to fur than feathers.

The animal gave an aggrieved shriek and snapped, flapping its wings. I pulled back my hand, and then gasped as the creature pressed its delicate head into my fingers, turning this way and that.

It liked to be stroked, I realized. The poor little thing was motherless and new.

"Dear God," I whispered, my voice trembling. "Am I dreaming? This must be a dream."

Tentatively, I scratched behind its head, on the neck. It cooed, turning big, yellow eyes to peer at mine.

It was more reptilian than I'd imagined from those German descriptions of the skeletons. These were more like a lizard's eyes than a chicken's.

The pterodactyl made sweet, unsettling squawks as I looked it over, marveling at every feature, each line and curve of the skin and flesh and filament. The first shock had receded, and my thoughts started up again, now racing a thousand paths.

What would it eat? Could it fly yet? Would the mother have tended the hatchling, like a bird, or left it to fend for itself like a reptile? How on earth was *I* supposed to care for it?

I heard a distant call and finally remembered that Lucy was waiting for me, probably terrified I'd been caught in a cave-in.

Of course. Achilles. The relief was immediate.

Just after Lucy had returned to Lyme Regis for good—she was seventeen and newly banished from her father's house—she'd rescued an injured baby raven, orphaned by a cat. Lucy hand-reared the chick and trained him like a hawk. Achilles was half wild now; he nested mostly in the trees outside Lucy's cottage, but sometimes scratched on the door to be let inside, to sleep on his perch by her fireplace.

Lucy would know exactly what to do.

I didn't want to keep her waiting any longer, but I needed to get the mother's skeleton out, too. The cave could collapse or, almost as bad, another fossil hunter might climb in to claim it before I returned.

This was just the kind of situation for which I'd held my magic in reserve.

I clasped the ammonite in my left hand, over my breastbone, and held my right hand above the jumbled pterodactyl fossil in the rock.

I focused on my intentions, the way Father taught me as a girl, when he first helped me string another ammonite to serve as my reliq.

The stone around the mother's fossil was once mud and sediment, and with my palm pressed to the ground, I willed it to be so again.

Transforming things into other things usually needed a great deal of magic from multiple reliquaries. But I had only the one. I had to hope this magic was small enough, because I wasn't transforming, *per se*. Just asking it to revert to a prior state. *Soften*, I thought. *Remember what you were.* I willed it to be water, and soil, thick, and slow-moving. To go *back*.

I let go of my reliq and pressed both hands to the cave floor now. It was working. Silty water rose around my fingers, and the hardened rock melted, slowly, into mud.

The hatched pterodactyl hissed angrily as cool brown water rose and covered its feet.

The mud squelched and sucked at my hands as I quickly gathered the fossilized bones and slipped them into my satchel.

Just in time, too; my reliq went cold. The magic had run out. I exhaled with relief and said a quick prayer of thanks as the mud hardened back to stone.

I turned my attention to the creature again. I couldn't put him in the satchel now that it was full of bones, so I tore off a strip of my petticoat. After it nipped a few times at my fingers, I managed to bundle the sticky, wriggling thing into a makeshift sling, which I looped across my chest.

I crawled to the entrance, the pterodactyl squirming unhappily the whole while.

"Hush," I chided. "I'm trying to help you."

I poked my head out of the cave mouth. "Lucy!" She immediately resumed cursing the day we met.

"I'm climbing down now," I called.

The rain had picked up, and I nearly slipped and fell to my death as I attempted to get into position for the climb.

But after a few harrowing minutes, I planted my feet solidly on wet stone.

Lucy was at my side at once, fussing. "You lunkhead, you *fool*—fine! Yes, I see how it feels now, if that was your point!"

"I wasn't trying to make a point." I plucked my top hat from her hands and set it on my head firmly. "Now—"

"And oh! Your cheek is split." She pulled a bit of shale from the cut, and I hissed.

"Just a scratch." I wiped away the hot blood on my cheek and tried again to tell her about my discovery.

But Lucy rolled her eyes. "Let me heal it."

"Oh, no thank you," I said, trying to dodge. Just because Lucy *could* do most magic didn't mean she was good at all of it. And I'd learned from painful experience that she was particularly unskilled at healing.

But she grabbed my face and pressed her fingers against the cut.

I yelped and squirmed as the skin knit closed. The healing was ten times more painful than the scrape itself. But it was done, and the tenderness faded quickly. I touched my smooth cheek, marveling, as always, at the power of her magic. It would have drained my whole reliq to do that.

The pterodactyl made a croaking sound.

"A bird? Why didn't you say so?" Lucy's eyes lit, and she reached for my sling. "Is it injured?"

I hesitated. "Not a bird, exactly." I opened the fabric.

Sensing an opportunity, the baby creature flailed wildly, and I quickly tied it shut.

But Lucy had seen.

"Mary." Her eyes went wide, lashes fluttering. "What is that?"

"Well. If I am not mistaken—and I don't think I am—this is a pterodactyl."

Chapter 6

"Buckland. I must write to Buckland," I muttered, as I ran around the shop lighting my candles. I had no reliq-lamps—only the rich would spend a week's worth of magic on something that burned out and had to be replaced every morning by a fresh reliq. I gathered ink and quill next. Buckland and Catherine would likely be at the London house, since he only taught at Oxford in the fall.

The pterodactyl sat on my worktable and chirped. Lucy's wide eyes swung between us both, a pendulum of shock.

"But *how* is it *alive*? You're sure it came from a fossil?"

"Yes! From a fossilized egg! At least I *thought* it was fossilized. And I don't know how it's alive!" I spilled ink on my hands and dashed it across my skirts.

"Maybe you're a witch, too," she mused, and I scowled.

"Don't be ridiculous. I have to use a reliq like all the rest of us."

"And did you tap your reliq to resurrect the creature?"

I paused, mid-stride. "No. But that's because I didn't resurrect it. I didn't have anything to do with that. I was just the person who happened to be there...."

That sounded silly, even to my ears. The odds were too great. But what part could I have played?

I wrote the note to Buckland matter-of-factly, before I could second-guess myself. I'd found a near-complete pterodactyl fossil in the cliff. And a live one, too. I assumed the Society would be interested in procuring both specimens, the living and fossilized? I requested a prompt response. Signed and sealed.

Lucy grimaced, studying the pterodactyl as it walked cautiously across the desk. It moved on all fours, the wings tucked like a bat's. "It looks rather ... demonic, don't you think?"

The pterodactyl did look, unfortunately, like a demon, with those bat-like wings and the hooked, pointed teeth jutting out of its orange beak.

This was going to be difficult to explain, wasn't it?

An entirely new species no one had seen before? Hatched from an ancient egg? Who was going to believe that?

I could only hope Buckland had some better ideas about how to introduce this creature to the wider scientific community, and the public, in a way that didn't end with the pterodactyl killed and my reputation destroyed.

"What should we feed it, then?" Lucy asked. "A human soul?"

I scowled. "It's *not* a demon."

I should have thought to feed it. Well, to be fair to myself, I had thought of it, and then I'd forgotten in my haste to write to Buckland.

It wouldn't do anyone any good if I let my specimen starve to death before I could hand it over to the Society.

"Fish seems like a safe bet for now," I said, studying the shape of its skull and the pointed fangs hanging from its beak like icicles from a gable. "Until I can more thoroughly examine its teeth."

Lucy cocked her head. "Or, you could just offer it different things and see what it likes."

"I—" I laughed. "I honestly hadn't considered that."

Lucy laughed, too, and then the pterodactyl joined in with a screech, flapping its wings and sending my letter flying.

Lucy took the letter and promised to come back with some food for the creature, which meant I was alone with the pterodactyl again, and somehow more nervous than I'd been in the cave. Maybe it was just starting to hit me. The responsibility all at once feeling real.

I had to care for this creature. Feed it. Keep it safe. Keep it alive. Except living things weren't exactly my area of expertise. I'd be far more at ease if I'd only found its fossilized egg.

But that wasn't thinking like a geomagician. That was the way a frightened woman would think. I needed to think like Buckland.

If Buckland were here, he wouldn't be afraid. He would grasp the opportunity presented. As Lucy so astutely pointed out, this was a chance to study the habits of a live specimen of a long-gone animal. A chance to learn about its diet. Understand its habitat. Watch its behaviors. Measure its intelligence.

We had so much to learn, and there was so much the pterodactyl could teach us.

I offered the creature my hand. It stretched its neck forward to rub against my palm, and I could feel the thin bones of its neck. I studied it, carefully and curiously, as I scratched behind its head.

The skull was something like a puffin's, with a large, rounded beak slashed with a yellow stripe. The golden eyes were wary as I ran my hand down its short neck and across the small body, only a little bigger than its head. The long, whiplike tail ended in a feathered fan.

It made an unhappy noise as I moved down its wing, following the bone from shoulder to claw, the way you would reach to shoe a horse.

"I won't hurt you," I said softly, and it settled at my voice.

The wings didn't fold like a bird's. They arced back from the claws in a sweep, a sort of jutting elbow. I'd never seen any creature like it. Not even in sketches.

"You, my friend," I said, "are going to be the subject of *so many* papers."

Lucy returned with a bit of dried fish and bread crust.

We set a strip of fish between the pterodactyl's front claws. It bent forward and poked with its beak, then flung its head back and gobbled it down.

Thank goodness. At least I wasn't going to have to chew its food first, as mother birds do for their offspring.

I put down a little more fish, just ahead of the pterodactyl's beak this time, so that it had to walk to pick it up. All four sets of claws clicked on the tabletop; it moved like a lizard rather than a bird, the body curving with each step.

The creature looked at me expectantly after it swallowed the fish.

"It's learning to trust you," Lucy said softly.

The pterodactyl chirped, looking at me expectantly. Still hungry. Before I could set out more fish, it launched itself off the table, gliding smoothly down to my feet.

Lucy and I yelped, both of us jumping back as the creature trotted over and sat before us, looking disconcertingly like a dog. It opened its beak, colorful jaw yawning wide. A thick, gray tongue extended. It squawked insistently.

I dropped the last of the fish into the open maw with some nervousness. The beak slammed shut, and the fish disappeared.

So, the thing could glide already, and far better than any baby bird would be able to this close to hatching. I mentally composed some notes. *The pterodactyl is born with functional wings, and able to glide from a height soon after hatching. This suggests it did not require significant maternal nurturing after birth.*

I held very still as the pterodactyl experimentally rubbed the ridge of its head against the folds of my skirts.

Lucy knelt and stretched out a hand. She clicked her tongue softly, and after a moment's caution, the pterodactyl let her stroke his head, closing his eyes as she scratched at the back of his skull.

"What are you going to call it?" she asked.

"The German specimens are called *Pterodactylus antiquus*, but this one is much larger than either of those examples."

"I meant a name."

I frowned. "Oh. I don't know. What do you think I should name him?"

Her eyebrow twitched. "Him?"

I looked down at the pterodactyl weaving around my skirts. I doubted a visual inspection would tell me anything—it seemed most likely the creature had a cloaca, given its similarities to birds and reptiles both.

But I didn't have to look. I couldn't explain it, but I knew, somehow, that the pterodactyl was male.

He tilted his head, swinging his golden eyes to mine.

I shrugged. "I can't just keep calling it *it*."

Lucy straightened. The pterodactyl poked curiously at her boots.

"He is sort of cute, isn't he?" I said, as he opened his toothsome maw again.

Lucy snorted. "That's what mothers always say."

I hung a sign in the window, CLOSED FOR RESEARCH, then ran upstairs to the flat and packed a bag of clothing. Together, Lucy and I managed to trap the wriggling pterodactyl in a wicker basket.

We both agreed it would be best to head to Lucy's farm, and even better to do so under cover of dark. Otherwise, someone would surely catch a glimpse through the shop window of the strange, flying demon, and the gossip would be all over town before I could count to ten.

Lucy's cottage was isolated and rarely visited. Ideal conditions for keeping the pterodactyl secret, and safe, until Buckland sent someone to fetch it.

My hand was on the key when I remembered the rent.

"Wait. Mr. Bolington is coming tomorrow. I have to stay."

Lucy shook her head. "Don't worry about him."

"You don't understand. Last time he said he'd throw all of my fossils into the street if I didn't pay. Every one, he said."

"I just told you. You don't have to worry about him," she said again. "Let's leave before the rain picks up."

I narrowed my eyes.

"Luce. What did you do?"

She finally turned to look at me. "I paid him." She wrinkled her nose. "After I posted the letter."

I went rigid.

"Please don't be angry, Mary. Consider it an early thirtieth birthday gift, if you like."

I couldn't be angry. How could I be angry with Lucy simply for being Lucy? She saw a way to help, and she helped. She saw an injustice; she tried to right it. That was who she was.

No, I wasn't angry. I was grateful—so grateful—and with that gratitude came a flood of hot, oily shame.

"I'll pay you back." I swallowed hard. "As soon as I sell the pterodactyl."

Chapter 7

Achilles was perched above Lucy's front door, sulking under the eaves to stay out of the rain. He cawed in greeting as we walked up the garden path, sailing down to Lucy's shoulder and eyeing my basket with obvious curiosity. The basket rattled against my hip.

Inside, the roof was leaking. Rain dripped through the thatch into a small puddle on the honey-wood floor.

"Thought I fixed that last time," Lucy grumbled, and spun her wrist. The thatch in the roof rustled as it knit itself together around the hole.

I set the pterodactyl's basket on the table as Lucy enchanted a fire in the stone hearth. I sighed with pleasure as I stripped off my wet socks and hung them to dry.

Lucy's cottage smelled like lavender and honey, no matter the season. The floors were always swept clean, and her walls and ceiling beams were garlanded with bundles of dried flowers from her garden. Her shelves boasted a few books but not a bone or fossil among them.

She'd traded three of her mother's diamond necklaces for the cottage and surrounding land. I was there; the farmer's eyes had bulged alarmingly when seventeen-year-old Lucy, freshly disinherited, stood on his doorstep and offered him a fortune in jewels.

The cottage, with its small main room and even smaller bedroom, was a far cry from her father's manor. The only vestiges of that first life were the two small portraits she'd stolen when she fled home and came to Lyme Regis for good. The paintings hung in twin dark-oiled frames over her hearth: one of the late Viscountess Marienne Murray, née Radcliffe—Lucy's mother—and one of Edgar.

The viscount in the frame wasn't far from the one I'd first met, with his boyhood platinum locks and the too-large ears about which Henry had mercilessly teased. During his visit last summer, Edgar had tried to convince Lucy to replace the portrait with a more flattering one.

"I like it," Lucy had said, patting his shoulder. "Keeps you humble. Lord knows something should." Even he had to laugh at that; our Edgar had never been one for modesty.

The table across from Lucy's hearth took up the bulk of the main room. It looked quite similar to my own work desk, covered in papers and dried inkpots. Achilles had followed us inside and hopped up beside the wicker basket, cocking his head in obvious interest. The basket rocked.

Lucy cleared the papers, but my eye caught on Latin. My own prejudice immediately assumed it must be the name of some flora or fauna. But *Libertas Magicae*—freedom of magic—wasn't a species. It was a rallying cry. The slogan of the Prometheans.

I picked it up, skimming quickly. *The condition of magic . . . the blessing of the Lord our God . . . as to render us unequal.*

"New pamphlet?"

Lucy nodded. "A woman in Exeter died trying to quick-fill a reliq on commission. Fainted and never woke up." She exhaled. "Her children were starving. Skin and bones, from all accounts. Poor woman just needed a little coin." Her eyes flashed fury, but I heard the anguish in the crack of her voice.

"But that doesn't even work, right?"

We were taught from childhood catechisms that magic was exhaled with breath. *From first breath to the last is magic,* so the saying went.

I wasn't an expert on current theomagical doctrine, but the fundamental notion was that reliqs, when worn directly against the skin, captured this holy breath.

Technically, you could wear more than one reliq, but the charge would be divided between them. The quantity of magic a person produced was finite, though not exactly fixed; maybe you generated a tiny bit more magic some days, a little less on others.

Charlatans sometimes claimed reliqs could be quick-filled by breathing faster through hyperventilation or strenuous exercise, or by wearing multiple reliqs. Some of the worst offenders even pretended to sell manifold reliqs—because if a back-alley quack did find the Holy Grail of reliquemistry, they'd sell it for only a couple shillings. *Ha.* But, like this poor woman, there were always some who were desperate enough to believe.

Lucy narrowed her eyes. "Does it matter? It was her only option."

I shrugged. "Guess not." I skimmed through the rest of her draft. "This is good, though. You make her story very sympathetic."

Lucy arched a brow. "I'm not making anything. I'm just telling the truth, so people know what happened."

"Good thing 'the truth' supports your cause, huh?"

"Don't be so cynical." Lucy snatched the paper and bundled it with the others, clasping them to her chest, as if to protect them from me.

"I'm not! It's a good tactic, and you know it, too, or you wouldn't be trying to turn her into a martyr with that pamphlet of yours."

Lucy's scowl deepened, and then she exhaled, nostrils flaring.

"You're right. And I feel terrible about it." She sat down across from me, tapping her fingers. "But the London council is planning demonstrations to support Edgar's rate-increase bill, and this might be just the heat we need to light a fire under folks, and get them into the streets."

"Yes, really singe their arses."

Lucy laughed. I was forgiven.

For all the times Lucy had to listen to me drone on about fossils and scientific papers, I had listened to her talk about the myriad evils of the reliquary system. "The cruel economy of magic," she called it once. I told her that *definitely* needed to go in a pamphlet.

Lucy and Edgar's mother had been a witch, and their father an unrepentant villain. Randall Murray had let his viscountess die rather than call the physiomagician, taunting his wife to save herself, if she could, with her own "foul witch magic."

So maybe it was no surprise both Murrays grew into reformers: Edgar, in his political career, and Lucy, with the Prometheans. They'd both seen firsthand what could happen when the powerful controlled another's magic.

Edgar, of course, had to pretend to condemn the Prometheans' methods, and call for reform through politics rather than protest.

But secretly he was one of the London council's most generous funders.

Lucy had divulged many Promethean secrets like that over the years. Code names. Tactics. Pamphlet distribution channels. Printing schedules. She trusted me, because she knew I'd keep her secrets safe—one, because I loved her, but two, because I couldn't be bothered to care to remember the details, even under torture.

Lucy's passion—reforming the reliquary system to be more just—was a noble goal, and a worthy cause. It simply wasn't mine.

Even the raven leaned forward as I untied the leather holding the basket shut.

The pterodactyl, nestled in its towel, looked up and chirped. The filaments around its neck, now dried, were soft and feathery. It could almost pass for a fledgling bird, except for those leathery, folded wings.

Achilles cawed, hopping across the tabletop, his own black wings beginning to spread.

"Don't be jealous, Achilles. Go to your perch," Lucy said firmly, and the raven rose and flew as commanded. He cawed again and turned his back to us, spreading tail feathers wide and sulking.

The pterodactyl nipped at my finger with his toothed beak. I chuckled and stroked between his eyes.

"He's bright," Lucy said. "Look at how his eye follows you. He knows you already. He'll grow to be as smart as Achilles, I'd wager. You should have no trouble training him."

I looked at her in alarm. Training him? I'd thought I only had to keep him alive.

We were straying quite far from geomagical territory now. A

geomagician might correspond or even collaborate with naturalists and biomagicians, trading books and research and observations. Buckland was actually quite well-versed in current biomagical research, and he'd often urged me to invest more energy in the studies of living creatures to inform my own work.

But I had never wanted to be a biomagician. I once had a dog, as a girl, and I quite liked her, but beyond that, I had no interest in the magic of living animals. I cared only so far as they could tell me about the dead.

"Now put your wrist at the stomach, under the chest," Lucy instructed, and for some mad reason, I did.

He didn't hesitate; he stepped right up as if it were a branch, then twisted his head to show those golden eyes and the scaled ridge above them.

Lucy went to the kitchen and returned with something fluffy and yellow and striped red.

I gasped. "Is that a chick?"

"Yes. Don't tell me you're squeamish," she huffed when I recoiled. "Didn't you once boil a drowned fox to examine its pelvis?"

I fed the pterodactyl, feeling only a little ill as a pale chicken foot disappeared down his gullet, and tried not to be charmed when he made a soft purring sound and settled onto his feet contentedly, as if my wrist were the nicest nest in the world.

Chapter 8

Morning mist shrouded the field, a veil that coyly shifted and swirled around Lucy and me as we walked. Our breath caught frost in the air, and my skirts were heavy with dew. The mighty oak at the heart of the sheep pasture, shading clusters of ferns, was our destination.

The sea was south. Once the mist burned off, I would catch a glimpse—a strip of glittering blue caught between the curve of the hills.

I'd been at Lucy's three days now, and it was the longest stretch of time I'd ever spent away from home. These were the first three days of my life that I hadn't walked the beach each morning hunting for fossils, and I was surprised how much I missed it. This was pleasant enough, walking the farm with Lucy, Achilles, and the pterodactyl in tow, but I missed the gravel and sand under my boots, the smell of brine, and the silence of my own thoughts.

We reached the oak, and Lucy murmured to Achilles. He

lifted from her arm and flew to the branches, looking down with a cocked head.

"Go on, then. You, too. Just like yesterday," I said to the pterodactyl, and gently brushed him off my shoulder as I pulled out my notebook.

He hopped down to the grass, then lumbered toward the tree with his strange, four-footed walk.

I'd guessed that at some point, he would begin to walk like a bird, with wings folded against his back, but that turned out to be a faulty assumption. *On land, the pterodactyl is quadrupedal, with all four limbs involved in walking, much like a bat,* I'd written yesterday.

"Have you chosen a name yet?" Lucy asked.

I blushed. "I . . . was thinking of calling him Ajax."

Lucy clapped. "Oh, because he's cousin to Achilles!"

"I know it's a little silly. The two obviously aren't really related, but—"

"Well, why not?"

I frowned. "Because they're distinct species," I said after a moment. "Like the mammoth and the elephant. We know from comparing fossils and skeletons that they were similar, but not the same species."

"I guess that makes sense." Lucy shrugged, then shouted at Achilles to stop chasing a sparrow.

But I was still mulling over Lucy's question. *Why not?* Without meaning to, she'd touched on the heart of all the most contentious geomagical debates of our time.

As I'd said, the mammoth and the elephant were the classic geomagical example of species differentiation. Buckland, the great defender of traditional geomagical theory, would say that they were distinct, separate creations, each perfectly formed by God.

Except that elephants appeared far, far later in the geomagical strata than the mammoth, long after mammoths vanished from it.

So where, exactly, had the mammoths gone? And the plesiosaur, or the ichthyosaur, or the pterodactyl, for that matter?

The Scriptures said, in Genesis: *And God saw every thing that he had made, and, behold, it was very good.*

Which posed a simple enough question: why would the Creator make the ancient beasts, only to destroy them later?

Buckland said that in the early days, when the Geomagical Society of London was first formed, the anathema word had been bandied about in whispered tones: *extinction.*

But that theory—and its threat to the Church—nearly unraveled our new science before it was even born.

It was Buckland, dedicated clergyman and geomagician both, whose infamous lecture upon his appointment at Oxford, *Vindicae Geomagicae, or the Connexion between Geomagic and Religion Explained,* brought about a tentative truce between Church and geomagical science.

I was only ten at the time, but I wish I'd been there to see it. Buckland told me about it later: how the audience of Oxford dons and students and other clergy sat rapt as he declared that the Great Deluge, Noah's flood, was responsible for the displacement of the ancients. Not extinct at all, he argued, only flung and scattered far across the earth.

And so things stood, more or less, until Henry Stanton—damn him—published his own counter theory last summer.

Of course I read his book, *Natural Disasters and the Magical Transmutation of Species.* Wasn't it possible, Henry posited, that the mammoth was actually an ancestor of the elephant, which had morphed or transmuted over the great stretch of time?

Henry went on to argue that catastrophic natural disasters initiated a magical process of transformation in surviving species, essentially turning them into new ones. That would explain how species disappeared or emerged in the fossil record during roughly the same periods that we saw evidence of significant geomagical change.

Not only did Henry's theory directly contradict Buckland's Church-approved Noachianism, it toed dangerously close to true heresy. According to Church of England doctrine, magic was exclusively the province of humans—the result of the Fall of Man—and not an external force at all.

Henry had named his theory "Catastrophism," which was unnecessarily dramatic.

Still, ever since I finished *Natural Disasters and the Magical Transmutation of Species*, I hadn't been able to fully dismiss the idea. Not that I would ever admit such a thing to Buckland.

Ajax wasn't an especially competent flier. So far, he was more comfortable launching himself from a height and then gliding to the ground.

I thought he might be able to launch himself skyward, eventually. He was still just a baby, after all. Time would tell.

Ajax climbed the trunk of the oak tree, claws hooking into the bark. He moved just as easily up the side of Lucy's house, or the leg of her table, as he did the oak.

If I'd found only the skeleton, we would never know he was such a skilled climber. I certainly wouldn't have guessed it from the claws.

The pterodactyl reached his perch overhead and settled, his wings flared like oversized shoulder blades. Lucy was right about his intelligence. *The pterodactyl adapts quickly to novel situations and challenges, demonstrating a surprising level of intelligence, similar to that of juvenile corvidae*, I jotted down quickly.

I held up my arm, and Ajax came at my summons, his leathered wings sweeping wide. He launched up from the branch, then arched through the sky, and I felt the warmth in my chest as he flew to me. *Good fellow.*

Ajax landed lightly, and I fed him bits of chick from a pouch with my free hand. I was surprised how much he preferred the poultry to fish, given his coastal habitat. Lucy had loaned me a set of elbow-length leather gloves, which helped minimize the scratches. Satisfaction curled around my heart with the trusting clutch of his claws.

Achilles, soaring above like a black shadow, cawed. Lucy's head snapped up, her eyes narrowing. She flung out her arm, and Achilles dove to land.

"Someone's coming up the hill."

I hoped it was Buckland. But it could just as easily be a stranger. We quickly reviewed our cover story: Ajax was a stowaway bird, found on a ship from New South Wales that had recently docked in Brighton.

I could only hope that was believable enough to stave off the parson and pitchforks awhile.

I heard the horses first, the patter of hooves on the packed-earth road, and squinted to make out the two riders as they came into view, the horses' legs swirling the mist like sea-foam.

"Mary, is that you?"

Sheer relief rolled down my spine at the familiar voice. My arm must have dropped a little, because Ajax squawked and poked at my ear.

"Yes! Yes, Buckland, it's me!"

Relief turned to shock as I recognized the man riding beside him. A younger face than Buckland's, and no hat on that head of thick, dark waves.

Shock turned to anger, and anger crystallized to fury. Even from the distance, I recognized those black curls and that wry smile—that damn, damned, damnable smile—as the stupidly handsome face of Henry Stanton.

Chapter

9

My heart pounded with every step Henry's horse took.

Lucy clutched my arm. "Is that . . . ?"

"Yes. It's him." My mouth was dry, the words hoarse.

"He got so *tall*."

My teeth ground together, and my fists clenched. How dare he? How dare Henry come back here? He had no right. No right at all.

Lyme Regis was my home. Not his. Not anymore. And Ajax was my find. My *triumph*. So of course, here was Henry Stanton, to spoil it all.

The pair reined in their horses and dismounted, crossing to us in a few strides. Both wore dusty breeches, riding coats, and tall, fine boots. I scowled, but neither noticed.

William Buckland—round-faced, with laughing wrinkles at the corners of his eyes and thick, caterpillar brows—stumbled forward and threw his hands to his chest, above his heart.

His mouth worked a moment, without any sound. It was the first time I'd ever seen the great William Buckland speechless.

I pointedly refused to look at Henry, but I could sense him standing perfectly still. *Observing.* He probably wore the same smug expression he had as a boy, explaining that "verteberries" were really "vertebrae."

Ajax shifted, pressing the side of his head against my cheek.

I had a living pterodactyl on my shoulder. Even Henry Stanton couldn't ruin this for me.

The animal's movement finally drew Buckland's eyes to mine. "It's real," he breathed. "It's alive. God in Heaven. It's *alive.*"

"Yes. Isn't that what I said in my letter?"

Buckland laughed. "So it is."

Henry stepped forward, and my head swung toward him, despite my best efforts. Something flickered over his face—shame, I hoped—but he hid it quickly.

Lucy was right; he *was* tall. Henry had been a nice-looking boy, but he'd become an alarmingly handsome man. He'd grown into his broad nose and strong chin, and his posture had improved significantly since our childhood. And from the tilted smirk on his mouth, I had the impression he knew what a striking impression he made, even in the brown traveling coat and leather boots.

"It's good to see you, Mary," he said quietly, then cleared his throat.

Our eyes locked, and the weight of the memories pulled me under like the tide. Because the last time I looked into those dark gray eyes, like the sky before a storm, I was fifteen years old—on the cusp of sixteen—and God, I had loved him.

I first met Henry on the beach, below the cliffs. I was kneeling on flooded stone, trying to chisel out an ichthyosaur jaw, when a skinny boy walked up and peered over my shoulder.

I glared back at him, squinting in the sun. The boy was lanky, with eyes too big for his face. "Can I help you?"

"Actually, I was hoping that I could help you." And he knelt beside me, and cold water soaked the knees of his breeches.

We spent every day together after that. For a full year, until we met the Murrays, it was just us two. Henry was my first friend. I think I would have loved him for that alone.

That year, I taught him all my father had taught me: how to walk carefully over wet stone, with a wide, bent-legged stance and heavy steps. I taught him the best time to search the cliffs—after a storm, when the winds and rain would flay and strip the rock to unveil new layers and bone. How to read the clouds for signs of such a storm on the horizon. How to clean and prepare the fossils we found. We were like two wanderers cast back through time, into a world before mankind. I was happy for the first time since Father died.

Henry's family was wealthy, but new-moneyed. His late father had been an industrialist whose textile factories earned a fortune with the adoption of the power-loom. He was introduced to Edgar almost as soon as the Murrays arrived in Lyme Regis the next June.

I'm sure Henry's mother hoped he would spend his time with the future viscount rather than the pauper fossil girl. Instead, Henry brought us all together. We were no longer a pair, Henry and me, but I didn't mind. I'd thought one friend was a gift. Three was a bounty I'd never dreamed.

Lucy was wild, her rosy cheeks still plump with childhood, her mouth always curved in some mischief. She liked to clamber over the rocks with Henry and me, though she didn't care for the fossil hunting itself. She annoyed and delighted me in equal measure, the sister I'd always hoped for.

Edgar had the same restless spirit. He could never sit still, and he spoke too quickly, switching topics so rapidly that he often tripped over the words. But—perhaps to survive his father's fist—he'd learned to channel that energy more strategically than his sister.

When she wanted to escape their governess, Lucy climbed onto the roof. Edgar, though, would claim he wanted to practice his Latin and settle the old woman in the plush armchair by the window—so the warm sun shone on her cheek—and read from Tacitus until she fell fast asleep. That usually bought the Murray siblings a few hours.

Edgar didn't care for fossil hunting, and Lucy was more a liability than help. So Henry and I spent less time on the beach that summer, and more time in his family library.

I'd showed Henry the *how* of fossils—where to find them, how to clean them—but eventually he wanted the *what*, and *why*. What were these creatures, these shapes we were finding in the cliffs? Why were they there? What did they *mean*?

I'd asked these questions, too. Only I had no way of finding answers except in conversation with Buckland. There were few books in Lyme Regis, fewer on geomagic—the science itself lacking even a name back then—and none at all available to a poor girl of low birth like me.

Nothing was barred to Henry and Edgar, though. Henry's stepfather kindly wrote to friends on Henry's behalf, and to members of the Royal Magical Society. Edgar, as a favor to us, wrote to the curator of the British Museum itself. And when Buckland next came to town, I eagerly introduced him to my new friends. Henry would go on to study with Buckland at Oxford, years later.

But back then, the study of geomagic was being birthed, and soon we were inundated with books and articles and even correspondence with some of the leading fossil collectors. All addressed to the boys, of course.

I'd never been to school. I could read, and write neatly, and draw a little. The truth was, I'd thought myself quite clever—certainly cleverer than the wealthy girls in town, trapped forever indoors with dull tutors and boring lessons while I learned by the sea, under the open sky.

I was Henry's teacher out there, but inside the sitting room of his stepfather's house, reading by reliq-lamp, the others had to guide me. My education was as patchwork as my skirts, and here it showed its seams, even as I tried desperately to hide them.

Henry, Edgar, and even Lucy all spoke elegant French. The boys read Greek and Latin, and knew the work of poets, writers, and scientists of whom I'd never heard.

At least I knew my Bible; Father read me scripture nightly before he died. Still, I could only half follow when discussions turned to theomagical matters.

"What Pierce argues here can't possibly be correct," Edgar might say, raising his index finger. "The King James translates this word as *enchantments*, but it would be more accurate to translate the Hebrew as *secret arts*."

"Someone should alert the archbishop," Lucy would tease, probably swinging her legs as she did. "Tell him to put seventeen-year-old Edgar Murray in charge of a new biblical translation."

That would make Edgar lift his chin. "Perhaps he should; mine would certainly be less . . . florid."

"You'll have to master your Greek verb tenses first," Henry might chuckle, and Edgar's face would sour.

"So sorcery, then?" Henry would ask, oblivious to Edgar's annoyance. "If we assume Moses's staff to be a reliq, and the scripture takes care to note that Pharoah's magicians are performing something different, then it *must* be sorcery, right?"

"Yes. That's the conventional interpretation." Edgar would frown. "But if I am right, then what if there is some other magic—this *secret art*—that the magicians can access?"

"What do you think, Mary?" Henry always asked, but I rarely had a clever answer.

"I—I think it's an interesting thought experiment," I would mumble.

Henry sometimes frowned; then a wrinkle between his brows, and fear would glaze my eyes. Was he testing me? Or mocking me? Or was he oblivious? I could never be sure, and I think that doubt was the first sign of some chasm forming between us.

Henry and I were alone on the beach that day, the last day, wet and laughing and covered in sand. Edgar and Lucy were trapped at home with their governess, and Henry and I had collected a pile of limestone nodules to crack open once the Murrays were released from their French lessons.

Henry stood, dusting palms against his thighs. I looked up from the limestone I'd been brushing. Henry had changed over his two years in Lyme Regis. He was sixteen now, and his shoulders and calves were muscled from our climbs.

"I must tell you something, Mary."

"Eh? What is it?"

Henry stood with his back to the sun, and I had to squint and shade my eyes.

"Wait, move that way a bit first. You're right in the sun."

Henry laughed and pulled me to my feet. I started to tease, but cut off as he gripped my hands tighter instead of letting them go.

Henry had never touched me like this, had never looked at me like this.

I'd seen that expression on his face—hard and focused, his lip twisted and caught between his front teeth—but it was usually directed at a particularly interesting puzzle he was keen to solve.

Now that look was directed at me. As if I were the most fascinating fossil in the world. My knees started to tremble, and my heart pounded into my ribs. I was afraid to move, in case I broke whatever spell it was that was making Henry Stanton stare at me like that.

But I was even more afraid that what he was about to say would break my heart. It would be something banal and devastating like, *I'm hungry, let's go back for lunch,* or *Do you see that ugly seagull over there?*

Only he was still looking at me, and I knew I needed to strangle this hope before it bloomed any further.

"Mary." Henry stepped closer. So much closer. I was afraid to meet those eyes. I looked past him, down the beach.

"You know, we should walk down to Charmouth. The innkeeper said he would put out some of my finds for his customers and—"

"Mary."

"And it's such a lovely day. I do love a blue sky, don't you? Of course you do. Everyone does. Silly thing to say. No one prefers a gray sky to blue, except perhaps you and me, because it means a storm, and fossils."

"Would you stop?"

Henry's thumb brushed my cheek, and all the breath left my lungs. I finally looked up, frozen by shock.

"I am trying," he said, and rolled his eyes, "to tell you that I love you."

Chapter 10

I GLARED AT BUCKLAND AND JERKED MY THUMB TOWARD Henry. "I wrote to *you*, didn't I? So what is he doing here?"

Buckland reluctantly tore his gaze from the pterodactyl. "When I alerted President Davies to your discovery, he thought Mr. Stanton ought to accompany me in his function as treasurer of the Geomagical Society of London."

Buckland said *Mr. Stanton* with the appropriate level of disdain, which I appreciated. I relaxed my hackles, just a bit.

Henry idly patted his horse's neck. "I'm the one authorized to actually spend the money."

Buckland's face twitched. The two men had their own rather complicated relationship, separate from each of ours. Henry had once been Buckland's star pupil. His protégé. And yes, it had rankled; I was honest enough to admit that.

Buckland never knew the details of what happened between Henry and me—only Lucy and Edgar did—but I thought he might suspect. In the time they worked together, Buckland was always careful not to speak of Henry Stanton. That held true until only a few years ago, when they had their own falling-out.

I can't say I wasn't delighted when Buckland finally felt the sting of Henry's betrayal. Henry Stanton would hang his own mother if he thought it would advance his ambitions.

And his current ambition was the society presidency. Same as Buckland's.

There was no need for introductions. Buckland and Lucy had met many times over the years of his visiting Lyme Regis, and of course Lucy and Henry were well acquainted.

The cold glare she stared at Henry warmed my heart. I could feel the chill just standing beside her.

Buckland was still giddy, hardly breathing through his chatter.

"What a marvel! Look at his claws! The beak is extraordinary; such a cheerful color!"

Buckland circled us; Ajax nervously shifted his weight on my shoulder from foot to foot.

"That orange shade! You said you found a skeleton of the mother? These *wings*! You wrote that they were leathered, but I struggled to picture it. They are just like a bat's! And one can see light through them? How many teeth does he have? And two types, you said? I assume the mother's skeleton is in the shop? The Society is prepared to offer you a handsome sum, of course, to take possession of both. A very handsome sum."

I raised my eyebrows.

Henry rubbed the bridge of his nose. "Perhaps we ought to sit down, at least, before we discuss the terms of sale." He stepped forward and reached out a hand. To take my arm? To gesture?

Whatever he meant to do, Ajax didn't trust it, either. With a sudden squawk, the pterodactyl lunged forward and clamped Henry's hand in his beak like a brightly colored trap.

Henry yelped, and I burst out laughing.

"So the shell was hard when you first picked it up?" Buckland asked.

We sat around Lucy's table as I described the egg's hatching for a third time. She'd poured tea, and I nursed it slowly, glaring across the table at Henry in between answers to the geomagicians' queries.

"It was definitely hard."

"Fossil? Or shell?"

"Fossil. Stone."

"You're certain?"

Am I? "I—I can't be certain, no. But it was very hard."

"Hmm. Very well. And then?"

"And then, all of a sudden, it was soft."

Ajax sat on his perch with Achilles, waiting patiently for some command. *I should give him a snack. He's being very good.*

"Did you do anything before it softened?"

"Not that I can recall."

Henry cut in sharply. "You didn't speak? Did you use any magic? Tap your reliq?"

I shook my head. "I only held it in my hands."

"And the color and texture changed while you were looking at the egg?" Buckland asked.

"I think so." I frowned. Had it? Or maybe own memory was growing malleable. "I'm fairly certain it changed as I was looking. But it was so gradual, I didn't notice at first."

"Aha, see! You didn't mention that before!" Buckland scribbled a note furiously.

Henry idly ran his fingers over his knuckles and glanced over his shoulder at the pterodactyl.

"Calm down; he didn't even break the skin," I muttered.

"Now, when you noticed—"

I threw up my hands. "What's the point of this?"

Buckland didn't look up from his notes. "Pardon?"

"I've told you all I remember. Why are we going over this again?"

Buckland kept writing, his quill dashing across the parchment. "Obviously I'm trying to see if it can be replicated."

"Replicated?"

Buckland met my gaze then, his eyes round with surprise. He set his pen down with deliberate care. "The resurrection."

I swallowed, finally understanding. "You—you think *I* did something? To make the egg hatch?"

"That's what I'm trying to determine," Buckland said, avoiding my eyes.

My throat tightened. "You're afraid it was some kind of sorcery." This was precisely what I'd feared.

My thoughts reeled. Daily magic—normal magic—was intention based.

If you burned your hand, you wanted it to stop hurting and to heal. You would touch a reliq and hold that desire, and magic did the rest until the reliq was empty or you released the desire. *I want that water to be cold. I want that fire to be lit. I want that tear to be mended.*

One of Edgar Murray's theomagical books had described magic as "the small prayers." Because magic, as every child learned in the catechism, was rooted in desire. The original sin. The fruit of the tree of the knowledge of good and evil.

The punishment for using magic, which Adam and Eve had stolen from God, should rightly be death. Only by Christ's sacrifice was humanity spared the commensurate punishment for our sin. But under the new covenant, believers could use magic without risking Hell.

Sorcery, though—as best I understood it, which was admittedly little—tapped the very language of creation. It was the breath of life. The Word of God. It was forbidden. Condemned. Anathema. No one burned witches anymore, but sorcerers? We would spit on their ashes and call it grace.

I shook my head. "But—"

"It's time," Henry interrupted. "I'm going to do it now."

Buckland's mouth tightened, and his eyes held fear as he nodded.

"Time for what?" I asked. "What are you going to do?"

Buckland reached across the table and grabbed my hands. "Mary."

I was startled by the solemnness of his face. The usual playful light in his eyes was gone.

"As sworn representative of the Geomagical Society of London and the Church of England both, I must ask you nonetheless."

His grip didn't slacken. It tightened, pinching the webbing of my fingers.

Under my shirt, my reliq grew warm against my skin, as if I were doing magic. Warm—warmer—then suddenly *hot*.

"My reliq," I gasped, and tried to pull my hands free, to move it away from my bare flesh. But Buckland held firm.

"What are you doing to her? Stop that!" Lucy's chair clattered as she sprang up.

Henry caught her by the shoulders. "It will be much worse for her if you interrupt."

I squirmed as the reliq singed my skin, and I gritted my teeth to stop from crying out. I refused to give Henry the satisfaction.

"Do you now, or have you ever, worked magic with words of sorcery?" Buckland asked. His eyes bored into mine.

"What?" I gasped. "No. Of course not."

"Have you now, or have you ever, stolen magic through vampyrism, in service to the Devil?"

"No." My voice was steadier this time. I understood what this was now.

It was an inquisition. An old, old, *old* method for rooting out witches and sorcerers—very popular back in the sixteenth century.

After I'd answered the three questions, I would have to show where my reliq hung. So long as the skin was unburnt, I would be declared innocent.

"Have you now, or have you ever, communed with the dead through necromantic magics?"

"No." I said it firmly, and after a moment, the ammonite on my chest went cold. It was done.

"I'm so sorry," Buckland said, his hands fluttering. "But of course you understand. We had to be sure."

"We still need to see," Henry said, and I glared, cheeks hot as I pulled down the top of my blouse. I wore my reliq over my sternum, and I lifted the ammonite to bare the flesh there, staring defiantly at Henry.

His cheeks heated. "That's sufficient."

The skin on my chest was white and unmarred. I'd passed the test.

"Did you two really think she'd done sorcery?" Lucy rolled her eyes. "How would Mary have managed to get hold of a book of spells anyway?"

I glowered. I liked to think that if I *wanted* to become a villainous sorcerer, I could have found a way. But I thought better of saying so.

"Of course not," Buckland said, "but President Davies insisted."

Ah—now that explained why Henry was *actually* sent along.

Buckland and Henry were known rivals, each the unofficial leader of an unofficial Society faction of like-minded members. Buckland, the Traditionalists, and Stanton the Catastrophists.

If both men returned with the pterodactyl and claimed the same explanation—decidedly *not* sorcery—it would carry much greater weight than Buckland's word alone.

Ironic, really, that the two of them had to forge this temporary alliance on my behalf.

I didn't trust Henry Stanton any farther than I could throw him. But I *did* trust that he would put his own ambition first. He wouldn't have wanted Buckland to have all the glory. The man who presented a living pterodactyl to the Society would be celebrated for the rest of his life—and it certainly wouldn't hurt a campaign for president. I'm sure each of them would have preferred to take the credit alone, but shared glory was better than none.

A sliver of a notion had started to widen in my thoughts, like a seam of light around a doorway. But before I could inspect it further, Buckland leaned back.

"There's really only one answer left. The simplest explanation." Buckland relaxed in his chair, the tension gone out of him.

"And what's that?" I asked.

"That you didn't play any part in the pterodactyl's resurrection. In fact—it wasn't a resurrection at all."

I nodded fervently. "Yes, exactly. I really don't think I had anything to do with it." I certainly hadn't done anything magical; my reliq was almost full until I used it to loosen the mother's skeleton from the mire.

"As you know," Buckland said, beginning to raise his voice, taking on the tone of the lecturer-preacher he was. I don't think he could even help himself. Henry rolled his eyes as Buckland gestured.

"I have long theorized that the ancient beasts were distributed to far-flung regions in the wake of the great flood. Scattered to the ends of the earth. But why, some ask—as you, yourself, Mary, have often wondered—if the beasts still walk the earth and swim its waters, then why haven't they been seen by human eyes? Why do we have no reports, then, of a mammoth wandering in Tunisia, or a plesiosaur in the Mediterranean? Perhaps, we have postulated, they simply settled far from civilization, in numbers so small they have slipped through history unnoticed, outside of legend."

Buckland leaned forward, and his gaze danced with delight, but his voice was solemn. "But now, you and your pterodactyl have given me the inklings of a new theory, Mary. A new answer for the riddle. Perhaps, rather than destroy or alter His first creations, as some have claimed . . ." He glanced, sidelong, at Henry. "I begin to suspect our Lord God, in His infinite wisdom, simply laid some of His creations to a long and quiet sleep, rather than erase them entirely."

There was silence around the table. Disapproval—disagreement—radiated from Henry, but not surprise. Buckland must have pitched this theory previously, perhaps as soon as he received word of my discovery.

The theory *did* make a certain kind of sense, if I squinted hard enough. And it *did* solve—quite neatly, in fact—that thorny theomagical problem of potential species extinction.

Buckland grinned in triumph as he concluded, "A sort of hibernation, we might even say. A divinely prescribed period of rest. Perhaps following the flood? And you, my dear Mary, have found one that has at last awoken."

I understood William Buckland better than he knew, I think. I studied the smooth lines of his shoulders, and the looseness in his jaw. *He believed it.* Buckland really believed this theory.

But he wasn't a fool, either—he knew, we all knew, that this theory would dearly please the Church, further tying geomagic and faith together in the braid that Buckland was always working to strengthen.

He could believe it to be true *and* believe it was a good strategy. Not to mention his theory would shield me from any accusations of sorcery.

"Yes," I said slowly. "I suppose you must be right."

Buckland nodded happily, but I wasn't looking at him. I was looking at Henry instead, because he was being awfully, awfully quiet, and I didn't trust it one bit.

Chapter 11

"Now, Miss Anning," Buckland said, pulling out a file of papers from his satchel. "Shall we turn to the rest of our business?"

I smiled. *Miss Anning*, was it? I leaned forward and tented my fingers on the tabletop, then blushed a little when Buckland chuckled fondly at the motion.

Damn him, it did undercut the image of a cutthroat businesswoman when he smiled at me like I was a ten-year-old asking for a sweet.

"Perhaps we need not consider this a negotiation at all," Buckland said pleasantly. "But rather, an agreement between friends." His blue eyes sparkled.

I snorted. I was ten years old when I first sold William Buckland a fossil: a trilobite from the Blue Lias.

My father was dead by then, and Mother already staring at the wall. We were surviving on parish relief, Mother and I splitting a crust of bread a day as our evening meal and taking turns to visit the slicks.

I was still gathering fossils each morning, though. Partly because I enjoyed it. Partly because I had nothing better to fill my days. Partly because I could usually find a thing or two to sell, and help keep us from the slicks for a day or two.

But mostly because I missed Father, and it felt a little like he was there with me when I was on the beach.

Then I would brush my wild black hair, put on my least-ripped frock, stand outside The Three Crowns, and thrust a tray of fossils toward tourists as they walked to the beach.

"Fossils and curios from the cliffs!" I sounded desperate, and I hated it. I couldn't help it. I *was* desperate.

A few bought my wares. Most ignored me.

But William Buckland bent and studied each carefully. His wife, Catherine—they were on honeymoon, surveying geomagical sites—stood back, smiling kindly. She was wearing a yellow-lace dress and looked to me like the stained-glass angels in the parish church.

"You're Richard Anning's girl," Buckland said, and a lump rose in my throat. I could only nod. "I dealt with him a few times. I was very sorry to hear of his death. He was an excellent collector. You have his eye for quality."

He fingered the trilobite and then turned it over in his palm to see the articulated legs.

"How much would you ask for this?"

"Only a pence, sir," I said eagerly. One pence would buy the night's bread, and another day's.

Buckland shook his head, though. "Oh, no. No, no. This is a fine specimen you have here. You must always know the true worth of what you have, Miss Anning. Tell me, what do you think this is worth, to someone who would cherish it? Who would recognize it for what it is? What would you charge then?"

It was the first lesson he taught me.

I grinned. "Alas, I know the worth of what I found."

"Yes. I was afraid you would," Buckland said, and chuckled ruefully.

"But"—I raised a finger—"precisely because we *are* friends, I have not yet reached out to any other geomagicians. I wanted to offer you the chance to procure them first."

Buckland's shoulders relaxed almost imperceptibly. He'd wondered, but was too polite to ask.

"However," I continued, "if we cannot come to an agreement, I won't hesitate to enter negotiations elsewhere. Including abroad."

He bristled. "You can't possibly mean the French."

"I will consider all offers," I teased. "Including any from the Société Géologique."

One of Buckland's regular rants was about the travesty of British fossil finds making their way abroad to France.

"If I may interject. What precisely," Henry said smoothly as Buckland grumbled, "are we negotiating?"

"Is that not obvious?" I scoffed and gestured at the pterodactyl.

"For sale, then? Or on loan?" Henry asked.

Buckland's brow wrinkled. "But—you are offering him for sale, aren't you, Mary?"

I swallowed. That's what I'd said in my letter. That's what I'd meant to do. I found things, and I sold them to Buckland. That's how it had always been.

And this sale would pay my rent and my debts. Cover Mother's care.

Besides, what else would I do with him? Keep the thing as a pet, like Achilles? I couldn't do that even if I wanted. Ajax looked like a demon flown straight off the margins of an illuminated Bible.

He wasn't, of course. He was a prehistoric creature of Earth, not Hell, which seemed rather a significant difference.

But not everyone would agree. There were still good odds I'd find my skirts singed if I went around with the creature squawking on my shoulder.

It would take more power than mine to convince the good people of Lyme Regis that Ajax wasn't a demon. Power like that of the Geomagical Society and the Church of England. And Buckland, as both a geomagician and minister of the Church, was far better positioned than I in that regard.

He is a specimen, I told myself firmly. I wouldn't look at Ajax. *Not a pet. This was always the plan.*

"Yes. I intend to sell him."

A strange expression flickered over Henry's face, but Buckland sagged in relief. "Excellent. Most excellent. And I can assure you, we will give you the credit for the discovery. As I always have, for all your excellent finds."

Credit. A brief mention of my name in the speech when he and Henry took the praise.

"Now," Buckland said, "how much do you want for them? The beast and the skeleton together?"

I told him. He sputtered, but I knew it was an act. We'd danced this dance before.

"Six hundred pounds? *Six hundred pounds?* You would bankrupt the whole Society!"

I raised a brow. He'd told me stories of their parties. "I doubt that. And again, I know what this is worth. The plesiosaur skeleton sold for two hundred only two years ago. The mother's skeleton alone is worth three."

"The most we can offer you is four hundred," Henry said.

I tapped my chin. "That's a shame. And a good thing the French are more generous."

"Gah," Buckland said. "Four twenty-five."

"Six hundred."

Lucy brewed another pot of tea and watched us with amusement.

After this second round of tea was gone, Henry cleared his throat. "If I might suggest—"

"No," Buckland and I both said in unison.

Henry put his hands up, leaning back in amusement. But Buckland was beginning to look troubled.

I'd refused to drop below six hundred pounds. I'd started at six hundred with every intention of negotiating in good faith, to find a price at which we both felt satisfied. Except I hadn't counter-offered once.

I knew I was being difficult. I just wasn't sure why.

"Five hundred thirty pounds," Henry said softly, interrupting my back-and-forth with Buckland. "That's the highest I can go. Or, frankly, the professor and I will both be expelled from the Society."

"That would already be twice the highest purchase the Society has ever made," Buckland added.

They were telling the truth. I knew it. Five hundred and thirty pounds would be enough for my debts. Enough for years of my rent and expenses. It was all I'd wanted, and more than I'd hoped.

So why was I resisting?

Behind me, the pterodactyl cooed, its claws clicking against the wooden perch.

I held out my forearm without really thinking, and the pterodactyl sailed to my shoulder. Buckland yelped at the rush of leathery wings, and Lucy laughed, but Henry only watched with curious, if wary eyes.

Ajax pressed his toothy beak against my cheekbone, and I ran a knuckle along the soft down of his chest, my swirl of thoughts crystallizing into clarity: *This is my chance.*

"I need to speak a moment with Buckland," I said, looking at Henry and Lucy. "Alone."

Once Buckland and I were alone, I sighed. "You know what else I want."

He closed his eyes and scrubbed at his chin. "I do."

"I want you to put my name forward. I want to be nominated."

"Mary, I—"

"You think I am unworthy?" My voice cracked. "Is that it?"

"On the contrary," Buckland said. He frowned as he shook his head.

"Then why won't you even try?" I'd shed very few tears since my father died—that day wrung them all out of me—but I felt them pricking now.

"It isn't that simple. No woman—"

I bit my lip, shook my head. I was afraid. Everything could very well crumble away. But I had to try. I would never have a stronger case for membership. I would never have better leverage.

"I won't sell," I said, fighting through my panic. I had to hold strong. "Unless you promise to nominate me. At the next meeting."

Buckland looked stricken. It broke my heart. *Whatever he says, he doesn't really think I deserve it.*

For a very long moment, I was afraid he would refuse. Then I really would be forced to write to the Société Géologique.

Buckland reached over and took my hands. His were sun-spotted and wrinkled. Mine were cracked, nails chipped.

"You're right," he said, so quietly I almost didn't hear. "Of course you're right. Yes. I will nominate you, Mary."

There was a catch in my chest as I breathed, as hope hooked on fear. It was finally happening.

If the Society elected me—and they *better*—I would be a geomagician.

"Thank you," I said, my voice choked on emotion. He squeezed my hands, his eyes warm and wide.

"I will do everything I can to see you join our ranks, Mary."

I swallowed, overcome. Buckland looked away, to preserve my dignity, and I was grateful.

"There is one thing, though." He cleared his throat. "You'll need to trust me, Mary. For this to work, I will need to campaign quietly, and win your allies carefully, lest we find ourselves derailed."

"Understood."

He did look at me then, eyes brittle. "In other words, dear. Don't tell Stanton."

Henry drew up the contract, and we signed. I sold the pterodactyl skeleton and Ajax—the live specimen, rather—to the Geomagical Society of London, care of William Buckland, for five hundred thirty pounds.

Henry blew on the ink to help it dry, and Lucy rose, bustling around the cottage and humming. I didn't pay much attention—Lucy was often bustling and humming—until Buckland pursed his lips.

"Are you traveling somewhere, Miss Murray?"

I saw now what Lucy was diligently filling. A fine leather travel satchel.

She frowned. "I assumed we'd be departing for London today. Or did you plan to stay in town awhile first?"

Buckland blinked, struck silent. Apparently, Lucy was planning to travel back to London with the geomagicians. I felt a twinge of jealousy, and then chided myself. I had what I wanted. I had the nomination.

But Henry laughed, suddenly, a burst of amusement. "Ah, that's what clinched the bargain, then? Mary comes along to present Ajax to the society?" He clapped, and my gaze whipped around in time to catch Buckland's wince.

"I—" I started, but Henry interrupted.

"Well, I think it's an excellent idea. You are, of course, very welcome to stay at my home. You too, Luce." Henry's eyes sparkled. "There's plenty of room for all."

I was as tongue-tied as Buckland. Me? Go to London? To the Society? I had the promise of nomination. It was enough.

Wasn't it?

Buckland muttered something, but I was looking past him. To Ajax. The pterodactyl perched contentedly, scratching at his soft brown chest with that orange beak.

He wasn't mine. I'd just signed the paperwork saying as much. And yet. And yet, he *was*.

I'd thought I would be satisfied with a little money and credit. Just a bit of recognition, and the nomination. But, really, that was only a fraction of the respect I was owed.

The truth—and I felt it now, hot and golden—was that I wanted more. Maybe I had for a long time, only I'd been too afraid to admit it.

But now the idea of staying here as Henry, and Buckland, and

Ajax went off to London and flipped the world on its head? The idea made my stomach twinge and twist with jealousy.

The geomagicians were going to make history. And I wanted to be part of it. All of it.

"Yes," I declared. "I am coming to London. That was the bargain."

Buckland arched a brow, but what could he say? He was the one who insisted we keep our deal secret in the first place.

"Yes"—Buckland exhaled—"but, as I already said, Mary, you will face a great deal of scrutiny in London. Frankly, your ... *reputation* may be better served by distance."

Reputation, Buckland said aloud, but he meant *nomination*.

He was suggesting I might be more likely to be elected *in absentia*. That the idea of me—the odd fossil woman from Lyme Regis—might be more palatable than the truth of me, in the flesh.

I bit the inside of my cheek. The worst of it was I couldn't even say he was wrong. I wasn't one of them. Not a scholar. Not a man. Not wealthy. Not even educated.

"For all your many charms, Mary, I am not sure you are prepared for the scrutiny you will face."

God, it hurt. It stung, nettle-sharp. I had thick skin, truly I did. But that cut through.

"But I am," Lucy said, walking over to put a hand on my shoulder. Her fingers curled like Ajax's claws. "It has been a while, yes, but I know well how to move in these circles. I can help Mary."

I looked up at her gratefully and then at Buckland.

"I understand. If they ... dislike me, they dislike me. It won't be on you, Buckland. It'll be my own damn fault. I won't blame you. I swear it."

My old friend's face softened, cheeks plumping in a warm smile. "Mary, dear. As you said, the bargain *was* already struck. You don't need to convince me further. If you want to come to London, then of course you shall."

Buckland sniffed, pointedly looking away from Henry. "But you and Miss Murray will stay at my home, yes? As previously discussed?"

My lip twitched in a smile. "Of course. As previously discussed."

Chapter 12

GIVEN MY LOVE OF THE OCEAN'S MARVELS, IT WAS A GREAT twist of irony to discover I was terribly prone to seasickness.

From the minute we boarded the *Unity*, only hours after Buckland and Henry had disembarked from it, my stomach began to heave. Lucy and I had been assigned a small cabin next to Buckland's, and after we dropped our trunks, I'd collapsed onto the narrow pallet, moaning into the crook of my elbow.

"It's all right," Lucy said automatically, patting my back. "It will pass."

"You promise?" I groaned.

"Well, no. But I can try to help, if you'd like."

"No, thank you." I groaned again and burrowed my head into the pillow. I had enough experience with Lucy's healing skills to know she could only make things worse.

Buckland knocked on the door and cracked it open. "We're about to get underway, if you'd like to come up for the sailing? How are you feeling, Mary?"

I answered with more groaning.

But I didn't want to miss the departure, so I let Lucy help me up and followed them to the top deck.

Unity ran the weekly trade route to London from Lyme Regis, and over the years, I'd sent off plenty of fossils, packed in crates and straw, in its cargo hull.

Ajax was down there now. Buckland had borrowed a special crate from a friend at the Royal Menagerie. The crate was constructed with a crosshatched wooden floor to allow solid waste to fall into a bed of straw below, and there were air holes drilled into the top. I'd given him a water dish and a few old rags to try to pad the corners. Still, Ajax had been ... vociferous in his disapproval when we closed the door. Henry said he told the captain that Ajax was a rare bird; the stamped PROPERTY OF THE ROYAL MENAGERIE on the crate helped the argument. As long as no one peered too closely between the slats, we should make it to London without trouble.

We walked up to a platform, out of the way of the crew's work. It was early afternoon. The sky was clear, the sun warm. Henry was already there, ankle hooked over one knee and a book across his lap. Round spectacles perched on the edge of his nose, and his brow wrinkled in thought.

I was half tempted to ask what he was reading, but I resisted the impulse. Instead I forced myself to look over the harbor, watching the shifting water and bobbing boats. My gaze lingered a little too long on my own storefront, now dark and locked.

Lucy had paid my rent. I'd sent money to Aunt Patricia for Mother. I'd taken Buckland to view the cave in which I found Ajax and his mother's skeleton. Then we boarded the *Unity*.

It was a little painful, actually, just how easy it was to leave.

With Lucy coming along, there wasn't even anyone to whom I needed to say goodbye. Just lock the door and go.

I leaned against the rail, breathing in through my nose and out through my mouth.

The captain called out, and the deck under us erupted into action. The sails billowed like white clouds, and then we were away.

For all that I wanted to be a geomagician, there was a reason I'd never traveled to London before. I was terrified.

It was one thing for the geomagicians to buy my fossils and respond to my letters. But there would always be a canyon between us—even with Buckland, as much as I counted him a true friend. I was an oddity, a curiosity as rare as my fossils. I wasn't one of them.

I watched Henry from the corner of my eye, the wind tousling his dark hair. *He taught me that lesson first.*

I was no fool. I knew who and what I was. For all the Greek and history and philosophy that I'd stuffed into my brain since Henry left, I was still just a poor, uneducated girl mucking about on the beach.

At least in Lyme Regis, I didn't have to hear the laughter. The whispers and snickers. Those learned men in their book-lined offices could deny me, refuse me, even reject me. But at least I wouldn't have to hear it.

Only now I was going to London. And there was no turning back, because the ship was underway.

The captain came up a few minutes later and knelt beside Henry.

"That won't be necessary," Henry said, shutting his book. "As I said before, I will be quite comfortable."

"But sir—"

Henry laughed and put a hand on the captain's shoulder. "Keep your quarters. It is only three days."

"What's that about?" Lucy asked when the captain nodded and hurried back down.

"Oh, he was offering me the captain's suite." Henry had gone back to his book.

Lucy snorted. "What? Why would he do that?"

"Hmm?" Henry flipped the page. "Oh. Because I bought the shipping company before we left London."

I snorted. Then groaned and clutched at my middle with a wave of fresh nausea.

But of course he had. They'd wanted the *Unity* to depart seven days before schedule, with no other passengers aboard? Easy solution—buy the whole company.

It was hard to remember that Henry Stanton was richer than the queen, since I still saw the shadow of an awkward, lanky boy in his face. But that boy was now one of the richest men in England. I should probably try to remember that.

He'd started with his father's fortune and then, after university, made some wise investments in mining companies operating abroad, then purchased them outright. Now Henry Stanton was the world's largest supplier of natural bitumen—a key ingredient, of course, in the reliquemical serum.

"I have a tincture that might help with your seasickness, Mary," Henry said, still not looking up from his book. "I get a touch queasy at sea myself, so my physiomagician keeps me well supplied."

"I'll manage," I grunted in response. I didn't want Henry's fancy remedies any more than I wanted his pity.

"Well, do let me know if you change your mind." He closed the book and stood. I tried to surreptitiously read the spine: *Geo-*

magical Uniformitarianism, by Charles Lyell. "Or if you'd like to borrow the book." He winked before strolling off.

I spun to Lucy after he'd disappeared. "The absolute gall of that man. He's *insufferable.*"

"Yes, because everyone knows the way to best offend a woman is to offer her"—she raised an eyebrow, and I could tell she was trying not to laugh—"a book."

I wrinkled my nose. "I *would* like to read Lyell's book, though. Maybe you could ask to borrow it?"

Lucy did laugh then, and I huffed off to see if Buckland had a copy on board.

After dinner—I managed to choke down half a stale roll—I crept down to the cargo hold with a reliq-lamp, navigating around barrels and wobbling stacks of boxes. I'd taken some of the dried fish and boiled eggs for Ajax's dinner.

I called softly. "Ajax?"

I swung my light around, studying crates for the ROYAL MENAGERIE stamp and listening for the sound of rustling wings.

"Ajax?"

Finally, I heard a small hoot, and followed the sound.

"Hello, friend. It's me," I murmured, as I popped the locks and lifted the hinged crate top, trying to position my torso so he couldn't fly out when I opened the lid.

I needn't have bothered. I'd expected Ajax to fling himself up and try to escape. But the pterodactyl hardly moved. In fact, his beak only twitched a little, and his eyes were glazed and milky. The smell of sick was choking.

"Oh, no." I gasped. "Oh—oh, no, no, no."

I hugged Ajax against my breast and stumbled back toward the stairs. His body was limp, his heartbeat distant. *Oh, God. Please, no.*

My room wasn't far. I kicked open the door. "Lucy? Luce?"

She wasn't there. And Buckland's room was empty and dark.

A door swung open across the narrow hall.

Henry. He was in a burgundy dressing robe and slippers. The ready smirk slid off his face when he saw Ajax in my arms.

"Bring him here. Quickly, now." He hurried us inside. "I can help."

"Please," I cried, as we lay Ajax on Henry's bed. The pterodactyl's head lolled listlessly. "Please, Henry. He's—important." I swallowed.

"Of course he is," Henry murmured as he yanked the reliq from his nightshirt—a belemnite on a golden chain—and pressed his other palm to Ajax's chest.

"It will take more than one," I said, and pulled off my own reliq, tossing it onto the quilt. "Where are your others?" Henry was rich. He would have a stash, somewhere. I turned to search his chest of drawers.

But Henry shook his head. "Don't need 'em."

I would have been annoyed, except I could tell he was concentrating. His eyes were focused, and a vein pulsed in his brow.

Ajax let out a pitiful, guttural sound, then closed his eyes and went still.

"No!" I threw myself forward, reaching for Ajax, but Henry caught me around the waist with his free arm and held me while I fought.

"Trust. Me. Mary." Henry grunted.

"Let me go!"

"Just . . . a second . . ." Henry said as I flailed. "And . . . there."

Ajax opened his eyes, then popped to his feet, cocking his head inquisitively.

Henry released me and I leapt to Ajax, stroking first his head, then his belly and tail.

"You gave me quite a fright," I chided, bopping his beak lightly. Ajax squawked.

"I'm sorry," I said sheepishly to Henry. "I must have overreacted. I really thought he was almost dead."

Henry's dressing robe had come untied in our struggle, and I could see whorls of dark chest hair above the gap of his nightshirt collar.

His face flushed as he hastily tied the sash. "Seasick, I think," he said, and cleared his throat. "Though I suspect he was suffering from dehydration. He's lucky you found him in time."

"You think he really was ill, then?" I frowned. "But I asked if you needed more reliqs, and—"

"And I said we didn't need them," Henry said calmly.

"Then he can't have been that poorly. I've seen healings before, Henry; I'm not an imbecile. Last time I had an ingrown toenail, the physiomagician said it would take three or four reliqs to heal."

Henry sat next to Ajax on the bed. Ajax laid his head on Henry's knee, and Henry scratched under the pterodactyl's chin.

"Yes. Well. I think you might want to sit down for this." He gestured to the wooden chair.

I crossed my arms. "What kind of game are you playing?"

"No games. It's just that this"—he opened his fingers to show the belemnite still on his palm—"is a manifold reliq."

My knees buckled.

Henry was up at once to catch my fall. "See, now, that's exactly why I thought you might want to be sitting."

Chapter 13

"Impossible."

Henry shook his head.

"You're lying."

His lips curved into a smug smile.

My stomach lurched. A manifold reliq. A real, true manifold reliq.

"Please, Mary. Sit down, and I will explain." He gestured for me to take his seat on the narrow pallet next to Ajax. The room was so small, our knees brushed as Henry settled into the single wooden chair.

"It isn't a lie, and it isn't a trick, either. That fossil in your hand holds the equivalent of seventy conventional reliqs," Henry said. "That's how I was able to heal Ajax so easily. Test it, if you'd like. It's practically still full."

Tentatively, I did as he suggested. There was no perfect metaphor, but if tapping a normal reliq was cupping water out of a pail, then this was peering into a deep, deep well—or standing at the edge of a ship and looking around at the vast expanse of the ocean.

From first breath to the last is magic.

The amount of magic that any given reliq could contain was a factor of both its material and the size of the object. While a small jewel would hold more magic than, say, a large rock, a larger reliq could store more magic than a small one of the same material. But anything too big quickly became impractical, since reliqs required contact with the skin to charge. I did once read that it was fashionable for knights and ladies to wear hammered gold breastplate reliqs, which seemed like a sweaty nightmare. But nowadays, most folk just wore a necklace or bracelet, and switched out when necessary. Well, the rich did.

These limitations were the whole reason we had the slicks. People like me just waited until we'd filled our personal reliqs back up.

But if you could afford it, there was no reason not to buy as many reliqs—filled by others—as you liked. I'd never had multiple reliqs of my own, but I'd seen Buckland work enchantments with them before. When clearing a dig site of debris, for example, he methodically pulled from one after the other after each drained out. But even then, you couldn't *combine* them. You couldn't multiply their power or use them together to amplify the effect.

Which isn't to say people didn't try.

No one knows where reliqs were first developed. The Bible never mentions reliqs at all, and the earliest hard evidence of their use in these isles comes from the accounts of occupying Roman soldiers, who wrote of a king with a magic sword called Caledfwlch. And the oral histories of many peoples beyond our islands claim their ancestors used reliqs even before that, as early as the invention of iron.

But all of history since is bloody with attempts to achieve precisely what Henry was claiming to hold. The manifold reliq.

It was the stuff of fairy stories and cautionary tales. The Girl with Bright Fingers, who killed her brothers and sewed their reliq-ringed fingers to her palms to try and make herself more powerful. Charlemagne, famously promising his throne to any man who could produce a manifold reliq, and whole armies dead in the attempt. The Crusaders, strapping stones to captured Muslims and burning them alive to test whether heated flesh would do it. The Aztecs, sacrificing a thousand souls at the temple to try.

There was a glow of pride on Henry's face, the shine of success in the curve of his lips as he calmly took the reliq and slipped the chain around his neck.

Cold slid down my back like ice.

"Did you do this?" My voice was hoarse.

"I think you already know the answer." His voice dripped with self-satisfaction—if I weren't so afraid, I would have rolled my eyes.

I rose, lurching for the door.

He shot up, face flashing confusion. "Wait—oh, dear—Mary, where are you going?"

"To tell Buckland what you've done." I gathered my courage and burst from his room, running for the stairs.

I glanced over my shoulder with every second step, expecting at any moment to find Henry with his knife at my throat.

He'd made a manifold reliq.

I'd known he was selfish. I'd known he was ruthless. Ambitious. But I'd never guessed he was capable of *this*. On one point, all the legends and stories agreed: manifold reliqs could only be forged with blood. Who had died for Henry's?

I gulped cold night air. The ship was quiet, the waves gentle, and the stars bright.

I ran through the scattered crew members, sleeping on pallets or tossing dice, up to the deck where we'd gathered earlier.

Buckland was reading by reliq-lamp, feet propped up on a small crate.

He frowned and set the book on the bench beside him. "Mary? What's the matter?"

I staggered. "It's Henry. Ajax was sickly, and I took him to Henry's room. Oh God, I left him in there; I didn't even think—what if Henry hurts him?"

I started to run back, but Buckland caught my arm.

"What did Stanton do?"

"A manifold reliq," I said, shuddering. "He's made a manifold reliq."

"Ah." Buckland's shoulders dropped. "That."

My eyes bulged. I stepped back, catching myself on the railing. I could see the truth written on his face. "You knew. You already knew."

"It's not what you think," Buckland said. "It's a machine, you see—"

"What's going on?" Lucy's head popped up, and I gave a strangled scream. She climbed over the rail, her golden hair wild with the wind.

"Where did you come from? Actually, never mind," I snapped. "Apparently Henry has created a manifold reliq."

Lucy gasped.

"Right," Buckland said, running a hand through his hair. "Well, as I was just saying—"

"I would wager," Henry said, swaggering over to the stairs—Ajax snuggled against him like a kitten; Henry had taken the time to dress in his day clothes again—"the professor was just about to tell you that the mechanism was his own idea."

"It *was*," Buckland said, eyebrows knitting. "And I know what you're thinking, Mary. But it is a safe process. No one died for these reliqs, Mary, I promise. It's simply a machine."

"A . . . machine?"

Both men seemed to think we were having a perfectly normal conversation on a perfectly normal topic. Only Lucy looked as shocked as I felt.

"The theory has always been quite straightforward, you see," Buckland continued. "A basic exponential function. When the magical reserves of one person are compounded with those of another, and those are—"

"And in practice," Henry interrupted, and Buckland's lips pulled tight, "it's a bit like weaving. Many threads combined into something greater. Which is why, when I designed the compounding machine five years ago, I named it *the Loom*." His eyes glittered. "Can you imagine the things we shall be able to do? Even I have trouble comprehending the scope of it! Enough magic in the palm of your hand to sail this ship when the wind is dead. Or keep your hearth lit for a week in winter. Or heal a fatal wound. Or a sick pterodactyl," he added with a smirk. "When before someone would have needed a barrelful of reliqs, now they will need just one."

"*Or,*" said Lucy sharply, "the bearer might sink the ship, or light their rival's house on fire, or cause that wound in the first place."

Henry arched a brow. "You have a poor opinion of human nature, Lucy Murray."

"Comes with experience," she said.

"Well, if one had ill intent against their fellow man, couldn't they do any of those awful things now, just as easily, with enough reliqs on hand?"

Lucy scowled, conceding the point.

"Only," Henry continued, "it would cost seventy poor souls a week or more of their magic—when this costs only seven men or women the magic of one day. *One day!* And I can assure you, they are compensated handsomely. One shift at the Glasswater Mill pays a wage of one pound seventeen shillings per day."

"Hell's bells!" I clapped my hands over my mouth.

"I told you," Henry said. "They are paid very well for work that requires nothing more than sitting still for a few hours. Far, far better than a lifetime of servitude to the slicks—wouldn't you agree, Luce? Your brother certainly does."

Lucy's chin jerked. "Edgar would never condone such a thing."

"On the contrary. Ed is one of Glasswater's leading investors."

Lucy looked to Buckland, who shrugged. "It's true. Viscount Merlton has been very supportive."

"Well . . . well, then." Her face twisted, pulled between distaste and loyalty to her beloved brother.

Henry made at least some effort to hide his smirk, but Lucy and I both scowled in return.

Buckland scrubbed at his brows, pacing. His cabin was only three strides wide, so he pivoted constantly.

It was just us two; Lucy had taken Ajax to our room, and Henry knew better than to follow us into Buckland's cabin.

"This wasn't how I wanted to tell you. I had a whole presentation prepared for when we arrived at Palmanaeus House," Buckland said, and sighed.

I snorted. "Is that supposed to make me feel better?"

"Yes." Buckland blinked. "The manifold reliqs are still new. The project is in partnership with the Reliquemical Guild—they supply us the serum for the procedure—but other than that, few outside the Society know of its existence. Though that will change soon; Stanton has been renegotiating the Society's contract with the guild."

"Why?"

"Oh, it's boring and complicated." Buckland waved dismissively. "The Geomagical Society is currently barred from selling fossils directly to consumers for use as reliqs. Which has never been a problem before. None of our members want to waste their own time selling fossils and rocks."

He didn't mean it for a slight, and I was careful not to let him see how it hurt.

The Society filled its coffers by providing fossils, gems, and minerals to the Reliquemical Guild. Society members were responsible for submitting a set number of artifacts each year, as part of their membership dues. But they earned that value back, many times over, in the annuity paid out of the Society's treasury.

Buckland continued. "Of course the Society would prefer—and I'm sure some of our potential customers would prefer—the discretion and ... oversight provided by a more direct distribution model."

In other words, the Society wanted to control who got those manifold reliqs. That was probably for the best; it wouldn't do for some rich maniac to get their hands on one in the slicks and level half of London.

"As I said. Boring and complicated."

But I didn't find it boring. Now that I'd gotten over the shock that they even *existed*, my brain was spinning with the potential. I could see why both Henry and Buckland wanted to claim credit for the invention.

I caught my breath. "Wait. This was why you fell out, isn't it?" Henry said he'd designed the Loom five years ago. That was about when Buckland and Henry's friendship ended.

Buckland inhaled deeply. "Stanton spoke often of his father's factories and the steam-powered looms when he was at Oxford with me. It was like a revelation; I realized that such a machine might be used to distill magic from multiple parties into a single reliq.

"After Stanton graduated and joined the Society, we spent almost a decade collaborating on the Loom's design," he said, and I recognized the wistful tone, even through my jealousy. What I wouldn't have given to be the one entrusted with that.

"And then?"

"And then we argued." Buckland sighed. "He was working on his book. His grand theory. *Natural Disasters and the Magical Transmutation of Species?*"

"I've read it."

"And what did you think of the argument?" Buckland tapped his hands. "That it is actually natural disasters that generate magic?"

"Well, I remember thinking, *Oh, Buckland will hate this.*"

Buckland chuckled. "I did. I do. Stanton would take God out of the matter of magic completely. As if magic were not the Creator's design for the redemption of man's soul. As if it were simply a result of some natural law."

"Like gravity," I said, remembering Stanton's argument from

the book. "But that was all? You argued theomagic, and he cut you out of the project?"

He frowned. "Yes. Well, no. You see, Henry had a specific theory about..." He hesitated. "About the nature of magic. One that I believed to be particularly blasphemous. Dangerous, in fact."

"What was it?" I was hard-pressed to imagine any theory much more blasphemous than the ones Henry had already published.

He frowned. "I think it best not to say. But eventually, I took my concerns to President Davies."

I winced. "Ah."

"Davies commanded him to strike the theory from the manuscript. Or Stanton would be disbarred as a Society member. Stanton was furious, but in the end, he agreed. On one condition."

"You were cut off."

"Yes." His mouth was tight with resentment. "And so, the Loom is Stanton's now."

Ajax was curled on my pillow, Lucy stroking his spine. She popped up as I entered.

"Can you believe the two of them?" she said furiously. She'd been stewing. "And whatever Henry wants to claim, I'd wager a hundred pounds it's a deeply unpleasant experience to fill those reliqs, no matter what wage they're getting. I will be having words with Edgar about this, have no doubt."

I ignored her. "How is Ajax?"

I checked him over carefully, running a hand down both legs and then along his spine and each winged arm. He seemed uninjured, as far as I could tell, and he calmed under my touch. I scratched his chin, and he cooed a little.

"He's perfectly fine," Lucy said dismissively. "And working conditions aside, it seems terribly reckless to loose such powerful reliqs on the world."

I patted my lap, and Ajax warily climbed over to settle on my thighs.

"Has he showed any more signs of illness?"

She shook her head. "Did Buckland say what they're going to do with the manifold reliqs?"

"Sell them," I said. Ajax snapped at my hand with his toothy beak, searching for a snack. "Don't you dare bite me"—I wagged my finger—"or I'll put you right back in that crate."

"Mary." Lucy's tone was serious. "I'll have to tell the others. You know that, right? This changes the whole game."

The Prometheans. I nodded slowly. I think I'd known as soon as Buckland confirmed manifold reliqs were real.

"Yes. I understand. But Luce . . ."

She nodded for me to go on.

"If it really is a faster, more efficient process? And those wages . . . Henry's right, Luce. The pay is good. I suppose my point is, maybe the Prometheans should support the mill instead. Honestly, this might be exactly what you've all been looking for. A way to really reform the system for the better."

"That's exactly what I'm afraid of," Lucy muttered, so softly I don't think I was meant to hear.

Chapter 14

Our path to London hugged the southern coastline, and we passed the famous White Cliffs of Dover early next morning.

Lucy and Buckland had sailed this route before but were generous enough to humor me. I pressed my chest against the railing and marveled at the cliffs, like great, glittering teeth.

I peppered Buckland with so many questions about the chalk and its gray-flint veins that he promised to show me samples once we reached London.

"But I'll warn you," he said, "the fossil yields from chalk aren't all that impressive. Your Blue Lias holds a far richer trove than these."

I preened a little at the thought that *my* beach was best. Its bluffs might be grayed and chipped, but the treasures were grander than those in the shining white cliffs. It was a silly thing to think, but I thought it nonetheless, and was pleased.

Lucy cleared her throat. "Henry's walking over here."

I turned from the railing too quickly and winced. I had to move slowly, or the queasiness caught me.

"Mary," Henry called.

I was still furious with him—for all the usual reasons, yes, but now also for this manifold reliq business. Henry'd made me look a fool, letting me run off to Buckland like that, only to learn *I* was the one in the dark. I could only assume it was all calculated to ensure maximum humiliation for both Buckland and myself.

Henry broke into a stupid little jog and caught my arm as I tried to hurry away from the railing.

"Are you all right? You look pale."

I yanked away. "I am perfectly fine."

Lucy forced him aside and looped her arm through mine. "I was just about to escort Mary back downstairs to our quarters to rest."

"Yes, of course." Henry nodded. "I only wanted to ask if Ajax—"

I caught my breath. I'd been down to check on him only an hour ago, with a breakfast of bread, sausage, and fresh fish. He'd been a bit morose, and had ignored the fish, but seemed otherwise fine. "What's wrong with Ajax?"

"No, no, nothing's wrong," Henry assured me. "I was just wondering if you'd like to let him out on deck tonight. I thought the fresh air might do him good."

"No," Buckland said. "We can't risk him being seen."

Henry scoffed. "Come now, Professor, in the dark he only looks like an odd bird."

"Buckland's right," I said loyally. "It's too dangerous."

Henry arched his brow, but then inclined his head. He looked at me with an expression I couldn't read, and I gazed coolly back.

"Very well," he said. "I'll tell the captain we won't need the deck cleared tonight, after all."

He walked away, and I glared at his back, watching the wind run like fingers through his dark curls.

The cargo hold had the thick smell of perpetually damp wood. It took a few deep breaths to adjust to the heavy wetness of the air as I made my way to Ajax's crate. I slid off the lid and scooped him up.

He made a squeak as he fluffed himself, flexing his wings and nuzzling into my palm.

"You seem to be doing better." I chuckled and scratched his neck.

"He does, doesn't he?"

I yelped in surprise, knocking over my reliq-lamp.

"Sorry, sorry, it's only me," Henry said quickly, shadows morphing horribly over his face as he righted the lamp atop the barrel. Ah, yes, that was exactly why open flames were banned aboard. "I saw you come down." He raised his palms. "I only want to talk."

Ajax squirmed in my arms, and Henry eyed him with amusement.

"Why? Do you have any other world-changing inventions to tell me about?" I said, too sweetly. "Any inventions that you stole from someone else?"

Henry's brows knit. "Is that what he told you? That I stole the idea for the Loom?"

"You cut him out of the project, didn't you?" I lifted my chin.

He stepped forward. "And did he tell you why I chose to do so?"

My tongue caught behind my teeth. I wished now that Buckland had said what, exactly, he'd objected to. "He said you had a theory. A dangerous one."

"Ah. He did not tell you," Henry said, smiling in a pleased way that I didn't like. "I see."

What on earth was this theory that neither of them seemed willing to explain? More secrets from which I was excluded, apparently.

Henry glanced at Ajax, still wriggling on my chest. "You could let him down to stretch his legs—and wings—don't you think? No one will see him here."

"I was just about to do that," I said, though I had planned no such thing. But it was an annoyingly good idea, so I set Ajax between my feet and nudged him gently with the toe of my boot.

"Go on now," I said.

Ajax rose and moved forward tentatively with his wobbling, four-clawed walk.

"He's not exactly the picture of elegance, is he?" Henry said, and, though I had similar thoughts, I shot him a glare.

Ajax stepped cautiously at first, placing his claws carefully and swiveling his neck as he wandered between the rows.

I had to remind myself he'd only been alive for less than a week, and most of that had been spent on the lush, wide meadow around Lucy's house. A ship was unfamiliar terrain to us both.

But Ajax grew bolder after a few minutes, almost excited. He began peering in between the boards and barrels and crates, poking around with the end of his beak. He opened his wings and hopped awkwardly along, nosing at the wood. Henry and I followed with the reliq-lamp.

Something small and dark burst out and scurried across the boards, just past our toes. I yelped, but Ajax made a squawk and pounced.

I grabbed Henry's arm in excited realization. "It's a cockroach! Henry, he's hunting insects!"

It was with breathless, hushed wonder that we both watched Ajax, this ancient creature, gulp down a cockroach and promptly search for more, racing along the seam between boards.

"With those teeth, I never would have guessed he would eat insects," Henry said in a hushed tone that matched my own.

"Never, if we'd only seen the skull, and teeth."

I hadn't taught him to hunt like that, and he hadn't learned it from Achilles, either. This innate ability was more evidence that pterodactyls likely didn't care for and teach their young in the way birds did. They would have been more like reptiles, the young left to fend for themselves from hatching.

"We will have to let him continue to hunt wild as he ages," I said quietly to Henry. I didn't want to distract Ajax, who was happily poking around a barrel of turnips. "To see if he is really an insectivore, or—"

"Or if it's only juveniles of the species," Henry finished.

"Precisely. Because we know he has the taste for fresh meat, too," I said.

"But likely not the hunting skill, or size, to catch any larger vertebrates."

I thought of all the fish I'd offered, which Ajax only begrudgingly ate, if at all. "He doesn't like fish, either. Dried or fresh."

"So his species were not piscivores. I wonder why," Henry mused.

I did, too. My first guess was the pterodactyls were simply graceless fliers, unable to swoop low and catch fish from the surface the way a seabird might. But I could be wrong.

It was still possible Ajax would grow into his skill as a flier and develop a taste for fish later. Another hypothesis was—and oh, an exciting one—that they'd existed contemporaneously with another species of pterodactyl, which *had* specialized in hunting fish. And still another theory: that the oceans of his time were too dangerous for his kind to hunt, given the plesiosaurs and ichthyosaurs that could catch a winged flier and drag it to the deep.

I laughed, nearly breathless at the glory of it; the buzz of curiosity in my chest, and this new thrill—the incredible, wonderful, wondrous fact that for once all the questions we had could be answered. We wouldn't have to guess. We could watch Ajax grow, and learn, and we would know. And there was nothing more satisfying than *to know*.

I was alarmed to realize I was grateful to be with Henry.

Now, *that* was a deeply unsettling notion. I crossed my arms, as if the protective motion could defend me against such foolishness.

But it was true. I was glad to be watching Ajax with someone who understood the significance of the experience. Even if it was Henry.

Henry shifted, pulling me from my thoughts. He was breathing so loudly I could tell he wanted to say something.

"What?" I asked—surprising us both with the softness in my voice.

Henry cocked his head. "What is what?"

"All that huffing and puffing." I waved in his direction. "What is it you want to say?"

He smiled wryly. "You've made it clear you don't want to hear anything I have to say."

"I'll make an exception this time."

His cheek twitched.

I expected more commentary on pterodactyl dietary habits,

but instead, Henry looked at me. The shadows hollowed his face, and his pupils were enormous and black in the darkness. I felt terribly off-balance, like the earth had shifted beneath my feet and left me stumbling.

Then his shoulders loosened, and he chuckled. It was rueful. Amused.

"I've missed you, Mary." He reached out, to cup my cheek, maybe, but I twisted out of reach.

How dare he. How dare Henry Stanton claim he *missed* me. All that silly, misplaced gratitude—which was far too close to forgiveness—evaporated as I tumbled into memory.

Chapter 15

On the beach, on the last day, sixteen-year-old Henry rolled his eyes and said, "I am trying to tell you that I love you."

The waves themselves went quiet to hear the pounding of my heart. His thumb brushed over my cheekbone, the line to my parted lips.

I loved him, too.

Of course I did. I'd loved Henry Stanton from the first moment, when he knelt beside me in the sand to dig free an ichthyosaur skull and share my giddy joy at the long teeth and spiraled eye.

I'd loved him for the way he walked beside me on slick rock, letting me catch his arm and catching mine in turn when we slipped. I loved the frown between his eyes when he chipped at a fossil. I loved the heat in his voice when we read a scientific paper and he encountered an argument he didn't think well made. I loved that he teased, but never about my mother. I loved that he snuck extra sugar into Lucy's tea. I loved that he told Edgar when he was being obnoxious. I loved the way he hummed to himself when walking. I loved him.

I loved him. And I had never imagined Henry Stanton would love me, too.

And I was afraid of it. Didn't trust it. Dreams like this didn't just come true. Not without a cost.

But when Henry ran a thumb down my cheek and curled his fingers into my hair and confessed that he loved me, I didn't care.

Later, when the letters stopped, I would look back on that moment and see that I was wise to fear. I should have listened to that instinct.

"I love you, too, Henry," I said, and relief turned his face boyish and bright. "I love you, I love you, I love you," I cried.

Henry laughed, and then pressed his lips against mine. We fumbled a moment—hands and mouths finding a rhythm—and then sank into the sweet heat of it. My chest fluttered and my limbs tingled, and I kissed Henry Stanton with all the hunger of longing, of nights where I'd lain awake, imagining exactly this.

He kissed my neck. He cupped my head and pulled me close. He brushed a palm over my breast, and I caught my breath.

"Mary," he breathed, and groaned into my ear, burying his face in my neck, his hands groping for my skirts.

I was willing. There's no point pretending otherwise.

But then Henry pulled back with a shudder, his hands on my elbows, holding me away.

"We shouldn't." He shook his head. "Not until we are married."

I didn't mean to laugh, but I couldn't help it. Henry looked shocked and hurt, so I tried to stifle it quickly, but the damage was done. He released my arms as if I'd burned him.

"Do you—would you not wish to marry me?"

"Oh, Henry," I said softly, "of course I want to marry you."

But we were too different. I knew what I was. Henry's family was kind to me, but that was as an eccentric companion for their son. They would never want me for Henry's bride.

I was plain and poor, ill-mannered and odd. His mother must simply have trusted that Henry would never see me as a potential object of desire, or she never would have let us spend so much time together.

And even then, part of me wondered if Henry understood what else it would mean to love me. What it would mean to his future. To his own prospects. To his dreams.

Henry had inherited his father's fortune, but to climb—to *really* climb, to the heights he dreamed—he would need a suitable wife at his side. Not a half-literate wild-child with no name or dowry to speak of.

I loved him. I did. But even then, my joy was shadowed by doubt.

I tried to explain this to Henry. I tried to tell him. But he grinned madly.

"Since when have you ever cared what others have to say?"

"But Henry—"

He took my hands. "Listen to me, Mary. Please."

God help me, I listened.

"I'm leaving Lyme Regis. Tomorrow. I'm going back to school with Edgar. His father's got me a place."

My heart fell out of my chest.

"That's why I had to tell you today. Even if you didn't love me back, I needed you to know, or—or I would have regretted it forever."

Henry was leaving Lyme Regis. I'd known it would come, eventually; his time here was always borrowed. But it was so much sooner than I'd imagined.

"But now? Now that we both know how the other feels?" He laughed happily. "I hardly mind leaving at all."

"Oh, good," I said sarcastically.

"Don't you see? This is just a step toward our future. A brief moment where we are parted, and then a lifetime to share. Ed has some grand ideas, Mary—you know how he is. This way, I can help him. Which will help *us*.

"In two years, I will go on to university. I plan to study geo-magic, of course, with Professor Buckland. And we will wed, then, Mary, and you can come with me. As my wife. As a woman, you won't be allowed at lectures, but I can share my notes with you, and my books, and we can work together. And then when I am done with university, I'll join the Geomagical Society. Buckland will nominate me, surely.

"You know I have plenty of money, Mary. We can travel the continent. Travel the world! All while hunting fossils. Think of what we can do! Together."

The vision was intoxicating. A future of fossils, and freedom, and Henry. I would be the wife of a geomagician. It was more than I'd ever dreamed for myself, and once it was laid out before me, I couldn't imagine any other life.

"What do you say? Be my wife, my love. Marry me, Mary."

And he smiled so earnestly that I took his offered hand and said, *Yes*.

An odd expression flickered across Henry's face as he watched mine. That furrowed brow and twisted lip would shatter all my hard-won dignity.

Was it pity? I could take his contempt. I was accustomed to contempt. Pity, though? Pity would unravel me.

But Henry was still talking. "I mean it, Mary. I've followed your career, you know. Studied your finds."

"I know," I said. "I've read your papers."

He raised an eyebrow. "You have?"

"I read *all* the papers."

He nodded. A muscle moved in his jaw. "I thought of writing. But I assumed you wouldn't want to hear from me. Not after . . ."

I laughed, lightly—at least, God, I hoped it was light. "After what?"

Henry frowned. "After how we left things . . . between us." He swallowed, his mouth twisting uncertainly. I had him off-balance. *Good.*

"Oh, you mean all *that*?" I waved dismissively. "I haven't thought about it in years. I had almost forgotten, really."

As if I could have forgotten. As if he hadn't left me shattered. As if he hadn't broken my heart.

We parted, that day, on the stairs to his stepfather's house, this secret engagement a golden chain between us.

"Goodbye for now, Henry," I said, and smiled with a meaningful look. I was already imagining his ring on my finger. The veil on my hair.

"Goodbye, Mary." He grinned back. Then he turned to go inside, and took my heart and my hope with him.

How young we both were.

The letters came steadily for a few months. I tore them open and pressed them to my breast, imagining I could smell Henry on the page or touch him through the ink.

Then the time between letters began to stretch, longer and

longer, and the words of love and longing were slowly replaced by short sentences about his days at school.

I wasn't a fool. I sensed the shift. And I whispered into my own letters, before I sealed the envelopes, my own kind of magic: *I love you, I love you, I love you. Love me, love me, love me.*

And then one day I counted the months and realized it had been seven since he'd written back. I waited one more, to be sure.

I wrote to Edgar then. He, at least, still answered my letters. *Please. Please—has Henry forgotten me?* I begged.

I am sorry to say I do suspect so, Edgar wrote back from school, and I could read the sorrow in between the lines. *Henry has a great deal of ambition, and little patience for anything that may hinder his climb.*

That was two years after Henry vowed his love and life to me on the beach. He would be off to university soon. And whatever he'd said that day, whatever he'd promised, I suppose I'd always suspected the truth.

I knew it was over. I gathered all the letters, and I brought them to the rocks by the sea, and I lit a candle and fed them one by one to the flame and scattered the ashes in the white surf.

Henry never wrote again.

Here, now, in the dim hold of the ship, a grown Henry ran a hand through his hair. There were scattered gray strands in it now, and more lines around his eyes. But he was still the same man who'd broken his promise.

"Oh," he said, his brows drawing together. "Well. That's good, then."

"We were just children. I never really believed you wanted . . . what you said you wanted."

I couldn't even say it aloud. Marriage. A life together. A life with me. Because of course I had believed him.

I bent to pick up Ajax so that Henry couldn't see my face. He chomped happily at the beetle in his beak as I carried him back to the crate.

Ajax made a small sound of protest but settled quickly. I closed the crate lid and turned back to Henry.

"You know"—his Adam's apple bobbed in a swallow—"when I agreed to accompany the professor, I thought that now, after all this time—I hoped perhaps we could be friends."

Maybe if I were a more forgiving woman, it would have been possible. But I had nursed this grudge from the cradle on my tears, and I wasn't about to send it to the grave now.

"I believe trust is a required condition for friendship," I said sharply. "I said I had almost forgotten the whole thing. That doesn't mean I forgive it. I have no need of your friendship, Mr. Stanton."

"Ah. I think you will find you do, *Miss Anning*. The Society is . . ." He drummed his fingers on one of the barrels. An annoyed huff came from Ajax's crate, and Henry ceased his tapping. "Traditional. You will need more allies than Buckland."

"Is that a threat?"

"No, Mary." He gave a half smile, mockery or pity or both, I couldn't tell. "It's an offer."

Chapter 16

We sailed into London just after noon the next day.

I'd thought myself prepared. Buckland often brought me copies of *The Times* and *The Morning Post,* so between the accounts of London's political scandals, innumerable murder trials, the new General Post Office, fire at the orchestra, and riots at the workhouse, I felt I understood the great city.

I was terribly wrong.

Lucy and I leaned over the railing, the wind cold on our cheeks. We shared the fog-cloaked Thames with scores of other vessels, headed upriver and down—small fishing boats and trading sail ships and even two hulking, belching steamboats. A small wood-hulled barge, its deck stacked with timber, passed below us, and her crew shouted obscenities that made my cheeks heat and Lucy laugh.

The river was hemmed by concrete embankments and wooden jetties onto which armies of dockworkers hauled brick, hay, and grain. Below, small figures—children, I realized—waded through the mud where low tide exposed the foreshore.

"Mudlarkers," Lucy said and sighed, before I could ask. "Poor things are searching for scrap metal to sell."

I watched the pack of grime-coated children and felt a warm spark of kinship for the mudlarkers hunting their treasures. Then I gagged as the wind carried up the smell of something rotten.

"You get used to the stench," Buckland said cheerfully, as he joined us at the rail. Henry was with the captain, near the bow. I looked away quickly when he turned toward us. *You will need more allies than Buckland,* he said last night.

He wasn't wrong; I *would* need to win other geomagicians to my cause if I wanted to earn my place in their ranks. But I knew Henry; he hadn't offered out of the goodness of his heart. So what game was he playing?

Buckland rattled off the names of churches, customhouses, and municipal buildings whenever they emerged from the gray fog. Soon after we passed under the almost-completed new London Bridge—still dressed in wooden scaffolding—the *Unity* docked.

I went into the hold to transfer Ajax to a lidded wicker basket and clutched it to my chest as we disembarked. Buckland and Henry arranged for coaches, and Lucy sent word to Edgar. I stood awkwardly, whispering to Ajax, though it was more to soothe my own nerves than his.

I'd assumed we would go straight to Palmanaeus House, but Buckland insisted on his own home first. "Catherine and the girls can help you freshen up," he said meaningfully, with an eye on my old dress. But he would send notice to all London members, he said, for an emergency Society meeting this evening.

Buckland was a showman by nature, but he was also cautious. The combination had served him well.

I understood his calculation. An urgent missive and emergency meeting would build anticipation, and Ajax's unveiling would be a true, revelatory spectacle, with no trickle of rumors to undermine the surprise. It would be the performance of Buckland's career.

Henry's elegant coach was soon drawn round, pulled by four prancing black geldings under the reins of a stiff-coated driver.

"I will see you tonight, then." Henry's eyes danced with some private amusement. I refused to smile back. "I hope you're ready. There's no going back now."

The wheels rumbled and hooves clacked on the cobblestones, and Henry was gone.

And good riddance, too.

Buckland, Lucy, and I climbed into another coach—less grand than Henry's, but still the finest I'd ever been in. I kept the window shade open to watch as we joined the swell of carriages and carts, carrying humans and sheep and chickens, or barrels of ale and baskets of turnips, or pallets of wool and silk, and all of us caught in the churn of the city, tumbling down too-narrow roads, wheels dodging pedestrians and the occasional loose pig.

The uneven stone of the road shook the teeth in my skull.

"Easy. We'll be there soon," I said softly to Ajax, when he squawked indignantly from inside the wicker basket.

The scene outside the coach windows changed as we traveled away from the river. We'd entered the wealthier neighborhoods; the houses stood in neat attached rows, in red brick or white stucco. There were lush hedges on either side of the road, and I caught flashes of more green, from parks and back gardens, as we passed the narrow alleys that ran behind each sumptuous row of houses to their mews.

Our driver turned down one of these lanes, and Buckland announced that we were nearly to his house. I stuck my head out the window again.

A young girl, maybe five or six, was half dangled from an open black iron gate, peering intently at our coach. She was the spitting image of her father. I waved. That had to be Blythe, the youngest of Buckland's three.

The girl squealed and darted up the steps as we pulled through the gate and into the back garden courtyard. Buckland's wife and other two daughters tumbled out the back door after the little one, all talking excitedly as their husband and father bounded out of the coach and sent Lucy and I rocking.

"Father, Father! You're back! Can we see the pterodactyl?"

"Hush, Blythe, you're not supposed to talk about it, it's a secret."

"But they're back now, what's the harm?"

"Darling," Catherine Buckland said, then grinned and kissed her husband. "The girls and I have missed you."

Two footmen appeared out of thin air and took the luggage. One tried to take Ajax's basket from my arms, and I yanked it away.

"This stays with me," I sniffed.

"Oh, is it in there?" the middle girl—Jane, I recalled—breathed.

"Patience, darling." Catherine Buckland laughed as she helped me down from the coach.

The garden was long and narrow, red-bricked walls on either side for privacy. The beds running along the far wall were tidy and neat, even in their winter rest, and two leafless trees stood guard at each end. The other wall, and part of the mews along it, had been converted into a menagerie, barred cages and covered doghouses and even a packed dirt pen with hurdles, something like a small-scale horse arena.

This was the *smaller* menagerie, I knew; most of the Buckland creatures were kept at their home in Oxford. I'd heard, through the years, tales of the hyena, and the eagle, and even a small bear that Buckland had kept until it escaped and ran through the Balliol garden.

"We only brought the guinea pigs and the prairie dog this time," Catherine said, noticing my examination, "and those live indoors and sleep with the girls. Well, and Silky, too," she said, gesturing toward the miniature horse, now craning its neck to see us over the half door of its stall.

"So, your pterodactyl will have plenty of space." Catherine grinned her motherly smile. "It is so good to see you, Mary. I've told William for years that I would like you to visit us and meet the girls."

"It's good to see you, too, Catherine," I said, as we embraced.

Catherine Buckland was an acclaimed scientific illustrator in her own right. In fact, she and Buckland were first introduced when Catherine was commissioned to illustrate one of his books.

In the early days of their marriage, back when I was a girl, Catherine accompanied her husband on most of his journeys down to Lyme Regis. But understandably, after they had children, she came less frequently, though Buckland always brought a trinket or sweet for me, courtesy of his wife.

The staff stabled the horses and put away the carriage as the rest of the introductions were made.

Elizabeth was the oldest daughter, at eighteen. She was tall and slim, with a heart-shaped face and wheat-warm ringlets.

Jane was next oldest, twelve and frowning, pulling unhappily at her skirts. The youngest, Blythe, was a whirl of perpetual motion, circling around our legs until her father swept her into his arms with a laugh.

"It's a pleasure to meet you all," Lucy said warmly, and Elizabeth Buckland blushed as she curtsied.

I had envied the Buckland girls, I think, since the day each was born. Those girls were the delight of their father's life. Though I knew Buckland cared for me—and as much as I cared for him—it wasn't the same.

I was a charity case, at first. A kind impulse, probably made to impress his new wife; I'm sure the truth was William Buckland never expected to see me again after our first interaction.

Only, he did. And then he was generous enough to keep buying my finds and, eventually, to teach me. He had classes full of students back at Oxford, but he always took time to answer my questions. To encourage my inquiry. He sent me articles and brought me books and connected me to his friends in the Society. Over the years, we'd turned from mentor and mentee to friends. And in my most secret of hearts, I had to admit that, yes, I sometimes thought of him as something like another father.

But I would never be his daughter. And maybe that wouldn't have been so painful if I had never known what it was to be loved so dearly, and then have lost it so suddenly.

Buckland swung Blythe up to sit on his shoulders. She pulled off his top hat and put it over her own yellow curls.

I told myself not to be sentimental. I was a grown woman, and my father had been decomposing in the ground for twenty years now. No need to keep moping around about it.

"Well, shall I let him out now?" I said, probably more sharply than I'd intended. "The pterodactyl," I clarified, needlessly.

"Yes!" shouted Blythe.

"I don't see why not," Catherine said, and her husband nodded. One of the servants trotted to shut the back gate.

"Then gather 'round, my dear ones," Buckland said, with raised hands and spread fingers, "and let us behold the great miracle of our age. The ancient brought back to us. The great beast revived. The old made new. The prehistoric dragon returned!" he said, and threw open the top of the picnic basket.

The dragon raised his head and squawked pitifully.

"Oh, dear," murmured Elizabeth.

Ajax was curled in his small towel, looking mostly like an aggrieved, brooding chicken.

"He's awfully small for a dragon," Blythe said.

"Is it sick?" Jane asked, peering over the side of the basket.

I plucked him out and clutched him to my breast. "*No*, he's not *sick*. He's just been stuck in boxes for far too long."

The girls crowded around me eagerly. Ajax squirmed unhappily, so I let him climb to my shoulder.

Once situated, he rose, stretching, and spread his wings, one behind my head and the other past my shoulder. He swiveled his head, golden eyes roving over the gathered admirers, flashing his colorful beak in that toothsome grin. The girls gasped.

"You can touch him, if you'd like," I said proudly. "He likes to have the top of his head scratched."

Jane was bravest. "He feels like Gerald!" She giggled as she scratched between the ridges over Ajax's eyes.

"Gerald is the caiman," Catherine explained.

I let Ajax down to the ground to hop around, and Blythe and Jane shrieked with delight and chased behind as he explored the garden, poking his beak curiously under the hedges.

Catherine herded the rest of us inside for tea, but Buckland went straight to his study, since he had to coordinate couriers to send word to the Society members for tonight's session.

He exchanged a quick kiss with Catherine, and I caught the flash of fear that slipped over Catherine's face.

"I hope you know what you're doing, love," she murmured in her husband's wake, before turning to us brightly. "Come, come. You must be starving."

Her naked fear was sobering, and I turned it over as the hot tea settled in my belly.

It was a reminder of the danger to us all in presenting Ajax publicly. I'd assumed Buckland's insistence on secrecy was to keep from spoiling the surprise, but I understood, looking at the anxious lines of Catherine's brow, that it was also a protective measure. She and Buckland were worried. If things tipped poorly tonight, we could all of us be branded sorcerers and thrown into prison.

I watched out the window as my little demon stood on his rear claws and flapped his leathery wings. He opened his toothed jaw to let out a cawing shriek that sent the hair on the back of my neck pricking.

I, too, hope Buckland knows what he's doing, I thought, and sent up an earnest prayer that I wouldn't spend tonight in a cell.

Chapter
17

EDGAR SENT A COACH FOR LUCY SOON AFTER, AND SHE bounded down the front steps with a perfunctory wave. "I'll see you tonight!" she called over her shoulder. "It will be wonderful, I just know it!"

Catherine was subtle about it, but it was obvious Elizabeth had been charged with attending me in Lucy's absence.

"I don't need a nursemaid," I protested, as the girl led me through the narrow back entryway and into the first-floor parlor.

"I'm only showing you to your room." Elizabeth smiled primly.

The house's walls were papered in green and gold and lined with warm reliq-lamps. Marble busts of scowling men and porcelain vases perched on pedestals, and a large oil painting hung above the piano. But this was William Buckland's home, after all, so the painting was of the animals entering Noah's Ark, and skeletons and fossils—neatly labeled with species and date of discovery—filled the alcoves and topped the tables.

"How does your father afford all this?" I murmured, gently poking a small marble statue of a snake.

Elizabeth flinched.

I had known Buckland wasn't poor. He was an Oxford don and church minister, and drew salaries from both. Plus he earned small profits from his books and the occasional well-attended public lecture.

But whenever I pictured Buckland at work in his study, I imagined him at a cramped desk in the corner, Catherine in a chair on the other side of the room at work on an illustration.

Obviously, in retrospect, I should have known the Bucklands were wealthy. After all, the family kept two houses, with staff, one in Oxford and this one in London.

"I didn't mean to be rude," I said, cursing my tongue and leaving the snake statue alone. Apparently I did need a nursemaid. "I only mean your father has been so kind to me, I suppose I imagined his station must not be too dissimilar from mine."

Elizabeth's face softened. "It's all right. My grandfather was a farmer, you know."

I was genuinely surprised. "I didn't. I thought Buckland's father was a metallumagician?"

We were flanked by more paintings in the hallway, one of a blue-and-white plesiosaur breaking the waves.

"No." She looked at me sideways, like she was surprised I didn't know this. "Grandfather knew the work of a metallumagician, but he never earned the title. 'His schoolroom was the field and fen,' Father likes to say." It was a good impression.

"But Grandfather taught himself to locate metal deposits. He hired himself out to the mining investors, at a lower price than a metallumagician. Then he invested back into the mining companies." She reddened. "That's why we're—well, as you said—I mean—"

"Wealthy."

"Yes." Her cheeks were shining apples. Her eyes flicked to mine and then away. "Father says you remind him of Grandfather. How you came from nothing, but earned a reputation for yourself nonetheless."

Then she darted forward, and I followed stiffly. I heard no obvious mockery in Elizabeth's tone, but her words—*from nothing*—hung in the air and left me uncertain.

I nearly laughed aloud as we passed the open door to what was obviously Buckland's real study. The lower half of each wall was glass display cases, filled with curiosities, and above these were shelves of books, all the way to the wood-beamed ceiling. A ladder tracked around all four walls to reach the tallest shelves.

No cramped corner workstation here. The desk was like a ship, at sea among piles of papers and stacks upon stacks of worn books.

On the other side of the desk, opposite the chair, stood a freestanding case, the upper half of glass and gold. Inside, resting on purple velvet, was a foot-long lower jawbone.

I paused in the doorframe. "Megalosaurus."

"You can tell that from here?" Elizabeth peered around me.

"Yes." I'd known immediately, from the size and shape of the bone. "I recognize it from drawings. But I've also heard your father go on and on about that thing for enough years, I'd probably know it from a hundred meters."

I remembered when Buckland first bought a few enormous fossilized teeth off a trader in Stonesfield, back in 1815. He'd spent years trying to identify the species, comparing it to every living creature and dead. They were lizard-like in structure, but too large for any known reptile; such a creature would have to be at least twelve meters in length.

The way he'd told the story, half the Society members jeered when he presented the hypothesis. Certainly the teeth were large, yes, but no lizard could grow that long, they said. It would collapse under its own weight. And where was his evidence, besides a bag of loose teeth?

Buckland and his friend William Conybeare came to Lyme Regis just after that failure of a meeting. We'd drunk together in The Three Crowns, and Buckland complained bitterly that he'd ruined his chance of discovering something truly new.

"Take it from a fossil hunter," I'd said, "there are always more bones. And if you don't find them, someone else will, and they will steal your discovery."

After that, Buckland bought every fossil out of Stonesfield that he could get his hands on.

Then came the jawbone—this jawbone—and five years ago, in 1824, Buckland presented to the Society the jaw, a piece of pelvis, a thigh bone, and several vertebrae the size of two men's fists on top of each other. *Megalosaurus*, he called it, and the applause was thunder.

In the letter he wrote to me after, Buckland called it his greatest triumph. *I owe you my deepest thanks, Mary, for I was lost and doubting and you gave me hope.*

I'd wept when I read those words. At the kindness in them. At the envy I felt, for the applause I would never hear.

"It's your father's proudest accomplishment," I murmured.

"Until now," Elizabeth said quietly. "Your pterodactyl will make him president, he says."

The tangle that left in me—of pride and jealousy, again—was too familiar.

"He still wants it, then? The presidency?" I was certain that he did, but I was curious what she would say. Curious what she knew of the matter.

"Desperately," Elizabeth said, as we climbed the stairs. "Davies is retiring this summer, finally, and Father says this is his last chance, before he's too old."

She pointed out the other rooms on this level: hers, Jane's, and then mine and Lucy's. The bath had already been drawn inside, the water steaming. My feet throbbed in anticipation.

The bed was four-poster, spread with a pink, rose-patterned quilt. The walls were painted butter yellow, and the wardrobe was nearly as wide as the bed frame. Bundles of dried lavender lay beside the pitcher and water bowl and across the pillow.

"I do hope Father wins. He has so many ideas for how to improve the Society." Elizabeth sighed. "Of course, you know that best of all."

Blythe barreled up the stairs and pitched into the room, followed by a laughing Jane and Catherine.

"Did you choose one already?" Blythe asked.

"Not yet," said Elizabeth. "I thought she'd want to bathe first."

"Choose what? And where's Ajax?" I said anxiously.

"Safe, I promise," Catherine said, and pulled aside a curtain so I could see into the back garden. Ajax was in a small, penned arena, poking around for bugs, I assumed. A knot between my shoulder blades unloosened.

"Choose one of the dresses!" Blythe squealed, prancing to the wardrobe and flinging open the door.

A rainbow of soft color hung in the wardrobe, in fine silk and cotton, lace trim and satin, embroidered flowers and puffed sleeves. My hands itched to touch them—to run my fingertips down the skirts and over the collars, just to feel the stitches, but I didn't want to get my dirt on the fine fabric.

I laughed. "Are you suggesting that perhaps I should not wear this to the Society this evening?"

I gestured over my body, at the mud-stained, mostly shapeless brown frock and the wrinkled floral kerchief that were my usual fossil-hunting uniform.

"You can't wear *that*," Blythe screeched. "It's wretched!"

"Blythe!" Jane and Elizabeth both gasped.

Catherine, thankfully, knew me well enough to laugh.

But still I stared, a moment too long. I had never worn a dress so fine as even the plainest in the wardrobe. Not once in my whole life.

I gave up dreaming of dresses like these a long time ago, when I put away fantasies of young bridehood and beauty. From the ache in my chest now, I knew they were only sleeping, never dead. But I was old now—nearly thirty—and wise enough to know those dreams were another girl's.

I could borrow a lovely dress, and let Elizabeth plait my hair and rouge my cheeks, but I couldn't unspool the years.

Catherine read something on my face and in my silence. "I'm sorry they're not new," she said. "We didn't have time to have dresses made, so these are mostly last season's fashions. But I think they will look stylish enough." She wrung her hands. "I hope you don't mind?"

Those hands were long-fingered, pale, the nails neatly filed. She had no calluses, I'd wager, but her knuckles were ink-stained a tawny gray.

Catherine Buckland should have been the most celebrated geomagical illustrator of our time. She had a gift. She should have studied in Paris. She should have apprenticed in Japan. She should have been hired in every nation, on every continent, to illustrate their artifacts. Her name should have been as well known as her husband's.

But she was a woman. And for all her talent, Catherine had

been beautiful, too, and she'd probably worn a dress like this the day she met Buckland. And Catherine probably pinched herself for happiness, to find a husband who admired her for her mind, and talent, and did not resent it.

If I'd married Henry, I would have lived Catherine Buckland's life.

If I had married Henry, I, too, would be the wife of a famous geomagician. I would be a mother, surely, with children of my own. I would have kept a home, or two, and I would manage a staff. I would wear fine dresses, and silk slippers. My husband would have been modern in his thinking on women's rights. He might have encouraged me to keep my hobbies—even to keep collecting fossils, if it brought me joy. And I would have counted myself lucky beyond measure.

But then there would have been babies to tend, and the house to maintain, and appearances to keep, and how did it really look, after all, if a lady went clambering about the rocks? What kind of example was she setting for her children? Didn't her husband mind?

If I'd ever had a trove of dresses like these, as a girl, or as a young bride, I wouldn't be here now. I would have slipped into another life. I would be happy, maybe, but not great. A wife, yes. But never a geomagician.

It was a sudden freedom, to realize I didn't want Catherine Buckland's life, or her daughters', either. But that didn't mean I couldn't appreciate a gorgeous gown.

"Thank you. They are beautiful. Truly." I laid my hands on Catherine's, and she relaxed with relief. "Blythe, why don't you pick out your favorites while I wash off some of this muck."

Chapter 18

Sir Jonathan Davies, President of the Geomagical Society of London, did not seem like a man often anxious. He had the kind of solemn face that had settled into craggy granite folds over the years. With his white hair, icy blue eyes, and a nose like a mountain peak, it was easy to imagine Davies staring down a wayward geomagician or addressing the assembly in his deep Welsh baritone.

But the man was nervous now. Sweat shimmered at his retreating hairline, and his fingers tapped. Unlike Buckland, Davies, and myself, Henry didn't seem nervous at all.

There had been some tense debate about the speaking order, but it was ultimately determined that Davies would open, Buckland would speak next, and then Henry would conclude the presentation. I could tell from their small smiles that both men thought they'd received the better slot.

The four of us were waiting in the wings of the Palmanaeus auditorium, separated from the stage and the gathered crowd of geomagicians by black velvet curtains. I held Ajax, stroking his head and chest, but any minute now I would transfer him to the wheeled cage beside us, with its golden filigree like fluttering wings. It was originally commissioned, Buckland said, to house a kookaburra gifted to the royal menagerie from the governor of New South Wales. I didn't want to ask what became of the bird.

The black curtains did little to muffle the collective speculation of our audience. Based on the snatches of gossip, most of the geomagicians seemed to think that Davies was about to announce his immediate retirement, with either Buckland or Henry—who, they had noticed, were not among the gathered—to be named interim president until the meeting in June.

"How many are there?" I asked.

"About forty, I expect," Davies said. "Current Society membership is sixty-four, but of course not everyone could be reached in time."

Forty gathered geomagicians. And we were about to deliver the shock of their lives.

My God, we really are about to change the world.

My stomach pitched with mingled excitement and fear. I pressed a hand to my waist, over the smooth yellow satin of the gown Blythe had chosen, as if that could settle the butterflies.

I'd imagined this moment a thousand times since we left Lyme Regis three days ago, but now that it was here, I felt mostly terror.

"It will be Stanton, surely," said a blustering voice over the fray, beyond the curtain. "The old man's time is long passed."

Someone scoffed loudly. "Your master isn't here, Whaley; no need to wag your tail."

Henry chuckled.

I caught only snatches after that, as the shouts rang over one another—furious phrases such as *how dare you*, and *decrepit*, and *impudent fool*—until a nasal voice rose above the fray.

"Gentlemen, gentlemen. Perhaps we ought to hold our speculation until we know what this emergency session is actually about."

I recognized that nasal voice: William Conybeare. He was the Society's master of fellows, and Buckland's closest friend and ally. He'd visited Lyme Regis many times, and while we were always cordial, he and I had never warmed to each other, despite Buckland's efforts. I'd always found Conybeare cold and haughty, and he found me, well, a woman, and therefore less than worthy of his time.

But what had Buckland told him? Did Conybeare already know what waited behind the curtain?

"It's time," Davies said, and when I didn't move, Buckland put a hand on my shoulder and looked pointedly toward the cage.

Ajax snuggled closer to my chest, chirping sweetly. The tip of his beak was sharp through the thin silk of my borrowed dress. I stroked at his head, a sudden heat in my eyes as he nuzzled against my palm.

It feels like goodbye.

But it wasn't. I would be a while in London, a few weeks, at least. I could still see him.

Still, I kissed the top of his scaled head as Buckland opened the cage door. A few thick branches were placed at different heights for perching, and I poked Ajax until he stepped onto one.

"Good fellow," I murmured, and stepped back, throat thick. Buckland closed the door.

He needs a place for a nest, I thought; *he doesn't sleep perched, he sleeps curled up. He needs his blankets. I should have brought his blankets.*

But Davies was already sweeping out through the curtains. The emergency session of the Geomagical Society of London was called to order.

⁓☙⁓

Davies spoke, but said nothing. He blathered on for a few minutes, thanking everyone for gathering on such short notice. He promised it would be worthwhile.

Buckland paced, muttering his speech. Henry was silent, his face calm stone. I crept forward to peer at Davies's back through the curtain. The lecture theater stage was a semicircle, with velvet-upholstered benches in a half moon and a narrow overhanging gallery at the back.

Conybeare sat near the center of the front row, his back stiff as iron. I could pick out a few more faces—geomagicians who'd come to visit Lyme Regis on occasion, to hunt fossils under my guidance or to buy from me. I wondered which one was Gideon Mantell. We'd exchanged a few letters over the years, and I'd sold him several specimens on mail order, but he'd never come to Lyme Regis. And which one was Archibald Taylor? I was looking forward to sharing my corrected copy of his plesiosaur paper. Samuel Enys had to be among the crowd, too. His analysis of my first ichthyosaur find still gave me a headache to recall. My chest quivered with excitement.

Davies was about to call out Buckland. "For you see," he said, "our very own William Buckland and Henry Stanton have returned to London with the most important discovery of our time."

Buckland transformed as he strolled from behind the curtains.

His chest broadened, shoulders stretching wide as if pulled with a wire. He was somehow taller, too.

So, this was the showman—the Professor and Reverend William Buckland that students lined up to see lecture.

"Summon in your minds, if you will," he said, somehow softly and booming at once, and the buzz in the hall quieted as he walked to the center of the stage and raised his hands. "The great cliffs of Lyme Regis, the crumbling rock and the crash of the sea. The ancient Blue Lias formation, in which so many specimens of ichthyosaurus and plesiosaurus have previously been discovered. You know this place. Many of you have walked there, with that dear friend of the Society, young Miss Mary Anning."

Henry was holding my hand.

I realized it with a sudden start, and nearly jerked away. His fingers were twined with mine, steady pressure. I hadn't known my hands were trembling. I didn't let go.

"We gather tonight, under these expedited conditions, because that same Miss Anning has recently found the skeleton of an unknown species of that most rare and curious of all reptiles, the pterodactyl."

Through the gap in the curtain, I saw a few frowns and exchanged looks at that declaration. Annoyance, that they'd been called from home for this. Yes, an English pterodactyl was exciting. But an emergency meeting? A smile tripped on Henry's lips.

"The creature she found is of a genus that has yet been recognized only in the upper Jura limestone beds of Eichstätt and Solnhofen, in the lithographic stone, which is contemporary with the chalk of England. The specimen is extraordinary.

"The creature somewhat resembles our modern bats and the vampyre species, but has its beak elongated like the bill of a woodcock and is armed with teeth like the snout of a crocodile.

Its vertebrae, ribs, pelvis, legs, and feet resemble those of a lizard, and the three anterior fingers terminate in long hooked claws like that on the forefinger of the bat. Over its body is a covering of scaly armor like that of an iguana, and small, hairlike filaments. Can you see it? Can you hear its cry? Imagine—flocks of these creatures, clouding the skies, soaring above the waters in which the sea-beasts dwelled."

Buckland's voice soared and dipped, and even I could picture the creature he summoned with the power of his words.

The crowd was with him now, despite their annoyance. The gathered men, from oldest to youngest, their faces rapt, leaned forward to catch Buckland's every word.

"In short," Buckland cried, "a monster, resembling nothing that has ever been seen or heard of upon Earth, excepting the dragons of romance and heraldry."

I didn't know how he did it, but his body somehow stilled, like all the vibration had gone out of his limbs.

His voice dropped, low and solemn. "But the skeleton Miss Anning found did not perish alone. For with her—clasped to the mother's breast—was a single, precious egg."

Well, that wasn't quite accurate, but I couldn't very well correct him at the moment.

Buckland let this linger for a moment, the powerful image of the dying mother and her egg. I remembered how I'd felt when I found it: the way it had moved me, even as I knew it was foolish anthropomorphizing to think the mother felt such a human emotion. Now Buckland worked the same trick on them all.

"Mary picked up the egg, and cradled it in her gentle hands," Buckland continued quietly, miming the actions. "And by some miracle—by some act of God—"

"That's my cue," Henry said, and slipped his hand from mine.

He grasped the bars of the golden cage and began to push, wheels squeaking softly as they gained speed. The heavy black curtain parted around them, and I heard a sound I'd never imagined: a sea of people gasping at the same moment.

The curtains closed behind Henry, and once again I peered through a narrow slit, this time as the audience erupted.

"The creature *awoke*," said Henry, and even I was caught in the spell of his voice, the smooth, confident musicality of it.

He's as good as Buckland, I thought, as a hundred expressions flickered across a hundred faces. Shock, and awe, and disbelief, and joy, and fear, and every combination thereof.

A few men leapt to their feet and began shouting. One man threw himself to his knees and began praying loudly, asking God to forgive us, to forgive him, to save us from the coming damnation.

"It is a miracle," someone cried fiercely, tears streaming down his face. "A miracle."

"That can't possibly be real," blustered another voice. "It must be a hoax. It has to be."

"Please," said Henry, raising his hands for order. But I could tell he was delighted. "Please, my friends. It is no hoax, and no demon, I promise. Come. Come and see. Come and see the creature, and make up your own mind."

"I told you," declared a giddy man in his forties with prominent gray sideburns. "All creatures return in cycles. I told you. I was *right*, and you all called me a fool!"

I smiled; that had to be Charles Lyell. I'd managed to steal Lyell's newest book from Henry's cabin before we disembarked. Lyell was infamous for his—obviously incorrect—hypothesis that Earth's features were formed by gradual, cyclical phenomena like erosion rather than climactic occurrences such as volcanoes and floods. That itself was a relatively harmless unorthodoxy, but Lyell had been mocked from the lecture stage, and by Henry, most memorably, for claiming that animal and plant species waxed and waned alongside these gradual cycles.

I knew Ajax didn't prove what Lyell hoped, but the man was practically dancing a jig, and I couldn't help but find his enthusiasm charming.

More men came forward, some hesitantly, others nearly leaping rows to race to the stage. A few refused, gathering in clusters to whisper and cast dark glances at my pterodactyl. But most of the geomagicians came.

Ajax squawked and spread his wings, putting on a good show and eliciting more gasps and excited chatter. The men crowded around his cage, commenting on his beak, his claws, the gold of his eyes, wondering what he ate, when he slept, how he flew.

I could answer all of those, if they let me.

He isn't yours, though. You sold him; he's theirs.

"See," Buckland was saying. "No hoax. You have seen the sketches of the German pterodactyl skeletons; this is the same."

"And for once, the professor and I agree," Henry said smugly.

The most surprising reaction was Conybeare's. He must not have known, because his already pale face was white with horror. He grasped Buckland's elbow. "*William,*" he hissed. "You said—you told me—"

"Is it not miraculous?" Buckland said pleasantly.

But Conybeare shook his head fiercely. "No. No. That is a demon. A devil. That creature . . ." He drew a shuddering breath. "Sorcery. It must be. It has to be."

Buckland frowned at his friend in alarm. "You misunderstand. Mary has—"

"Then she has ensorcelled you, too."

Buckland protested, but Conybeare was backing away, muttering a prayer of protection under his breath. "I cannot abide it. I must not."

He pivoted, walking quickly for the back door. A few others turned to watch, with worried looks. Two followed.

I chewed at my nail nervously. So, that was three who thought me a sorcerer. But Buckland didn't seem concerned.

"Ah! Lyell," he was saying already, "I see you have noticed the beast's claws. Do you see the three fingers? His grip is quite strong."

"Why don't we bring her out? You can ask Miss Anning yourself. She's only through there."

I jumped at the sound of my name in Henry's voice. He was standing with a cluster of geomagicians. His smirk widened when I met his eye, and he strode toward me, brushing the black curtain aside.

"Won't you come and meet your admirers?" he said, offering an arm.

"Davies said to stay here, and Buckland—"

"Yes, the professor does like to keep you all for himself, doesn't he," Henry said, and I bristled. He was trying to get under my skin, but that didn't mean it wasn't working.

Henry led me out from the curtains and through the gathered crowd. I swallowed as the conversation fell, and every eye turned to us. My fingers tightened unconsciously on Henry's arm.

Ajax, at least, gave a hoot and flapped his wings when he caught sight of me.

"Gentlemen, allow me to introduce Miss Mary Anning, of Lyme Regis," Henry said, as we stood in the center of the crowd, beside the aviary. "Our great discoverer."

"Is it true? Did the egg really hatch in your hand?"

I blinked, trying to find the source of the called question—a young man in his thirties with a patchy red beard and flushed cheeks.

There was a burst of chatter, heads turning to fellows and dropping whispers.

Buckland watched all of this with a neutral expression, and I wished I could read the thoughts in his skull. Did he disapprove?

Well, he couldn't always be my protector. I couldn't live in his shadow forever. The geomagicians would need to accept me or reject me on my own merits.

I squared my shoulders and waited for a hundred small decisions to be made, my fate in every one. The murmured discussions rolled over me like a river.

Crowds were fickle. Where would the waters carry this one? Would they doubt me still, or believe? Would they conclude it a hoax? Or sorcery, like Conybeare? Would they laugh—even if they believed—and push me out, even with Henry and Buckland both on my side?

"Yes," I said, at last.

I bit my tongue, fighting the urge to ramble on. Let them doubt me, if they wanted. I'd told the truth, and it needed no further defense. Still, my pulse thudded in my ears.

"Could it fly from birth?"

The question cut through the rest, addressed to me and not another geomagician. It was the young man with red hair.

"Not fly," I said. "Ajax still doesn't fly as a songbird. But he could soar soon after hatching. Within the hour, I would say?"

"Within the hour!" an elderly gentleman with half-moon spectacles declared.

"That suggests very low parental involvement, then. Like a lizard, or crocodile," another muttered thoughtfully.

"The mother was found with the egg, you say? So, she must have tended the nest before hatching."

The spectacled gentleman cleared his throat. "And was there any evidence of nesting materials?"

"No. I didn't see any imprints of sticks or twigs or other organic material at the site."

"Perhaps they buried their eggs, then."

"Yes, in moist sand, I think," I said slowly.

"That seems reasonable. Then, Miss Anning, did you find . . ."

And on it went, the geomagicians asking their questions and me answering, until my cheeks ached from the effort required to keep from grinning.

Once introductions were made, the redheaded young man was revealed to be none other than my friend Gideon Mantell. I laughed when he finally sheepishly introduced himself.

Even with only correspondence to go on, I had always been fond of Mantell. His father had been a shoemaker, which made him unique among geomagicians for his lack of pedigree. I always assumed that Buckland first put us in touch because of our similar backgrounds.

"You will have to come to dinner and meet my wife," Mantell said, grinning warmly. "Ann has long admired your career."

Frankly, I had little interest in entertaining a bored housewife, but I gave a polite response before Henry's hand on my back moved me smoothly along to meet others.

The bespectacled man who'd asked about nesting materials was Elias Goldsmild.

"An honor to meet you," he said earnestly, when we shook hands, and I was immediately put at ease by his warm smile.

"And these"—Henry gestured at a cluster of three—"are Misters Thomas Reed, Thomas Whaley, and Samuel Enys." Whaley and Reed looked to be about forty, but Enys was probably in his mid-twenties.

Whaley was glaring furiously at Goldsmild. Ah, it must have been Goldsmild who'd chided him earlier. Was the older man allied with Buckland, then?

And Samuel Enys, at last!

"You wrote a paper about my ichthyosaur," I said eagerly.

He beamed. "I did indeed."

"You misidentified the tail kink as a result of postmortem damage."

His smile slipped. "There were few specimens available at the time with which to compare," he said defensively.

"Well, yes, until I found them."

Henry laughed and clapped the red-faced Enys on the shoulder.

"Now, gentlemen. Lady,"—Henry inclined his head at me; I couldn't even tell if it was sarcastic—"I propose that we move this fascinating discussion to my estate, perhaps over some whiskey. Nothing formal. You'll come, won't you, Miss Anning?"

"Oh, I don't think—"

"I'm sure the professor will allow it," Henry continued, as if I hadn't spoken. "Won't you, Buckland? You are also welcome, of course."

I could see Buckland wanted to decline—for the both of us—but the crowd was already in motion, men excitedly gathering coats and hats.

"You will come, won't you, Miss Anning?" Goldsmild asked, and Mantell added, "Stanton always opens up his private collection. Did you know he has a partial saber-tooth tiger?"

Buckland came up behind me. "Please don't make me go to Henry Stanton's house," he muttered so only I could hear. "Haven't we had plenty of the man, these last few days?"

I snorted. "More than enough. But . . ." I chewed my lip. "Don't you think I ought to go? Eventually, I will want their votes, won't I? And it does seem like I am making progress. . . ." *Maybe even friends,* I thought, glancing toward an expectant-looking Goldsmild and Mantell.

Buckland rubbed his brow, and sighed. "One more night of Stanton won't kill me. I suppose."

Chapter

19

Henry Stanton was proved a liar yet again.

Nothing formal, he'd said. *Ha.*

Our coach rumbled down the long stone drive to Henry's estate. A row of willows was planted on either side of the road, their drapery twined with strands of mirror shards that glittered and tinkled pleasantly as the night breeze stirred the leaves. Music drifted on the wind, too, the energetic strains of pianoforte and raucous laughter.

At least I no longer needed to worry that I was overdressed. The gown I'd changed into for the evening was a deep sapphire blue embroidered with tiny stars across the bust and hem. It was cut below my collarbone, across my shoulders, and had puffed sleeves and a full skirt that swished when I walked. Elizabeth and Catherine had agreed that I looked like a princess.

But despite the gown and the glitter of it all—and because of it—part of me was already regretting the whole venture. I was nervous. I'd wanted to be part of things—that was why I'd come to London, wasn't it? But it was still nerve-racking. This was another world from my seaside town. It felt like I was about to step foot on another planet, with only hope that I'd be able to breathe the air.

At least Buckland was in a good mood. Presenting Ajax had been more successful than I think he'd imagined. Even a journey to his archenemy's home couldn't deflate his spirits.

I tried to keep my own disappointment about Lucy's absence in check. She hadn't come to Palmanaeus House for Ajax's reveal, and she hadn't returned to Buckland's in time for our departure. *She hasn't seen Edgar in almost a year,* I reminded myself. *Don't be churlish.*

As for Ajax, we'd left him behind in his golden cage. I hadn't realized we would be leaving him at Palmanaeus House overnight until Buckland began turning off the reliq-lamps and Ajax started screeching and fluttering around the cage. I'd just assumed Ajax would be coming back to Buckland's house. But Buckland had plans for converting a permanent place in the exhibit hall, and said there was no point moving him until then. It made logical sense, but I couldn't very well explain it to Ajax in those terms. He just knew I was leaving him, yet again, in a dark and unfamiliar place.

Elizabeth Buckland had looked almost as sad when we left her behind.

"You're *so* lucky. Women never, *ever* get to go to these geomagical receptions," she'd said, sighing, while plaiting my hair over the crown of my head. "Not even when Father hosts them here."

Henry's Heronstone Manor came into view: a sprawling redbrick house, white columns at the entry and climbing vines curling toward a slate roof. A row of coaches was parked out front in a neat line, and footmen swarmed as our driver pulled to the back of the queue.

I wasn't sure what protocol was—I'd never even seen a house so fine, let alone been invited inside—but clearly Buckland knew how to do this sort of thing. I told myself not to be a country fool and followed the butler up the stairs.

He led our party through the open wood-and-iron doors and then into a cavernous great hall, where I couldn't help but catch my breath.

We were greeted by a curving double staircase, like twin scrolls unfurled to the marble floor. Sunbursts of flowers, lush as summer, decorated the railings with ribbon, and a chandelier of glass and reliq-lamps hung from the ceiling and cast gold sparkles across the room. A servant took my coat as I stood struck and silent, and then Henry Stanton was striding toward us from the open set of doors between the staircases.

"Ah, Professor," he began, and then he stopped short, almost stumbling, and the usual ever-present smirk slid off his face. "Mary."

I looked around, then down at my blue dress, afraid I'd done something terribly wrong. Maybe I was overdressed. Or maybe he was expecting me to bring Ajax?

But before I could work it out, Edgar Murray, Viscount Merlton, strode into the room, Lucy bouncing beside him.

"Surprise!" Lucy exclaimed.

"Mary, my dear!" Edgar clasped my hand. "You didn't really think we'd miss your great triumph, did you?"

Unlike Henry, who even I could admit was unnaturally good-looking, Edgar had never been handsome. But Edgar Murray had never met a situation he wasn't certain he could improve—his appearance included. His dark-blond hair was stylishly arranged to hide the top of his ears, and the double-breasted brocade waistcoat made him look broader-chested than he really was.

"Now, if you'll follow me"—Henry gestured—"the festivities are out back in the gardens."

"Should I collect my coat?" I looked around for the servant who'd taken it.

"It's terribly ostentatious." Lucy sighed, looping her arm through mine. "But no, you don't need a coat. Henry's done something to the air—"

"It's my working, actually," Edgar said, raising his index finger.

"And an ingenious one, too." Henry clapped him on the shoulders. Edgar had improved at concealing his thoughts over the last fifteen years, because the tightening around his eyes was almost imperceptible, except that I knew to look for it.

Edgar fell in beside me as we walked through the ballroom, which was more sumptuous even than Buckland's, gilt and landscapes painted on every wall. "I'm glad you've finally come to London. It will be refreshing to converse with someone who can keep up." He smiled.

I felt a wave of something like vertigo, thinking about the last time the four of us were together—a gang of lonely children with the whole of life before us, glittering and gold.

Before my own dreams turned to ash.

I tried to squash the resentment curdling under my ribs. I didn't want to be angry with Edgar. I had never asked him to choose my friendship over Henry's—just as I'd never asked Buckland. It was Henry who'd shattered my heart and left me behind, a discarded sacrifice to his own shining future.

I smiled back. "I was actually going to write to you—have you read *Deontolomagica, on Ethics*?"

"Have I read it?" Edgar snorted. "I gave Bentham the idea. What is a good action? You see, it depends on one's definition of *good*."

I didn't especially care; I just knew Edgar would enjoy the subject. The walls were decorated with nearly as many fossils, skeletons, and mounted exotic creatures as there were paintings—at just a quick glance, I spotted a snarling polar bear in the corner, a plesiosaur spine, a stuffed dodo bird, and a deerlike creature with curled devil horns.

Three geomagicians lounged on couches at the back, deep in earnest discussion, the air around them thick with cigar smoke.

But the back wall was wholly glass, and Henry and Lucy were telling the truth: the party was, somehow, being held outside, despite the April chill.

The garden trees had the same mirror-shard strands as the drive, scattering the moon and reliq-lamplight in dappled silver across the spiraled stone of the patio.

"... and the highest good, therefore, would be that action or moral decision which achieves the most good for the most people—"

"Why, it's an ammonite," I exclaimed, interrupting Edgar as I recognized the full shape of the patio.

"Nature's golden ratio." Henry turned. He'd been listening. "Mary, would you like a quick tour of the grounds?"

I didn't want to give Henry the satisfaction, but I couldn't resist. Buckland declined and went to join a small cadre of geomagicians, but Lucy, Edgar, and I followed Henry onto the grass.

His house—his estate, rather—was like something from a dream. The air was enchanted to be warm as mid-July, and coats and jackets were strewn across the lawn. Men gathered in small groups, on chairs and chaises and standing in huddles, and I caught snatches of conversation as we walked, gossip about recent geomagical finds, debates about theory, and discussion of fossil-hunting methods. My urge to leap in was tempered only by my desire to absorb all the rest.

Glowing orbs—not reliq-lamps, but simply amorphous, flickering balls of pure yellow light—floated overhead, buoyed on slow currents of air. And no one was playing the instruments. They'd been enchanted to play themselves: a jaunty pianoforte pressing its own keys, and a harp plucking its own strings. Violins and cellos floated in midair, bows gliding across the strings on their own. Someone handed me a crystal glass of some kind of port, so warm and sweet I had to be careful not to drink it all at once. I wanted all my wits about me tonight.

"It's obscene," Lucy chided Henry as we followed him through the greenhouse, where ripe oranges shimmered like jewels. "How many reliqs does this take, just to keep these trees alive in the dead of winter? And those floating reliq-lamps. How many men and women gave their magic to light your vanity moons, hmm?"

I hadn't been thinking in those terms, but of course Lucy was. This kind of luxury would require extraordinary amounts of stored magic, probably thousands of reliqs. Even running this home on a day-to-day would require a huge number of reliqs.

The poor sold our magic to the slicks, and the rich bought it, and that was just how things worked. But I'd never thought much about what the rich did with their reliqs. In all the years I'd heard Lucy rant and rage about the unfair economics of reliquary trade, I clearly hadn't been creative enough to imagine harps and floating orbs, all enchanted with the reliqs one of us peasants would otherwise have used to start our hearth or repair a ripped seam.

But Henry didn't flinch. "Seven men and women, to light them all, and most of the rest of this, besides. One manifold reliq filled at the Glasswater Mill, and *voila*"—he gestured with one hand, the light sparkling in his champagne flute—"all of this."

"Yes, yes. That's precisely the benefit of the manifold reliqs," Edgar added eagerly. "As I explained to you earlier, the combined—"

Lucy put up a palm. "I don't want another lecture on the schematics of your little machine."

"The Loom is a very large machine, actually." Henry tipped his glass cheekily.

Edgar groaned. "You're not helping."

"I want you—both of you"—Lucy's glare swept over Henry—"to consider whether this is really a good idea. Right, Mary?"

I was too slow to respond, apparently, because Lucy's face fell. I could see why she was upset, but I couldn't muster quite the same outrage.

"My dear Luce," Edgar said gently, taking her arm. "As I was just saying to Mary, *good* is really a question of proportion. And the manifold reliq Looms provide a scalable solution to free the poor from reliance on the slicks."

Lucy let her brother guide her back to the greenhouse door, but the furrow between her brows only deepened.

We returned to the patio, where Buckland was holding court. Even here in the house of his rival, he was loose and loud. Wine sloshed in his glass as he told some joke and the geomagicians around him laughed.

"I invite the professor to these receptions every time, you know, but this is the first one he's attended in years," Henry said, low enough that Edgar and Lucy didn't hear.

"I wish I had known," he continued, "that to step out of his shadow would mean the end of our friendship."

I knew it was manipulation, but still, I heard the ring of truth in his words.

"Come," Henry said when I didn't respond, "I should not monopolize your time, as I know there are others who are very eager to speak with you."

He led us toward a cluster of geomagicians near the enchanted self-pouring champagne. I recognized the warm smile of Elias Goldsmild, and blushed at an eager wave from red-haired Gideon Mantell. Young Samuel Enys was trying to hide his dislike, but poorly, and the Thomases, Whaley and Reed, were indifferent to me, but were sharply focused on Henry's every word.

I was introduced to Charles Lyell and to Archibald Taylor.

"Mr. Lyell, I am so looking forward to reviewing your new book. And Mr. Taylor! I read your recent plesiosaur paper. I was hoping you would be here."

Taylor preened. "You enjoyed it, I hope?"

Lucy coughed and pinched my arm, and I swallowed down my first response. I'd already made an enemy of Enys, clearly—it would be best not to make another.

"Oh, I thoroughly enjoyed annotating it," I said, which was true, but left Taylor with a baffled expression.

I noticed, with a mixture of alarm and pride, as the other geomagicians peeled from Buckland's crowd to join our circle.

"Would you like to see, Miss Anning?" asked Samuel Enys, loudly interrupting as Henry introduced me to a stooped, white-haired geomagician he called Mr. Lawson. "They're very expensive; I doubt you've had many chances to examine one."

"Examine what?" I asked curiously, turning from Mr. Lawson.

Thomas Whaley, with whom Enys had been speaking, waved a hand and said, "I was only showing Mr. Enys my new bezoar. Recently retrieved from an ichthyosaur skeleton, in Charmouth."

I managed not to snort. "A bezoar, you say?"

Bezoar stones, found in animal intestines, were once believed to counter any poison. I'd read that for a while in the Middle Ages, goat-stomach bezoars were the most popular reliq for the upper class.

True bezoars are caused when an animal swallows some non-organic material like a pebble, and the stomach reacts by coating the material with layers of calcium and phosphate. But this was no true bezoar.

"I'd love to see it," I said.

Whaley presented his treasure on a silk scarf with a flourish. Enys looked smug. There were admiring sounds all around.

"So dark!" someone said. "Dark as pitch."

"Or ink," I mumbled, which perhaps wasn't polite. But none of them seemed to notice. Buckland wasn't around to give me a warning *look,* and Lucy didn't know enough to know she ought to.

Whaley said he would be taking it to the slicks soon, to be turned into a reliq. I bit the inside of my cheek.

"May I hold it?"

Whaley was clearly reluctant, but he let me pick it up from the silk and turn it over in my hands. Sometimes these were mistaken for petrified fir tree cones. But I'd pulled enough from the intestines of ichthyosaur skeletons to know it. Like the other "bezoars" I'd examined, this one was long and cylindrical, roughly cone-shaped.

"Would you like me to tell you what it is?" I asked, handing it back to Whaley.

"I know a bezoar when I see one," Whaley snapped, as Enys scoffed openly.

"Have you ever cut one open?"

He scoffed. "Why would I do that?"

"Hmm. Very well."

The other geomagicians looked between us, loyalty to Whaley warring with curiosity. Henry cocked his head but said nothing. A smile played over his lips.

"Well, I want to know," said Elias Goldsmild.

I shrugged. "I think I must defer to Mr. Whaley."

"Fine," he snapped. "What do you think it is, Miss Anning, if not a bezoar?"

It was difficult to keep the glee from my voice. Lucy tried to pinch me, but it couldn't be helped.

"Why, it's feces, Mr. Whaley."

Henry burst into laughter, and he wasn't alone. Edgar snorted. Samuel Enys gasped, but then began to giggle wildly. Whaley's face was a rapidly ripening tomato.

"We can cut it open," I said, "if you'd like to see. You'll almost certainly find small fish bones. And the black color is, I believe, from the ink of belemnites that the ichthyosaur consumed. My own studies suggest they were a regular part of the ichthyosaur diet.

"See, Mr. Whaley," I said—in all earnestness—"just think of all we can learn about the ichthyosaur's diet from your 'bezoar.'"

Whaley seethed, his eye twitching, but Goldsmild asked if I had interest in collaborating on a paper about the subject. And apparently Enys had forgiven me, too, because he suggested we find a mallet right away to open up the bezoar with haste.

Chapter 20

Henry leaned over, his breath warm on my ear. I glared, and he stepped back, putting the appropriate distance between us.

"Would you like to see the saber-tooth?"

Even if it was, lamentably, Henry's property, that wasn't the kind of invitation a fossilist ever turned down.

I started to follow, already eager. Henry had authored a paper about his saber-tooth tiger a few years ago, which I'd read, but since they were an exclusively terrestrial species, I had never had the chance to see a skeleton other than in ink.

Lucy coughed, and Henry's brow knit briefly. "You and Ed, too, of course."

Buckland and Henry might have different philosophies regarding the nature of geomagical change, but there was a great deal of overlap between their tastes in décor. A python skeleton hung from the ceiling of Henry's office, frozen in undulation by thin wire and clacking softly with a breeze from the open window. The built-in cabinets were a parade of fossils, carefully mounted and labeled, a clutter of delights. Henry's study was on the second floor, overlooking the hedge maze and the formal rose garden, and moonlight and the floating light-orbs cast a silvery glow through the room.

We huddled around the saber-tooth tiger bones, the yellowed-ivory skull nestled on red velvet.

"Beautiful," I murmured, as I ran my fingertips down the length of one perfect canine. The other was cracked near the root, the rest of the tooth lost to time and dirt. When Henry and I began debating how far the lower mandible must have unhinged for the beast to sink those terrible canines into the throat of its prey, Lucy and Edgar grew bored and drifted over to Henry's crystal collection.

Henry cleared his throat.

"There's actually another specimen I'd like to show you, while we're here." He crossed to one of the tall, dark cabinets with an iron handle. "I bought this fossil from a Mr. Peter Hawkins, two years ago."

It didn't ring a bell. "I don't know the name. Does he hunt fossils in Dorset?"

Henry shook his head. "Not a hunter. A collector." He slid one drawer open on smooth silent hinges. I recognized the specimen at once and gasped with delight.

The specimen was a complete sclerotic ring from around the eye of an ichthyosaur, a circlet of bony, segmented plates, like scales. It lay like a crown, pillowed on a bed of black velvet.

I remembered this eye-ring well. It was the best of my samples, the finest of the four I'd sold to the Swiss geomagician to repay Lucy.

I stroked it tenderly, remembering the pain of the selling, and the elation of its discovery. When I found that ring, I had to chisel it free over the course of one long, cold morning, my fingers slipping from wet and numbness. I spent an hour looking, but there was no sign of the rest of the skull. Only this near-perfect circle, the eye of a monster.

I ran my fingers over the stone plates, picturing the white of an enormous eye, a black pupil turning its gaze on me like some slippery prey. I'd never again found another eye-ring so complete, and I'd never read account of anyone having done so, either.

"Your original buyer—Mr. Hedinger, I believe—made some bad investments in the Americas and had to sell off most of his collection. His loss was Mr. Hawkins's gain, and now"—Henry said, gesturing at the eye-ring—"yours."

"I am very glad to see it again," I said, feeling strangely touched. "Thank you for showing me."

Henry laughed. "Oh, no, you misunderstand. The eye-ring is yours. It's a gift."

My very eyeballs must have bulged. I didn't know what to say. "I—Henry—"

My tongue tripped over itself as I wavered between refusal and acceptance. I wanted the ring, obviously, but I didn't want to be a pawn in whatever game Henry was playing now.

Buckland.

This had to be about Buckland. They were both vying for society president. Maybe Henry hoped to use me against Buckland. But how? Set me to spy on him, perhaps? It would be easy enough to do, with me staying in his house.

"I don't know what new scheme you have in mind, but I'm loyal to Buckland," I said firmly, "and I won't betray him, whatever fossils you try to bribe me with." I was proud that I managed to resist gazing longingly at the sclerotic ring as I said this.

Henry chuckled. "You mistake me, Mary. Not that I didn't consider it, but, no. That isn't what I want from you."

He'd admitted it, at least. He wanted something. "Then what *do* you want?"

From the corner of my eye, I saw Lucy watching with a wary look, spine straight. Edgar, having finally sensed the strange shift in the room, looked up and blinked in confusion.

Henry raised his voice. "Lucy. Ed. Might I have a moment to speak with Mary? Alone?"

My heart skipped a beat. *Don't be ridiculous,* I chided the fool thing. *This is only more of Henry's scheming.*

"Absolutely not; that's wildly inappropriate—" Lucy began, but Edgar touched her wrist.

"We can give you five minutes," Edgar said firmly.

Lucy started to protest again, but I shook my head. I wanted to know what Henry had to say.

Lucy huffed. "Fine, then," she said, and stalked out. Edgar cast us a knowing look that made my stomach flip just before he shut the door.

Henry turned back to me, his gray eyes like a storm over the sea. He stood very still.

"Mary."

My heart skipped again.

"The Geomagical Society has been beholden to fairy tales—to lies—for too long," Henry said, and I felt my stomach unknot.

Of course. This was about the Society. It wasn't some grand romantic declaration. Of course. Thank heavens.

Henry continued. "The truth is clear in stone and soil, but we are too cowardly to speak it plainly. And the work suffers for it."

"You speak of Buckland."

"I speak of all of them," he said, gesturing toward the window and the geomagicians beyond. "Even my own fellows and friends. Even myself." He shook his head. "But not you. You're not afraid."

I burst out laughing. I wasn't sure if he was earnest or mocking, but either way, it was a good joke.

Henry shook his head. "You're not afraid of the truth," he said fiercely. "You speak the truth, Mary, and damn what anyone else thinks. And there is nothing I value more, in man or woman."

I rolled my eyes. "Flattery isn't going to get you anywhere, Henry. Speak plainly."

"It would be easier to show you." He turned us toward the great desk, which gave the impression of a magnificent chestnut stallion at attention. Loose papers and books were scattered across the desk, and a quill rested on the tusks of a brass mammoth statuette.

One stack of notebooks and loose papers, nearly a fist high, was neatly bundled in green ribbon. *For Miss Anning,* read the attached note.

"My research," Henry said. "The sources behind my claims. About how species are changed."

"I read your book, Henry." I was familiar with his key hypothesis: that natural disasters—floods, storms, earthquakes, and the like—generated magic.

Henry argued that it was the lingering magic from these violent phenomena—catastrophes—that we accessed with reliqs. That intriguing blasphemy made up the first half of his book.

But personally, I'd found the second half more persuasive. Because Henry further argued that these catastrophes, and the enormous release of magic, caused animal species to *change.*

Henry postulated that the missing ancient species—even my

ichthyosaur or plesiosaur—had, in fact, changed into something new. *Molded like clay into a new shape*, he'd written.

I remembered, in particular, a fascinating chapter about the saber-tooth tiger. Henry suggested that a volcanic eruption 9,000 years ago in eastern Russia had transformed the saber-tooth into the Siberian. It was easy to picture him drafting the chapter in this very room, staring at his saber-tooth skull and chewing on the end of a pipe, deep in thought. I was irritated at how endearing I found the image.

"Then let me show you the rest," Henry urged. "Let me show you what Buckland wouldn't permit me to publish."

Oh, I *was* curious now. So, this was the secret—the terrible theory Buckland had decried. The reason the two geomagicians had fallen out.

He took my silence as agreement, which I suppose it was, and began shuffling through the mess of papers and maps, sketches of species and diagrams of skeletons, handwritten documents, maps, and typeset letters.

"Here it is." He pulled from the stack of maps one slightly larger than the rest, unfolding it to full size. It was a map of England, Scotland, and Wales, and had been marked with tiny numbers. The numbering seemed random, scattered across the whole of the map. But in several places, they clustered.

He spread it across the desk, and we leaned over, together. My initial guess was that the map must depict the locations of important geomagical discoveries.

But that didn't make sense. The area around Bristol had an especially large cluster, and as far as I knew, there weren't many major geomagical finds from that area.

And where I knew Lyme Regis to be had only three numbers—91, 242, and 533.

I tapped a finger on my hometown.

I thought, a little piqued, that if this map did show significant fossil finds, then the largest cluster should be here.

"What are these? Potential dig sites?"

Henry shook his head and grinned. "No. Not fossils. *They're witches, Mary.* You see"—his eyes were wide, sparkling—"witches are the key to it all."

Chapter 21

Henry grinned madly as I tried to gather my thoughts.

"You mean these dots are—?"

"Yes," he said, nodding eagerly. "Witches. Most suspected, some confirmed. Of course, there must be more, both historical and contemporary; I don't claim this to be an exhaustive compendium." He shuffled through the other papers and handed one to me. "Ah, here. The corresponding names. Lucy, you'll note, is number five hundred sixty-two."

I jumped quickly down the list, then to the next page, all the way to number 562. *Lucy Marienne Murray, 1803– , Place of Birth: Gloucestershire. Parents: Marienne Radcliffe and Viscount Merlton, Randall Murray.* Marienne Radcliffe was listed at 558.

I flipped back up to the earliest entry—*Taliesin, Approx. 530–590, Place of Birth: Unknown; Parents: Unknown*—and then peered at Henry with a new appreciation for his commitment to thorough scholarship.

"How long did this take you to assemble? This is impressive work."

"About twelve years." He pulled out another map and set it next to the first. "But, here. See?"

This second map was also annotated with dates and drawings, scrawled notes along the margins in Henry's familiar hand.

I looked at Brighton. "*Storm, 1703,*" I read aloud.

My eye darted between the two maps, comparing the clusters of witches with the marked locations on the other, and I began to understand what Henry was suggesting. Bristol: *Flood, 1607.* Dover: *Earthquake, 1580.* Edinburgh: *Blizzard, 1699.* Lincoln: *Earthquake, 1185.*

"No. No, that can't be," I murmured. "Surely someone would have noticed."

"They did," Henry said, and slid another document in front of me. It was a parchment fragment, the text faded and stained.

"*. . . for fiftene dayes we coulede not leave, th' sky was whitae and icae froze on thy brow . . .*"

I skipped to the next legible area.

"*. . . in th' wake ophe th' storm we, ten ophe our number claimede able to worke enchaunting without a relique, an was demonstratede in the villauge square . . .*"

"A terrible blizzard," Henry said softly. "In 1323. Crops, cattle, hundreds of people—all lost. The toll was staggering. This account is from a small village near what is now Hereford. See?"

Sure enough, there was a cluster of witch-dots near Hereford, and several dates of birth around that year. But there were many after, too.

"*. . . and th' reliques were burned lowe. And so the newe weirde folke, made hooly, for God's purpose, save'd the croppes. . . .*"

The reliqs were all drained over the course of the blizzard, and then the crops died. But somehow, some of the people had magic. Were *made hooly,* the document said. Ten of them, according to this account. And somehow, even without reliqs, they'd saved the crops.

"You're saying they were created," I said slowly. "That . . . that the blizzard *created* witches. People who could do magic without reliqs."

Henry shook his head. "*I* am not saying anything. I'm simply sharing the evidence I've assembled. You can draw your own conclusions."

I huffed, and he chuckled.

"No. It can't be." I shook my head. "We know that witchery is passed through the family line. That would explain these clusters." I tapped the one at Hereford.

"It certainly would. Many of the people who survived the blizzard and gained new powers would have procreated. As humans are inclined to do." His mouth twitched. "So the witchery would have passed to their children. But how does it *begin,* Mary? How does it get into the bloodline in the first place?"

Hundreds of years ago, when witches were put to the stake with some regularity, it was believed that they gained power by siphoning it from others.

We knew better now; some people were just born with witchery, the same way a man might be born with red hair, or buckteeth.

But Henry was suggesting something extraordinary. I could see now why Buckland and Davies had forbidden him from publishing this theory in his book. To suggest that animals could be changed from God's design by the force of natural magic was already stretching the limits of accepted theomagical doctrine. To go further—to argue that mankind itself might be shaped and changed by natural phenomena ...

Henry saw all of this cross my face, I'm sure. He watched me closely, gaze steady. He must have seen something there—I don't know what—because he took a deep breath and pulled a clip of a newspaper from the stack, and slid it across to me.

"One last thing."

My blood went cold. My fingers trembled as they ran over my own name, lettered in blurred, worn ink. *Three Dead in Lightning Strike in Lyme Regis, Infant Miraculously Survives.*

"You're number five hundred thirty-three."

I stared. I swallowed. My mouth was dry. I looked down at the newspaper clipping. I stared at Henry a while longer.

Then I laughed.

"You know, you almost had me."

"This isn't a joke, Mary."

I pushed the torn, faded paper back across the table. "For a minute there, I almost believed you." I tugged meaningfully at my ammonite reliq on its leather thong. That was obvious-enough evidence; I couldn't do magic without it.

Henry sputtered. His cheeks were red, jaw clenched. He blinked rapidly.

"You're not—I—look! See." He dug frantically through the stack of books, then shoved one—thick, the leather embossed in gold—into my hands.

Taxonomia Malleficarum: a Taxonomy of Witchery, by Heinrich Nachtnebel, read the gilt. The parchment was fragile, and smelled of dust and dampness.

"There are different kinds of witches," Henry said quickly. "For a while, witchery classifications were quite a popular topic in theomagical circles. The field fell out a bit after that shameful business over in Salem."

I winced. "I can imagine." The first British colonists in the Americas had been dissenters—notably, Calumnates—who held that any and all magic was sin. There were few geomagicians working in the Americas, but you could always pick them out; their work so often had an anti-magic slant to it.

"After that, witches were, well, a bit more hesitant to sit for anthropological interviews, even here."

I flipped through the pages of the *Taxonomia*, skimming chapter headings. *Green-witches. Water-witches. Paper-witches. Stitch-witches.*

"Nachtnebel theorized that many witches have a special affinity. Essentially, an area in which they do not need to use a reliq."

My nose wrinkled. "But that's the very definition of a witch. Someone who doesn't need a reliq for any magic."

"That's the *conventional* definition. But maybe the ones we think of now as witches—extraordinary people like Lucy, who have affinities for all magic—maybe that is only one category of witch? And what if there are others?"

Even as I followed this argument, a small part of my brain noticed that I liked to see Henry excited. I liked the way his eyes lit, and his mouth worked quickly; how the smirk fell away to reveal the truth of his joy in the work. It reminded me of the boy I'd known.

"If Nachtnebel is right, if *I* am right, think how many witches there may be, right now, living their lives in ignorance. Unaware of their potential. Men and women with some area of magic for which they wouldn't need a reliq. Who just have no idea of their gift, because it's simply not part of our framework for how witchery works. But such frameworks should—*must!*—adapt to new information. That's basic scientific principle."

"And what would that make me, then?" I asked, and realized, as the words fell out, that he had me half convinced already.

Henry's face softened, slackened, and his hand darted out across the still-spread map to catch my chin gently. His thumb stroked across my cheek, and my skin lit where he touched me.

"Isn't it obvious? Why, Mary, you're a fossil witch."

Chapter 22

*S*NAP. THAT WAS THE SOUND IN MY BRAIN AS ALL OF THE fog cleared, and everything became obvious.

I'd assumed Henry wanted to use me as a game-piece in his campaign against Buckland. I was right. I just hadn't understood how. I did now. I understood perfectly.

"You want me to support your theory," I said, laughing—it was all so obvious now. "You think I had something to do with Ajax waking because of some kind of *witchery*? Which would, not incidentally, directly contradict Buckland's proposed theory of flood-hibernation."

All that talk of my truth-telling and fearlessness. That's why he'd spoken before of being allies. Of friendship. Now, if I agreed with his conclusions, Henry hoped that my own conscience would force me to say so. And if I did, it would probably humiliate Buckland more effectively than anything Henry could do directly. Henry had caught me very neatly indeed. Because, yes, I was almost convinced by Henry's theory despite myself.

Except, if I really was what Henry thought—a *fossil witch*—

wouldn't I have managed to resurrect something before Ajax? In all my years handling fossils, why was this the first?

I said as much to Henry as I folded my arms.

His smile reappeared, cockier than ever. "But Ajax wasn't the first. No; the first was years ago. I saw it myself."

My mouth fell open. I had nothing to say to that.

Henry's eyes glittered. "Do you remember one morning, on the beach near Black Ven—"

"There were a hundred days like that," I said flatly.

His lip twitched. "Well, that morning, Lucy decided she was going to swim the Channel. She kept going out past the breakers. Edgar was terrified; he paced up and down the beach, insisting she come back to shore before she drowned."

"I remember." My voice was sharp to hide the pleading. *Please don't*, I meant. Because oh, I remembered that day. I remembered it all too well.

It was the day I knew I loved him.

While the Murrays were otherwise occupied on the shore and in the waves, Henry and I chipped several small trilobites out of wet stone.

"Do you think these were nests?" sixteen-year-old Henry had mused. "It's strange we always find so many so close together."

"Nah, breeding grounds, I bet," I said, grunting as I popped a large chunk of stone free. "I suppose if you have to die, that's not a bad way to go."

Henry flushed pink. Heat rushed to my cheeks; I hadn't even thought to be embarrassed until I saw he was.

"Yeah, I guess so," he said, with a nervous laugh, and went back to his work.

But I couldn't move. My pulse raced, and my palms dampened.

It felt like lightning in the air, as if the very atmosphere between us had changed. Like *everything* had changed.

A lock of hair fell over Henry's brow, and his arm muscles strained as he chipped at the rock. He looked at me furtively, eyes darting away when I caught him.

I tried to focus on the fossil in my hand instead. I always found trilobites beautiful, with their armored plates. I ran my thumb down the little humps, imagining this creature scurrying across the seafloor, scavenging for food.

"Here, I'll clean this one; you pluck out the next," I said, and reached for one of the wire brushes. Henry thrust it out.

Our fingers brushed. Henry sharply inhaled, and I dropped the trilobite. It tumbled down into a crack in the rock, and I sighed and picked up one of the others. Best to keep occupied before I said something foolish about the shape of his hands.

That was it, really.

We cleaned the trilobites and headed back to town for lunch.

Henry avoided me for a few weeks, talking dull philosophy and theomagic with Edgar instead of fossils with me. But by the middle of summer, we'd found a new balance, carefully avoiding any subjects related to sex. Well, up until the very end, when the whole thing fell apart.

But I certainly hadn't resurrected anything other than horrible, useless *feelings* that had bought me nothing but trouble.

"We cleaned trilobites," I said uncertainly.

Henry nodded. "And you dropped one. Do you remember?"

I cocked my head. "Yes, I dropped it into a crevasse." *When our fingers brushed, it was like my skin was on fire.* But I had no idea where he was going with this.

"It didn't fall into the rock, Mary. It scurried down there. It escaped. Because it was *alive*."

I blinked. "That's impossible."

"I thought so, too. Even then, as a boy, part of me thought I'd imagined it," he said. "But I knew what I saw. I just couldn't explain *how*. It wasn't until you wrote to Buckland about waking Ajax that I understood what it must mean."

Henry leaned forward. *A lock of hair fell over Henry's brow.* I shook my head, trying to peel the past and present apart before they merged.

"Don't you see?" he said. "Forget Buckland's nonsense about hibernation."

"I—"

Henry gripped my hands. "It's you, Mary. You've done it before. *And you can do it again.*"

Henry's eyes searched mine. A muscle in his jaw tightened, and his hands twitched, and my pulse beat a wild rhythm.

The door flung open with a bang.

We leapt apart, and my lungs stuttered with fear at the pale look of terror on Lucy's face.

"The Inquisitors are here."

My knees turned to jelly. Henry caught my elbow. Lucy ran over, and they held me between them.

"How?" Henry demanded.

"Conybore? Conywear?" Lucy snapped. "Some geomagician."

"William Conybeare," Henry and I said in flat unison.

"Apparently he went straight to the Inquisitors this afternoon and accused Mary of sorcery. They're here now; Edgar and Buckland are trying to reason with them, but they want to bring you in for questioning."

"Do you have any idea who I am?" I heard Edgar sneering from the hallway.

Inquisitors. My head was all wet cotton, all my thoughts filtered through a haze of white terror. This was everything I'd feared, come at once.

"Damn it." Henry grimaced. "Buckland was sure we had at least a few days."

Anger flared in my breast. They'd expected this. Why hadn't Buckland said? Why hadn't they warned me?

But they did. Buckland hadn't wanted me to come to London. He'd wanted me to stay far, far away. I was the one who insisted on coming along.

Ajax. The fear twisted deeper, lodging like a hook. They'd execute him, too. Tear him apart, wing from wing, claw from claw. Tears welled in my eyes. I'd led Ajax to his death.

Footsteps outside. Lucy ran back to the door.

"Listen to me," Henry said, and turned me toward him, gripping my shoulders. "This is our chance. They'll want to know how you brought Ajax back. Tell them, Mary. You know it's true. I can see it—I see it now in your eyes."

"I can't." I shook my head, biting hard at the inside of my cheek. "You're asking me to carry my own sword to the executioner."

Henry's expression twisted, agony and anger and, finally, fear rolling across his features before it cleared. He stepped back, letting me go.

"Then keep your head and your wits, Mary. I will do whatever I can to see you safely through this."

God, be with me now, I prayed; then I inhaled, and exhaled, shoulders rising and dipping with each breath as we waited for the Inquisitors.

Chapter 23

My heart leapt to my throat as the Inquisitors entered the office, but I squared my shoulders and looked at them serenely.

"—as I was saying, as you can *see,* no one is trying to harbor anyone," Buckland said. He was clearly attempting to escort them into the room, but the lead Inquisitor brushed past him aggressively. Buckland huffed in affront, and Edgar's face was red with fury.

I gave a tiny nod when they both caught my eye. I could handle this. I hoped.

The Inquisitor's leader wore white and silver, but the other four wore black cloaks. All five had shaven pates, and silver reliqs in the shape of a cross hung on their foreheads. The one in white and silver swept forward, his cloak swirling at his feet dramatically.

"Good evening, gentlemen," I said, hoping he wouldn't catch the flutter in my voice.

"Are you Miss Mary Elizabeth Anning, of Lyme Regis?" asked

the one in white. He had heavy black brows and a square jaw. He might have been handsome but for the deep scowl-lines etched between those brows.

"I am."

He thrust out a piece of parchment and said, "Then by order of the archbishop of Canterbury, you are hereby summoned to appear before the high council."

"On what charges?"

"That most serious of all charges, I am afraid," he said solemnly. "Sorcery."

I could feel the sweat pooling under my arms and coating my upper lip.

"And I suppose this is about the pterodactyl? Very well. Should I hold out my hands to be tied? Put them behind my back? I've never been arrested for sorcery."

One of the Inquisitors cracked a smile but hid it quickly. The lead Inquisitor's scowl only deepened.

"It will be all right, Ma—Miss Anning." Henry reached for me, but black-cloaked arms yanked me back. Henry's fist clenched, and a muscle twitched in his jaw.

"Yes," said Buckland sharply. He raised his voice. "The truth will always prevail."

Apparently the only thing needed to bring Henry Stanton and William Buckland to the same side was my own arrest. Who would have ever guessed?

They bound my wrists behind me, though not ungently.

"And under which specific ecclesiastical statute is she to be charged?" Edgar looked more intrigued than I would have cared for—this was my life, after all, and not an interesting theomagical case study—but at least he added, "So that we might best prepare Miss Anning's defense."

The Inquisitor sneered. "I do not answer to you, Lord Merlton. We Inquisitors answer to no one but God. Now Miss Anning must do the same."

My room at Lambeth Palace was actually very comfortable. In some ways, it was even nicer than my flat back in Lyme Regis. There were no bedbugs, for one, and servants came regularly to tend the fire. I had a bed with a thick quilt, and there was an old Bible in the bedside table, so at least I had reading material. The only tiny complaint I might have registered about the accommodations was the thick layer of dust on the mantle and windowsill. It seemed I was the first person to stay in the heresy suite—as I'd taken to calling it—for a very long time.

The last person executed for heresy died forty years ago. A farmer, he was convicted of using sorcery to save his harvest after a blight. All the neighboring fields died, but his survived.

I remember thinking, when Parson Anders taught that story, that the farmer would never have been caught out if he hadn't been selfish about it. He really should have used his sorcery to save all the crops, and probably no one would ever have figured him out.

Sometime during the night—because despite everything, I was exhausted—I'd woken in a cold sweat, convinced that maybe I *had* accidentally used forbidden sorcery to wake Ajax.

I sat up in bed, clutching the covers and trying to steady my breathing. The candles had died, and the fire was embers. Long, black fingers with sharp, pointed nails stroked the stone wall across from the bed.

A scream gathered in my throat, and I pulled my knees to my

chest, eyes darting to the barred window, to the bare tree in the courtyard, as the nightmare cleared.

The blackened fingers were only the shadow of a tree branch swaying in the wind.

I couldn't get back to sleep after that.

I flopped to my side and opened the Bible. They'd taken my reliq, so I had no light, but if I tilted it just so, I could catch the moonlight enough to read. I started in Matthew before circling back to Genesis, and was halfway through Leviticus when the sunrise began to turn the gray wall a rosy pink.

In fact, I'd just gotten to one of the few verses about magic, Leviticus 20:27: *"A man also or woman that hath a familiar spirit, or that is a wizard, shall surely be put to death: they shall stone them with stones: their blood shall be upon them."*

If I remembered my history correctly—Edgar loaned me a book on the subject a few Christmases ago—it was Constantine the Great who convened the First Council of Nicaea, where a group of wise bishops determined that *actually*, these verses surely referred to sorcery, vampyrism, or necromancy, and not reliq-magic at all, which was spreading rapidly through the Empire.

Hard not to wonder whether Constantine, having seen the political and economic value of magic, hadn't applied some light pressure to the bishops. But I suppose God works toward His purpose in mysterious ways.

Not that it was a settled question, even after the Council's declaration. Christianity spread rapidly after magic use was sanctioned, but the history of Christendom is stained red over the technicalities.

Even now there are dissenters and separatists, like the Calumnates, who still believe magic is sinful, or the Fishers, who think magic corrupts the soul, or even the Catholics, who hold that a reliq must be regularly consecrated at communion, and that use of an unconsecrated reliq is a violation of God's law.

And a great many people still think *witchery* is sin, even three hundred years after Queen Anne Boleyn's reign and the Church's reversed stance. But they read that other famous verse—I flipped to it in the Bible—*Thou shalt not suffer a witch to live,* Exodus 22:18—and disregard scholarship, or context, or even translation.

My heart squeezed as I thought of all the witches who'd died screaming on account of that verse over the years. On account of one interpretation. I thought of Lucy, whose own father had believed as much. If she'd been born a hundred years ago, he probably would have stoned her himself.

And I thought, too, of Henry's theory: that *I* was a witch. A fossil witch, he'd said. A shiver ran down my spine.

I closed the Bible and set it on the quilt, wrapping my arms around my knees and staring out the window.

It was all interpretation. Not unlike geomagical scholarship, in truth. We had only these few verses, scattered like bones in the cliffs, and all anyone could do was try to make sense of what they found through some combination of context, knowledge, and experience. And the interpretation could always shift with new discoveries, or new theories, or even with popularity—with who was in favor and who was not.

It was not a comforting thought. Someone, or maybe several someones, would decide my case, and they would use these verses, and my life depended on the interpretation.

Because if they determined that my actions in reviving Ajax were done by sorcery? Or necromantic magics? If so—well, I would not spend another night in my comfortable cell, because I would certainly be executed before sunset.

And Ajax, too. My heart lurched as I pictured his adorably ugly face, his body clutched in black-robed arms. He wouldn't understand. He would only know I wasn't there.

I could picture the fear in those golden eyes, and hear the thin, confused squawks. Where was he now? Was he safe?

My fingers trembled as I opened the Bible again, this time to Psalm 121. My father's favorite psalm.

The Lord is thy keeper, I read, and prayed. *The Lord is thy shade upon thy right hand*—er, wing. *The sun shall not smite thee by day, nor the moon by night. The Lord shall preserve thee from all evil: he shall preserve thy soul.*

I didn't know if Ajax technically possessed a soul, but I didn't think God would mind.

"Amen," I said aloud.

Tears pricked at my eyes. Suddenly I was a child again, with thick thumbs and grubby knees, and my father's voice was soft in my ear, and his hand on my shoulder, strong and sure. I read the verse again and again, my eyes blurring over the page, until sunrise came to claim me.

It was almost noon when the thick-browed, white-robed Inquisitor collected me from the heresy suite.

There was no runner in the hallway, so our steps echoed on the ancient stone. The walls were windowless and bare except for a few reliq-lamps in mounted iron torches, spaced apart so that we passed through long stretches of darkness before the next.

White-robe stopped before a set of double doors, and knocked once, sharply.

"Enter," a voice commanded, and I obeyed, blinking and blinded in the sudden light. The ceiling was vaulted and beamed, and bright color spilled from the stained-glass windows, flooding the black-and-white tiled floor. A long table stood in the center of the room, empty chairs along either long side.

And at the head of the table sat the archbishop of Canterbury, tapping his fingertips on the tabletop. At least I guessed it was him based on the full regalia, robes, and triangle headpiece. He had hawklike eyes and high, regal cheekbones.

Between the doors and the table was a small, plain wooden bench.

"Walk," snapped white-robe. I stumbled forward and onto the bench.

The archbishop put on a pair of spectacles and bent down to read aloud. "Mistress Mary Elizabeth Anning, daughter of Richard and Molly, of Lyme Regis, Dorset. Twenty-nine years old." His voice wasn't cruel, or cold; it sounded like he was reading aloud from a mildly amusing book. It gave me some flicker of hope.

"You are accused of using sorcery to conduct necromancy."

I swallowed. "I am not guilty, Your . . . Excellency? Holiness?"

He squinted at me over his spectacles. "I did not yet ask your plea. You may call me Father."

I flushed. "My apologies, Father."

"I have heard the evidence against you, and for you, and now I would like to hear from you directly." He cleared his throat. "And how would you plead, to the charges against you?" He gave me a look that clearly meant, *Now you may say it.*

"Not guilty."

The archbishop took off the spectacles and folded them neatly. "Very well—"

A screech sliced through the thick silence. I knew that screech. I would know it anywhere. *He's alive. Thank God.*

"Where is he?"

I looked around foolishly, as if a pterodactyl could be hiding in plain sight. He had to be somewhere nearby. Maybe in the next room?

"Please, is Ajax all right? He is innocent, I swear it. Even if you have to execute me, maybe you could just let him go?"

I thought I saw sympathy flash across the archbishop's face. I could have sworn it.

But then he bellowed, "Silence," and held up a hand. "Bishop Price, please summon the others."

White-robe nodded curtly and disappeared, the doors shutting behind him.

The archbishop slumped a little and rubbed at his brow.

"What has Buckland gotten us into now," he muttered. "I swear the man brings me nothing but trouble." Then he said, gruffly, "Come here, child."

He gestured impatiently when I hesitated. The archbishop held out his hands as if I should take them, and cautiously I did. His palms were dry and warm. He was younger than I'd guessed, closer to fifty than seventy.

"You only need tell the truth, Miss Anning. The good Lord shall see to the rest."

He patted my hands and then shooed me away to my bench. I hurried back, reeling, and the doors opened again, only a moment after I adjusted my skirts.

Buckland himself was second through the door after Bishop Price.

"I told you," Buckland was grumbling, "she already cleared an inquisition, before we ever left Lyme Regis."

But the white-robed bishop said haughtily, "Not one of *ours*."

My heartbeat stuttered with fear, and I tried to soothe it. I had passed Buckland's inquisition. I would pass this one, too. I clasped my hands and tried to steady my breathing.

Henry, Edgar, and President Davies followed after Buckland. Henry's set chin and stony expression radiated a confident surety that did help my nerves. Edgar was attempting the same, but his twisting hands gave away his own anxiety. Davies merely looked annoyed.

I felt a bit like a maiden on trial in some old tragedy, whose knights had ridden to her aid. I tried not to think of how many of those tales ended with the maid and knights dead.

For the other side—my accusers—were two unfamiliar priests in black robes, led to the table by Bishop Price in his white robe. Each carried a golden plate of sorts, cradled on a black velvet pillow.

Price leaned over to say something to the archbishop, and I twisted my sweaty palms together, knuckles white.

"Miss Anning," the archbishop's voice boomed through the atrium, "has pled not guilty to the charges laid before her, of sorcery and necromancy. I have heard from both her accuser, and her"—he arched an eyebrow—"*many* defenders.

"I have examined the creature in question," he said, "and Misters Buckland, Stanton, and Davies have testified that it is consistent with the examples of prehistoric pterodactyl skeletons from Germany."

Bishop Price still looked too smug. This wasn't over yet.

"So, Miss Anning"—the archbishop tented his fingers; even from all the way down the long table, I could see his eyes narrow—"let us begin."

Chapter 24

THE QUESTIONS WERE THE SAME.

Do you now, or have you ever, worked magic with words of sorcery?

Have you now, or have you ever, stolen magic through vampyrism, in service to the Devil?

Have you now, or have you ever, communed with the dead, through necromantic magics?

The two assisting Inquisitors hung my ammonite reliq around my neck, then strapped my hands to the heavy golden plates. My fingers were spread with leather bands, tiny cogs whirring around them, brushing against my knuckles as Bishop Price asked the questions and the reliq burned against my chest until I thought the flesh must surely be melting away.

"Unmarked," one of the Inquisitors said, after they'd inspected the skin under my throat. "She speaks the truth."

They freed my shaking hands once the archbishop nodded, and I tried to wipe my tears surreptitiously with a sleeve of my dress. The pain was gone, and my ammonite reliq was cold again against my flesh, but the memory of agony still fired along my nerves.

It was over. I had passed the test. I would live. Probably.

The men were talking, voices heated. Price and Buckland sniped at each other. Henry was demanding my immediate release, and Edgar was citing historic ecclesiastical case law in my favor.

I tried to focus, but my thoughts were too scattered. I pulled at my reliq necklace, running my fingers up and down the leather and over the ammonite, working to try and calm my racing mind as the men debated my fate.

I followed the curl of shell with my index finger, over the fine ridges, and my thoughts drifted, carried on the slow currents out to an ancient sea. What remained now was only the shell, but once this empty case had housed a soft, strong body—large eyes, and tentacles. It would have been a powerful swimmer, propelled by spurting tentacles through the water.

This one had lappets, long prongs, at the shell opening, so it was a male. I could almost see it—darting through a rainbow reef to avoid the jaws of an ichthyosaur, or diving to catch small fish. I imagined it using those powerful prehensile limbs like an octopus to crack open a bivalve and slurp the slippery feast inside.

I thought of the ammonite, growing larger, year after year, diligently building itself a new home as it outgrew each chamber of the spiral, and then sealing it up behind. Always at home, and always trying to leave. Bound to its past. A record of a life.

If only humans carried our pasts so visibly, rather than as scars on our hearts. Perhaps we would be kinder to one another, if the past were bound to our backs for all to see.

"Miss Anning." The archbishop scrubbed at his brow.

I jumped a little at my name.

"Based on your testimony, I am sufficiently convinced that the pterodactyl's existence is not a result of any knowing act of sorcery on your part. Unfortunately, that is not proof of an absence of heresy." He raised a hand before Buckland could interject. "So what I'd like to know is, how *should* we explain the pterodactyl, if not with sorcery?"

My fingers stilled on the ammonite as I felt the gaze of every powerful man in the room settle on my face. Watching. Waiting. My cheeks warmed with the heat of their eyes. Henry's, especially. Henry's most of all.

I believe him.

The realization hit me like cold water. I believed him. The idea was mad, his theory absurd. Witches and catastrophes and magic and secret powers I'd never known—but knew now that I had always possessed.

Because the ammonite in my hand was *alive.*

A soft, warm tentacle probed at my palm, and another searched between my fingers.

I swallowed down the scream that rose in my throat.

Be still! Be stone! For God's sake, stop that! I commanded, and the tentacle disappeared. I wrapped my fist around the ammonite, and it was hard, dead stone once more.

It was Henry's voice I heard in my mind, urging me to tell the truth. Here was proof. Of his theory. Of my own magic. My own power. Evidence wrapped under my white knuckles.

It was true, and it was heresy. It was true, and it might see me killed, and Ajax, too, and both of us in an unmarked pauper's grave.

Could Henry save me from that? Did I even trust him to try?

I tried to speak but made no sound. I closed my mouth, working my tongue against my teeth. "I do not know how it came to pass," I said finally, speaking slowly. "But I know I played no part in the pterodactyl's waking. The miracle was God's alone; I was only a witness."

I bowed my head, my face flushed with the lie.

"Thank you, my child," the archbishop said, just as Edgar Murray leaned forward with a raised index finger.

"Did not our Lord reveal himself first to Mary Magdalene? Perhaps God, in His wisdom, intends here to remind us that it is the humble—the poor, the downtrodden, the *powerless*—who are closest to His heart, and most worthy of His miracles. Indeed, I am—"

"Save it for Parliament, Lord Merlton," chuckled the archbishop. "A valiant attempt, but my position on reform has not changed since our last conversation. The Church of England left the reliquary business three hundred years ago for good reason. I will not be the one who puts us back in the midst of it all."

The archbishop exhaled. "But I am satisfied there was no malicious magic at work. Very well, Buckland. Go on, then, tell me more about this new 'hibernation' theory of yours."

*

"When Miss Anning found the creature," Buckland said, "he was in a cave, with his mother and a clutch of eggs. I examined the cave myself, before we left Lyme Regis. There was clear evidence of diluvium throughout the cave, Your Grace."

I bit the side of my lip. I was afraid I knew where he was going with this. My eyes flicked to Henry, who was watching Buckland with a hard, blank stare.

"You say that like it means something important, but I cannot possibly guess at what," the archbishop said drolly.

"Diluvium is sediment. Gravel and sand," Buckland said. "It is evidence of flooding. In fact, I believe it to be proof of *the* flood, Your Grace."

The archbishop tapped at his chin. "You're saying—"

"I'm saying that the pterodactyl mother perished in the great floodwaters, but the clutch of eggs was covered with diluvium and sediment, and set by our Lord to a long and quiet slumber. Not destroyed," Buckland said quietly. "Nor made extinct. Only sleeping, for a time."

This time, Henry did meet my eyes, raising his brow.

Because it wasn't true. What Buckland was suggesting couldn't possibly be proven. It did appear that Ajax's mother had died in some kind of flood, but the geomagical strata in the lias immediately above that cave was *not* marine. I'd dug into that layer before, farther down the coast, and had found impressions of plant life and bird bones.

The evidence just didn't support Buckland's claim.

I wondered if he believed it, too, or if it was another lie. It was growing hard to tell now. Was this simply another strategy to help my cause? *Or to help his,* I thought, darkly. Or did Buckland really believe what he was saying?

Either way, I couldn't say anything now—I would undermine Buckland, for one, and second, the archbishop was laughing with delight and clapping Buckland's shoulder. I had chosen my path. Now I would have to follow it through.

Henry clearly made the same calculation. He pressed his lips tight in a thin line.

"You will have to help with the sermon, my friend. For there must be a sermon. A declaration! A great reveal! *The Geomagical Miracle! A Refutation of the Extinction Heresy!* The great marriage of science and faith, at last." The archbishop sighed. "I do always love a wedding."

The doors swung closed behind us, and we stood a moment in the dark hallway.

Buckland swept me clean off my feet and crushed me against his chest.

He set me down again as I tried to catch my breath.

"Are you well? Are you hurt?" His chin creased in a frown, and his eyes were intent as they searched my face. He looked like he wanted to hug me again, and my heart pinched at the lines of worry between his brows. It made my throat thick with emotion.

I took his hand between mine. "I am well. I am fine. My accommodations were honestly rather comfortable."

Buckland guffawed, and then he did hug me again, ruffling my hair like he used to do when I was a small girl and wore it loose down my back.

I flushed, but I couldn't really muster any annoyance, even with Henry, Edgar, and President Davies present. I was too grateful to be alive.

"I hope you know we are very grateful for your assistance in the matter, Lord Merlton," President Davies was saying, shaking Edgar's hand. "The Society is lucky, indeed, to have such excellent friends."

I might have rolled my eyes at Davies's obvious simpering, but Edgar looked pleased.

Another door opened down the hall, followed by a pinched squawk and the flapping of leathery wings.

"Ajax!"

I rushed toward the harried-looking servant who held Ajax in a small gilded birdcage. I snatched the cage from the startled fellow and opened the door, hugging Ajax to my chest and checking him over. He looked well, if tired. His eyes were glassy, and his happy chirps were muted. But he settled quickly in my arms, resting his orange beak on my shoulder. I held him tight.

"So, this is the infamous beast," said Edgar. "He's smaller than I expected."

"He's a baby," I said defensively.

"Do you think he'd let me touch him?" Edgar asked. His eyes were wide with wonder, round and bright as he stared at the pterodactyl.

I grinned. "Yes. Go ahead. He likes when you scratch here, under his chin."

"Hello there." Ajax closed his eyes and cooed softly as Edgar scratched him.

Then Ajax jumped from my hold, using Edgar's forearm as a ramp to climb onto his shoulder.

"I think he likes you," I said, and smiled.

Edgar stroked under Ajax's chin. "Come. Let's get you out of here before my sister loses her mind with worry."

It was nearly dusk when we made it to Buckland's house. I half stumbled, half leapt from the coach steps and into Lucy's arms. Ajax chirped from his birdcage, and Buckland put him on the grass to hop around the garden and stretch his wings.

"You're alive," Lucy whispered, burying her face in my shoulder and sobbing. "Mary, you're alive."

"Yes. I'm alive," I said. "So, please stop trying to strangle me."

She laughed. Edgar handed Lucy a handkerchief to dab her eyes.

"Thank you. For helping her. You too, Henry," she added, after a reluctant pause.

"Yes, yes, everyone was very noble and brave in coming to my aid," I said, scooping up Ajax before he could climb my skirts. "And I am very grateful. Thank you, Mr. Stanton. Good night."

Henry arched his brow, but dipped his head. "Of course, *Miss Anning*. I am—I am glad that you are well." He bid goodbye to the others and then strode toward the back gate, disappearing into shadows. Lucy tried to give me a meaningful look, which I ignored.

I said a more earnest goodbye to Edgar, and then Catherine Buckland shuffled us all inside to the parlor, where we told the rest to Lucy, Catherine, and Elizabeth. Ajax sat curled on my lap like a chicken, and I stroked down his spine until he drifted to sleep.

Buckland began to describe the sermons and presentations that were planned to introduce his new flood-hibernation theory, and then, next thing I knew, Lucy was patting my cheek.

"Mary? You fell asleep."

"What? I'm so sorry, everyone. What were you saying?"

Elizabeth smiled. "I was saying you look like you need to go to bed."

"I've set out a basket in your room so Ajax can stay with you tonight," Catherine said.

I protested, but feebly, and soon Elizabeth and Lucy were gently but firmly leading me upstairs. I still couldn't stop yawning.

Lucy whirled the moment she shut the door.

"*What* happened with Henry?" She and Elizabeth sat on the bed.

I blinked and yawned again, setting Ajax in the blanket-lined Moses basket. "What?"

"After you were taken away last night, Henry nearly lost his mind. I thought he was going to march into Lambeth Palace himself and try to break you out."

Had he really? There was a moment last night in his office when I thought—but no. He'd been trying to persuade me of his theory, to counter Buckland's. That was all. "We were . . . we were just talking about geomagic."

Lucy scoffed. "And tonight?"

"Lucy says you used to be lovers," Elizabeth blurted out.

"Lucy!"

Lucy flushed, fluttering her hands. "I didn't say *that*. I only said you were sweethearts, once, back when we were children."

I sat down on the floor beside the bed and groaned, head in my hands.

Elizabeth giggled, and I realized, suddenly, how closely the two of them were sitting—hip to hip on the bed.

Good heavens, had they started up the very minute we arrived in London? We'd been in town only two days, though it did feel more like two weeks, with all that had happened.

Anyway, I didn't have the energy to consider anyone's romantic life at the moment. Including my own.

"Move," I said gruffly.

They exchanged looks.

"Get off my bed."

Lucy and Elizabeth jumped to scramble.

"I'm going to sleep"—I flopped face-first on the bed, and my words were muffled by the pillows—"for a thousand years."

Chapter 25

Gossip traveled quickly in Lyme Regis, but even faster in London. By morning, the whole city was buzzing with talk of the pterodactyl.

I discovered this when I finally stumbled downstairs for breakfast the next morning, Ajax mounted on my shoulder, and found the Buckland household in a state of chaos. William Buckland shouted through the open door at the assembled crowd on his front steps, while Catherine gathered the younger girls in the sitting room away from the windows.

"You're in the paper, Mary!" Elizabeth hurried to my side. I snatched the pages from her. Sure enough, it was there on the front page, right above a story about the upcoming second reading of Edgar Murray's reliq reform bill.

DORSET WOMAN DISCOVERS ANCIENT 'PTERODACTYL,' DORMANT SINCE NOAH'S FLOOD.

"I've said you'll get a statement this afternoon, direct from Palmanaeus House!" Buckland shouted at the crowd outside.

"Where is the creature to be kept?"

"Will it be on display?"

"Should we expect other ancient beasts to wake as well?"

"Is Miss Anning there? Does she have any comment?"

"Go away, you're spoiling my breakfast!" Buckland slammed the door, sighing in exasperation. But he grinned when he saw me. "Mary! Oh, good, you're awake!"

"I'm so sorry about all this," I said. "I didn't mean to bring all this trouble to your house."

"No, no. It's precisely what I hoped," he said cheerfully. "Did Elizabeth show you today's paper? You like my headline? Front page!" He beamed.

I nodded. "Yes, but . . . but it isn't *true*."

His brows shot up, and he hurried me into his study, shutting the door behind us.

"Mary, you cannot claim something like that. Not even here."

"But Ajax wasn't really a victim of the great flood," I said, shaking my head. "Of *a* flood, maybe, but—"

"Then the evidence will show that. Eventually."

"But you told the archbishop—"

"Frederick is a practical man. Ajax posed a problem for him. You did, too. I thought it best to make you a tool to serve his purposes, rather than a hindrance."

I couldn't decide if it was reassuring or terrifying to know that we'd played such a game with the archbishop, and that he moved his own players, too. That I now was among them.

I heard Henry's voice in my ear, his words of condemnation. *The truth is clear in stone and soil,* he'd said. *But we are too cowardly to speak it plainly.*

"Mary." Buckland's eyes softened. With pity, maybe, though I couldn't understand it. "You want to be a geomagician, do you not?"

"More than anything."

"Then trust me. Someday—when you are safely ensconced within the Society, and all of this is a distant memory—maybe we can say it was an error in sampling. Or that new evidence was uncovered. But it will be long forgotten by then, and no one will care.

"How can I put this," he said, and sighed. "Ajax is a bridge now between the Geomagical Society and the Church of England. Which makes you both exceptionally valuable. Do you understand?"

"Yes," I said, and it came out as a whisper, because I didn't need the implications spelled out. If one side gave way—if either the Society or Church turned against us—then the other would as well. And I stood to lose everything in the fall.

I found Lucy out back, feeding an apple to the miniature horse. I let Ajax down to hunt bugs at our feet.

"Those newspaper men," Lucy said, wiping horse slobber onto her skirts, "are very persistent."

She jerked her chin toward the back wall. She'd enchanted the hedges to grow out thickly across the gate, but I could see figures trying to peer through nonetheless.

I exhaled. "Buckland's thrilled about all the attention. He thinks it'll be good for the Society."

"And you? How are you feeling?"

I was still reeling from my conversation with Buckland. All those long years in Lyme Regis, dreaming of being a geomagician, I had never imagined how much politicking would be involved. How naïve I'd been, thinking it would all be studying rocks and writing books.

"I'm just grateful I wasn't executed." I tried to laugh.

I could see Lucy knew there was more, but she also knew me well enough to see I didn't want to talk.

"Well, to celebrate your survival, Edgar has invited us to dinner tonight." Lucy dropped her voice low and looked around. "He's promised to invite a few friends, too. Gentlemen he thinks might be interested in allying themselves with the cause."

I managed to hide my grimace. An evening catching up with Lucy and Edgar sounded delightful. An evening listening to pompous philosophizing about reliq-reform? The opposite of delightful.

But Lucy's eyes were shining, and I *was* eager to see Edgar again; we'd barely had a chance to speak before I was arrested.

"Of course," I said, scratching the little horse's forelock. "Dinner it is."

The coach rumbled along, Ajax squawking in my lap as we were jostled over a deep pothole. I pulled the curtain aside as we neared Palmanaeus House and gasped at the gathered crowd. I clutched Ajax tightly, more to soothe my own nerves than his.

There were hundreds of people gathered in the park across the road, a mass of bodies held back by a row of constables.

"Well, look at that," Buckland said. "I'd bet my hat that not one of them cared a lick about geomagical history before today. And now, thanks to you, they will learn that we geomagicians are not the enemy of their faith, as they may have feared. Because of you, Mary, they will know we only reap the field that God has sowed."

I rolled my eyes. "Spare me the sermon, Buckland. Are you sure we can't just go in the back?"

He gave me a pointed look. "It's never a good idea to disappoint an audience."

I nodded grimly. We rolled to a stop a few moments later. I started to unlatch Ajax's carrying basket, but Buckland shook his head.

"On your shoulder," he said, "for all to see. Give them a show, remember?"

I took a deep breath, trying to steady myself. It was all a bit of show. And then I could get to work, studying Ajax as I'd intended, and proving my worth to the geomagicians.

"Go on," I said, and Ajax hopped happily to my shoulder, swinging his beak around curiously. I could only pray he wouldn't take the chance to demonstrate his flying.

Buckland flung open the door rather dramatically, and a footman helped me down. I ducked my head and rounded my shoulders, then scurried quickly up the wide marble stairs. Buckland sighed, but let me be.

Then a roar went up from the crowd across the street. I jumped at the sound. *That's the beast, and the woman who found him,* they were saying.

"Well? They've recognized you. Give them a wave, eh?" Buckland prodded, then demonstrated, as if I had forgotten how it was done.

I scowled at him, but I turned and waved my elbow mechanically to and fro, using my free hand to press Ajax's feet against my shoulder.

They cheered as Ajax rose and spread his wings.

President Davies swept forward to meet us at the top of the steps, shadowed by a gaggle of redcoats and constables.

"Welcome to Palmanaeus House, Miss Anning," Davies said,

as if I hadn't been here only days before. He gave a sweeping, low bow. I settled on an awkward curtsy.

Davies signaled two servants, and they lifted the iron latch and pulled open the double oak doors, hinges creaking.

Davies bent as if to kiss my cheek and whispered, "Will the beast fly on command?"

"No," I said, and Davies frowned. "I don't want him to be lost. But I can have him spread his wings again."

"Do it, then."

I turned my chin to meet one of Ajax's golden eyes. I raised the arm on which he stood, and he chirped and sidestepped out to my wrist. I wasn't wearing gloves, and winced at his claws. But I lifted my arm slowly.

I bounced my wrist—irritating the pterodactyl—and sure enough, Ajax rose and spread his wings wide. He followed this display with a mighty cry, a sharp crack like breaking ice, and a hush fell across the crowd beyond the road.

I lowered my arm then, and as I turned to follow Buckland and Davies through the double doors, the gathered found their breath and cried back to us, the sound as loud as thunder.

Chapter 26

THE DOORS TO PALMANAEUS HOUSE CLANGED SHUT, plunging us into an eerie silence after the roar of the crowd. Davies ignored me utterly, falling quickly into conversation about an increased security budget.

But I was distracted staring at the great skeleton, floating in the center of the entry hall just above my eyeline.

It was one of mine. A plesiosaur. I'd found it in 1823, six years ago. I sold it to the Society through Buckland for forty-one pounds.

"Mary," President Davies called, and I broke my gaze away from the great skeleton.

Davies and Buckland had been joined by a short man with a hooked nose and straw-colored hair, dressed in rough leather work clothes.

"Miss Anning, this is Mr. Burton. He is on loan to us from the royal menagerie's aviary. He is extremely well qualified, I assure you. Ajax will be in excellent hands."

My heart sank a little, but of course I wouldn't be permitted to care for Ajax alone.

My hand cupped over Ajax's sloping back as I whirled toward the hook-nosed man in leather.

"So, eagles and hawks, then? Ajax is very different, I will warn you."

Mr. Burton shrugged. "One bird's the same as another."

I nearly choked. My voice pitched to a screech. "A—a *bird*? Ajax is *not* a damned bird."

Davies made a shocked sound at my expletive and then twisted to arch his body over me. It was a blunt but effective tactic. Despite his stooped shoulders and shuffle, he easily passed six feet, and towered above me. My righteous anger shriveled under his gaze. It was difficult enough to stare up and meet his blue eyes.

"Were you a man, Miss Anning," he said, his voice a cold murmur, "I would tell you that such displays of emotion are not permitted in Palmanaeus House, and I would ask you to leave, and not to return."

I swallowed, my lips dry. I'd assumed President Davies to be rather ineffectual—past his time and prime, pushed to a reluctant retirement by his cabinet members snapping at his heels. But with Davies's stare on me and that threat over my head, I could hardly remember that he was stooped and graying.

"But you are not a man," Davies said, and continued staring down his nose at me, "and I cannot in good conscience punish you for following your womanly nature when faced with disappointment."

He straightened, and I ducked my head—not only to seem suitably chastened, but also to hide my anger. *My womanly nature?* Inside, I seethed, even as I apologized to Mr. Burton.

"Very good." Davies nodded approval. "Now, Mary, if you would be so good as to hand over the creature? A number of fellows have already signed up for slots to examine him."

Of course. And they would write the papers and the books. Once again, someone else would make their name and reputation on my work.

"But I will still be permitted time with him, won't I?" I said, looking to Buckland for assurance. He looked to Davies, who frowned.

"Whatever for?"

"For my own studies, of course." It was offensive that I even had to clarify.

"I didn't know you had such ambitions," Davies said stiffly.

And *I* didn't know how to respond to such a foolish statement.

"Mary has grown quite fond of the beast," Buckland said smoothly. "Surely it wouldn't hurt to let her spend some time with him. And she will be a familiar face to him, after all. A comfort, during the transition."

Davies grunted. "I suppose that would be acceptable. On occasion."

Mr. Burton held out his gloved hand expectantly, and I realized he meant for me to hand Ajax over.

I lifted Ajax from my shoulder, stroking at his eye ridges. He tilted his head to look at me curiously.

"I'll see you later," I murmured, and resisted the urge to kiss his toothy beak.

I am very fond of him, I thought, a lump rising in my throat as the bird-keeper took him from me. I supposed there was no point pretending otherwise anymore, even to myself. Ajax and I were bound and bonded.

But he wasn't mine. He belonged to the Society now. The zookeeper took him onto his gloved hand, another hand laid over his back to hold him firm. I watched as Ajax was carried in this manner, squawking, up the curved steps, and my heart pinched with every furious screech.

Someone cleared their throat.

"Buckland. President Davies. Might I have a word?"

My spine went rigid. William Conybeare stood in the archway to the library, wringing his hands, his beady green eyes downcast. The geomagician who'd run straight from Palmanaeus to the Inquisitors to report me for suspected sorcery. Conybeare was the reason I'd come perilously close to execution.

"This is not a good time," Buckland said coldly, turning his back to Conybeare in an obvious dismissal.

Conybeare ignored this and came forward. "Please, my friend." He sighed, heavily. "I never should have doubted you."

But of course he said this to Buckland. Not to me.

"No, you shouldn't have," Buckland said sternly, but I heard the depth of hurt in his voice. Conybeare was not only his closest ally in the Society, he was Buckland's dearest friend. "All these years of friendship, and you could not trust my word when I said that Mary was innocent of sorcery?"

Conybeare's eyes landed on me for the first time, and even then he could hardly keep the disdain from flickering across the hollow bones of his face.

He resents me, I realized, feeling the cold chill as his gaze brushed mine.

Conybeare had played a bold hand in running to the Inquisitors. Perhaps it had been driven by true belief. Or maybe it was only the natural growth of his long suspicion of me. Or maybe he'd been playing for his own power and reputation, as the only one who'd seen through the evil sorceress and her ploy.

But whatever had driven Conybeare to the Inquisitors, the gamble had failed.

Conybeare hung his head. "And I will live with that shame every day, my friend."

I started to speak, but bit my tongue when President Davies narrowed his eyes. I wasn't eager to be chastised for my womanly nature again so quickly. Besides, I trusted that Buckland could see his old friend's motivation well enough.

Buckland clucked his tongue, and I lifted my chin, expecting the professor to chide him, or—at least—to demand Conybeare apologize to me.

"You only did what your conscience felt was right," Buckland said instead. "How could I fault you for that?"

As I gaped, Buckland took his hand from my arm and held it out for Conybeare to shake.

Conybeare smiled with thin, pale lips. He didn't need to look my way; I could feel the smug satisfaction rolling off him in waves.

"Now, come," Buckland said, gesturing for Conybeare and Davies to follow him through to the library. "And I will tell both of you more about the flood-hibernation theory that so captured the archbishop."

He did turn to me then, pressing his lips together. "My office is upstairs, left down the hallway. Wait for me there."

The three geomagicians vanished through the arch, into the dim library, and I was alone now, standing before the plesiosaur.

I swallowed down my disappointment, and my anger.

I was here, wasn't I, standing in Palmanaeus House? I was here.

Scattered reliq-lamplight flickered across the white bones of the great beast. The plesiosaur was supported by only a thin rod jutting from the floor, and had been wired together—the jaw hung open, paddles in motion to give the impression that it was swimming through the dark cavern of the hall, as if it might dart at any second into one of the branching hallways, sailing under white arches and columns like smooth coral.

I ran my fingers lightly over the finger bones in the strange, paddle-like fins.

Plesiosaurus, of the Jurassic Lyme. Collected by William Buckland, September 1823.

I remembered finding it. The way my heart leapt as I uncovered more and more, frantic fingers scraping bloody in the sand and stone. I'd been so sure this plesiosaur would turn the key to the Society's door.

Something twisted in my stomach, and I had to close my eyes for a moment and let myself feel the wood under my feet. I was inside the damn door now, and somehow becoming a geomagician felt more impossible than ever.

"I remember when they brought it in. I knew at once that it was your find."

It was Henry's voice, close to my ear. "It is a beautiful creature."

I kept my eyes closed just a moment longer, imagining that I was at home in Lyme Regis, on the beach, the sea washing white over my bare feet.

I exhaled, letting it slip back to sea. We were side by side, shoulder to shoulder, facing the skeleton.

"You were right." My voice was a whisper. "I woke my reliq. An ammonite." His shoulder jerked, twitching against mine.

What am I even doing?

Up until I said the words, I hadn't been sure I would. But now they hung in the air, and I couldn't take them back even if I wanted.

Henry's office was smaller than I'd expected, certainly less grand than his home study. There were the standard dark wood walls and crowded bookshelves, but something about the office felt almost homey. The couch was threadbare in spots, and a tartan blanket was tossed haphazardly across the back. *He sleeps here, at least sometimes,* I realized.

"Can I get you a drink? Tea? Coffee? Something stronger?"

I'd expected Henry to launch immediately into an interrogation. It took me a moment to realize he was as nervous as I was, and leaning on manners to disguise it. We were both avoiding eye contact.

"Tea, please." I smoothed my skirts as I sat on one of the velvet couches.

"I'll call for it," he said, and touched a reliq embedded in the wall. "Tea to Stanton, please. It's connected to the kitchens," he explained, as I stared.

"Palmanaeus House has its own kitchen?"

"Of course. And a café. Did Buckland tell you nothing?"

"There's hardly been time," I said defensively.

"Ah, too true. It has been rather busy since you arrived in London, hasn't it?" He sat on the couch across from me and rested an ankle over his knee, tapping his fingers on his shin.

A young page brought the tea, and we both jumped at the knock. Then he was gone again. Neither of us moved for the tea. Was Henry waiting for me to speak first? The grandfather clock ticked the minutes, and I chewed my lip.

Damn it. "Do you really think—"

"So the ammonite—"

We both stopped short. I swallowed.

He laughed and leaned forward, elbows on his knees. "It's rather exciting, isn't it? You can wake the *dead*."

Henry's smile cracked wide, dimpling his cheeks. Not the smirk or the coy, haughty smile he usually wore. This was a true smile. And that sent a spike of fear down my back.

I sprang to my feet. "I can't do this." I hurled myself at the door.

"Mary, wait!" Henry caught my wrist just before the doorknob.

I shook my head frantically, breaking his loose hold. "No. You were there, Henry! I already told the archbishop of Canterbury I had nothing to do with Ajax's resurrection. And Buckland's already off and running with his flood-hibernation theory."

Henry's voice matched mine, a hoarse whisper. "But don't you want to know the truth?"

"I—" My gaze dropped. It shamed me, curdling in my chest.

Henry continued. "Don't you want to know what you are? What you can do?"

My chin snapped up, and I laughed. "Don't pretend this is about me. This is about *your* reputation. You want me to prove your theory. To prove Buckland wrong. Well, I won't be part of it. I refuse to be a pawn in your game against Buckland."

"Then you are the pawn in his," Henry shot back. "I admire your loyalty to the professor, Mary. Truly I do. And I understand—"

"No. You don't. You have no idea."

I didn't have to believe Buckland's hibernation theory to trust that it was the wisest tactic for the Society, and for me.

That was the heart of it. I trusted Buckland. He had proved himself, a hundred times. A thousand times.

"William Buckland saved me." My voice was thick with emotion, but I couldn't help it. "He bought my pitiful shells and stones when no one else would. He bought from me when I had no reputation at all; just a tray of curiosities from the beach. Some nights, his coin was all that kept me from the slicks. Or the whorehouse. Or from eating garbage, scraps of half-rotted fish for my supper, which I did plenty of, I assure you. But never when William Buckland came to town."

Henry's face was pale. "Mary—"

"You *left*." The words tore from my throat. Hot tears threatened, and I blinked quickly. I wouldn't cry. Not in front of him.

Henry's chin jerked, and I stepped back, drawing strength from the door against my spine.

"But Buckland was there. Every summer, he came back to Lyme Regis. And it wasn't just charity. My pride couldn't have stood that. No. He gifted me books, and then asked what I thought of them. As if it mattered. As if he cared. He wrote to his friends, and he said, *She is the cleverest fossilist I have ever met*, and then they came to buy from me, too."

My chest rose and fell rapidly with my breath. "Everything I am, everything I have, is thanks to William Buckland."

Embarrassment pierced my fervor, and I stopped short, suddenly tongue-tied.

Henry stepped close. Too close to be appropriate. I had to lift my chin to meet his eyes, my own narrowed. He caught my hands before I could pull away and held them to his chest.

"Don't." His voice was rough.

I was so startled by the force of his anger that I froze. I felt his heartbeat, and his breath, under my palms.

"Buckland was there when—" His eyes fell, dark lashes fluttering. "When no one else was there. Of course you're loyal to him. You wouldn't be you if you weren't."

His fingers tightened. "But don't give Buckland credit for what you've made of yourself. He may have helped you to—to *shine*—but you were always the diamond."

Henry's Adam's apple jumped, and his lips parted. He wasn't ... was he?

I caught my breath. But then he let go, dropping my hands as if they burned and turning away from me with a shudder.

My arms hung in the air a moment before falling to my sides.

My thoughts were tangled, my own doubts fertile soil for his words.

"But. But I understand now." Henry was still facing away. "You think that if you investigated this theory of mine—this power of yours—that you would be betraying Buckland."

I nodded miserably, though he couldn't see.

"And so you betray yourself instead," Henry said softly. He paced to the window, hands clasped behind his back. "The Mary I knew would never leave truth buried because unearthing it would be ... inconvenient."

I flinched. It was all still manipulation, but it hit the intended target. His words were working. My resolve was weakening.

I certainly didn't want to be someone who ignored the truth. But it wasn't only inconvenient. Henry's theory was downright dangerous—for the Society, and for me.

"It isn't only Buckland." My voice dipped low, reedy with fear. "Henry, I don't want to be *executed*."

He looked at me in shock. "What? You have to know I would never do anything to endanger you."

I scoffed. "The only reason I left Lambeth alive is because Buckland convinced the archbishop I had nothing to do with Ajax's resurrection. Do you really think he'd take kindly to your new, heretical explanation instead? One that upends hundreds of years of theomagical consensus?"

Henry's brow smoothed, his shoulders relaxing. His mouth curved into that damn smirk.

"Ah. I believe we are suffering from a misunderstanding. One that I can easily rectify. I am not asking you to support my theory with the archbishop, or even within the Society. As you said, Buckland's foolish flood-hibernation theory is to be the official explanation for Ajax's resurrection. There's not much either of us can do about that now."

"But," I stammered, "the other night, you wanted me to tell the archbishop I'd woken Ajax with . . . with fossil witch magic."

"Yes"—Henry sighed and waved a hand—"there was a window, but as you've said yourself, that's likely closed now."

"Then what do you even want from me?" I nearly laughed, torn between confusion and frustration.

"And finally, the lady asks." His mouth quirked. He turned away again and opened one of the drawers in the cabinets along the wall.

"We're both scholars, are we not? I thought it would be obvious what I want." Henry stretched out his arm in offering. A dark-gray belemnite lay in his hand. "I want us to study *you*."

Chapter 27

I stared at the small black bullet in his palm, my breath fluttering.

"We don't have to tell them," Henry said softly, jerking his chin toward the door, to the rest of the Society. "We don't need to tell a soul. But at least we—you and I—we would *know*, Mary."

I stepped back, away from the temptation of the fossil, and the answers it held. "I don't believe you. You want this because it supports your theories. Whatever you promise now, I know you'd ultimately want to publish. How could I trust you? You'd want to make your name, whatever the cost to mine. Or to my life."

"Mary, please, listen." Henry's voice held something eager, almost desperate as he stroked a thumb across the belemnite. "Yes, I care for my reputation, and my name. As you do, too. Don't deny it. But those are nothing—*nothing*—next to truth. I've spent fifteen years thinking, wondering—dreaming, really—about that trilobite darting into the rock, straight from your hand. *If only I'd been faster*, I've cursed myself. Think of what I could have learned. The geomagical knowledge that could have been gained, if only

I'd been quicker to catch that damn trilobite, before it slipped away."

He took my wrist and rolled it over. I didn't resist. His words were like hypnosis. He tipped the belemnite into my palm.

"You told me you woke the ammonite," he said, curling my fingers around the spiral, under his own. "When you could have taken that secret to the grave. But you told me the truth."

He was right. I looked down, at our clasped hands, to avoid his eye.

We didn't have to tell Buckland, Henry said. We didn't have to tell anyone. We could do this, just us two. I could bring the fossils to life, and we could study them.

But could I trust Henry to keep his word? Or would he reveal my secret the moment it proved advantageous to his career?

I chewed my lip, weighing the risk of betrayal against my own desire.

Because it *was* desire. If Ajax was just the start? If I could bring other specimens back? Examine *live samples*? The idea of studying living fossils, even in secret, even with Henry, was ... intoxicating.

"But I told you the truth." I looked up, meeting those storm-cloud eyes.

Henry's hand peeled off mine.

I nodded once, sharply, squared my shoulders, and then closed my eyes, trying to pay attention to the smooth texture, and the hairline cracks. That's what I'd done with the egg, and the ammonite, wasn't it?

Come to life? Please?

Even in my thoughts, it was hardly a confident declaration.

"There's no rush," Henry said, and I opened my eyes for a quick glare before shutting them tight again.

I tried to remember what I'd done with the ammonite, before the archbishop.

I searched my memory, searching through the rush of fear I'd felt in that room, my fate in their hands.

What had I been thinking of, when it woke?

Oh—I imagined it alive. My fingers tightened around the fossil as my heart jumped with excitement. *Yes. That was it.*

I imagined the little creature swimming through shallows. I pictured its large, searching eyes, probably just below the rostrum, over long, thin tentacles that propelled it through the warm Jurassic waters as it hunted. I saw the creature darting away from a predator and squirting a black cloud of ink to aid its escape as it raced away from outstretched jaws, and sharp, curved teeth, and—

The tentacles were slick and cold.

My eyes flew open and then my palm, as I thrust the belemnite toward Henry.

He gripped my shoulder, and we stared, in awe, in shock, and in joy, at the squid-like creature cradled in my hand.

"Oh, my—oh, good Lord." My voice was a squeal. "It worked. It *worked*. But what—Henry, what do we do with it now?"

A moist, salmon-pink skin had formed over the bullet skeleton, with a spade-like flare of flesh at the head. Ten tentacles wiggled and flexed over my hand. The rolling black eyes showed clear distress.

"Water. Right?" Henry ran for the pitcher on his desk, water splashing as he held it out. The cephalopod tumbled off my hand and plopped into the water, just as Henry exclaimed, "Christ—wait, that's fresh water."

He gripped his reliq. "Maybe I can make it salt water? But how salinated?"

"I'll just turn it back," I said, then practically shouted, "Be—be still. Be stone!" Isn't that what I'd commanded the ammonite?

But the belemnite showed no signs of fossilization; it darted furiously back and forth, and then the pitcher filled with a black cloud of ink.

I plunged my hand into the graying water and wrapped my fist around the squirming belemnite.

"Be still," I said, desperately willing the cephalopod to return to its fossilized state. As I watched, the flesh and tentacles vanished, a sort of fading to nothingness that felt like double vision. And when I pulled my hand out of the water, I clutched only the hard bullet shape of the fossil.

My shoulders sagged with relief, and my fingers trembled as I held it out to Henry. Then, with the same motion, we looked down into the water, still dark with ink.

"Well," Henry whispered, then cleared his throat. When he looked up at me, his eyes were shining. "I suppose we ought to send for some seawater from Lyme Regis."

I'd hardly recovered my breath, let alone my wits, when Henry nodded firmly, as if something had been decided.

"You'll need an office," he said. "I don't think that should be a problem, though. There are plenty of open rooms."

"An office? At Palmanaeus?"

"Of course." He ferried the pitcher over to his desk and poured a small sample of the inked water into a glass, raising it to the light. "All the other research assistants have offices."

"Research assistant?" My jaw dropped. Oh, Buckland wouldn't like that *at all*.

"It's perfect," he said cheerfully. "You and I can continue these experiments under the guise of traditional research. And, of course, being my assistant will give you a formal attachment to the Society."

I chewed my lip. Henry made a very good point.

"You discovered Ajax, yes," he continued. "But really, you're still only Buckland's houseguest. The other geomagicians will tolerate you—for a while—as a novelty. But you can't join the Society. You have no training. No education. No official reason to be hanging about Palmanaeus.

"Eventually, the others will grumble, and then they will complain, and then you will be asked, politely but firmly, to remember your place."

My stomach twisted. I couldn't discount a word he said. It was true; I'd experienced just a taste of it this morning. It was too easy to recall the bitter flavor when Buckland led Conybeare and Davies away, without a thought to invite me, too.

I had hoped to convince the other geomagicians to support my nomination in June, but what if Henry was right? What if they tired of me—of my *novelty*—long before that opportunity came?

Ultimately, my real question had to be: Would it help my cause for membership, to be a formal research assistant to Henry Stanton? Or would it hurt my chances of Society election?

Buckland thought my case for nomination would be strongest with distance—he'd wanted me to stay in Lyme Regis altogether, I reminded myself. He would never approve of this course of action.

I almost asked Henry his opinion. It was a mark of how much had changed between us that it nearly slipped out: the deal I'd made with Buckland to put forth my nomination. But I pressed my lips tight at the last second. *Don't tell Stanton,* Buckland said. And I'd promised.

He frowned. "What's wrong?"

"I can't be your assistant. Buckland would be so disappointed."

Henry scoffed. "By what right? He could have hired you himself. Why hasn't he?"

My tongue was tied. I had no answer. Had Buckland considered and dismissed it? I pressed my hands to my thighs.

"I'll tell you why," Henry said, rolling his eyes, which then brushed over my chest. His cheeks reddened. "It is because you are a woman."

He was probably right. The idea of a woman research assistant—even one as accomplished as me—might never have occurred to Buckland. Buckland was always concerned with precedent. With how a thing might look to others. Always concerned with how it would impact his own standing and reputation within the Society. Whether it would hurt his case for the presidency.

"But not you?" I pressed. "You don't mind that I am a woman?"

"You are not a regular woman." He waved a hand dismissively. "You? You are Mary Anning."

A warmth spread down my spine.

"Besides," he said, "Roderick Murchison's wife assists him. And Mantell's wife was the one who found that damned iguanodon tooth of his in the first place. Even Davies's wife likes to play at fossilist."

"Yes, but those are their wives."

Henry threw up his hands. "Mary, how can I put this gently? Those in power do not need to concern themselves with the opinions of those without. The professor's influence here is waning. Buckland knows this. *You* know it. Davies knows it, too—two months ago, he as good as promised me his personal endorsement for the presidency."

I caught my breath. There was no way Buckland knew that. Or did he?

It certainly explained why he'd pushed so hard for the flood-hibernation theory. Strengthening the Society's reputation and ties to the Church would buy a great deal of goodwill from Davies. Maybe enough to steal that endorsement from Henry.

"I am offering you a place, here. A place you deserve," Henry said quietly. "Can the professor say the same?"

For just a moment, I let myself feel the sting of betrayal, of Buckland shaking Conybeare's hand, then disappearing into the library and never looking back.

I'd already agreed to work with Henry. He was right; being his research assistant made perfect sense.

And so what if Buckland was disappointed? As Henry just pointed out—he could have asked at any time. But he hadn't.

"All right." I took a deep breath. "Yes. I will be your assistant."

Chapter 28

Henry gave me the tour of Palmanaeus House. The upper level was mostly offices and specimen display rooms, the shelves filled with fossils, minerals, and rock samples.

"I was thinking of this one for you," Henry said, cracking the door. Henry waved a hand, and the reliq-lamps flicked on. "It's been empty since Alfred Ejlersen passed last year. Go on, then."

I stepped inside cautiously. The still air had a musty smell, but not unpleasant. The windows were draped in a worn, patterned velvet, a chaise and two armchairs upholstered to match. The walnut shelves were empty, only patiently waiting for books and fossils to fill them. The desk was enormous, stretching half the length of the left wall, with built-in shelves and slots and spaces for papers.

"It's magnificent," I managed to breathe.

A fierce squawk undercut my words. *Ajax*. My fingers twitched as my head whipped toward the familiar sound.

"He's just next door," Henry said softly. "I thought you might like to be close by."

"I'd like to see him," I said, and Henry nodded, as if he'd expected as much.

Ajax was being kept in a converted specimen room, in the golden aviary from our initial presentation. Rows of benches had been added on each side, to enable observation. Eight geomagicians were already gathered, scratching notes and sketches as Ajax hopped across the bottom of his cage. I recognized a few. Gideon Mantell gave a cheerful wave as we entered, and Elias Goldsmild nodded respectfully. Thomas Whaley scowled before smoothing his features, and his companion, Thomas Reed, looked quickly between Henry and me before plastering a false smile on his own face.

The pterodactyl screeched when he caught sight of me, his wings spreading and flapping. One of the men began sketching furiously.

I wanted to run and crouch next to Ajax and stroke his head through the bars, but I keenly felt the eyes of the geomagicians on me.

"Join us, won't you?" Mantell said, patting the space beside him on the bench.

"I will, later," I said, grateful for the warm welcome. "Mister Stanton is giving me a tour of the Society."

"Yes, Miss Anning has agreed to serve as my research assistant," Henry said, and every eyebrow in the room shot up.

Thomas Whaley's jaw dropped open as well. "But—Stanton—she's a—"

"*She* is a very accomplished fossilist," Henry said sharply, and Whaley took the rebuke with a wince.

I winced as well. Now I would have to race to tell Buckland myself, before someone spilled the news. I'd hoped there might be a bit more time.

"That she is," said Goldsmild. Whaley's Adam's apple bobbed, but he nodded stiffly.

Henry's palm pressed at the small of my back, and I nearly jumped. "Would you like to see the library now?"

"One moment," I said, and walked—confidently, I hoped—toward the golden cage. I knelt and poked my fingers through the bars. Ajax crept forward and slipped his scaly head under my hand, closing his golden eyes as I scratched at his ridges. He made a soft croaking sound that shattered my heart.

"I'll see you soon, my friend," I whispered, then straightened, swallowing the lump in my throat. "Ready."

Geomagical theory divides fossils into two categories: body fossils and trace fossils. In a body fossil, all of the hard-body components of an animal have been preserved and are intact.

Body fossils are my bread and butter: the rare and precious skeletons of ichthyosaurs and plesiosaurs, yes, but also the shells and internal structures of mollusks and cephalopods like ammonites and belemnites.

Trace fossils are overwhelmingly more common than body fossils. It was the nature of fossils for pieces to be lost to time, for the earth to consume the body and leave only the trace. So much of the geomagical evidence we have is in these traces: footprints in the rock, or the imprint of a fern, or the outline of a body long decayed. These traces are a vital record, and an important tool for geomagicians working to piece together a geomagical timeline or understand a species.

But there's a reason I trawl the beach in Lyme Regis hunting for the rarer body fossils: only body fossils can be turned into reliqs.

So this was the first hypothesis Henry and I decided to test once we finished our tour of the ground floor of Palmanaeus House.

My heart hammered with excitement as Henry set up the table, and I quickly scrawled in my notebook:

Hypothesis:
- *Reanimation requires the skeleton—or body fossil—of a creature. An imprint or trace fossil will be insufficient.*

From his drawers, Henry selected several salamander-like samples he'd collected in Scotland. We'd both agreed to wait on aquatic creatures until we could procure some seawater. He had also gathered and prepared a four-sided glass tank—just in case.

I took a seat, and Henry laid out three samples on the table between us: a trace imprint of a hind leg and tail, a full imprint of a skeleton, and an intact skeleton. The tiny, fossilized bones were too fragile to remove from the stone in which they were embedded, but it was a body fossil nonetheless.

I sketched them quickly. *Figures 1A, 1B, 1C. Hypothesis Body Fossil: Alpha Attempt.*

"Are you ready?" Henry grinned boyishly, and I grinned back. I was more confident this time. I knew I could do it. Still, my breath fluttered nervously as I laid a hand over the trace imprint. I tried to keep my expectations low. Maybe I could only reanimate creatures from the Lyme Regis region anyway. *Well, if this fails, then that can be Hypothesis Beta,* I told myself.

I'd hardly closed my eyes when I opened them again.

"There's nothing." I shook my head. "The trace won't work."

"How can you tell?" Henry leaned forward. "What does it feel like?"

"It's like . . ." I frowned, thinking how to describe the strange sensation. The sudden *knowing*. "When I reach out, I find only darkness. No . . . no thread of life at all. There's nothing to grab hold of."

We each dashed off a few sentences in our notebooks. I laid my hand on the next, the imprint of the salamander. All the tiny bones had long ago dissolved instead of becoming fossilized.

I felt a flicker, that time. I sat straighter, trying to picture the salamander, crawling through the wet mud and moss. But where the other fossils—Ajax, the ammonite, the belemnite—had pulled me deeper, had turned into something richer and more real than my own imagination could possibly summon, this was a shallow, pale image. It was my own thoughts, and nothing more.

I shook my head again, and we didn't even speak before dropping heads to our journals.

But we both held our breath as I laid hands on the fossilized salamander skeleton. I started again with my own, conjured image. But it quickly transformed, and my heart leapt as I was pulled into the scene. *It was working*. The glittering ferns, slick with dew. The smell of wet earth, and the feel of it, the dirt breathing under tiny, pattering feet. The air, washing over glassy gills, sweet and clean.

Henry whooped with joy, and I threw off my hand just in time to watch the salamander rise from its bed of stone, leaving a hollow in the shape of its body.

Henry scooped the salamander into cupped palms.

"Hello, little fellow," he said softly, stroking gently with his thumb at the orange-brown head. "And welcome back to the world."

We ran the experiment several times more with other salamander fossils, trying to pinpoint the exact conditions required for resurrection, before settling on a revised working hypothesis.

Revised Hypothesis:
- *Reanimation requires at least 95% (approx.) of a complete skeleton—or body fossil—of a creature. (See Figures 13-18A)*

I reanimated one salamander that was missing its front leg bones, and the creature rose up nonetheless with four intact limbs. Henry and I both jumped from our seats and actually embraced across the table. But when I tried with another incomplete specimen that was missing its back half, I couldn't catch hold of the thread.

After another test, we settled on the ninety-five percent completeness as a "tipping point" threshold, but agreed we ought to try again later with another specimen.

By then we had three salamanders in our glass tank, and the sky outside Henry's window was pitch black.

"I suspect this means you'll be most successful with invertebrate marine species," Henry said, as we returned the fossilized specimens to their drawers.

Invertebrate marine species, like the belemnite, ammonite, or bivalves, were considered unaltered fossils. Their hard-body component—the shell—was already in one piece. No fiddly little bones to get lost to time.

I nodded. "I was thinking the same. And we can also rule out any difference between altered and unaltered fossils."

"Oh, excellent point. Shall we make that Hypothesis Gamma, then?" Henry proposed.

"Perfect," I said happily, nestling a salamander imprint back in its drawer.

Marine shells were already formed of geomagically stable minerals like calcite or aragonite, so they simply bounced along through time and geomagical change until someone like me dug them up.

But the salamanders were altered fossils. In an altered body fossil, the original bone was long gone. The skeleton had, over many thousands of years, been replaced by other minerals, like silica, dolomite, or hematite. My great discoveries—the plesiosaurs, and ichthyosaurs, and even Ajax's mother, the pterodactyl—were all altered, their bones turned over time to stone as they lay in the earth.

A little giddily, I wondered if Henry was thinking the same thing I was. That maybe, just maybe, I could resurrect those, too.

"Now, what are we going to do about *those*?" Henry gestured at the three live salamanders in their tank. "Do you want to ... er ... put them back?"

I frowned. We hadn't yet tested what would happen if I tried to reanimate something I'd put *back*, as Henry said. I was hesitant to test the possibility on the salamanders. "Let's keep them," I said. "Do you think you could smuggle them out?"

Henry nodded. "Shouldn't be a problem. But I do wonder if we won't need a longer-term solution."

"What are you thinking?"

"Well, if we're going to build out a little menagerie"—he said the word playfully, and I chuckled—"then we may want to start doing these experiments away from Palmanaeus. I have a flat only a few blocks away that we could use. I can even hire caretakers for the specimens you reanimate. Discreet ones, of course."

I cocked my head. "You've thought about this."

"I told you, I already knew you could resurrect them. I was just waiting on you to catch up." He shrugged, a little sheepishly, and I saw a hint of pink rise in his cheeks.

Heat rose in mine, as well, as I realized I was staring at Henry and feeling, well, rather *fond* of him.

He believed in me. He trusted me.

I was not so foolish to believe our partnership was wholly altruistic, but still, it was a partnership.

Henry gave a little jerk of his shoulder, and his fingers twitched at his side. "Listen, Mary. Earlier, when you said that—that I left. I need you to know—"

I shook my head. "It doesn't matter. Please. I told you before, on the ship. All of that was so long ago. We were children, playing at love. It was nothing." I tried to laugh, but it came out a hoarse, strained chuckle.

"It wasn't nothing. It was everything." He stepped toward me, his lips parted so I could see his tongue slide over the edges of his teeth. "I have regretted leaving Lyme Regis every day since. I—" Henry's voice cracked.

"Don't," I managed to whisper.

He was very close now, his face above mine, and an ache in his gray eyes. I wanted to slap him. I wanted to kiss him. I wasn't sure which I wanted more.

I cleared my throat. "Don't be silly." I waved a hand, as if that could clear the tension from the air, then opened and closed a random specimen drawer, just for something to do. Somewhere to look that wasn't his face. "You said you wanted to be allies. Well, we're allies. Now, let's just focus on the work, shall we?"

Chapter 29

I rapped my knuckles on Buckland's office door, trying to calm my racing pulse. I'd practically fled from Henry, and my thoughts were tangled and wild.

Buckland called for me to enter, and I stepped inside his office.

He winced and smacked his brow. "Oh, my dear Mary, I'm so sorry, I got wrapped up in some other things and completely forgot to come and collect you after my discussion with Davies."

I managed a smile. "It's quite all right. I've managed to entertain myself."

"Good, good," he said cheerfully, glancing at the darkened window. "Let me finish this last letter, and then we can be on our way home, yes?"

I sat in one of the chairs, listening to the scritch-scratch of his quill and tapping my toe anxiously. He hadn't heard about my employment with Henry, that much was clear. Or there would have been a thick line of consternation between his brows when he greeted me.

I would have to tell him. Any second now he would sign his letter, and I would have to tell him.

"So," he said, still not looking up from his letter-writing, "you are to be Henry Stanton's research assistant."

I caught my breath. "You heard."

"I heard," he said softly, laying the quill on his desk and folding his letter into neat thirds.

"I wanted to tell you myself. I—I was just about to."

Buckland didn't answer. He held a lit candle over the parchment and let the wax drip onto the fold, sealing it with his ring. Over the course of our friendship, I had received a hundred, maybe a thousand, letters sealed thus.

What had I said to Henry? *Everything I am, everything I have, is thanks to William Buckland.* Guilt was slippery in my throat.

Yes, but what was it Henry had said in response? *He helped you to shine*, he said, *but you were always the diamond.*

Still, I couldn't look at Buckland. I stared at my hands, clenched white fists.

His lips were a thin, pressed line. "Mary—"

"You could have asked me yourself," I whispered. "To be your assistant. I would have said yes in a heartbeat. But you didn't. And Hen—Stanton did. So, I have to do this. Even if it makes you angry. Even if it makes you hate me." I forced myself to look up and meet my old friend's eyes.

They were unreadable in the dim light. Buckland cleared his throat, and I braced for his disappointment.

Instead he said, "I understand."

"You do?" I managed to stammer.

He nodded. "Henry Stanton presented an opportunity for advancement, and you seized it. Just as I would have advised."

"I—" I was lost for words. I'd used them all up in my useless tirade, apparently. He wasn't even angry. "Well. All right, then."

"Yes. All right, then." He squared his shoulders and said cheerfully, "Now, I believe Catherine said the cook would be preparing roast goose tonight. Delicious, roast goose. Tastes a bit like flamingo, did you know? I had flamingo once. A little gamey, but overall very satisfying. Perhaps I will see if Catherine can get her hands on another."

He chattered on—about flamingo and parrot and puffin and their relative merits as dinner—as we climbed down the stairs.

"Do be careful, though, won't you," Buckland said, interrupting his description of a fried parrot wing as we reached the last steps. "I don't want to see you. . . ." He paused as we stepped out into the night to wait for the coach to be brought round. "Well, I suppose I don't have to warn you about Henry Stanton's loyalty, do I?"

I stumbled a little, blinking in shock. He knew. All this time, I thought I'd kept my heartbreak secret.

"How did you know?" I managed.

"Oh, from the very beginning. From the first day you introduced me to your new friend, Henry, it was in your eyes. But I did not think it my place to say anything, or to offer warning. I am"—he smiled, fond and sad together—"well, I am not your father. And there are some lessons that must be learned by the young."

I thought of the moment where I'd considered kissing Henry. How I'd imagined what it might be to press my lips to his once again. The desire, long dormant, but waking again.

Apparently I'd never learned my lesson, after all.

All thoughts of Henry vanished the second I saw Lucy, sitting stone-faced in the Bucklands' parlor. Elizabeth was beside her, looking smugly pleased.

"Oh, no," I gasped, hands flying to my mouth. "Luce—I'm so sorry."

"Don't worry," Lucy said stiffly. "I sent word to Edgar that we wouldn't be coming, after all."

"I have no excuse." I knelt in front of her chair. "I completely forgot. Henry asked me to be his research assistant, and—"

"I thought you said no excuses." Elizabeth sniffed, and I scowled.

"I'm just so sorry, Lucy. I'll make it up to you. And Edgar! I'll make it up to you both, I promise."

Lucy sighed. "Well, if you promise," she said, catching hold of my fluttering hands and finally offering a tiny smile. "I'll hold you to that, though. Now, did you say Henry Stanton asked you to be his assistant?"

"Research assistant," I said. "I have an office and everything."

"But you're a woman," Elizabeth said sharply.

"Yes. I am."

"So you can't have an office at Palmanaeus."

"Well, I do." My voice was terse. Elizabeth wasn't even part of this; this was between Lucy and me.

"Elizabeth, darling, can you give us a few minutes? I need to speak with Mary," Lucy said, and I tried not to look *too* pleased. Elizabeth made a disapproving noise as she flounced away unhappily, but she didn't argue.

Lucy arched her brow. "Research assistant?"

"We ... actually make a good team."

"Hmm." She looked as if she might say more but then shook

her head and clapped. "Now, about that promise to make it up to me."

I chuckled. "Calling it in already?"

"There's a meeting tonight. Come with me."

My eyes widened. "A Promethean meeting?"

She nodded eagerly. "We're coordinating to support Edgar's bill."

I hesitated. I had no real desire whatsoever to get caught up in Lucy's politics. But I *had* just let her down.

I nodded. "All right. I'll come with you."

Lucy clapped. "Oh, wonderful! We'll leave around midnight; Edgar will send a coach to the back gate."

"We're sneaking out?"

Lucy looked coy. "Do you really think Buckland would approve if we announced we were taking his daughter to a Promethean planning committee?"

I wrinkled my nose. "Elizabeth is coming?"

Lucy lifted her chin. "Yes. She is very devoted to the cause already."

I rolled my eyes. "You've only known her about three days."

A soft, glassy look passed over Lucy's eyes. "She's sweet, Mary. Smart, and kind. But she's got a fire in her, too."

"You really like her."

Lucy's nose flushed red. "I do."

"Then I do, too." I squeezed her hand. "Midnight, you said?"

"Midnight. Oh, and wear dark colors."

The coach came to a stop under a streetlamp, and we stepped out into a round pool of silver light.

"We'll be back in one hour," Lucy said, slipping the driver a coin, and he nodded and flicked the reins.

Lucy led us down an alley off the main road, which quickly dumped into a promenade lined with gentlemen's clubs. We joined a stream of happy drunks and eager night-hawkers.

This was a wealthy neighborhood, and the men were top-hatted and tailed. Constables were posted at regular intervals under bright streetlamps, blue uniforms starched and stiff. But Lucy led us farther, down narrower, darker alleyways, where pub signs and doorframes needed repainting and the crowd was sparser.

I frowned as we turned again, down a converted back alley, narrow and crowded, lit only by a few reliq-lamps hanging in interior windows. Men and women hung in the doorways, calling out to the darting, scurrying crowd and making furtive exchanges. There were no bobbies here, to be sure.

I couldn't quite believe Lucy had brought Elizabeth to this part of town.

An addled man stumbled in the road in front of us.

"The queen is in the castle," he croaked in a singsong, showing a row of blackened teeth.

Lucy flung an arm in front of me defensively as the man tried to lurch forward, his eyeballs rolling in his skull.

"But the walls are made of silk, and now the worms revolt." He laughed, and then urinated on the road just in front of us.

Elizabeth screeched, and I jumped back from the splash.

"It's just there," Lucy said, and hurried us both forward by the elbows, around the drunkard. She led us to a sagging wooden structure. The upper level was half-collapsed, and two of the windows were shattered. The shutters were closed, their paint peeling, but a sign above the doorframe read, THE EAGLE AND FLAME.

"Rather obvious, don't you think?" I muttered, and Lucy rolled her eyes as she rapped on the blue door.

An eyeball appeared in the crack.

"Password?"

"Meadowlark."

The door swung wide, and we followed the tiny, stooped bearer of the eyeball—the innkeeper, I assumed—inside. The room was warm, and warmly lit. There was a bar, and small round tables, and all the usual features of a cozy common room.

Lucy was greeted like an old friend, and a pair of men in tailored suits vacated their table so the three of us could slide in instead. I studied the gathered as the innkeeper brought us each a small glass of brandy. The clothing ranged from fine, like the two gentlemen's, to plain, dirty workwear.

"Now, where were we," said a man with dark stubble along his jaw. He was one of the ones in workwear—a laborer of some sort, from the dust and mud on his trousers—but the whole room turned to him in polite attention.

"Logistics," said a woman in a black widow's veil.

"The protest will take place a fortnight from tonight. Cell leaders, please get word to your cells as soon as possible. In the meantime, we will be rallying support. We'll be converging just south of the Covent Garden slicks, two Thursdays hence, at four o'clock sharp."

"What did we decide on the armband proposal?" asked a man with a port-wine stain.

"It makes it easier for the bobbies," the innkeeper said.

"Yes, but also easier to identify one another," countered one of the suited men.

"What do you think?" the leader asked, turning to Lucy. I realized for the first time that none of the Prometheans had used her name—or any names, for that matter.

Lucy pursed her lips. "I think yes. Reports from the Nottingham leadership suggest that even when people don't actively join in, they may don an armband in support."

The Promethean leader nodded. "I agree. All in favor of armbands?"

He counted the votes carefully, an ultimate tally of thirteen in favor, seven against. Elizabeth raised her hand to vote, but I kept my arm down.

"The ayes have it. We'll do black, to match the Nottingham movement. Now, each of you be sure to remind your cells—allow people to access the slicks as they need. This is *not* a blockade, or a boycott."

"Not *yet*," muttered a girl even younger than Elizabeth, in a factory uniform.

The leader nodded. "Not yet. Of course, we will escalate if we must, but for now this is a rally to support Lord Merlton's proposal to raise the national reliq-rate. We will not be engaging in any violent action. This is a peaceable protest. Is that understood?"

A previously silent man with a long, drawn face and dusty clothing raised his hand.

"And if the bobbies get violent with us first?"

The Promethean leader grinned, a spark of something cold in his eye. "Then we give it right back."

Chapter 30

I WAS STILL TROUBLED COME MORNING, AS HENRY AND I worked to sort his collection of ammonite and nautilus fossils to determine which I should resurrect first. Henry had furnished three rooms of his London townhouse with glass tanks in varying sizes. Only one was filled: a tank we'd outfitted with carefully arranged mud and ferns for our Scottish salamanders. We were waiting on the water for the rest now, but Henry expected it to arrive by tomorrow midday, along with a shipment of small bait fish and mealworms. In the meantime, we sorted, and I worried.

I loved Lucy. She was my dearest friend. And I agreed with her cause. Truly, I did. The system *was* broken. Or perhaps even worse, the system was operating just as it was designed.

But in all the years Lucy had been involved with the Prometheans, I suppose I'd considered the movement mostly academic: a reformist analogue to the Geomagical Society, essentially.

I realized now that had been simply my own willful misunderstanding. Lucy had described plenty of the group's actions to me:

protests, and boycotts, and even violent clashes between Prometheans and authorities. But it had always been so far away from our little world in Lyme Regis; it was easy to dismiss. And I couldn't dismiss it now.

Because I kept seeing the cold look in the Promethean leader's eye, at the end of the meeting, and the current of . . . what was it, exactly? Resignation, perhaps—a general acceptance that things might escalate. Probably *would* escalate.

And yet, I knew the desperation that drove people to the slicks, and the bone-deep shame that followed. I knew the sting of handing over your own magic, unspooled from your own soul, and for what? Mere pennies. The way it made you feel small, and hopeless, and empty. I'd tasted the poison of the slicks enough times to know that Lucy—and the Prometheans—were right.

If Edgar's proposed legislation really could get the reliq-rate raised, it would be a huge boon for those who sold in the slicks just to buy their daily bread.

I must have looked troubled, because Henry glanced up from across the table of swirling ammonites. "What is it?"

I waved a hand and scrawled in my notebook, *Experiment 54: compare ammonite and nautilus diet.* "It's nothing."

Henry cocked his head. "Tell me, please. Maybe I can help."

We were in the upstairs study of his home, which was decorated like the rest, in that fusion of velveted luxury and scientific clutter that the geomagicians seemed to favor.

I chewed my lip. Frankly, I was curious to hear Henry's thoughts on Edgar's proposal.

I closed the notebook. "You know, I assume, that Edgar Murray has introduced a bill to raise the national reliq-rates?"

Henry snorted. "I told him it'll never get out of the Lords."

"It's a good idea, though, don't you think?" I pressed softly.

"The rates haven't been raised ... well, certainly not as long as I've been alive."

"It is a fair proposal, yes," Henry said thoughtfully. "And I'll certainly agree the reliq-system is long overdue for reform. Even more reason the bill won't succeed."

"Why not?"

"Because too many people with power benefit from the system as it now operates—our Society itself, for one. We provide raw materials to the Reliquemical Guild, which in turn become reliqs. If the payout rate was raised, that would impact our own coffers." He shrugged. "And the Society is only one such example. Even if it were to somehow make it through the Lords, half the members of the Commons hold investments in my own bitumen mining companies—which, I'm sure you've already realized, would be affected by such an enormous ripple in the reliquary economy."

"Of course."

His smile suggested he knew I had realized no such thing, but was kind enough not to say.

"You think it's pointless, then?"

He started to say something, and then, thinking better of it, pursed his lips and said, "Let me put it this way. Edgar and Lucy can do all the politicking and protesting they'd like. But they're still trapped in an old stone wheel, one set rolling down its hill long, long ago. The most Edgar can manage through his bill is to shift that wheel's path by a centimeter. Maybe an inch." He shrugged. "I'm not saying it's *pointless*, I'm saying it's not enough."

I huffed, bristling in defense of my friends. "And when exactly did you get so interested in reform?"

"Since I created the machine to make that wheel obsolete," he said coolly.

Ah. Right. "The Loom."

"Imagine"—his gray eyes were eager—"a network of mills, all running my Looms, stretching all across the country, offering fair, high wages for low-skilled labor—far higher than Edgar's proposal could win for them."

"And earning you a fortune in the meantime." I arched a brow.

He chuckled. "Mary, darling, I have a fortune to last a thousand lifetimes. Is it really so impossible to believe I might have other reasons?"

I was so thrown by the *darling*, I didn't have a quip ready.

"Anyway, I suspect even Ed knows his Reform Act is bound to fail. Hunt couldn't manage to get his own bill through the Commons, and that was much less radical, and Hunt a far more inspiring orator than Edgar." He shrugged. "Ed's skill has always been in the ... subtler aspects of politicking."

"Then why bring the bill forward at all?"

Henry cocked his head. "Perhaps to prove that such efforts are futile."

I snorted. "That makes no sense."

"I'll say this: I learned a long time ago never to underestimate Ed." He chuckled. "You've played chess with him. You know."

I smiled fondly. Lucy and I swore off matches with Edgar after being roundly beaten so many times, but Henry persisted. When Henry finally claimed a win, Edgar sent for a stack of books on chess strategy. Henry never managed to repeat his victory.

"Then what is it he wants?" I asked. I could ask Edgar, but I was curious what Henry would say.

Henry rose and walked to the window, looking down at the street with hands clasped behind his back.

"Change," Henry said softly. He was quiet a long time, staring out the window, before turning back to face me. "Do you remember the mouse?"

I blinked at the shift in topic, but I knew what he meant. Henry and I once captured a mouse, with plans to run it through a series of cognitive experiments. Edgar vowed never to speak to us again if we didn't let it go. We released the mouse at once, traumatizing Henry's butler. It was the only time I'd ever heard Edgar raise his voice.

I nodded.

Henry ran a hand through his dark hair. "When Buckland and I designed the Loom, I must confess we were thinking only of the Society. Of the potential power of the manifold reliqs. It was Ed who recognized the greater potential—what power it might give the powerless."

Henry didn't need to say it. I knew we were both thinking of the viscountess. Edgar and Lucy's mother. Her sickness, and the servants sent away. Lord Merlton hiding the reliqs and taunting his wife to use her witchery to save herself if she could. And the two pale-faced children hiding in the shadows, jumping at their father's tongue and cowering from his fists.

Henry sighed as he shrugged. "I can't claim to know all of Ed's plans—"

"He'd probably say we were too simple to comprehend them anyway," I quipped, and tried to tell myself it wasn't to make Henry smile.

But it worked. "He would indeed." Henry laughed fondly and then gave a small shake of his head, as if to clear the heaviness from the air. "Now. Would you like to see the tank I've commissioned for our ichthyosaur attempt?"

I gasped, abandoning all thoughts of reform, and magic-collecting looms, and Prometheans in my wake as I raced to follow him through the doorway.

Henry spread word around that I was assisting him on a comprehensive survey of British Ichthyosauria. I was well positioned to assist in such an undertaking, having made most of the significant finds, so no one questioned our cover story. Though, admittedly, the geomagicians of London had far more pressing things about which to speculate than what exactly Henry and I were getting up to together.

By the end of my first full week in town, nearly every geomagician in Britain had descended on Palmanaeus House, drawn by the irresistible lure of a living, breathing pterodactyl specimen. The Society was full of noise and bluster, arguments and examinations and men in every corner, furiously drafting papers and proposals, all working to put their own mark on Buckland's grand hibernation theory.

Buckland once joked that if you put three geomagicians in a room, only two will ever agree at any given time. So I was surprised, and frankly, a bit appalled at how easily the professor's theory was accepted among the geomagicians. Granted, there were already a few splintering theories and theomagical debates around the subtler nuances. For example, one faction swiftly declared that hibernating species were gradually being triggered to wake by a warming in the climate, while others were becoming convinced the wakings were related to patterns of human migration.

The timeline, too, was subject to great debate. Buckland, in his presentations, posited that small pockets of ancient species must have been waking in random, staggered fashion through all of human history, which would explain tales of dragons and sailor reports of sea monsters in the deep. Others—Charles Lyell chief among them—posited instead that species woke in repeating cycles, and that we had likely entered one such cycle.

Lyell presented his theory one afternoon in the lecture hall and then promptly set out for Switzerland to pursue reports of a mammoth sighting in the Alps. Others followed suit, planning field expeditions in search of all manner of lost creatures, based on rumor. As Society treasurer, Henry had to authorize the funding, and he grumbled to me—privately—that it pained him to waste Society coin on what were likely to be, in some cases quite literally, wild-goose chases.

Because of course we were the only two who knew the truth. None of the geomagical expeditions would yield any resurrected species in the wild forests and mountains they planned to explore. If only they knew what was swimming around in Henry Stanton's extra bedrooms.

Almost every grand room of Henry's London flat now held rows of tanks, and I'd filled them dutifully with all manner of delightful wriggling, swimming, crawling things from Henry's private fossil collection.

The ichthyosaur tank—still empty—was roughly the size of a four-poster bed; the glass smith said that was as large as he was willing to build in a residential structure. But we had a pack of sea snails in the library, and belemnites in the study, and tanks of ammonites and trilobites in the bedrooms. Fish and sea-rays and the lily-like crinoids took over the dining room table, and Henry's own office now held the largest ammonite I'd ever seen. We were receiving new shipments of seawater every day, and Henry brought on a staff of four—young men loyal to Henry and reliq-sworn to absolute secrecy—to manage all the feeding and tank cleaning.

Henry and I were feverish with sketching and measuring and observing, the specimens and me both. I kept careful logs of each resurrection attempt in this journal, along with notes about my diet, sleep, menstrual cycle, time of day, weather, and my personal mood.

We had, by now, a fairly comprehensive understanding of my power and its limitations. And my attempt on a dead lizard, killed by Elizabeth Buckland's cat, proved conclusively that I was unable to revive a newly dead thing.

Henry and I had nervously laid out its stiff, delicate body on the desk, on top of a lace tea doily. He leaned forward to watch as I touched the cold reptilian skin.

But rather than the tingling warmth I felt with fossils, a chilled, oily sensation spread through my chest, flipping my stomach, and I'd immediately vomited into one of his Dutch blue vases.

"Well, I think that proves you're not a necromancer," said Henry, as he gently rubbed my back. "Which is probably for the best."

I laughed at the understatement of the year, then groaned as my bile rose again.

It was almost too much. I felt, at any given moment—chatting in the library at Palmanaeus House or sitting at the Bucklands' for dinner—as if I were about to burst apart with the pride of my secret. I was bringing back the dead.

I was bringing back the dead.

No hibernation. No Godly hand of divine intervention. My power. *My* magic. *Me.*

And no one would ever know.

It was a bitter pill. I was the one who'd insisted on this secrecy. Not once had Henry broached the topic since we formed our initial agreement. I'd accused him then of caring more for his reputation than my safety, but now I was the one doubting the trade-off.

Would I truly be charged with heresy if the truth came out? Surely I wouldn't *really* be executed. This wasn't the Middle Ages anymore.

Maybe we could find a way to successfully spin my power. A blessing from God, perhaps?

And then we could throw open the doors. Show the geomagicians our tanks of treasures. I could publish. The world would know. *I* would be known.

One evening I looked up from my notebook mid-sentence to see Henry settled on the rug in front of the belemnite tank. He'd rolled up his sleeves to work in the tanks, so his forearm was bare where it rested on a propped knee. There was always something catlike about Henry Stanton, with that confident swagger and knowing smirk, but he looked especially feline now, watching the dark tentacles curl and uncurl.

I almost said as much, but the teasing words died on my lips. Reflected blue light flickered over his face, limning his cheekbones and dipping into the hollow of his throat. He was still, and rapturous, and I wanted to touch him, wanted to trace the shifting shadows and light with my fingertips.

I couldn't move. Couldn't *breathe.*

But Henry turned then, and patted the rug beside him. "Come

and sit with me." His smile was earnest and wide. I knew better than to trust it.

I collected myself as I sat, hands tightly clasped in case they decided to reach for his face of their own accord.

"Nothing." His voice was soft. He was staring at the squid again. "No publication, no accolade, no presidency. Nothing I might earn or do or write or discover. Nothing could come close to this."

I care for my reputation, and my name, he'd said before. *But those are nothing*—nothing—*next to truth.* The knowledge alone would be worthwhile, he said, when I'd doubted his motivation. He didn't need the recognition. Only the truth.

I believed him now.

I pretended to marvel at the squid, but really I studied him from the corner of my eye, this man I'd considered a ruthless, status-seeking climber. It was an unsettling realization to discover that perhaps Henry Stanton was a far nobler scholar than I.

Chapter
31

WE FOUND A SMALL ICHTHYOSAUR IN ONE OF THE DUSTier storage rooms of Palmanaeus. It wasn't one of mine; my complete ichthyosaurs were all the monstrous variety, stretching five meters or more. But none of those would fit in our tank.

Henry loosened the collar of his shirt and rolled his sleeves, panting. He'd carried the fossil slab all the way from Palmanaeus.

"It isn't that heavy," he'd scoffed when I suggested he ask a page for assistance. So I had to laugh as he mopped the sweat from his brow.

He chuckled sheepishly. "It's very warm in here."

The ichthyosaur skeleton was still embedded in stone. But the fossilist had done a thorough job, and I felt fairly certain we had ninety-five percent of the bones.

I knelt beside it on the floor, my heart stuttering. Henry knelt across from me.

"Are you ready?" his voice was husky. My mouth was dry. I nodded and brushed my fingers over the skull.

There it was. The spark of life.

My hands shook as I ran them down the curving spine. My thoughts went still, and quiet, now flooded with images of the sea—the crashing waves and the warm water on powerful flanks, tiny fish darting in the shallows.

But something was different. Wrong.

I gritted my teeth, trying again. Diving into the flickering images of sea and stone and coral.

But whatever the thread of life was made of, it slipped out of my grasp. As if it were just out of reach.

"I can't ... grab hold ..." I mumbled, and my vision started to blur.

"Mary!"

Henry threw himself across the stone slab. I slid, limp, against his chest. The magic vanished as my fingers twitched, leaving a newly carved hollow in my stomach.

"I'm sorry." My voice was slurred, and my hands weren't cooperating. Everything sounded very far away—except for Henry's heart, pounding under my ear. "I don't know what happened. Why it didn't work."

"Don't be sorry," he said. "All power has limitations. It's no shame on you. We'll simply focus on the little ones."

"But—"

"Hush." His arm tightened around my waist. "You're safe. That's all that matters."

What a damnable man, I thought, and closed my eyes, letting my breathing steady to the rhythm of his.

I protested weakly, but Henry forbade any more resurrection attempts for the day. So after I was recovered, we walked back to Palmanaeus House for an afternoon of research instead.

I assumed Henry would go to his own office, but instead he followed me to mine. He settled into the dark-blue chair by the window and pulled a book from his satchel—*Occidental Cults and Rituals*—and crossed an ankle over his knee.

I'd always preferred to work alone, but somehow Henry's presence didn't annoy me. It was even comforting, rather than obnoxious, to hear his steady breathing and the crinkle of paper as he turned pages.

Ajax cawed unhappily through the wall, the cry like a hook in my ribs, breaking my concentration. The squawk was followed by male voices—cries of alarm.

He probably tried to bite someone again, I thought, my lips twitching with a smile.

"Do you remember the day we met?" Henry's voice was so soft, I wasn't sure I'd even heard correctly until he continued. "It was on the beach. You'd found an ichthyosaur."

The muscles between my shoulder blades pulled tight. "I remember."

"I was looking for you. Did you know that?" He chuckled. "I'd been bothering Mother for weeks at that point, ever since they sent me home from school. She told me to go outside, to get some fresh air and leave her alone.

"I was wandering around down by the seawall, just kicking rocks. One of them was strange. It had an imprint of a bivalve. The lines were so clear. A sailor hauling in fish saw me studying it. 'There's a girl,' he told me. 'Odd. But about your age. She finds lots of those things on the beach. Sells them for coin. If you want to see more of 'em. Name's Mary.' Or something like that. And then the man went back to his catch. He didn't even wait for me to respond."

Henry's fingers tapped idly on the page of his book. His eyes were distant.

"That man changed my life. Isn't that strange? He's probably never thought again of the boy with the seashell. But I was curious. I walked out on the beach, the way the man had pointed. And eventually, sure enough, there you were. You were kneeling in the sand, digging away with such single-minded purpose at this dark-brown skull. I could see the pit of the eye, and the jawbone. Like a monster. Your dress was soaked from the knees down.

"You looked up at me with this annoyed scowl, as if I'd interrupted you. Which I suppose I had.

"But I was fascinated. From the moment I first saw you, I was fascinated."

It was like his words and the memory had cast a spell, and I was afraid that if I moved, or blinked, or even looked away, it would break.

Henry broke it himself. He cleared his throat and looked down at the book in his lap.

"I'm headed out of town for a few days," he said quickly. "It's been some time since I've checked on operations at Glasswater Mill. I should go and see how things are progressing with the Loom."

"Of course," I said lightly, but my heart dropped. *How long?* I was bursting to ask. And, worse, so much worse: *Take me with you.*

Henry wasted no time; he was gone within the hour. But he left me the keys to the London flat.

So the next day I walked through thick morning fog from Palmanaeus to Henry's to continue the work alone.

The butler greeted me with a drawn face the moment he opened the door. My stomach sank. "What's wrong?"

He exhaled. "Come and see for yourself."

I followed him upstairs to one of the tank-storage rooms.

My dread deepened when I caught the eye of one of the pages we'd hired to care for the revived specimens. The young man stood in the corner near the salamander tank, wringing his hands. His eyes were glassy. He shook his head.

I raced to the tank, pressing my hands against the glass and peering inside. Dread clawed at my chest and slithered into my throat as I caught sight of the still, tender bodies, and had to tear my eyes away.

"No." My knees nearly buckled. "Please. No."

"They were gone when I arrived. I swear it, Miss Anning."

I reached in and lifted one of them from their mossy bed, stroking with tender fingers.

The black-olive eyes were dim and lifeless, and the skin was dry and cold.

I sank to the floor, my pale-green dress pooling around me, and I stared at the tiny, stiff creature in my palm.

All my powers were useless. The salamander was no longer a fossil. It was a body. A corpse. It was gone.

And the poor salamanders were only the start.

It was one of the belemnites next. I found it the following morning, floating lifeless at the top of its tank. And on Tuesday afternoon, one of the smaller ammonites passed, and I discovered three dead sea snails—one of which had vanished completely. I could only assume the others had scavenged its remains.

Early Wednesday morning, a trilobite died, simply stopped in its tracks, as its many legs suddenly stilled.

That's when the quiet worry, which I'd been trying to dismiss, burst into true fear.

Something was wrong. With the creatures. Or me. Or my magic. Maybe all the resurrections were temporary. Maybe—

By that point I was already running back to Palmanaeus House, my skirts clutched so indecently that a gaggle of street youths whistled as I raced past.

If it had just been the snails, I wouldn't have worried. But the others were long-lived creatures. They should have had years and years left.

I flew up the stairs, ignoring the startled pair of geomagicians forced to scurry out of my way. I flung the door open, my heartbeat pounding in my throat.

Ajax chirped and scurried toward me in his awkward gait.

I sank to my knees and folded myself around his body, still half in the doorway. I pressed my cheek to his, inhaling the musky animal scent. Relief softened my hands, warmed my palms as I stroked his head. Ajax was fine. He was *alive*.

"Can I help you, Miss Anning?" The voice dripped annoyance.

I looked up, the scene taking shape. There were four men in the room, and eight raised eyebrows. Three geomagicians. Jonas Finch, Adam Harrelson, and Matthew Turner—an expert on Crinoidea I'd been hoping to impress. And the zookeeper. Mr. Burton. Burton had bits of bloody meat in his leather glove. It must be feeding time.

Burton spoke again, as if I were very simple. "Is there something you need?"

My cheeks flushed. I pulled my face away from Ajax with as much dignity as I could muster.

"I'm sorry to interrupt." I stood, smoothing my skirts to avoid their eyes. "I—" Ajax flapped his wings and hopped. He wanted to be picked up. I bit my lip, resisting the urge to do so. I'd made a fool of myself and couldn't even tell them why. But I had to say something.

"I missed him." I winced as soon as the words were out of my mouth.

Burton sneered, but Jonas Finch smiled indulgently. He was Buckland's age, an erosion specialist with a fondness for good wine. "My wife is the same about her little dog. Percival. Damn thing bites at my ankles, but Etta won't hear a word against him."

"A tender heart is a credit to any woman," Turner said, and I wanted to melt into the floor.

I inclined my head. Ajax squawked for my attention, but I didn't glance down. "My apologies for having disturbed you, gentlemen."

I hurried from the room, forcing myself not to look back at Ajax, even as I heard a flutter of wings and a pained yelp that suggested Ajax had bitten someone again.

I stalked back to Henry's house, cursing myself. I'd gotten worked up over nothing, and now I'd have a reputation as a soft-hearted, sentimental woman no better than Finch's wife with her little dog.

Of course Ajax was fine. It had to be an environmental issue. The creatures' diet, maybe, or their water quality. We certainly couldn't replicate Jurassic conditions in a glass tank.

At least I could ensure the deaths were not in vain. I collected my notebook, a scalpel, and the icebox in which I'd stored the dead specimens and set up a necroscopy laboratory in Henry's kitchen.

I sketched out internal structures and soft tissue as I went: the flesh lost to time, muscle no human had ever seen before. I told myself this was good. Worthwhile. I was still learning. Still collecting knowledge, even with the deaths. Failure—death—was simply the cost of scientific progress.

I was glad the stink of dead fish had cleared the staff from the kitchen, because I cried every time I set my knife to a cold tentacle or pried open a protective shell. *The geomagicians were right to be so patronizing,* I thought miserably as I fought back the tears. Apparently I was like any other woman, quick to resort to emotions.

I wept alone, in the thick silence of the kitchen, and cursed Henry Stanton for leaving once again.

I lunched later that day with Gideon Mantell and Elias Goldsmild in the Palmanaeus cafeteria, poking at my broiled chicken and half listening to their discussion about sedimentary composition in the Highlands.

Maybe I should try a different diet with the belemnites. They seemed content with the mix of fish and crustaceans I'd offered, but a different type of fish might improve outcomes.

"... what do you think, Mary?" Mantell asked eagerly.

I started. "I'm sorry. I was thinking of—something else. What were you saying?"

"We've been working on a proper name for your bezoars." Goldsmild smiled. "Gideon here has proposed *coprolite*. Kopros, from 'dung,' and lithos, from 'stone.'"

"It was my wife's idea, actually," Mantell said, dropping his voice low.

"Coprolite," I said, trying it out on my tongue. "Certainly more scholarly than fossil-feces."

"Exactly." Goldsmild chuckled. He and Mantell exchanged a glance, and Mantell gave a quick nod.

"Mantell and I thought perhaps we could write a paper on the subject."

"Of course," I said, fighting back my envy. "You came up with the name."

Goldsmild cocked his head. "We mean *with* you, dear."

"I don't know how much availability you have, given your commitments to Stanton's research," Mantell said, "but if you have the time, we'd love to have you."

I blinked as the offer sank in. The geomagicians wanted to work on the paper with me. As partners. Co-authors.

It wasn't exactly how I planned to make my mark as a scholar, but I *had* been the first to identify the bezoars—*coprolites*—for what they were. But between my work with Henry and a co-authored paper with Mantell and Goldsmild, my reputation as a geomagician could only be bolstered. Every chance to prove my worth as a scholar was an opportunity to gather votes for my eventual election.

My cheeks warmed as I stammered out, "I'd be honored to work with you both."

For the first time since I'd discovered the dead salamanders, I smiled.

And I smiled through the rest of lunch, fantasizing about my name heading a geomagical paper, and soon my name signed to the Charter of the Geomagical Society of London.

It was gray and wet when Buckland and I rode home that night in the coach, puddles on the cobblestones and halos around the streetlamps.

He was delighted by news of my planned co-authorship.

"And you simply must give a talk as well. I can help you practice! I'll have much more time to assist next week, after the public lecture."

Said public lecture on flood-hibernation theory was to be held in St. Paul's Cathedral, no less. Ajax would be on display for the public in his golden cage as the star exhibit.

"Do you think the archbishop will attend?" I asked.

"He will," Buckland said, preening. "He is most eager to show his support for the Society."

"That's good. I wonder—"

The coach lurched to a halt. Buckland frowned; we hadn't been driving nearly long enough to be at our destination.

A voice barked at our driver, and Buckland and I both poked our heads out the windows to see what was the matter. The street was oddly deserted, and a prickle raised the hairs on my neck. *It's too quiet*, I thought, just as I was blinded by a white light. I yelped and leapt back from the bright beam.

"Sorry, miss," said a gruff voice, and the light shifted to sweep over the coach's interior.

"What is the meaning of this?" Buckland asked.

"Apologies, sir," the constable—I could see his hat and coat now—grunted. "There's rough types out tonight. Prowling the streets. Causing trouble and bothering good folks like yourselves. We've blockaded the roads ahead to limit to residential traffic only. Your address, sir, if you would?"

The protest, I realized with a start. I'd quite lost track of time over the last fortnight, but it had to be the Prometheans. Edgar Murray's reform bill was to have its second reading in the House of Lords tomorrow.

The officer squinted, but Buckland said, "And we are very

grateful for your concern, and diligence." He gave his address, and the constable waved us past with one last, skeptical glance my way.

We rumbled on. Now that I was paying attention, it was impossible to ignore the eerie absence of sound, beyond the turning wheels and clattering hooves.

Lucy would be out there. Somewhere in the darkness across the city. I prayed quickly for her safety.

"I wonder what that's all about," Buckland mused.

I pulled the curtain aside to look out the window at the empty street and lied. "Your guess is as good as mine."

Chapter 32

"Pass the butter, Blythe dear. Jane, don't slouch."

Poor Catherine Buckland, always trying to keep order among the chaos.

As Blythe passed the butter, a loose guinea pig ran zigzag across the table, leaving footprints of jam on the cloth. Lucy cried in shock, and Blythe squealed in delight. "George! You naughty boy!"

I was still reeling from the dead specimens, and anxious about Ajax—despite what I told myself about dietary mishaps or water salinity causing the other deaths. Still, it was difficult to sulk at the Buckland house.

"No guinea pigs on the table, please," Buckland said, not looking up from his newspaper.

"Yes, Papa," Blythe said. She scooped George into her front pocket, and Lucy and I both giggled.

I caught her eye, and she grinned, but I was hit with a wave of guilt.

Breakfast at the Bucklands' was the only time I really had with

Lucy these days. Since I'd started my work with Henry, our days overlapped very little, busy as she was with Promethean business.

I had always been able to tell Lucy the truth—even the complicated bits. But for the first time, there were secrets between us. The truth about my work with Henry, for one. The way I feared I was beginning to feel about him, for another.

I'd always planned to tell her. She was probably the only one I *could* tell about my strange magic, and what Henry and I were up to, reanimating all those species.

Except there'd been no time to do so. Lucy rushed off each morning and came home late at night, and when we did have a moment, all she wanted to talk about was reliqs and protests and Parliamentary bills. And the truth—unflattering and self-centered as it was—was that I resented it.

I tried to quell that ungenerous feeling when it rose. Lucy was following her own dreams. Just as I was.

And yet, I still hadn't told her that I could resurrect the dead.

Maybe you don't trust her, I thought, and my hand flexed.

That couldn't be true. Could it?

"Pass me the toast, would you, E?" Lucy asked, and Elizabeth reached for it. "A guinea pig seems to have run across mine."

Elizabeth laughed a little louder than was called for as she handed over the basket.

Little Blythe was practically writhing with boredom by now, so the governess, Tabitha, hustled her and Jane to the nursery.

I stabbed at my eggs. Was it really possible that I trusted Henry more than Lucy now?

"Ah, Mary," Buckland said, folding the paper behind itself and tapping at the headline so I could see. PROTEST FOR RELIQ REFORM TURNS VIOLENT. "That must be what the constable was going on about last night. See, here: 'Reliquemical Guild issues statement condemning the violent intimidation of its members and patrons,'" he quoted, then clucked his tongue disapprovingly.

"That's a lie," Lucy said sharply. "It was completely peaceful."

Buckland's eyebrows shot up; honestly, I'd never seen them rise so high.

"And you know this because . . . ?"

Lucy lifted her chin. "It's my business to know. They *were* rallying in favor of my brother's proposed bill," she said, rather artfully dodging the fact that she'd snuck out of his home in the night to participate.

"Ah, yes," Buckland said dismissively. "The reform bill."

"Yes," Lucy said. "Edgar is proposing a reform resolution for reliq-trade. To raise the national base-rate paid to sellers."

Buckland made a dismissive noise and flipped the page. Elizabeth and Lucy exchanged a look.

Lucy shook her head—I do not think Buckland saw—but Elizabeth ignored her and said, sweetly, "What, Papa, you don't think the reliq rates should be raised? It has been sixty-three years since the last rate adjustment, did you know?"

Buckland looked up finally, frowning at his eldest daughter. "Sixty-three, you say?"

Elizabeth nodded eagerly. "Oh, yes. They were due to be raised in 1803, but it was deferred because of the war. Do you know how much inflation has risen since 1766? I certainly did not."

Lucy kept her face carefully blank, but I was watching Catherine's instead and noticed her eyes dart to Lucy.

"I had no idea you were so interested in politics, Elizabeth," Buckland said, setting his paper down and looking closely at her.

"Well, I wasn't much before," Elizabeth started, then stopped at the sudden flare of Lucy's brows. Catherine noticed that, too, I saw.

"But this is more than politics," Elizabeth continued, "it's a matter of human dignity."

I realized my fork was hanging halfway to my mouth and put it down quickly. The Bucklands weren't exactly political, but they *were* wealthy. As Henry so recently pointed out, that usually made one rather resistant to the type of reform that could disturb a balance of power currently hanging in their favor.

And now here was their dear oldest daughter, spouting reform slogans, the night after a protest. This breakfast conversation was about to get very interesting indeed.

"Hmm. And what dignity is to be found in selling one's magic?" Buckland asked, tapping his fingers on the tablecloth. "Is not the greatest dignity to be found in honest work?"

"Yes, of course." Elizabeth nodded eagerly.

"But if the rates were raised—if, say, a man could earn a living selling their magic—wouldn't it only encourage more of the behavior?"

"Of course not! Papa, did you know that the most common reliq-seller is a mother? These are simply women and men who want to feed their families, and provide a life for their children. Seamstresses who have been put out of work by the steam looms. Thousands of women and men who lost their livelihoods." Elizabeth shook her head. Her face glowed with the conviction of a new convert. It was almost hard to watch, like a woman skipping toward a cliff.

"No one *wants* to sell their magic, Papa. It is a last resort. There are simply too many poor, and too many others eager to buy the magic they have earned."

"I see. And you believe raising the rates to be a sufficient solution to these problems?" Buckland asked pointedly. "You do not think, for example, that the whole system should be abolished altogether? The sale of reliqs banned—surely to be driven underground, to become unregulated? You would not advocate, would you, for violent measures, and the destruction of property in your aims, would you?"

Elizabeth hesitated. Even she could recognize now the real inquiry under his words: how radical had his daughter really become, under Lucy's influence?

Lucy herself was worrying at her lip, though I don't think she realized it.

"I think," Elizabeth said carefully, "that Viscount Merlton's proposed bill is a good start."

"Oh, is it?" Buckland did look at Lucy now, with arched brows.

Lucy lifted her chin, taking the invitation to jump in. "Yes. It is. And you can come and watch the reading and debate today, if you'd like. You all are welcome, in fact. You would be my brother's guests."

Buckland watched his daughter. "Perhaps I will."

Elizabeth clapped. "Oh, yes, please, Papa, do come! And Mary, you must come as well!"

I shook my head. I had absolutely no desire to get involved with this family argument. "Oh, no thank you. I have Society business to attend to."

Elizabeth looked confused. "But—but you've sold in the slicks, haven't you? So you know it's a terribly unfair system. Surely you want to see it changed?"

If I'd dropped my fork at that moment, I think we all would have jumped ten feet.

My cheeks burned. Both Catherine and Lucy stared anxiously. Buckland politely avoided my gaze, a furrow between his bushy brows.

I stared at the sickly golden, congealing egg on my plate rather than meet their pitying eyes. I'm sure Catherine and Buckland already knew. They'd seen my home. They'd watched me struggle in the years after Father's death. I'd been too poor, for too many years, *not* to have sold in the slicks. But it just wasn't the kind of thing you ever mentioned. It was as if Elizabeth had casually announced that I'd once worked in a brothel.

I knew Elizabeth didn't mean any harm by it. She was just a girl. She didn't have enough experience of the world to realize how it would shame me to have it said aloud.

It was Lucy with whom I was truly furious. How could Lucy have told her? I had thought her flirtation with Elizabeth relatively harmless. Charming, even. But that was before she dragged my secrets into it, for Elizabeth to spill out across the breakfast table.

Catherine reached for her oldest daughter's hand. "You have a tender heart, my dear. That is to be admired. But people choose the slicks for all sorts of reasons of their own. Perhaps we should leave it at that."

Elizabeth pulled her hand away and turned to me. "Mary. Tell them. If—"

"This has nothing to do with me," I said harshly.

"You needn't be ashamed—"

"Enough, Elizabeth," Buckland said firmly. "Go and join your sisters. I need to speak with Miss Murray alone."

Elizabeth tried to argue.

"Now." His tone left no room for debate, and Elizabeth hurried from the room, with a last apologetic look—to Lucy.

Buckland shook his head. "Mary. I am . . ." He sighed. "I am truly sorry."

"It's all right," I said, my throat tight. "I know she didn't mean anything by it."

"It was still cruel," Catherine said softly. "And you did not deserve that."

I looked away.

"As for you, Miss Murray," Buckland began, "I am afraid I must insist that you refrain from further engagement with my daughter on this topic. We have been very glad to have you in our home, and hope to keep you as our guest. But in the future—"

"No, no, of course," Lucy said, quick to nod her agreement. "I do hope that you can forgive me. I have spoken too freely with her."

"Your business is your own," Catherine said, and I wondered if her husband also knew about Lucy's evening activities, because Catherine surely did. "But Elizabeth is a girl with a bright future, still unwritten. You must leave her out of it."

"Of course," Lucy said. "And Mary, I am—"

I rose abruptly, not bothering to excuse myself. I stalked from the room before Lucy could catch me.

"Let her go, love," I heard Catherine say, and I sent her a silent thanks. I didn't want Lucy's apology, and I certainly didn't want to hear whatever justification she had to offer.

I was still fuming, up in my room, yanking a hairbrush through my tangles. I suppose the Buckland girls would use their reliqs for this: a quick bit of magic to braid the hair or lace the backs of their corsets. I'd even seen Elizabeth use her reliq to magic a bit of rosy color onto her cheeks and lips.

But I'd been too long conditioned to hoard magic to use it in such a frivolous fashion. I'd never known when I might need to sell my reliq to afford a bit of bread.

You needn't be ashamed, Elizabeth Buckland had said. I furiously plucked strands of black hair from the brush. What did she know of that shame? What did Lucy, for that matter?

I'd done what was needed to survive. I'd fought and sacrificed and *worked* to get where I was. I wasn't ashamed of anything. But that didn't mean I wanted my life story used as part of some political narrative like something in Lucy's Promethean pamphlets.

There was a knock at my door.

"Go away," I snapped. "I don't want to talk to you."

"I know." Lucy opened the door anyway.

"I mean it."

She shut the door behind herself and came inside. She had a little basket in one hand, filled with bunched cloth.

"That's too bad. Because I need to apologize."

I whirled in my chair and crossed my arms. "And if I don't want to hear it?"

She rolled her eyes. "Do you remember the time you accidentally suggested to Mayor Payne that I had kissed his wife?"

I winced. "I do."

In my indignation with Lucy, I had neglected to consider that the problem with dear, longtime friendships was that you had inevitably wronged them at some previous point, which they would be sure to reference when you were very reasonably and righteously angry with them.

"And what did I say, when you tried to apologize?" Lucy put her hands on her hips.

"You told me to go eat a toad."

"I did. And what did you do?"

A smile threatened to crack across my lips. "I went outside—"

"—and found some poor, innocent toad, and put the fat little fellow to your mouth and—"

I chuckled, despite myself. "And I made you swear to forgive me, or I would eat him."

"Well, Blythe helped me search the garden," Lucy said, drawing open her basket.

I gasped. "Lucy, you didn't."

She reached into the basket and pulled out the fattest, most indignant-looking toad I had ever seen. She twisted up her face, and raised the creature toward her lips.

I rushed to her. "Oh, ew, ew, don't do it, that's disgusting!"

I caught her wrist and yanked, and the toad went flying, landing with a thud on the rug. Lucy and I gasped in unison as we ran over.

Lucy scooped him up, and he *ribbit*ed solemnly, apparently none the worse for wear.

We burst into laughter, both collapsing onto the divan.

"I was wrong to tell Elizabeth," Lucy said, wiping at tears of laughter with her free hand. "I shouldn't have."

The image of the toad in midair popped into my head again, and I hiccupped in laughter.

"I do forgive you. Of course I do." I held out my arms. Lucy set the toad back in his basket, and we embraced. Her hair smelled like lavender, like the bundles she hung over the mantel in her cottage in Lyme Regis. Like home. I squeezed her tight before I let her go.

"You know," Lucy said, as we pulled apart, "despite what her ... *zealousness* this morning might suggest, Elizabeth would much rather work with you than me."

"What? Me? Why?"

"Because she idolizes you." Lucy looked at me in disbelief. "You really didn't know? Elizabeth's spent her whole life hearing from her father about the wondrous Mary Anning, the prodigy of prodigies, the cleverest fossilist alive, the future of geomagic, the hope of womenkind, the light of science in the dark of ignorance. Et cetera, et cetera." She waved her hand.

My chest was tight. "Buckland said all that?"

"Apparently. Did you know that as a girl, Elizabeth begged for bones? So her father would catch rats and boil off the skin and meat for her, and give her the skeleton in pieces, so that she might practice fitting it back together. So that she could learn to assemble a fossil skeleton, if ever she found one. And he brought her real fossils, too, still cased in stone. So she could practice digging them free. Like you."

"But Elizabeth's hardly said a thing to me," I floundered. "And nothing at all about geomagic."

Lucy chuckled. "It may not occur to you, Mary, but not everyone is quite so bold as you. It can be difficult for some people to march up to their heroes and tell them you'd like to speak with them about, I don't know, pleasasaur bones."

"Plesiosaur."

Lucy groaned as she laughed. "Just, maybe you could speak to her? Then perhaps she will stop whining that you think she has brains of cotton."

I stammered that I didn't think Elizabeth had brains of cotton. Lucy looked skeptical.

I reached for her hand. "I mean it. She picked you, didn't she?" Lucy's neck flushed pink, climbing to her ears. I didn't need to tell Lucy to be careful. She knew the risks of a romance with a well-bred young lady; the ruin it could bring to Elizabeth's reputation, and her own.

And if she had to choose between my secrets or Elizabeth's, which would she keep?

The realization was painful, but clear. I couldn't tell Lucy the truth. Not about the reanimations, or the tanks of ancient creatures at Henry's house. Not about Henry's theory of magic, or even that I was some kind of witch with a special affinity for fossils.

The toad interrupted my thoughts with an unhappy *ribbit*, and I plastered on a smile.

"I'll speak with Elizabeth. I promise."

"Thank you. Now, come on," Lucy said, picking up the basket. "I told Blythe she could feed him a cricket before we put him back under the roses."

Chapter 33

Together, Lucy and Elizabeth were surprisingly forceful. It was a testament to their combined power of persuasion that the pair eventually convinced me, and then Buckland, that we really ought to attend Edgar's speech.

Listening to a series of pompous speeches sounded like a rather boring way to spend an afternoon to me. But it was clear this meant a great deal to Lucy. Besides, there wouldn't be many other chances in life to visit Westminster, let alone as the personal guest of a member of Parliament.

I insisted on going to Palmanaeus for my daily welfare check on Ajax, but Lucy hardly let me stroke his beak before hurrying me back to the coach.

We passed through a packed crowd on our journey, the shouting protestors holding signs scrawled with LIBERTAS MAGICAE and WE DEMAND REFORM and chanting, "Raise the rate."

"So many," Buckland murmured, and I had to agree—I was frankly shocked at the sheer mass of humanity. There had to be hundreds, maybe even thousands, gathered outside. Lucy sat up straighter, her face shining.

A few minutes later, we passed through the gates and were then escorted up a back staircase to take seats in the tiered guest gallery, looking down on the floor of the House of Lords.

Lucy took a seat at the very front row, leaning forward over the railing. Elizabeth claimed the only open space to Lucy's right, so Buckland and I settled in behind them.

Lucy tapped her fingers on the wooden armrest and bounced her knees. I leaned forward and put a hand on her shoulder. "He'll be fine."

She nodded but continued to fidget. "Edgar is . . ." Lucy began, in answer to Elizabeth's questioning look. She exhaled. "My brother is very clever. Sometimes that gets in the way of communicating with the rest of us."

"Edgar's not the best public speaker," I translated.

Buckland coughed, covering a laugh, and Elizabeth looked horrified that I would speak so frankly of a viscount.

"He's well prepared, though," Lucy said quickly. "He's been reading all the greats—Burke, Pitt, Wilberforce."

"Can't study your way to personality," Buckland murmured, too softly for Lucy to hear.

The gallery was quickly crowded, and the energy on the floor below was tense, visible in the quick, over-shoulder glances and stiff spines. There were a scattered handful of other women in the gallery, but not many. I fidgeted nervously, affected more than I'd imagined by the anticipation heavy in the air. It felt like the moments in the archbishop's chambers, before they'd begun to argue my fate. Like a moment out of time, where the scales could still tip either way.

"Hello, Miss Anning."

Henry.

"You're back," I said, and cringed at the breathiness in my tone.

"Just returned to London this morning." Henry arched a brow. "I'll admit I am surprised to see you here."

"Stanton, please. They're about to begin," Buckland interrupted, as a narrow-faced, stern-looking man began marching forward. The crowd of gentlemen parted around him.

Henry took the open seat beside me.

"Lucy insisted," I whispered. I folded my hands in my lap. I certainly wasn't eager to do so, but I knew I had to tell him about the specimens dying. "Henry, have you been to the London house yet? I'm so sorry, the specimens—"

"I know. I saw." Henry set a hand on mine and squeezed once. "Don't trouble yourself about it. These things were bound to happen."

I doubt I managed to keep the relief from my face. He wasn't angry.

Buckland cleared his throat, but Henry ignored him. "That's the prime minister," he continued.

Another man, harried-looking and thin, rushed toward the great gold podium—something very like an altar—at the front.

"And the lord chancellor. He'll preside over the debate," Henry added.

The lord chancellor had a nasal voice, and there was a long bit of formal-sounding and procedural business to which I paid little attention until Viscount Merlton, Edgar Murray finally came forward, inclining his head at the attending peers.

The sunlight through the upper windows fell on Edgar, but it made him look pale rather than golden. He squared his shoulders and raised his chin, as both Henry and Buckland had when they presented me to the Geomagical Society. But something—maybe the tightness around his mouth, or the squint of his eyes—belied his confident stance.

"I rise today in answer to Her Majesty's most gracious urging, at the opening of this present session," he began, his words too quick, butting up against one another, "that this body might carefully consider the cry of her people."

He paused and cleared his throat a few times. My heart went out to my old friend.

"Come on, Ed," Henry whispered. "You can do this."

When Edgar began again, it was slower. Better. "With all humility," he continued, "I feel convinced that the speedy and satisfactory settlement of this question becomes daily of more pressing importance to the security of the state, and to the contentment and welfare of the people."

He put emphasis on the right words and looked appropriately solemn, but something was forced about his delivery, almost as if it were an imitation.

"It is therefore not only for the sake of the measure itself, which calls for a reasonable increase in the established rate of exchange in government-sponsored Reliquary Trading Houses, proposed at a twelve percent increase, but also with regard to the recent state of the country, that we endeavor to effect speedy and satisfactory settlement of the question."

Edgar clasped his hands behind his back, and I realized it was an imitation of Henry. Perhaps that's why the performance felt wooden to me, even as the men behind us murmured praise for Edgar's intellect—though they deemed his position too radical.

Edgar went on, and from our vantage in the gallery, I could see every sidelong glance and stiffened shoulder, and these outweighed the nodding heads two to one.

Even before Edgar finished speaking, I knew the proposal would fail.

After he inclined his head and returned to his seat, other peers rose, one after the other, to argue against the measure from every conceivable angle:

The economy was too fragile for an increase.

The economy was strong, precisely because of the low rates.

Did this body really want to encourage sloth by reducing the incentive for the poor to seek gainful employment?

To sell a reliq was no better than prostitution. The government should never have condoned it in the first place.

"He sounds like a papist," Buckland grumbled, as the man was shouted off the stage.

The measure should be tabled for another year, to give the House time to commission a formal study on economic impacts.

There was no need. An analysis by the Reliquemical Guild estimated that reliqs on the market would drop by twenty-seven percent. (This figure cracked through the floor like a whip.)

Lord Merlton had designs for prime minister; wasn't that obvious? He was trying to curry favor with radicals.

A national rate increase would not account for cost-of-living differences.

Rates shouldn't be determined nationally anyway; they ought to be set at the borough-level, with local approval.

Any rate increase would only embolden the protestors.

Sales of reliqs might increase instead, flooding the market and throwing the economy into chaos.

Did they really think the radicals would stop with an increase? No; they wanted to destroy the whole system. The whole economy, for that matter, probably out of spite.

If the pay-rate to reliq sellers was raised, then the purchase price would also increase. Those simple folk who purchased reliqs—to light their homes and grow their crops and feed their families—would have a lower quality of life. Why should their families be punished for the poor choices of others?

The military depended on reliqs; British national security would be threatened.

The lord chancellor nodded sharply in approval at this last speech, and that felt rather like a death knell. I looked to see how Edgar was handling it. I guessed he was aiming for stoicism, but I could read eager hope on his face.

"Poor Edgar," I whispered. Then, seeing Lucy's slumped posture, "And poor Lucy." She, at least, knew that the game was lost.

But Henry wasn't listening to me. I followed his sharp gaze to see a hunched, uniformed figure dart in through a side door.

The uniformed man whispered in the ear of another seated along the back wall, and that man rose and spoke with someone else, who then spoke with another. At first, few of the members down on the floor seemed to notice, but here in the upper balcony we had a perfect view of the message, running like a ripple through the room.

"Something's wrong," Henry said, pulling me by the arm. "Get up."

I yelped at the force of his grip. "Ouch, Henry!"

"Get *up*."

"To arms. To arms!" called a deep voice from somewhere below.

I gasped as everything broke into panic. The redcoats stationed on the floor below suddenly raised their rifles, in almost synchronous motion, and closed ranks, ushering the lords through a door behind the golden podium.

Up in the gallery, we were all on our feet as well, several people shouting at once.

"Please stay calm!"

"We're under *attack*!"

"Get to cover!"

"The damned rioters have broken in!"

A soldier, rifle held out, rushed down the balcony steps to the balustrade and commanded us to evacuate immediately.

Bang.

The building rattled. Windows shook. Voices cried out. The viewers' gallery broke into a chaos of shouts and clambering bodies as everyone rushed up the steps for the exit.

I swayed, catching my balance by grasping Henry's shoulder. He gripped my elbow, and I grabbed Lucy with my free hand. Buckland and Elizabeth fell in, and we joined the bottleneck of panicked visitors trying to squeeze through the singular, narrow doorway.

Another bang sounded, rattling my teeth. I turned to look down at the floor. Most of the lords below had been ushered through the secure doors, but there were still a handful remaining. One of these left-behinders was old, stooped, and white-haired.

I remembered his speech. He'd said that a rate increase would only make the protestors bolder.

What's next, he'd blustered, *demands for universal suffrage? Secret ballots? Seats in Parliament? If we give them a stitch, they'll unravel the gown.* A younger man supported him, but they were limping along slowly when the double doors on the wall opposite burst open.

Our group had been seated closest to the front, so we were last to the doorway. We were nearly there when I glanced back, down to the floor. Had the old man escaped?

I paused on the top step.

He hadn't. The pair still hobbled, a trio of soldiers around them as escort. But the men's faces—one old, one young—were pinched white with terror. *Hurry*, I willed the pair silently, *hurry, hurry.*

"Mary! Come on!" Lucy tugged at my arm.

But down below us, in a swirl of gray smoke, stood two men in tall boots and loose trousers, one in suspenders and the other in an oversized coat.

Their gazes were hard, but for the briefest second, shock and bewilderment flickered over their faces, as if they had not expected to get in, and didn't quite know what to do now that they had succeeded.

The man in suspenders said something I couldn't hear and then raised his gun at the old man.

Henry tried to shove me through the doorway, but I shook him off.

"Wait, Henry, we have to—no, look out!"

At first I didn't realize I was the one who had shouted the warning, even as my cry echoed through the hall.

It only dawned on me after the gunshot rang out, as something slammed into my shoulder.

"Oh." I frowned at the blood blooming over my heart. "I think I've been shot," I said, just before I lost consciousness.

Chapter 34

I DRIFTED IN AND OUT OF CONSCIOUSNESS. LUCY'S TERRIFIED face above mine. Elizabeth, screaming. Buckland's hands, covered in blood.

Henry, pulling something from his coat pocket and hurling it off the balcony, down to the chamber floor. The room exploding in white.

Bloody hell, what was that? a voice said. *They're dead,* another said. *They're dead, aren't they? But who were they? Radicals. Fools.*

So many voices, shadows, flickering in the darkness.

Hold on, Mary.

Save her, Stanton—

Please.

—You must have more.

Prometheans.

In the space under my collarbone, above my left breast, someone was striking a hammer against chisel, digging deeper.

The stone must be shale; it fell apart in flakes of blood and flesh. The fossil they were unearthing would be very fine indeed.

Is the girl—

—dead?

You can't let her die. You must have another.

Goddamn it, Mary. Don't you die on me.

—it's her heart. The girl who was shot—

—saved Lord Knackbull.

—Do it, Henry.

Don't they know—

—Idiots.

They're hurting their own cause?

Soft hands cradled my back. Searching fingers probed into the hole above my breast.

A boulder on my chest. I couldn't breathe.

Stay with me. Oh, God. Stay with me. This will hurt, but then it will help, I swear.

The hammer struck hard, splitting bone—*Oh, no,* I thought, *surely they've broken the fossil*—and everything burned white.

I woke in a forest, a bower of solemn greens and smooth, dark woods. Soft morning light filtered through thin, young leaves, warm across my cheek. I lay beside a rosebush, full white blooms like clouds bending toward me with the smell of sweet summer wine.

"Oh, thank God. You're awake."

I blinked, Edgar Murray's face coming into focus.

"Where . . . where am I?"

"My house," Edgar said. "The Green Room."

I could see now that it wasn't a forest at all; it was a bedroom, and I was in a bed with twisting wood posts and a draped green canopy. The arched window above my head was stained glass, a family crest in green and gold. The rosebush was, in fact, a vase of cut white roses on the side table, though anyone would forgive the mistake; it was fifty roses, at least, the vase itself buried under fronds of draping greenery.

"What are these?" I muttered.

"Roses," Edgar said. "Courtesy of Lord Charles Knackbull, Earl of Harewood. You saved his life yesterday."

Ah. That had to be the old man. I tried to sit up, then stopped short. I'd just remembered. I was shot.

I frowned, peering down at my shoulder. Someone had dressed me in a crisp white shirt. My arm and chest twinged a little, but it certainly didn't feel like a gunshot wound. It felt like I'd tweaked a muscle, and weeks ago at that. Not like I'd been just shot in the heart.

"Are you all right?" Edgar gently helped prop a pillow behind my back.

I poked at my shoulder with my other hand. "I thought . . . for some reason, I thought I was shot. But—did I just pass out, then? What happened?"

"Oh, no, you were shot. Just above the heart." He chuckled. "You bled out all over the visitor's gallery, I hear."

I stared. That didn't make sense. Had Edgar drugged me to kill the pain, then?

Henry banged on the other side of the door; I knew it was him, because his shout accompanied the frantic knocking.

"We can hear her, goddamn it. Let us in, Murray, or God help me, I'll—I'll break both your kneecaps."

Edgar rolled his eyes, but rose to unlock the door.

Henry barreled past him, his eyes blazing. Lucy and Buckland rushed in behind. My chest tightened as Henry claimed Edgar's place in the chair beside my bed.

"Praise God," Buckland said, shaking his head solemnly.

"You're alive," Henry breathed. "You're alive."

"Apparently," I said, my fingers brushing over my chest. "But—how? Edgar said I was shot."

Lucy, Edgar, and Buckland looked at Henry.

"I healed you," Henry said quietly, and uncurled his fingers to reveal a small bivalve on a leather thong. A reliq. "Here. It's empty now."

Back home, rich Mr. Jenkins once shot himself through the foot cleaning his musket, and it took the physiomagician sixteen reliqs to close the wound, and even then Mr. Jenkins limped for two weeks.

But I'd been shot near the heart and healed with only one.

Henry nodded, seeing that I understood.

One of the manifold reliqs. I took the shell. I could feel its emptiness, the lack of the telltale hum of stored magic. Only a fossil, again.

"I wasn't even sure it would work." He looked down at his hands. "You'll have a scar, but I—I did what I could."

I didn't wait for the men to look away as I pulled aside the top of the clean white blouse to look at my chest.

I stared, with some combination of shock and awe, at the puckered scar, running in parallel below my collarbone. My fingers brushed over the uneven skin, almost like a rough seam. The skin around the wound was pink. Blood had been wiped away, leaving a stain. But my body was whole. Healed.

If I'd had these, back then . . . if I'd carried a manifold reliq the day Father fell from the cliffs . . .

And—and *Mother*. If a manifold reliq could heal a wound to my heart, could it also heal her mind?

I shivered and covered myself quickly, as if that could distract me from my own overwhelming thoughts. "And the others? Did everyone else make it out all right?"

"Fine. All fine. There were no other injuries."

"Well, at least not until the riots began," Buckland said.

"I wouldn't call them riots, exactly," Lucy countered, archly.

I frowned. "Riots?"

"After Westminster evacuated, the soldiers went out to disperse the crowd and—well, they did not hold back."

"That bad?"

"Worse." Lucy's lip jutted.

"It's a wonder you slept through it all, honestly," Buckland huffed. "The rioters marched to the Shoreditch slicks and burned it half down. When I took Elizabeth home this morning, Catherine said they could smell the smoke even from there."

Edgar leaned over to peer out the stained-glass window. "Things seem to have run their course by now. Only smashed glass and a few drunkards left on the street out there."

"And ruffians," Buckland grunted. "With their pamphlets. Saw several of those on my way back here. Trying to start the chaos all over again."

I exchanged a look with Lucy at the mention of pamphlets. I had to imagine the riots would be an unfortunate setback for the Promethean movement. Lucy's dour expression suggested I was right.

Henry looked almost as solemn. He'd been quiet since he'd handed me the manifold reliq. There was no sign of his usual smirk, and his brow was drawn tight. He must have been deeply shaken by the attack on Parliament.

I started to climb out of the bed. Buckland put a hand on my shoulder. "And where do you think you're going?"

"Let me up; I'm healed. You all saw," I protested, as Lucy and

Buckland wordlessly colluded to press me back gently but firmly. Healed or not, I was weaker than I should've been; the effort of pulling myself up left me almost breathless. "I need to check on Ajax."

"What you need," clucked Lucy, "is rest."

"You don't understand," I said, as Lucy arranged my pillows into a fluffy barricade. I couldn't explain my fear, but it made my voice thin and high. "I have to know that he's all right."

Buckland patted my hand. "Not to worry. The riots didn't go anywhere near Palmanaeus."

"I'll go." Henry was already striding to the door. He looked more like himself now that he had something to do. He grinned as he put on his top hat and tipped it forward. "But if I am struck down by *ruffians* while in your service, Mary, you must promise to weep on my grave."

He was gone before I could properly scoff.

Chapter 35

I WOKE, LATER, TO THE SOFT STACCATO OF VOICES.

It was dark, just past midnight according to the reliq-clock on my nightstand, and only a little light spilled through a crack in the curtains and around the doorframe.

With a grunt of effort, I pulled myself from bed and hobbled to the door, pressing my ear against it.

Male voices. Two, I thought, though I couldn't make out the words.

My chest ached, and I would have shrugged and taken back to bed if I hadn't heard my own name next.

"—and Mary!" The voice faded again, and I turned the doorknob.

Before bed, Edgar's maids had bullied me into a bath, heated with a never-ending basket of reliqs, and had dressed me in a blue nightdress, finer than any gown I'd ever worn. The soft silk swirled around my ankles as I padded down the hallway toward the voices.

"—they could have been *killed*, Ed."

I paused, hand on the wall. That was Henry. I didn't like the way my heart fluttered at his voice. It had fluttered earlier, too, when he returned to assure me that Ajax was biting his handlers especially viciously in my absence.

"Just promise me," Henry continued. "I couldn't bear it if—"

He cut off abruptly. I froze.

"You can come in, Mary," Edgar said wryly.

I winced. Of course he'd set a ward of some kind. Silly me, forgetting again how many ways magic could be used when it was always at your fingertips.

Sheepishly, I entered. Edgar and Henry sat in plush leather chairs, a decanter of whiskey on the table between them and glasses in hand.

My heart raced a little when Henry's gaze met mine—as it always did now, the stupid organ. Henry's eyebrows rose, and my cheeks flushed as I realized I hadn't worn a robe over the nightgown.

"I heard my name," I said, folding my arms across my breasts.

"Sit, Mary. Please," Edgar said, and gestured. "Can I pour you a glass? You're in luck; Henry was just chastising me. A favorite pastime of his, you may recall. Perhaps you'd care to join?"

Henry leaned back with one arm thrown over the chairback, an illusion of ease that might fool someone else. But I could see the tension in the curve of his shoulder.

Edgar sat as he always did—back straight, elbows on the armrests—as if the seat could barely contain his restlessness.

I accepted the glass of whiskey and lowered myself into an empty chair. "And why is it you require chastising?"

"We—the government, I mean," Edgar continued with a

wave, "received some warnings that such an attack might be forthcoming. Henry is quite furious that I allowed my sister and yourself to attend yesterday's session in light of that intelligence."

"Allowed us?" I arched a brow.

Edgar gestured at Henry, in a show of, *See? I told you.* Henry scowled.

"The risk of a successful assault was considered very, very small," Edgar said. "And truly, Mary, if I'd understood the seriousness of the threat, I would have pushed to delay the whole thing. As I wish I had now. I had so hoped my proposal would lead to change. Instead, all I've managed is to throw London into violence."

"More protests? Is Lucy . . ." I trailed off, nearly afraid to ask.

"Under house arrest? Apparently," said a cross voice.

We turned; Lucy stood in the doorway. She, at least, had remembered her robe. Her yellow hair hung over one shoulder in a loose braid, and her feet were bare. She sank into the fourth leather chair, across from mine.

"As I said, dear sister, you are more than welcome to venture from this house tonight over my cold and rotting corpse," Edgar said cheerfully. "Otherwise, it'll have to wait until morning, I'm afraid."

It was impossible not to compare this man with the one who'd spoken in Parliament. Edgar was clearly at home here in his study, surrounded by his friends and his books, his energy lending a lively warmth to the room.

Lucy scowled and curled her feet under herself. "Well, have you heard any more news? Any idea who was behind the attack?"

Edgar shook his head.

"It wasn't Prometheans?" I asked.

"Of course not," Lucy sputtered.

"Who were they, then? Those two men?"

"I don't know." Lucy scrubbed at her face. "They could have been Libertines. They're far more radical than we—though much smaller, too," she mused. "Or Dunnites, I suppose. But they've been rather hesitant to do anything besides stage a few small sit-ins."

"My money would be on the Libertines," Henry murmured. "They used to sabotage my father's factories, back when I was a boy."

"Libertines? Dunnites?" My head spun.

Lucy looked surprised. "I'm sure I've talked about them before. There's not just *one* reform movement, after all."

"No. These things are always growing and splintering, sharing some aims and not others. Similar goals. Different tactics." Edgar swirled his glass and grinned. "Rather like us, in fact. Will it be Lucy's rabble-rousing that secures that fairer world of magic? My politicking, poor as it is? Or will it be the promise of Henry's great Loom?"

Henry chuckled. "And Viscount Merlton, Lord Edgar Murray, behind them all."

"If you want something done right, you've got to do it yourself," Edgar said, and shrugged.

"Well, you know how I feel about your 'Loom,'" said Lucy. "The very concept of manifold reliqs concentrates magic in the hands of the wealthy, rather than expanding the right to self-determination of one's own magic."

I was only half listening as Edgar countered that the Loom would provide financial independence, if not magical; and was that not an intermediate step toward freedom? I was thinking instead of the old viscount, who had so feared his witch wife's power that he let her die in agony. I hoped he rotted deeper in his grave every time his son or daughter spoke of magic and freedom in the same breath.

"It is no replacement for direct action." Lucy was shaking her head. She sighed and wrapped an arm around her knees. "I should have been out there yesterday."

I startled. "But if you'd been among the protestors—"

"Mary, don't you dare say whatever inane thing you're about to."

"What, that you could have been killed?"

"They're my *people*. I should have joined them," Lucy said.

I tried not to let her see that it hurt me. Wasn't I her people, too?

"Is it so crazy that I don't want you to die?" I snapped. "It just seems like all of this is getting a bit out of hand."

"All of this?" She stared. "All of *this*, Mary, is my life's work. Wouldn't you risk it all for yours? At least *I* am trying to make a better world."

I was stung silent, and Henry caught his breath.

"Luce." Edgar said her name softly. "That wasn't fair."

Lucy flushed. "You're right. Forgive me, Mary."

I nodded, but my cheeks were hot with shame. Was that really what she thought of me?

"This has been a trying time for us all," Edgar said, as if that could set the matter to bed. "But I must admit, I have been glad to have us four together again." His cheek dimpled. "That summer in Lyme Regis was the best time of my life."

"Of mine, too," Lucy murmured. She flashed a smile. "Which is shocking, really, given that you three spent most of your time talking about old books and bones." She groaned and waggled her eyebrows. "Remember Ed's obsession with Pharaoh's magicians? The 'secret arts'?"

"Oh, to be young again." Edgar laughed. "Ah, well. I suppose we all have to grow up sometime, don't we?"

Henry chuckled as he poured more whiskey. "To Mary. Who brought us together. Then, and now."

I stayed quiet as the others toasted my name, and knew that each was remembering that summer, with sweetness and sorrow both. Just as I was.

Lucy caught my eye over her glass. *I'm sorry*, she mouthed.

I nodded, accepting the apology, but I understood now that something—some vital cord of trust between us—was beginning to fray.

I followed the physiomagician's orders dutifully for three days so that on the fourth, when I insisted on attending Buckland's public lecture at St. Paul's, he begrudgingly consented.

"But do make sure she takes it easy, Lord Merlton," the physiomagician said, sighing and pushing the spectacles up his crooked nose. "You *appear* healed, Miss Anning, but we can't be sure how your heart is recovering. And you come straight here after the lecture, you understand?"

I agreed, but Edgar caught my eye when the satisfied physiomagician left the room.

"You'll be headed back to Buckland's, then?"

I grinned. He knew me well. "I need to get back to my work." *And to Ajax and the other specimens.* Henry brought me updates, but we couldn't speak openly in front of Edgar or the staff, so I was eager to check on things myself.

"Look after yourself, all right? Don't let my sister get you into trouble. Things out there are still unstable." Edgar jerked his chin toward the window. "Now, we better get going. William Buckland will have my head if I'm the reason you're late for his great triumph."

I knew Edgar wasn't much for hugging, so I swallowed a lump in my throat when he wrapped an arm around me. I'd long considered Lucy a sister. But while Edgar was dear to me, we'd never been *close*. For all our letters and Christmas dinners at Lucy's cottage, I often had the uneasy sense that I didn't quite measure up. That Edgar was always waiting for me to prove myself worthy.

But now, as Edgar ruffled my hair, I thought back to all those letters and dinners and wondered if I'd missed the depth of his affection all along.

It cost two pence to enter St. Paul's. How different my life was now; one month ago, I wouldn't have been able to afford the entry fee to see my own discovery on display.

Fee or no, the crowd out front already swelled, bursting against the rope barriers erected to make order from the chaos. Constables patrolled around the edges, searching the crowd for signs of trouble. But, having quite recently seen an *angry* crowd, I could clearly see this was a different mood altogether. Men and women and children were dressed in their finest clothes, grinning and laughing, and hawkers strolled through the crowd, selling snacks and ale and—amusingly, since I had no idea what the artists had based them off—commemorative paintings of Ajax.

"A real live *dragon*, son," I heard one man in threadbare trousers exclaim to the small boy hoisted on his shoulders. "It's a miracle."

I was grinning, too, as Edgar and I were ushered from the coach and into an entrance at the back of the cathedral.

Ajax *was* a miracle. I shouldn't let myself forget that. And he was *my* miracle.

"Mary!" Catherine Buckland called out, when the viscount and I entered. She rushed toward us, catching my hands.

"Thank God you're all right. We've been so worried. But William said you've been recovering well?"

"Yes, very well, thanks to Viscount Merlton," I said.

Catherine thanked him profusely as Edgar demurred. I scanned the room, saw President Davies, Buckland, and the archbishop deep in conversation, and Henry with a cluster of geomagicians. Other important-looking folk in fine dress milled about, claiming their seats in the front section. The general public would stand behind the red ropes, once they were admitted.

"Where is Ajax? And is Lucy here?" I hadn't seen her since the other night in Edgar's study, and even with her apology, I had the sore, nagging worry that things still weren't quite right between us.

Catherine pointed toward the row of white arches along the nave. "Lucy and Elizabeth are observing Ajax with some of the other ladies."

I excused myself to join them, passing under the great white eye of the dome as I walked to the altar from which Buckland would give his lecture.

Ajax was behind a golden curtain, strung over the altar to hide him from the crowd until the last possible minute. I slipped behind it, and when I saw him, it took my breath away.

He was perched in a metal tree next to the lectern, the graceful branches of molded copper and the trunk painted gold. More gold wrapped around his left ankle, a thin chain that bound him to the tree. He'd been positioned just so to allow the sparkling light of the stained glass to fall across his chest.

The archbishop and Buckland had done well. The pterodactyl

looked every inch a gift from God. My eyes filled. My precious, darling, adorable Ajax.

He caught my scent, maybe, or my face, and rose to his full height, spreading his wings wide and calling out in distress. He tried to hop, pulling the chain at his ankle taut.

"Oh, hush, love," I murmured as I climbed the altar steps. "I'm here now, aren't I?"

"You can't go up there! It isn't safe!" blustered one of his handlers, a blond man with elbow-length gloves. He wasn't one I'd met before.

Lucy's laugh was like gentle rain. "Don't you know that's Mary Anning? He won't hurt her."

The handler hesitated, and I crossed the rest of the distance to Ajax. He cooed and clucked, hopping happily. If I could have reached that high, I would have thrown my arms around him and buried my face in his neck. Instead I settled for stroking his soft belly, and then, when he bent his neck to me, his eye ridges and chin.

I missed him. I missed him so much.

I wished I could blame it all on Davies, or the handlers. But I'd let myself become distracted. By the other resurrections. By Henry. By the dramatics with Lucy. But no more. After today, I would visit him daily. I would insist upon it.

Ajax needed me. And I needed him.

Lucy was next to me then, her hand on my shoulder. "They're about ready to open the doors to the public."

"Luce," I said thickly, still battling the wave of emotions from seeing Ajax. "I know, the other night, you and I—"

"I shouldn't have said it," she interrupted, clasping my hands. "I was fearful, and frustrated, and I took it out on you."

I nodded, fighting not to cry as we embraced. I gave Ajax another quick pat on the chest and told him to be good. He protested with a few squawks but settled quickly.

A pretty redhead beelined to intercept us.

"Marged Davies," she said in a charming Welsh accent, thrusting out her hand.

This was President Davies's wife? She had to be half his age, at least; hardly out of her twenties, if I had to guess.

"Is it true you found that gorgeous plesiosaur in the entryway of Palmanaeus?"

"Why, yes," I said, surprised and a little flattered, despite myself. "It was one of my earliest finds."

She smiled conspiratorially. "I have my own theory about the plesiosaurus, if you are int—"

"Ah, Marged, I see you've already found the woman of the hour," Davies declared. Marged stiffened at his booming voice, too loud in the echo of the cathedral. But she smiled as she turned toward her husband, now marching in our direction with a white-haired man in tow. I recognized him at once—the old man from Parliament. He was flanked by two younger, harried-looking staff members. Buckland followed at a pace, slipping in beside me.

"Miss Anning," Davies said grandly, "I am very pleased to introduce to you Lord Knackbull."

"Miss Anning." Lord Knackbull thrust out a hand.

I took it, unsure if he meant me to shake or kiss it, but instead he brought it to his own wrinkled lips.

"I owe you my life." His eyes glistened with tears. "A hero. A true hero. I am honored to meet you."

"Oh," I said, flustered. "I only did what anyone would do."

"Nonsense. You risked your life to save mine," he said. "Please, Miss Anning. If there's anything I can do to be of service, to you or"—he took in Buckland and Davies, like a true politician—

"your Society, please do let me know. I would be most gratified to be of assistance. I admit that I know very little about your work."

Buckland's sly eyes lit. "Perhaps you'd like to attend the reception this evening, at Palmanaeus House?"

"Oh, yes," Davies said smoothly, catching on to Buckland's idea. "We can share with you more about our Society, and perhaps some of the ways we might even be able to assist you, sir, and the government."

Buckland smiled. "I can at least promise an evening of enlightening conversation with other men of intelligence—something I am sure you find little enough of, in your line of work."

Knackbull barked a laugh.

Elizabeth Buckland was making her way over to us, but stopped short rather than interrupt the conversation with Lord Knackbull, and folded her hands neatly. But she bounced eagerly on her heels, and I remembered what Lucy had said about Elizabeth's interest in geomagic. She was probably as excited for today as her father.

I looked at Elizabeth, standing patiently by, and Marged Davies, behind her husband's shoulder, and I had a sudden thought. Perhaps I could extend an olive branch to Lucy by offering one to Elizabeth. Needling Davies at the same time wouldn't hurt, either.

"Actually, President Davies," I said—and his head swiveled in obvious annoyance—"I was thinking perhaps other women might be invited as well. *I* will be in attendance, so it will already be a gathering of mixed company."

Buckland grinned and looked indulgently at Elizabeth, whose eyes went bright with glee. Marged looked hopefully at her husband for his answer.

Before Davies could object, Knackbull clapped and said, "What an excellent idea. My son Laurence"—he gestured at one of the thin men I'd taken for an aide—"has a young daughter who would love to meet you, Miss Anning."

And it was settled.

"Well played," murmured Buckland as we took our seats in the front row. "You are getting the hang of politics, after all, aren't you?"

Before I could respond, the organist took his seat. The show was about to begin.

The onlookers flowed in a crowded, steady stream, their upturned faces a mix of wonder, fear, and delight.

The faithful who'd come to hear Buckland covered every square of the checkered black-and-white floor, stretching into the nave and quire.

The procession of the cross was followed by the reading of scripture, and then we sang together, a number of hymns. In some ways, it was just like any Sunday at home in Lyme Regis, with Parson Anders at the altar. But in others, it was nothing at all like the familiar worship of home. The attendees around me, for one, were not the fisherfolk and craftspeople I'd grown up with. Those types stood clustered behind us, shuffling patiently behind the red ropes. I sat among lords and ladies, viscounts and earls and countesses, draped in silks and jewels. I could only guess at how many reliqs they wore, pinned to ears and wrapped on wrists and braided into hairpieces. Enough magic to level the whole cathedral in just the first three pews. And our singing echoed through the nave and down the quire, rather than caught in the low, pigeon-infested eaves of the Lyme Regis chapel. I was struck with a moment of homesickness for the old chapel, and the smell of the sea.

The archbishop strode forward after the reading, and climbed the curved stairs to the carved wood pulpit. He gave a signal with his hand, and the golden curtain at his back fell away. A murmur whipped through the pews.

Ajax perched on his golden tree, looking down over all of us. With a harrowing cry, the pterodactyl spread his wings and beat the air. Voices gasped and swore around me, but I didn't turn to look; I was transfixed by the sight of my pterodactyl.

The archbishop began. A miracle, he called Ajax, in his low, soothing voice. A revelation: a window into the mind of God.

Buckland was leaning forward, mouthing the words as the archbishop spoke them. His fingerprints were all over the text of the introduction, and I could tell he was pleased with the archbishop's impassioned delivery.

The archbishop finished by listing the many accomplishments of William Buckland: Oxford professor, vice president of the Geomagical Society of London, and—most important—ordained and respected clergy of the Church of England.

Buckland beamed as he rose and climbed to take his place amid the applause.

It was strange to hear my own story retold with Buckland's flair for dramatics. *A determined young fossilist*, he called me, *Mistress Mary Anning of Lyme Regis*, and a hundred heads turned my way.

My cheeks warmed. How had I ever doubted Buckland? Here he was, with the greatest audience of his life, and it was my story he told. My name he credited.

Buckland described the heart-pounding scramble as the cliff

gave way and unveiled the cave. He captured the dry, earthen scent of the dark cavern, and the scraping of my knees as I made my slow crawl to the pterodactyl. My heart pounded as he described the moment I discovered the pterodactyl skeleton, and the egg.

"And then—whilst cupped in young Miss Anning's trembling hands—the egg hatched," Buckland said softly, into the quiet hush.

My guilt cut through the spell of his storytelling. Yes, true, Ajax hatched in my hands. I felt Henry's eyes, raising the hairs on the back of my neck. But it wasn't the full truth.

"Our Lord, you see, works all things to His purpose. He peeled away the rock and stone, to make way for Miss Anning, so that she could be there to bear witness to the perfection of His timing. To bear witness to this great revelation."

His voice rang through the cathedral, gathering strength from the murmurs. From the widening eyes. He cleared his throat.

"As geomagicians, we have dedicated our lives to understanding the Earth, seeking in her bones to understand her secrets—how she and her creatures were formed by the hand of God.

"And the best of our geomagical evidence demonstrates that the present system of this planet is built on the wreck and ruins of one more ancient, and there is nothing in this inconsistent with the Mosaic accounts. In fact, we have again and again proved the Mosaic account to be in perfect harmony with the discoveries of the modern geomagical science. Every discovery that has yet been brought to light by geomagical investigations confirms the truth of Scripture.

"But we who study the Earth have long been dogged by the sharp-toothed specter, with no answer to be found in scripture. I speak, you may already have guessed, of *extinction*." He spoke the word like a curse.

"How could a loving God—a perfect God, an infallible God—destroy his own creations? And on this, the Scriptures have been silent.

"I know many of you have asked this same question in your own prayerful hearts. I have asked it myself. *Lord, Lord,* my soul has cried, in search of an answer."

Buckland's voice was a roar and a rumble, as gentle and powerful as a river over rock.

"And here it is at last. Here is proof divine, an answer long sought. For this creature, the egg of the pterodactyl, was ensconced in diluvium: the substance left behind in the wake of the Great Deluge."

I bit hard on the inside of my cheek. *Not true, not true, not true.*

"Put to sleep in the silt of the universal deluge—the Noachian flood—the pterodactyl slept through the ages of man. Not extinct. Not a mistake. Only asleep, for a time. But now—now, my friends, the sleeping giants *wake* at last."

He flung one arm backward toward Ajax, startling him. The pterodactyl spread his wings and screeched in surprise. A terrible, beautiful sound to punctuate Buckland's terrible, beautiful lie.

Here Buckland paused, his gaze sweeping over his listeners, his eyes triumphant. I pressed my feet to the floor, stone cold and hard through my leather soles.

"We know that once there was an ancient Earth ruled by great beasts. A world that the Creator set to a sleep—a long and gentle rest—in the waters of His flood. A reprieve, perhaps, to allow the species made in His own image, and whom He loved best of all, to thrive. Time, He granted us, to become masters of all magics, and of the Earth herself, that we might be prepared when the beasts began to wake."

Chapter 36

I KNEW WHAT HAD BEEN WON TODAY. TO THE DOUBTERS, WHO read Genesis and questioned its account, the archbishop could say: *The science proves it.* And to the faithful, who looked at the science and questioned the geomagician's claims, the Society could say: *The Scriptures prove it.* The archbishop and Buckland had tied the Church and geomagic together and, in doing so, strengthened both.

I tried to focus on that outcome as I wandered aimlessly through the reception crowd and my brain chanted, *Lies, lies, lies.*

Given the ongoing protests, an entire battalion of infantrymen had been deployed to patrol the area around Palmanaeus House tonight, reliq-lamps and rifles at the ready.

None of the reception guests, arrayed in tails and evening gowns and milling about the entry hall, expressed discomfort at the row of stationed constables who had greeted them at the top of the Palmanaeus steps. In fact, I heard quite a few murmurs of appreciation for the security measures as I made my way through the crowd in the entry hall, dodging servers with trays of champagne. I grabbed two glasses and downed them quickly.

"I am relieved to see they've taken our safety seriously," I overheard one older woman with too much powder on her brow saying, as I squeezed between her backside and a glass display of mammoth tusks. The woman had her arm tightly looped through the arm of Augustus Ward, a geomagician with expertise in limestone composition.

"I'll admit I was sympathetic to their cause at first. It must be a terrible thing to sell one's magic. But surely destruction is never the answer."

"Agreed," said Mr. Ward firmly. "We simply cannot negotiate with the people terrorizing our city."

"But I thought the protestors weren't responsible for the attack on Parliament?" a young brunette responded. She had the look of a daughter, maybe, and wide, earnest eyes.

"So they claim," said the first woman darkly. "But I don't believe it."

It was probably a good thing Lucy wasn't around to hear her. But where the hell *was* she? And where was Henry, for that matter?

He'd visited every day during my convalescence, but with Edgar around, our conversations had been limited to the subject of Ajax.

But I needed to talk to someone, and Henry was the only one who knew the truth. About Ajax. About Buckland's theory. About me. My strange magic. I even knew exactly what I wanted—for Henry to put his broad hands on my shoulders and assure me I'd done the right thing. That I was safe. That our discoveries were worth the risk. That all would be well.

But, to my increasing annoyance, neither Henry nor Lucy was anywhere to be found.

Oh, there were plenty of *other* people eager to speak with me. Several wives of geomagicians had offered to set me up with this-or-that young country cousin of theirs. And Marged Davies had cornered me a few minutes ago to share her nonsense theory that plesiosaurs might have been exclusively ambush hunters, lying in wait on the seafloor and waiting for prey to pass above. I listened politely, gently explaining that it was most likely they used their long necks to scoop fish from above, nearer the surface.

I'd finally excused myself to fetch another drink. If I couldn't find my friends, at least I could try to locate someone who had *actually* spent time studying fossils and not inventing wild theories about them.

Still, I didn't regret forcing Davies to open the house to women for the night. Elizabeth had been ecstatic, and Lucy, grateful. Even Catherine Buckland thanked me profusely and solemnly.

It was clear that most of the women here tonight had never stepped foot in these halls, even the white-haired ones whose husbands had likely been founding Society members twenty years ago. I had to admit, it was gratifying to see the awe on the faces of wives and daughters as they stared up at my plesiosaur for the first time: the way their jaws dropped open and hands pressed to their breasts.

"*Oh,*" they all seemed to breathe, and it was like they were saying, *I see now. I understand.*

But it wasn't all delight. One young woman, Adam Harrelson's daughter, ran out screaming from Ajax's room upstairs, where he was on display for the evening. As she was escorted down the hall, the geomagicians chuckled knowingly. I clenched my fists as men around me murmured about "delicate sensibilities" and "ladylike dispositions." Fool girl; she'd just made the rest of us look weak by association.

I was still eavesdropping when I spotted Lord Knackbull through the crowd ahead, a young, doe-eyed girl, scarcely twelve—the granddaughter, presumably—at his side.

I tried to duck away, but Knackbull caught my eye.

"Ah, Miss Anning, there you are."

I straightened as the crowd parted to let him through.

The granddaughter's name was Alice. She trembled as she curtsied and murmured her greetings.

"Go on, dear," Knackbull urged. "Show her what you brought."

I don't know what I expected. A cross-stitch, perhaps, something feminine and delicate. But instead, the girl pulled from her pocket a thumb-sized chunk of amber, a winged shape trapped in the frozen liquid.

I was interested now. I'd never had the chance to see a creature trapped in amber.

"Grandfather gave it to me," Alice said in a quiet voice.

"It hails from the Baltics," Knackbull added, "or so I was told by the rare-reliq trader who sold it to me." He smiled indulgently at his granddaughter. "Our Alice is quite ... enthusiastic, shall we say, about insects. Her parents are, of course, scandalized by such an unwomanly passion"—he shrugged—"but what are grandfathers for, if not to indulge their grandchildren?" He winked, and Alice giggled.

"May I?"

"It's a gift, Miss Anning," Alice said shyly. "For you."

I rolled the smooth ball across my palm, studying the insect inside. It was a mosquito, remarkably preserved. I peered closer to see the tiny filaments along its legs, and the geometric shapes made by the veins in the wings.

I imagined the creature, its wings fluttering faster than the human eye could see, landing on the back of some warm-blooded, lumbering creature, and tasting copper in its strange mouth. The amber grew warm in my hand.

I could wake it. I could take it upstairs now, and crack open the amber, and reanimate the insect—

"I want to be an entomagician someday," Alice said softly, her big round eyes darting from mine as I looked at her in surprise. "I never knew that women could study the science magics, until I learned about you."

My heart lurched, and softened.

I took Alice's hand and placed the amber in her palm, curling my fingers around hers.

"Keep it safe for me, for now," I said, a lump in my throat. "And bring it back to me when you are an entomagician."

Soon a piano was fetched and set before the plesiosaur, and the well-bred ladies took turns playing jaunty tunes, and the men told ribald stories to uproarious laughter.

I took my search for Henry into one of the cigar-filled lounges. But the room fell to an awkward silence when I entered, the men clearly waiting for me to leave to resume a conversation.

I was still nursing that sting when Ann Mantell, Gideon's wife, lured me into the visitors' library off the entry hall by suggesting that she'd like my help finding a suitable book about lizards of the continent to help her husband with his research.

I'd drunk too much champagne. My head was spinning, the glittering light of reliq-lamps refracting in starbursts.

But through the sparks, I could see that Marged Davies was lying in wait, and she sprang from her armchair as I trailed in behind Mrs. Mantell. Another woman sat beside her, salt-and-pepper in her black hair. She rose more slowly.

"Ah, if it isn't the famous Miss Anning herself," said the unfamiliar woman, smile widening to show two charmingly overlapped front teeth. She introduced herself: Roderick Murchison's wife, Charlotte.

I ignored the hint of dismissiveness in her tone and tried instead to remember how I knew her name. It came to me as we shook hands. Henry had named her, and Ann Mantell, too, as the other women assistants of geomagicians.

I frowned, taking in the trio. "Did you two also have questions about lizard species?"

Marged Davies inhaled deeply. "Not exactly." The three women exchanged glances.

I narrowed my eyes. "If this is more about plesiosaur hunting—"

"It isn't," Marged said quickly.

"Though to be frank, you should at least consider Marged's argument," Charlotte Murchison muttered darkly, before Ann Mantell hushed her.

Marged ignored them. She smoothed her hands on her skirts. "Thank you for joining us, Miss Anning," she said, and it was suddenly clear that this was a practiced speech.

"Mrs. Murchison, Mrs. Mantell, and I have all spent many years supporting our husbands' work in geomagic. And we have learned a great deal through that experience. But all three of us have long admired your aptitude and talent—not only with fossil hunting, but even more so with your analysis of the specimens and samples that you've found. Your accomplishments in geomagical studies have inspired all three of us to learn more."

Even Charlotte Murchison nodded at that. Mrs. Davies continued.

"And while we know we cannot hope to match your genius, the three of us were hoping, well, we were wondering . . ."

She paused and looked to the others for help.

"We would like to learn from you, Miss Anning," Ann Mantell finished hurriedly. "We were thinking perhaps you might offer a lecture, and open it to women—"

"And I hoped you might be willing to set us a syllabus, for our own education," added Charlotte with earnest excitement. "My Roderick won't ever lend me his books."

"Maybe it could even be a series of lectures."

"*An Introduction to Geomagic for the Fairer Sex* would be my proposed title," said Marged, with flushed cheeks. "I am sure my husband would hate it. That's half the fun." She laughed.

"There has never been a woman geomagician, of course, but you've come closer than anyone. You've cracked the door, as it were, and perhaps one day it will be opened to us all," said Charlotte solemnly, and the other two nodded.

They looked at me expectantly—so hopefully—and a hundred thoughts raced through my head. I didn't think the ladies would like to hear any one of them.

The very idea of a lecture series on geomagic for women—forget Society election; if I tried to give such a talk, I would be laughed out of Palmanaeus House. My reputation would never recover.

I understood by now how Palmanaeus House operated; the way in which factions and relationships formed the structure of power, both social and scholarly. If I allied myself with the women—with the wives of geomagicians—I would be *seen* as a wife, even if I wasn't one. The men outside this library, their three husbands included, would never again see me as an equal. Not as a geomagician, or a practitioner. Not as a scholar in my own right. I was already losing the battle to be respected. I couldn't risk making it worse.

I felt a twinge of guilt, as I stood silent and their faces began to fall.

But I had fought my way to where I was. I'd shed sweat, tears, and blood in sea-rock. I hadn't married a geomagician. I hadn't asked some other woman to put her own ambition aside to help me with mine. What reputation I had, I'd earned myself. They could surely do the same.

"I can't teach you," was what I said in the end. "I'm—I don't have the time."

I turned and rushed out of the library.

Chapter 37

A MAKESHIFT DANCE FLOOR OPENED, AND THE MUSICIANS played a toe-tapping polka. Happy couples in fine gowns and soft shoes twirled across the checkered floor, in circles around the plesiosaur. The song slowed, easing into a waltz.

"May I have this dance?"

I jumped and glared over my shoulder at Henry. The quickening of my pulse made me snappish. "And where have *you* been all night?"

"I'll take that as a yes?" He slipped his arm around my waist and lifted my other palm, running a thumb over my knuckles. I shivered and scowled. I could feel the warmth of his palm through my dress, an imprint on my skin. Heat rushed to my toes.

"It isn't appropriate," I protested. "I'm your assistant."

"It's only a dance," he murmured, and God help me, I didn't drop his hand.

I was a poor dancer, but Henry was an excellent one, and he led us both with confidence of skill. His grip was strong but light on my waist.

"I've been looking for you. We still haven't had a chance to talk properly." I cleared my throat as he carried us around in time with the music, never minding my stumbles.

His eyes sparkled. "Oh?"

"About the salamanders. And—the others." *Belemnites, and trilobites, and ammonites, and sea snails, and, and, and . . .*

"Ah. That," Henry said, and he twirled me.

"I'm so sorry," I said, my voice cracking, when he caught me close again.

Henry's lips parted. "Oh, Mary. Not this again."

"But—"

He shook his head as we spun. "How could you ever think I'd blame you? There were always going to be losses. That's the nature of the experiment. The cost of the work. So don't dwell on what we've lost," he said, and his hand tightened on my hip, to pull me in. "Think of all we've gained."

I forgot, for a moment, that we were in a room full of geomagicians and lords and other important people, and considered kissing him then and there. I thought of raking my hands through his hair, pulling his mouth down, and catching his lips against mine.

And Henry's gaze held something hungry, too, as those stormcloud eyes stared into mine. He'd asked for my friendship, once upon a time, and I said I didn't trust him.

But that wasn't true anymore. And there was no denying we were friends now. Friends, and maybe—perhaps—

He doesn't want you. You're just drunk and making a fool of yourself.

I stumbled over my feet as the thought tossed cold water on my ardor.

Henry had to catch me. "Whoa. Are you all right?"

"Yes, I'm fine," I stammered, reeling away. "I only need some air."

I stumbled down one of the corridors, deeper into the bowels of Palmanaeus, a warren of storage rooms and study carrels and locked office doors.

I thought I'd been careful. I'd thought myself prepared. But here I was, once again, thinking of Henry Stanton's mouth and wishing his fingers would lace through mine. And this time, I didn't have the excuse of being sixteen.

The reliq-lamps in the hallway flickered in their iron sconces and mirrored-glass cases, mocking my foolishness.

"Damn Henry. Damn, damned, damnable man," I mumbled.

One of the reliq-lamps had burned out, a missing tooth in the row of neat lights. Silver was considered the best material for reliq-lamps, given its natural reflective properties, and I stopped in front of the burnt light, staring at a hammered circlet of silver behind the glass dome.

Someone had worn that. Nestled next to flesh, around their neck or tucked into their stays, or maybe wrapped around a thigh if they were particularly worried about theft. Some man or woman had probably leased it from a slicker. They'd worn it for a week, or maybe two, and then taken it back in exchange for a couple shillings. All their magic, poured into the metal. And what had they bought with it? Bread, or fish, or cheese? Had they saved it for medicine, or fuel? Maybe they had put it toward a debt to the cobbler, or the physiomagician, or the landlord. And now here was their reliq, burned low in one night.

I was too drunk for this. Drunk and lovesick.

I was just about to sulk back to the party when I saw two figures turn down one of the branching hallways ahead. I recognized Lucy even with the shadows; I'd know that determined walk anywhere.

I followed, and just as I was about to call out—*Where on earth has she been all night? Doesn't she know I need her?*—she and Elizabeth stopped, looked around furtively, and slipped through a doorway.

Ah. I blushed. I was loath to interrupt their chance at intimacy. I hurried away, thoughts flooded by upsetting images of Henry and myself, together in an empty, darkened office ...

Then I heard footsteps in the hall, coming from the other direction. And not the light steps of women, but men's heavy bootfalls. On a wave of instinct, I hid behind a bookcase.

Three men ducked quickly into the same room as Lucy and Elizabeth and shut the door behind.

Well, then. It appeared the two women weren't sneaking away for privacy. No; this was Promethean business.

I frowned. Lucy had no right to be sneaking outsiders into Palmanaeus House for her little meetings. Especially not tonight. It was dangerous—what if they were caught?—but it was also plain *rude*.

I'd always trusted Lucy's judgment, but she was once again testing the strength of that trust.

My brow and lips knotted as I grasped the door handle, ready to pull it wide and tell her off for being both careless *and* obnoxious.

"... a full assault seems extreme," said a man's reedy voice.

"I disagree," said another male voice, laced with cold anger.

"Polite politics and protests have bought us nothing. It's far past time we burn the whole damn slicks to ash, in every city in England."

Burn the slicks?

I didn't like the slicks. Obviously. Of course I didn't. But to burn them?

A heavy sigh. Lucy's. "Look," said my friend, "I want to destroy the slicks as much as anyone. I'd like to see every one of them wiped from every city in England."

My head spun. But—but what would happen to England? To society? We would be plunged into darkness—I glanced at the reliq-lamps along the wall—quite literally.

Surely there were other ways to make a point. Weren't there?

There was silence from inside the room, too. I could picture Lucy, shifting foot to foot as she searched for the right words.

"But the slicks are more than buildings and potions and weighscales. If we burn the quadrants down, they'll just rebuild. No. We have to think beyond the slicks. Beyond the physical. If we fail to change the hearts and minds of our fellow men, then I guarantee we will never see true change. In fact, I believe we'd see even the sympathetic common people turn against us."

"So what would you have us do instead?"

"We . . . we starve them out," Lucy said slowly.

"What do you mean?"

"A blockade on the slicks. We cut off their access to magic." I heard Lucy take a deep breath. Her voice grew stronger as she spoke. "Until Parliament passes the bill to raise the exchange rates, we lead a boycott of the London slicks. No one sells their magic. No one buys reliqs. See how fast they raise the rates then."

"There will be repercussions," said another, deeper voice. "And not just from the rich. Sellers will be furious, too."

"Then let them," snapped Lucy. "But it's the only way I can think to prove how valuable their magic really is. See if they complain when it *works*."

"I thought we were done with this foolishness about rates," the nasal voice said. "It isn't enough."

"No," said Lucy. "It isn't. But it's a first step. To show that the system—the way things have always been—can, in fact, be changed. And if something can be changed, then, eventually, it can be broken."

I listened a few minutes more, as they worked through logistics and assigned responsibilities.

When the meeting appeared to be winding down, I peeled away from the door. I couldn't let Lucy catch me spying; our friendship might never recover.

I exhaled through wrinkled nostrils as I crept back to the entryway. I wished, very much, that I hadn't gone spying on anyone. I didn't want to be a spy—I wanted to be a geomagician, for God's sake. I could have just kept drinking champagne and moping, and then I would be blissfully unaware of Lucy's plans. Because what was I meant to do now?

I knew Lucy well enough to know she would call her blockade collective action.

But I knew it would be violence.

If the Prometheans did manage to blockade the London slicks, the whole might of the British Empire would be thrown against them. Military. Constables. Mercenaries. There would be blood in the streets.

Lucy was a grown woman, and could make her own choices, and take her own risks.

But Elizabeth. Elizabeth was young, scarcely out of girlhood. Elizabeth shouldn't be out gallivanting in the midst of civil unrest that could blow into violence at the slightest breath. I could picture it, too easily: Elizabeth, falling, with red blooming from her neck, a river in the cobblestones.

I shivered. Elizabeth didn't deserve to pay the price for Lucy's folly. Something in the turning gears in my head locked into determined place as I set off to find Buckland.

Chapter 38

Two mornings after the reception, I lay sprawled with Lucy, Catherine, and Elizabeth on a hilltop, under a large tree, somewhere in the Oxfordshire countryside.

It was like I'd forgotten the wind. This one didn't carry the smell of the sea, but its scent of green, wet earth was enough to make me take deep, gobbling breaths, until Lucy told me to stop being obnoxious.

"I can't help it," I said. "It smells so clean."

The country air was good for Ajax, too. I had never seen the silly creature this happy. He clambered over branches, shaking leaves down into our hair, then leapt lightly and soared to earth, the sun shining through his papery wings.

He stopped to snatch a biscuit from Elizabeth's lap—I couldn't even scold him, he looked so pleased with himself—and then raced to scamper up the trunk again.

This area was known as Kirtlington Quarry. It was a solid site for fossils, if not as rich in deposits as Lyme Regis. But there were plenty of shark teeth and crocodilian remains to be found in the clay and the limestone cave system. The land was now owned by the Society, and given the proximity to Oxford, Buckland had often used this area as a training ground for his geomagical students.

Henry told me, on the carriage ride out, that of the reliqs sold by the Society for the slicks, a full thirty percent were sourced from the region. As a result, there was a permanent excavation at the site, managed by a local staff.

Kirtlington itself was a small village with a small inn, so the locals were busy now helping our geomagicians erect the field tents that were to be our home for the next two or three weeks.

And there were a lot of tents. William Buckland had received word that the laborers had recently opened up a new chamber in the cave system and discovered possible mammoth remains.

He'd invited any interested geomagicians to join him in the initial exploration. Conybeare, Mantell, Goldsmild, and a few others had taken him up on the offer, and the whole thing now had the air of a picnic. It was a chance not only to map the new cave area and collect mammoth fossils, we hoped, but also to escape the powder keg of the city. The chance to study Ajax in more wild environs—flying, hunting, thriving—was even further temptation.

I don't know whether Buckland really did receive word about mammoth bones or if that was exaggeration. But the invitation to join an actual Society fossil-hunting expedition had been too much for his eldest daughter to resist.

That night at Palmanaeus House, I had ultimately decided that, really, none of this politicking was my business whatsoever, and there was no good to be done meddling. My only obligation here, I determined, was to remove the people I cared about from imminent danger.

Still, I didn't tell Buckland the truth that night at the reception. The truth would have terrified him, and endangered Lucy, too.

Instead I spun a story—one that I knew would elicit the reaction that I ultimately hoped to achieve: getting Elizabeth out of London.

"She's seeing a young man," I said, when I pulled Buckland aside. "I saw her, tonight, meeting with him down near the study carrels."

Buckland's face darkened. He asked if I knew anything else. Who was he? How had they met? Had I caught sight of his face? Where did he go, after?

I told Buckland, regretfully, that I knew nothing more.

"But perhaps it would be wise to leave London for a while," I offered, as if the thought had only just occurred to me. "Take the girls back up to Oxford. These sorts of infatuations do tend to fizzle just as quickly as they begin, given some time and space."

"Yes. Very good idea, Mary. Excellent idea. And thank you for telling me." He set a paternal hand on my shoulder, and if I felt a little queasy with guilt, I told myself that he wouldn't really want to know the truth anyway.

But from there, the expedition to Kirtlington was all Buckland. I'd assumed that Buckland would simply send the family to their Oxford home for a time, which would at least remove Elizabeth from danger. But apparently he knew his daughter well enough to suspect that she needed another motivation to leave London. Thus, the expedition to Kirtlington.

As for myself, I practically leapt at the chance to get out of London for a while, especially when Buckland agreed we could bring Ajax along.

I was also looking forward to a little distance from Henry Stanton. Time and space would let me cool my head and heart both.

But when I shared our plans to go up to Kirtlington, Henry tapped his chin and said, "You know, that's quite close to the Glasswater Mill. I'll finally have the chance to show you the Loom."

I blinked. "You're planning to come?"

He cocked his head. "Of course. The professor's invitation was open to all geomagicians, wasn't it?"

"But I assumed—the specimens—"

"Will be just fine. I only hire the best." He waved, and then grinned slyly. "When do we leave?"

Lucy poked at my ribs, a little harder than necessary. "Are you listening?"

I started. "Yes. What? Well, no."

Catherine laughed. "It's all right, dear. I was only saying how nice it is to be on an expedition again. It's been too long."

Catherine Buckland was lying back, propped on her elbows. They'd left the two younger girls at the Oxford house with a nanny, and Catherine was clearly relishing her brief freedom; she'd taken off her hat and was letting the sun warm her cheeks.

"I used to go with William all the time on his fossil hunts," she continued. "Dashing around the coast after my mad husband. Even spent our honeymoon visiting geomagical sites. That's how we met; do you remember, Mary?"

I smiled. "Of course I do."

"You were such a small slip of a thing, and so pale," Catherine said, closing her eyes. I remembered I'd thought Catherine looked like an angel, in her lace dress and hat.

She had more wrinkles around her mouth now, but she still looked something like an angel.

"I remember after we met you, when we were back in the tavern, warming up at the fire," she continued, "William told me that trilobite you sold him was the best specimen he'd seen in years. 'We will have to keep an eye on her,' I remember him saying. 'Someone must help her to reach her potential.' He said he hoped we'd have girls. Clever, like you." She smiled warmly.

There was a lump in my throat around which I couldn't speak, but I saw the twitch in Elizabeth's lips.

"Why did you stop, then, Mama?" Elizabeth asked. "If you enjoyed fossil hunting so much?"

Catherine tilted her head. "Well, I enjoyed it, but fossil hunting and geomagic were never my true passion. Not the way it is for your father. Or for our Mary, here." She smiled. "So, when life got more complicated—babies, and animals, and homes to keep—I truly didn't mind letting that phase come to an end. You three were my true passion, after all."

She reached for her eldest daughter's hand and clasped it tight.

There was a hint of triumph in Elizabeth's eye, and I looked away, the brief bloom of jealousy sour on my tongue.

"I think I'll go down and see how things are progressing." I rose, wiping grass from my dress.

I left Ajax to his own devices in the treetop, trusting that he wouldn't stray far from Catherine—his second-favorite person, after me. He'd spent the coach ride happily bouncing between our two laps and ripping our skirts in the process with his claws.

Lucy stayed on the hill with the Bucklands as I clambered down to the campsite. She was pouting, I knew. But sullen was much better than dead.

When Buckland announced the expedition, I'd known Lucy would want to stay behind in London, given the Prometheans' plans.

But I needed to lure Lucy away from the city—and unfortunately, she was not interested in a fossil hunt. I had to lean shamelessly on guilt instead.

"Please," I'd begged, the night before we were due to leave. "Please. You said when we came here that you would be my companion. The Society election is in a few weeks. This is my last, best chance. I need you, Lucy."

"Yes, but the Prometheans—"

"Are you in London for the Prometheans, then? Or for me? Because I *thought* you came here for me, but I've seen little enough evidence of that so far."

I suppose it had such power because there was a kernel of real feeling in what I said. My voice caught. "I nearly died, Luce."

She flinched. "Yes, and I—"

"And then you ran off immediately for Promethean work. You are gone every evening, and rushing out the door each morning. You spend your free hours with Elizabeth, and I have not resented that joy. But you're hardly a suitable companion to me, let alone a friend."

My words slipped, and I blinked quickly, looking at my hands. It was all true, really. But I would never have said it aloud if I didn't have to; I certainly didn't want to begrudge her the work, or her romance. That was the worst part of me, not the best.

And Lucy's loyalty was the best part of her, and I tugged on it unfairly. Cruelly.

"Fine," she whispered at last, with glittering eyes. "I'll come with you. You win, Mary."

Her body was stiff when I hugged her, and though it broke my heart, it didn't matter. Lucy could be as angry with me as she wanted. At least she would be safe.

Chapter 39

WE EXPLORED THE CAVE FOR THE FIRST TIME THAT afternoon, once all the equipment was unloaded and our tents erected. The cave wouldn't fit all of our party, Buckland said, so we drew lots to divide into two groups. I drew in the first round, but awful old William Conybeare—who never approved of women doing much of anything—didn't think it proper for me to participate in the exploration. Thankfully both Buckland and Henry came to my defense.

"Mary is my invited guest," Buckland said, at the same time that Henry said, "Mary's my assistant."

The two rivals scowled, as if the agreement pained them, but I grinned.

"If you're uncomfortable, perhaps you ought to wait for the second group," I said innocently, as I tied up my dress so that my knees wouldn't be caught in my skirts as I crawled.

Conybeare sputtered, and Henry barely covered his snort with a cough.

I rolled my eyes. "Oh, you've all seen a woman's knees before."

Conybeare's eyes bulged, his face turning bright red. Henry laughed openly now, and Buckland scowled. "Don't encourage her, Stanton."

We entered the cave system through a natural, tear-shaped hole between several large boulders, the gap barely wide enough for my shoulders.

Buckland had a reliq-lamp strapped to his chest, but the light hardly reached me as we crawled deeper into the damp earth and were swallowed by the dark.

Everything inside the cave felt weighty. The air itself had a heaviness from the moisture and stillness, and the sound of my own breath and our shuffling legs echoed in the tight quarters as we dragged them through thick mud. The *drip, drip, drip* of distant water was nearly maddening. Under the mud, the stone was rough with mineral deposits and budding stalagmites. The short stalactites from the ceiling were like terrible teeth, scraping at the back of my head. I grinned as I poked at one and came away with a drop of water on my fingertip.

I was surprised how much I enjoyed exploring the Kirtlington cave. Most of my finds back home were exposed by rock falling or sliding from the cliffside during storms. I had to race the wind and water for my fossils, hurrying to unearth them before the sea grew impatient and tried to claim us both.

The Lucy-carved cave from which I'd extracted Ajax was the only other cave I'd explored. This cave system went deeper, tunneling into the white limestone hills.

Before too long, the passage opened quickly to a height that I could walk hunched over, and, peering best I could around Henry's rump—at least it was a nice arse—I saw Buckland straighten to almost full height. A few moments later, I stood, too, looking around at the small cavern in breathless wonder.

Buckland held up the lantern, sweeping it around. The beam was weak by the time it hit the uneven, pocked walls, where shadows shrank back like devils from the light. The ceiling was just above our heads, and Henry had to hunch.

"One of the locals said witches used to hide here during the bloody reign, whenever Inquisitors swept through the countryside," Henry said in hushed, almost reverent tones. The place seemed to demand it.

I shivered. It was almost too easy to picture those men and women, hundreds of years ago, hunched in the alcoves and hidden pockets of the cavern, curled in threadbare blankets, hoping they wouldn't be hanged.

Buckland led our party to the far end of the chamber and swept his light across to reveal a roughly oblong shape, low in the wall—so pitch black that it looked less like a hole and more like a gap in reality.

There was a mound of cracked stone below it that must have fallen loose, probably worn away in the recent flood.

"This is it," Buckland said. "One of the men sent his little boy in, and he came back and said there was something poking up from the ground, like a tooth. From his description, I feel sure it's a tusk."

I was listening, but I'd spotted something in the jumble of fallen rock. I knelt and picked it up. Even in the darkness, I knew the feeling of a seashell. And this one had a small hole through its center. I ran my fingers over the round edge and then tucked it into the satchel on my belt. Best to keep my suspicion to myself, for now. One shell did not a hypothesis prove.

Buckland took out a stack of reliqs and ran his hand over the edges of the black void as he did. The rock around the hole crumbled to a fine sand that dusted over our boots. It took him a few minutes and six reliqs, but soon enough, the gap was large enough to climb through.

We peered inside the small chamber that he'd opened. It was only about hip-high, and Buckland had to stay on his knees as he swept the beam of his reliq over the earth.

He caught his breath, and we craned our necks as Buckland took out a brush and swept away some of the dust and loose sediment—enough to reveal a foot-long stretch of smooth, yellowed ivory.

He grinned triumphantly. "Time to dig, my friends."

That afternoon, during his shift in the cave, Gideon Mantell found evidence of two other mammoth tusks, which sent all of us into a frenzy: apparently, we had *multiple* mammoths on our hands.

It took three days just to uncover the whole of that first tusk, even with the aid of reliqs. Buckland expanded the entry to the chamber, but the crawl space was only big enough for two people at a time, working on their knees. We took turns in shifts, chipping and dusting.

My muscles were pleasantly sore that evening as Mantell and I collected our supper of fish stew from the camp cook. I fingered the bit of shell I'd taken from inside the cave, now in my pocket.

Ajax climbed down my sleeve and hopped to the ground, pecking around our chairs for any dropped crumbs.

Conybeare and Goldsmild joined us around the campfire.

"Did you hear? Goldsmild found a molar fragment," Mantell said.

"Just now, as I was packing up," Goldsmild said, grinning. He was covered in drying mud—we all were, really—but pulled a clean white linen kerchief from his pocket and unfolded it reverently. The piece of mammoth tooth was still half buried in rock, but the straight-edged, vertical plates of dentine were obvious in the browned bone. We all gasped and cooed as he passed the tooth fragment around the circle for examination.

Even Lucy was impressed. "That's just a piece of a tooth, you say? But it's huge!" The shard lay the full length of her palm.

"Indeed," Goldsmild said solemnly. "They were mighty beasts, the mammoths. Far larger even than their still-living cousins, the elephant."

"Can you imagine trying to hunt an animal like that?" Lucy mused, passing it on to an almost-bouncing Elizabeth. "Like trying to take down a house."

"Well, very few humans would have had the chance to hunt them," Buckland said quickly. "The mammoths disa—I mean, went into flood-hibernation—long before Noah's progeny repopulated the Earth. Perhaps he had room aboard for only the elephants."

Henry made a dismissive noise in his throat. I hadn't seen him join us, slipping from the shadows to sit casually beside Goldsmild.

"Don't you ever tire of the knots you must tie yourself into, Professor?" Henry said.

Buckland's lips pinched flat as his brow knit.

"See here, Stanton—"

Catherine set a hand on her husband's arm. Some unspoken signal passed between them, and Buckland took a deep breath.

"On the subject of elephants," Catherine said softly. "There are reports of elephant graveyards in Africa, are there not? Perhaps the mammoths demonstrated similar behavior, and we've stumbled upon one such graveyard."

"Elephant graveyards are only legend," Conybeare said.

"And we haven't found any more of the skeletons, besides the tusks. And Goldsmild's tooth," Mantell noted.

"We have hardly begun the expedition," Goldsmild said. "There could still be all manner of bone in there."

"Well, we know the cave is prone to flooding," Buckland said. "Perhaps the tusks, being the heavier ivory, remained while the rest of the skeletons were swept away."

I bit my lip as they theorized, thinking of the seashell in my pocket. Ajax pressed against my knee, and I scratched the top of his head. I was already complicit in one lie about a flooded cave. I didn't want to join another.

"Or . . . what if it's a burial?" I said suddenly, before I could second-guess. "A . . . human burial?"

Even with the dancing fire, I could see the paired lines between Buckland's eyes deepen.

Henry straightened, across the fire.

I swallowed. Maybe I was wrong. It would be perfectly fine if I was. But I needed to say my piece nonetheless.

I pulled out the seashell I'd found and unfurled my palm. "This was in the rubble of the passage. It has a hole, for a string." I swallowed. "What if . . . what if it was a reliq?"

Chapter 40

Well, no one could say I didn't try. Mantell and I were assigned morning shift next day, and he awkwardly tried to bring it up as we chipped slowly around the tusks.

"If mankind—"

"We don't have to do this," I said quickly. "I wasn't trying to upend geomagical philosophy. I just thought it might be a reliq."

"It could still be," he said gently. "Even Buckland said as much."

Buckland had dismissed the idea of a burial site without comment—as if it were so foolish, it wasn't even worth a denial. But he'd agreed my shell could very well be an old reliq.

"Certainly possible," he said in a patronizing tone that made me wince. "We know the cave was used as a hideout. Someone easily could have dropped it."

It was almost a relief. I didn't need to meddle any more in faith and science. I'd presented my theory, and clearly, I was wrong. No harm done.

Elizabeth was waiting when Mantell and I emerged into blue sunlight. She handed us each a rag, and I wiped sweat and mud from my brow.

Ajax hooted and hopped around my boots until I knelt to scoop him onto my shoulder. He poked incessantly at my ear until Elizabeth fed him a strip of jerky.

"He's a menace." She laughed. "Wouldn't eat a bite while you were inside, now acts like I tried to starve him."

Conybeare and Goldsmild joined us a few moments later; their shift was next.

"Stanton wants to speak with you, Mary," Goldsmild said. "He's in the map tent."

"Thank you for telling me." I started to walk up the hill to camp, but Elizabeth caught my elbow.

"Wait," she said softly. "Could we speak privately, first?"

I nodded, and Ajax trotted at our heels as Elizabeth led me away from the camp. We walked toward a small wood at the edge of the meadow.

Elizabeth didn't speak, and I started to get nervous—did she suspect what I'd told her father? We were nearly to the trees when she whirled toward me.

"Lucy has been acting strange." Her eyes brimmed with tears. "Distant."

"Oh!" That was a relief; whatever this was, it wasn't about her father, or anything I may or may not have told him.

"Has she said anything to you?"

I shook my head. "No. I'm sorry."

She hung her head, and I patted her stiffly on the shoulder. I never quite knew what to do when people cried.

"I'm sorry I'm such a mess," she said. "It's just that—well—no one else knows. About me. Us."

Her eyes darted to mine.

"Your secret is safe with me, I promise." I smiled. "And for what it's worth, I can tell Lucy is very fond of you."

I thought for sure it was the right thing to say, so I was surprised when Elizabeth gave a choked sob. "Fond of. What a fool I've been."

I tried to explain. "I'm sure it's just that she's distracted with Promethean . . . stuff. And the protests. She does really like you."

I was wildly out of my element. I wished I was back in the cave instead.

Elizabeth sniffled, looking up. "You really think?"

"Yes!" I said, eager for this conversation to end. "In fact, I'm pretty sure she's annoyed with me, and not you at all."

Elizabeth narrowed her eyes. "You? Why would she be angry with you?"

"Because I strong-armed her into coming along, when I know she would rather have stayed in London."

"Oh." Elizabeth flushed. Her voice was very thin. "I thought she came because she didn't want to be apart from me."

I didn't know what to say to that. There was nothing you could say to ease that kind of anguish. Poor girl. I wasn't lying; I could tell that Lucy was fond of Elizabeth. But I wasn't sure it was love.

I thought, with some pain, of how I'd once loved Henry. And how it had broken me when love wasn't enough.

I bent down to pick up Ajax to give Elizabeth a minute to compose herself. He only protested a little as I put him on my shoulder.

"It may be more than fondness," I said, very carefully, still not looking at the younger girl. "Lucy might even love you. But I am not certain there is room in her head or heart for much beyond the Prometheans these days."

Elizabeth laughed, a cold cracking sound. "I should've known it was pointless to ask you."

I looked up in surprise.

"I try, and try, and try. But you just have to have everything, don't you? I should've known that meant Lucy, too."

Elizabeth was walking away, shoulders hunched.

"What?" I was frozen, trying to figure out what had just happened.

"Don't worry. You needn't be jealous," Elizabeth snarled. "They would all choose the brilliant Miss Anning if they had a choice."

I jogged after her, Ajax digging his claws painfully into my shoulder.

"Wait, please! I don't understand. I only meant that Lucy is so often preoccupied with her reform causes, and trust me, I understand how annoying that can be, I—"

"Annoying?" Her eyes were ice. "Lucy is fighting for what she believes in. She's fighting for all of us. God, she's fighting most of all for you! *Always* for you!"

Elizabeth jabbed a finger at the center of my chest, and I stepped back in shock.

"But of course you have no idea what that means. What it means to fight."

I caught my breath as I narrowed my own eyes. How dare she? I'd been patient, and kind. I'd tried to be a friend. But Elizabeth had been born into luck and luxury, and she had no right to speak a word about *fighting*.

"I have fought every day of my life," I said, heat in my voice. "Any respect I have earned, I have claimed with my own blood and sweat. So don't you dare say I know nothing of fighting."

"And what have you gained for others?" Elizabeth shot back. Her eyes brimmed with tears, and she shook her head so they scattered. "Nothing. I may not be the daughter my father always dreamed of—not clever and cunning like his beloved *Mary*—but at least I won't be a coward, either."

I gasped as she stormed away, the blow of her words like a physical weight as it struck.

Ajax chirped, and I stroked his belly, trying to steady my breathing. "Well," I said aloud. "*Well. That was certainly something.*"

Had she hated me so much, all this time? I had my flaws, but I certainly hadn't deserved that vitriol. A coward! She'd called me a coward! I honestly couldn't believe the absolute gall.

I was still stewing as I walked back across the rolling meadow toward camp. I squinted. That was odd. Henry was running toward me, through the yellow wildflowers. My heart skipped a bit.

I crossed my arms. "There's no need to run. I was on my way to meet you already."

"Mary." He was panting as he drew up before me. The wind bounced his dark curls fetchingly. "Come quickly. Goldsmild found a skeleton."

"Part of the mammoths?"

"No." He grinned. "Human."

Chapter 41

I set Ajax on the ground, then lifted my skirts and ran.

Ajax made a frustrated caw.

"Well, keep up, then," I called over my shoulder.

I swear he understood me. I glanced back as Ajax cocked his head, as if he were considering a new idea. He took a few, quick steps. Then he stopped, stretched out his forelimbs and wings with them, and pushed off from the ground in a powerful leap.

"Henry—Henry, look," I gasped, and stopped abruptly. But Henry didn't manage to slow. He was too close behind. With a cry of alarm, he wrapped an arm around my waist and spun, as if he were trying to fling me aside. But instead he landed flat on his back in the grass, the wind knocked from his lungs, and I fell atop him, our legs tangled together, my hand still on his chest where I'd tried to stop him short.

We lay there in a daze as the pterodactyl soared overhead.

"My God. He's flying. He's doing it."

I was already drafting my note. *Pterodactyls are capable of flap-*

ping flight, like birds, and bats. They launch themselves from standing with a mighty leap and generate lift with their wings, to—

Oh. Henry's arm was stuck in the crook of mine, and as he moved, it brushed against my breast. I looked down from the sky, from the flapping wings on the wind, and swallowed hard.

The weight of my body was on his. If I laid down my head, it would rest on his chest.

The rings of his irises were silver in the sunlight. There was something urgent in the look of them. He lifted a hand and brushed his knuckles across my cheekbone. A sharp pain and then a pleasant tingle slipped down the back of my neck, like the brush of a feather.

"You're hurt," he said softly.

"I'm fine." I jerked away, clambering to my feet. I dabbed at the small cut on my cheek. Only a scratch. "Probably your damn buttons."

But one second more and he would have kissed me, I was sure of it. *And would that have been so terrible?*

Exclamations and shouts drifted up the hill on the wind. They'd seen Ajax flying.

"Come on," I said gruffly, as I extended an arm to Henry. He flashed a grin and reached out toward my face.

I caught my breath, but he only plucked a bit of grass from my hair.

"Wouldn't want to give anyone any inappropriate ideas," he teased, and I glowered.

It was tight quarters in the cavern, our bodies squeezed together as we craned our necks to peer into the pocket chamber at the back, waiting turns to see the body. I chose a spot far from Henry, on the other side of Mantell and Conybeare. I'd tried to leave Ajax with Catherine, but he'd thrown such an enormous fit, I eventually let him follow. He was mostly behaving himself now, investigating the nooks and crannies of the cave.

Goldsmild had found the bones, so by tradition, he would claim the honor of first inspection.

"It's a pelvis, as I thought," he called through the gap. "And I suspect a femur, too."

We all spoke over one another.

"Is there sign of a skull?"

"Male, or female?"

"Adult, or child?"

"Are there any other shells? Or beads?"

"Can't be sure. Can't be sure," Goldsmild said. He was on hands and knees in the small, dark cave, running a brush gently over the bit of now-exposed bone protruding from the earth.

"Get him some more light," Buckland instructed.

Conybeare passed in another reliq-lamp, and Goldsmild angled it above the skeleton so the pale light flooded the floor.

"It'll take a long while to get her out," he said. "We'll need to go about it slowly, so as not to damage the bone."

"Yes, or . . ." Henry crouched and reached through the doorway, handing over a small belemnite. "We could have her out rather quickly."

Goldsmild frowned a moment, then nodded. He tucked the manifold reliq under his shirt and then knelt to press his hands to the earth around the bones.

The cave was tomb-silent as we held even our breath, waiting to see what magic Goldsmild would work with Henry's manifold reliq.

The ground began to tremble. Conybeare yelped and grabbed

my arm, then let go just as quickly, as if my delicate lady-flesh had scorched his palm. I smiled primly. Ajax squawked and ran to me, huddling between my legs.

I bent to touch his head comfortingly. The ground continued to quake, but delicately, like an old man's quivering hand.

Inside the small hole, pebbles loosened, and rose, tremulously, into the air. They drifted, a gentle, upside-down snowfall, toward the ceiling over Goldsmild, and hovered there. His head was still bowed, back arched in concentration.

"My God," Mantell whispered, speaking for us all.

More sediment and stone followed, shaking itself loose to pebbles and rising, like a rusted fog from the ochre-iron in the stone. And more followed, the earth carving itself from the ancient stone and peeling away from the bones.

Goldsmild crawled toward us, and we helped him through the gap as the rest of the cave floor inverted itself to settle on the ceiling instead. We waited with awe and impatience.

And then it was done. Now, through the small black archway, was a pit, a hollow, and the bones.

A naked skull. Arms. Scattered finger bones. The curve of a pelvis. Rounded, cracked ribs. It was whole, nearly perfect. If there were any bones missing, I couldn't tell. The body was laid out straight; whoever they were, they'd been put here after death, not caught in a rockslide or flood.

Tucked among and round the body were two more mammoth tusks, and a scrap of iron that might have been a blade. More beads, shells, and clay, scattered across the floor.

It was, in a word, extraordinary. Here before us was a complete human fossil and ... well, I couldn't even think of another skeleton like it, in England or abroad. Even Ajax's discovery was only a footnote, next to this.

Treasures beyond treasures, laid out as if on a table, and the covering sheet pulled back. Goldsmild had unveiled every secret in the cave in less than a hundred heartbeats. Hours—days—weeks of work, finished in moments.

There was no light on Henry's face, but I knew his eyes would be bright with triumph if there were. His manifold reliqs had proved their worth once again.

We were all still, held by the spell of awe. Buckland broke free first. He knelt and peered into the pocket cave.

"Let Mary," Henry said quietly, but firmly. I frowned. Goldsmild should still have led, by rights. Buckland hesitated before he turned around, but then said, simply, "All right," and moved aside as I came forward.

The roof of the smaller chamber was now only a few inches higher than the doorway we'd made. I had to sit and slide a bit, bumping down the sloping wall, then landed ungracefully in the lower chamber.

"You stay put," I said to Ajax, as he made to try and follow. He gave me a disgruntled look, but folded his wings and obeyed.

The air smelled metallic, of churned, iron-rich earth. I was careful to avoid the artifacts as I crawled over to the skeleton and knelt beside the skull.

The tableau told a story clear as words. They'd been a leader. A woman, I thought, from the many beads—probably once strands of a necklace, or a crown. A queen, maybe. Young, judging by the state of the many teeth still in her skull. Someone respected, and beloved. I imagined the mourners, weeping as they laid her to rest.

I imagined her face, serene in death, closed lids and limp body as a lover laid her down and wept into her long, plaited hair. I imagined the reliq across her breast, her arms folded to hold it close. I could see them, in flickering firelight, tearstained faces as they laid down their huntress-queen.

I touched the skull, my palm round on the crest of her brow, and it was warm.

I gasped and pulled back, catching my wrist with my other hand.

Not a woman. He had been a man. A hunter. I saw a flash of him, dark-eyed and tall, when I touched it. That was impossible. Wasn't it? But the tingle rolled down my arm, the thread of life. If I tugged, if only I pulled—

Except I knew what would happen.

It was one thing to keep a sea snail in a tank, to watch it live and die behind glass. It was one thing, even, to keep an ammonite—despite those dark and knowing eyes, the ammonite was still a simple creature of instinct. And Ajax was not so simple a beast, but I perfectly understood why he was caged, even if I didn't like it.

Still, as I grasped the man's skull, I couldn't help but think of the ammonites and salamanders, dead on the sand of their tanks.

I wouldn't wish that life, or death, on any creature. Not an ammonite or salamander, and certainly not a human.

His soul was with God. If I woke him now, would I tear him from that blissful rest only to see him caged?

"Mary?" Henry asked eagerly, and I knew what he was really asking—a question only I could hear. *Could I reanimate it?*

"Well, I think he was actually a male," I said quickly, to cover my odd hesitation. "From the shape of the pelvis."

I caught Henry's eye and shook my head quickly as I pulled my hand away, the tingle retreating down my arm.

Chapter 42

CATHERINE WAS BROUGHT IN TO SKETCH THE SCENE BEfore we removed anything. She was the one who found the coin.

"I see something," Catherine said, kneeling down with her lantern. "Metal, I think."

We quickly passed it around, and Conybeare declared it to be Roman in origin.

"Roman, you say? You are certain?" Buckland said sharply. It was hard to see in the shadows, but I thought his brow was wrinkled. I realized several things in sequence, and bit down hard at the inside of my cheek.

The mammoth tusks and the bones were contemporaneous. The man had lived, and hunted, among the beasts. I had seen a flash of him when I touched the skull. I had *known* he was a man, in the same way that I knew he died in a time far, far older than the Romans.

But, as Buckland had pointed out, men weren't supposed to

have dwelt with mammoths. Mammoths seemingly vanished—or went into *hibernation*—with the flood, when there shouldn't yet have been *any* humans in Britain.

Except that was wrong. And I was the only one who knew it for certain.

There was a heaviness in the pit in my stomach as I turned over the implications of this. It was revolutionary. It was terrible. It was thrilling. It was terrifying. It would unravel so much—too much?—of Buckland's carefully woven narrative of geomagic and biblical doctrine: either man had lived earlier, or the mammoth later, than we'd been taught.

I didn't know what to do. Henry stood still, watching me very, very closely. I turned my face aside.

Goldsmild's working had revealed all the cave's secrets in wondrous fashion, but it had done so in a way that made it impossible to reconstruct a relative timeline of the artifacts. We had not conducted the usual, careful analysis of geomagical strata that would normally be performed in such a case, logging layers as we passed through them to determine the relative age and type of rock. Without that, it would be impossible to prove that the mammoth tusks, beads, and bones were from the same period.

And now there was the coin, and no way to prove that it had nothing to do with the skeleton. Buckland had said it himself, before—people had probably been using this cave for centuries.

My only evidence was my own power. But to reveal that would reveal all of my secrets. And I couldn't risk that.

If I told them the truth now about my gift, Buckland would believe me. But would he still support me? Nominate me? The truth would undo so much of his careful work. Could our friendship withstand that?

And then there was Conybeare. He had been eager enough before to turn me in to the Inquisitors. I wasn't keen to hand him a fresh two-for-one heresy: resurrection *and* biblical rejection.

So. So, this would be another secret I would keep.

"I do believe there was a Roman outpost nearby," Mantell said excitedly.

"But why would she be buried here, alone?" Conybeare frowned.

"You still think it was a woman?" Catherine paused and looked up from her sketchbook. "But I thought Mary said—"

"The beads," said Conybeare sharply. "Likely from a necklace. A Roman man wouldn't have worn such adornments."

Buckland nodded, and then began to spin the story, pacing around the larger cavern. Maybe she was a prostitute, he said, tapping at his chin. A local Briton who serviced men at the outpost. That would explain the single coin, and her solitary burial. My heart sank with every word.

It was the sort of scandalous history that people loved, and I could easily picture it in the headlines, splashed across the papers: *Geomagicians discover remains of a Roman prostitute in Kirtlington Quarry Cave.*

And my name would be there beside the others: Buckland, Conybeare, Goldsmild, Mantell, Stanton, and Anning. But—did I want that? My name, beside another lie? My stomach was queasy.

"Mary?" Henry cocked his head. "Are you all right? You look a bit pale."

"I'm fine," I snapped. "It's a momentous occasion, is it not? I am simply overcome."

His eyes narrowed; then he smiled. "You don't think he's right. You don't think the skeleton is of Roman origin."

Damn him, damn him, damn him.

"I—I am not sure," I said, trying to force myself to meet Buckland's eye. "But I do wonder if it isn't . . . older."

"Hmm," Buckland said, stroking his chin and nodding. "Iron Age, then, you think? Could be. Could be. The beads could certainly be Iron Age. But the coin—"

I shook my head. "Older," I said softly. Oh, damn Henry Stanton to Hell. "I think his people hunted the mammoth."

Buckland's mouth fell open. I swallowed. The shocked silence grew to fill every black pocket of the cave.

Henry stepped closer. "What makes you think this?" Was he goading me?

I could still tell the truth. What I could feel. What I could do. *Fossil witch.*

But I knew Buckland too well.

He would go to the archbishop. Coordinate some rationale. Find some justification in the text of the Old Testament, maybe. Tell the archbishop it would prove the age of humanity, perhaps. Whatever it was, eventually, Buckland would ask me to try to raise the bones.

I must admit Elizabeth's accusation—*coward*—was ringing in my ears. *What have you gained for others?* she had asked me. And what answer did I have? But perhaps I could give one now, if only to myself.

Buckland might even promise that the man would live free, uncaged. But the promise would never hold. They—no, *we*, because in the end I would join them, whatever I swore now—would poke and prick and measure and test and examine the hunter. He would be a specimen. And he would never be free, until he died again.

If I were a better woman, maybe that would be enough. But I was not, and it was not.

Because I was afraid, too. I didn't want to challenge the Church, or upend geomagical doctrine, or society. I was happy to leave all that to Edgar and Lucy. I was not a radical. I never had been. I only ever wanted to be a geomagician.

And if I claimed, truly, that the body was older than Rome—older than we'd ever imagined man to be—the votes would slip away like water on oil.

So, was it cowardice? Maybe. Did it matter that I knew it was also right?

I dropped my gaze and shrugged. "It was just a silly idea."

<hr />

The celebration that night was raucous, as we emptied bottle after bottle of wine around the campfire, swapping stories of geomagical finds and expeditions.

Even Elizabeth stopped pouting when Goldsmild told the rapt audience about the fossilized shark's tooth he'd been sent by a Swiss naturalist.

"As long as my palm, finger to wrist," he swore. "Can you imagine the size of that maw?"

"Why, it would have to be taller than man," Mantell exclaimed, and he and Conybeare began trying to calculate how tall it would be, assuming such a shark kept the same number of teeth as its modern kin.

I crept away when Catherine pulled out her sketchbook, and the geomagicians leaned over to draw these potential shark mouths at scale. Ajax was already asleep, curled in a pile of blankets by the fire, and I let him be.

The moon was bright and full, so I had enough light to walk by. I'd taken my blanket, wrapped around me like a cloak, to keep warm in the cool spring night.

I wandered away from the cave, down the slope of the hill and over another, until the happy noise of the campfire grew distant, replaced by the sounds of crickets and rustling leaves. An owl hooted somewhere from the treetops.

My heart was heavy. I'd made my decisions, but I was burdened, still, by the weight of so many choices. The decisions. The politicking. The calculations. The lies. What was right, and what was wrong, and how did anyone ever decide at all?

Prometheans and Lucy and Henry and Buckland and Edgar and Ajax and the archbishop and the Society, and so many loyalties and demands, and I was only one woman, who'd simply wanted to be elected geomagician and write a few well-reviewed papers.

I should have listened, all those weeks ago, when Buckland told me to send Ajax to London in his care.

"Oh, what do you want now?" I snapped at the quiet footsteps that crept behind me, turning toward the man who'd joined me in the dark hollow of the hill.

Henry caught me by the forearms. I froze, stunned at the intensity in his gaze.

"You could have done it, couldn't you?" he whispered, searching my face. His eyes flashed.

"I didn't—"

"Come, Mary," he said, bending toward me. "I already keep so many of your secrets. What's one more?"

His face had a wildness I'd never seen before—as if all his careful restraint was slipping. Was he drunk? No; he'd only had a little wine, and he didn't smell of spirits. He smelled like the campfire smoke, and the spice of his cologne, and of himself. His sweat. His skin.

I swallowed. I lifted my chin, and my heart skipped a beat. "Is that a threat? I tell you, or you—what—destroy my career?"

"Do you really think I would do that?" Henry's eyes were cold, searching mine. He still held my wrists. I didn't pull away. I didn't know why.

"I think you'll turn on me." I freed my hands and jabbed at his chest. His face darkened. "The moment it suits your purposes. The second it serves your cause."

"You think you know my cause?" Henry's chest rose and fell with the effort of his breathing as he stepped—somehow—closer. "You think you understand me?" The fingers of his right hand curled into a fist. A warning prickle behind my neck tempted me to shrink away from the cold glare of those night-dark eyes, but I couldn't make myself move. I shivered.

"Maybe you do." Henry laughed, harsh and raw. I'd never heard that laugh before. "Is this your revenge?" He lurched away, turning his back to me. "To bring me low? To harry me to the brink of madness? Do you want me to grovel at your feet?"

Well, now he wasn't making any kind of sense. It was as if he'd gone completely—*ah*.

I bit my lip. Yes. Well. That would explain things. Henry was experiencing a psychological break. He *had* been under a great deal of stress, what with his campaign for society president.

I should probably fetch one of the others. Get him some kind of medical attention.

"Um. Henry?" I set a hand on his elbow. He flinched from my touch.

"Damn it, woman," he whispered, and ran both hands through his hair. His pupils were huge in the low light. "Very well. You've won. I will grovel." His hand cupped my chin, his fingers trembling on my cheek.

"I surrender," he said, with a hoarse, desperate whisper.

This wasn't anger, I realized, though my thoughts seemed to be slow, and thick as molasses. *Despair.* And desire.

His lips parted.

"Oh ... *oh*," I stammered, my hands fluttering. "I—I see—"

Henry kissed me.

His hands clasped either side of my face, insistent fingers threading into my hair. My arms flung wide in shock as he crushed me against his chest. He tasted like wine, warm and heady. His lips were soft as his thumbs stroked at my jaw. He made a sound. A groan torn from his throat.

"Forgive me." The cold air was a shock on my lips. A lock of black hair tumbled over his brow as he looked down between us. "I know—"

I stared at the broad shoulders, the coat rustling in the wind, his form a silhouette against the starlit sky.

"Oh, do be *quiet*," I said, and closed the distance between us.

I pulled him into me, my hands insistent and wanting. This time it was Henry who stiffened in surprise, and I laughed as I wound my arms around his neck.

Then our breath caught on warm, desperate lips, and everything was a blur of shadow, and touch.

I kissed him hard. His hands were on my cheek, my neck, then my hips, then circling my back.

This was nothing like when we were young. Fools; we thought we knew so much back then. The way he'd touched me then was sweet as honey. The way he'd kissed me then was gentle as a feather. We thought we burned, but, God, we were innocent— that was nothing next to fifteen years of longing and resentment.

Henry's lips roved along my chin. He groaned into my neck, sending shivers down my spine. His fingers shook as he brushed his hand over my breasts, and I threw my head back, laughing, shaking with want.

He kissed the soft, pale skin at the top of my breasts, his tongue darting circles as he worked lower, and I groaned.

"Are you sure?" he asked hoarsely.

Damn, damned, damnable Henry Stanton.

"Yes," I managed. "Yes, I am sure."

Chapter 43

WE LAY TOGETHER, WATCHING THIN CLOUDS DRIFT ACROSS the moon and letting our breathing steady. There would be time later to think about what came next. Things would change. They always did. But it was enough to lay with Henry now, still naked and warm, with quickly cooling sweat on my skin.

That's what I thought, at least, until Henry ruined it.

My thighs were pale, my belly soft and bare. The cool wind rippled the fine hairs of my legs and arms, and caught my braid, tangled and loose from our lovemaking. I felt like some kind of pagan goddess, of lust and earth.

"Pass me my chemise, would you?" I slipped it on, as Henry stepped into his own trousers.

We grinned at each other, half-dressed.

"You have no idea how long I have wanted that," he said, and kissed my bare shoulder before helping me adjust my blouse. Then he pressed his brow to mine.

"I love you, Mary," he said solemnly.

I felt like I was falling from a great height.

"I never stopped loving you, I swear it." He said it so tenderly, and earnestly, that it cut all the deeper.

I stared. My mouth worked, but no words came out. When Henry broke our engagement all those years ago, it had wrecked me. This man had left me shattered. But, with time, I picked up the pieces. And with wire and plaster and a bit of hubris, I put myself back together, just as I would reconstruct a particularly unruly fossil. I had managed all of that because I knew Henry didn't love me.

I stumbled back. Henry came after me, and I caught him in the chest with my palm.

"No. No. Don't you *dare*."

He frowned, then his eyes widened. "It's all right if you don't feel the same. I only wanted you to know."

"Oh, I love you, too." I laughed. "I wish I didn't. I wish to God I didn't love you, Henry Stanton, but I do."

He reached for me, but I stepped away, feeling terribly, bitterly sorry for myself. My voice was a soft, broken-winged thing. "But that wasn't enough before, was it? *I* was never enough."

He opened and closed his mouth twice, then spread his hands, fingers wide. They fell at his sides. "Oh, Mary. Is that what you thought?"

"What else was I to think?" I flinched, mouth trembling. I squeezed my eyes shut, remembering the letters I burned to ash on the sand, and all the others he never bothered to write.

"Look at me." Henry pressed a hand to my cheek and raised my face to his. "You have always been enough."

"Then why didn't you fight for me?" I could only whisper, choking back tears. "I would have fought for you."

"I know." He nodded, his chin jerking as he gripped my shoulder. "And if I could do it over, I swear to you, I would."

He bowed his head to kiss me again, but I pushed him back, gently but firmly, and wrapped my fingers around his muscled forearms.

"Will you fight for me now, Henry?"

Buckland had warned me: *He can't be trusted. Stanton will ruin it all*, he said. And I'd promised, because I hadn't known Henry—the adult Henry, as he was now. This Henry had been nothing but an ally and a friend. And he loved me, he said. And—God help me—I loved him, too.

"Every day. Until my last breath." He brushed a strand of hair behind my ear, and I leaned into his palm.

I swallowed at the tingle that raced down my neck at his touch.

"Then help me. Buckland plans to nominate me to the Society at the annual meeting. Help me get the votes."

I hadn't known what to expect, but I'd only imagined two potential outcomes: immediate agreement or rejection. What I didn't expect was confusion. It spread across his face, straightening his lip and pulling down his brows.

"He plans to ... *what?*"

"I just said: Buckland's going to nominate me."

"To the Society?"

"No, to Parliament," I huffed. "Yes, to the Society. Is that so incredible?"

I didn't understand what was happening. Why was this so confusing? And why was there something of a smile twitching over his mouth?

"I know a woman's never been nominated before, but you said yourself I deserve—"

"No, Mary." He shook his head. "It's not that a woman has never been nominated before. It's that a woman *can't* be nominated."

I didn't understand. Or I did. "What are you saying?"

"I knew it. I knew he had some other scheme!" He began to pace. "Let me guess, the professor made you swear not to tell me?"

"How did you know?" I stepped back, my heart lead in my chest. "What do you mean?"

"He can't do it, Mary." Henry spun toward me. "And he knew I would tell you the truth. Buckland can't nominate a woman, Mary. Even I couldn't nominate you. '*A male person of full age, having the qualifications in formal education or practical experience befitting a geomagician, may be nominated for election by any Fellow in good standing with the Society,*'" Henry quoted.

"But that's not in the Charter." I shook my head. "I've read it; I specifically checked. It never mentions men or women." My head spun. I was afraid I might vomit.

"No, it's not in the Charter. That's from the bylaws. You wouldn't have seen them. They're kept at Palmanaeus, under key. For Society-member reference only."

I hardly felt the sting of the betrayal. I was too numb—it was like Henry was speaking a language I'd never heard. Something so foreign, my brain couldn't even recognize it.

"That can't be right," I mumbled. "It can't be. He promised."

"And I suspect I know why he felt confident enough to make such a promise," Henry said. "Because if Buckland was elected president of the Society, he could amend those bylaws by unilateral decree. And it would take a two-thirds vote to overrule him. He was gambling, you see—if the professor won the presidency, he would be able to keep his promise to you."

"But if he lost . . ."

"You don't need to worry about that," Henry said fiercely. He took my right hand and kissed the center of my palm. "I only wish I'd known sooner; I could have set your mind at ease. Listen, Mary—whether it's Buckland or myself who wins the presidency doesn't matter."

"You'll rewrite the bylaws, then? If you win instead?" I asked sharply.

"Mary," he said, eyes solemn. "I would rewrite the whole world for you."

My fury burned white-hot as I marched back to the campsite, Henry at my side. I slipped my hand out of his as we came into view of the fire, and the others turned to greet us.

Henry had tried his best to re-plait my hair and pluck out the grass, but I'd been in a rush to confront Buckland, and from the knowing smirk on Lucy's face, I gathered it hadn't been sufficient.

I pushed aside the embarrassment. Let them think what they wanted. It didn't matter anymore.

I walked straight to Buckland, cutting between Goldsmild and Mantell in their chairs.

"Ah, Mary," Buckland said cheerfully, "we were just saying you should—"

"*A male person of full age.*" I was standing too close to the fire, his face caught in my shadow. The heat seared my back, and sweat broke out across my brow and lip.

Buckland's mouth constricted, then slackened. His gaze flickered to Catherine beside him, and she stiffened. My heart was rent again. She had known.

"It's true, then," I said flatly.

I felt like I'd been punched in the gut, and my knees nearly gave way.

Ajax had woken at the sound of my voice, and he ambled over from the basket to rub his head against my knees. I scooped him onto my shoulder.

The other geomagicians were speaking—to me, to Buckland, to one another—things like, *What is the meaning of this? Buckland? Surely this is a misunderstanding*—but I ignored them, and Catherine and Elizabeth, too.

"I was going to tell you. I swear it. I was going to tell you when we returned to London," Buckland said.

"You *lied*," I spat. Ajax made an angry hissing sound in echo, spreading his wings.

"Mary, wait, please." Buckland clasped his hands. "Whatever Stanton told you, it wasn't like that."

"Wasn't it, though?" Henry folded his arms and stepped half in front of me, blocking Buckland's view. "Did you or did you not neglect to mention that section of the bylaws when you made your promise to Mary?"

Buckland flinched but ignored him, speaking to me. "I told you from the first, Mary, these kinds of things take time, and careful maneuvering. But you made me swear to nominate you; do you not remember? You made it a condition of selling Ajax. What else could I say?"

"You *lied*!"

Elizabeth and Catherine were grim-faced in the firelight behind him, hands clasped together.

"I did not!" Buckland protested. "I never did. I intended to be president. I still intend it. And as president, I can change the bylaws. Not just for you, Mary, but for—"

"You're a liar!" I shouted. My throat stung with it. Elizabeth gasped as Ajax rose and spread his wings behind my head.

"You lie, and lie, and lie, and always, you find some way to justify it. You lie as you breathe, and tell yourself God will understand. Even then, I trusted you." I laughed, and Lucy gave me a worried look. "But no more. We are finished, Professor."

My heel ground the dirt as I turned. Ajax's claws tightened with the sudden movement, drawing blood. "Take us away from here, Henry."

He smiled grimly. "Gladly."

But Lucy didn't follow. She looked between me and the Bucklands—between me and Elizabeth, I suppose.

"Lucy?"

Perhaps I should have told Lucy she didn't need to choose sides; this wasn't her war. Maybe I should have said that this wasn't Elizabeth's fault. That I wouldn't blame Lucy, if she stayed. But I was full of fury.

So instead I said, sharply, "You wanted to go back to London, didn't you? Here's your chance." And Lucy came with us.

Chapter 44

Glasswater Mill was a square red thumbprint pressed to rolling green hills, its singular chimney thrust into the sky like a raised fist. I watched out the coach window as the mill vanished and emerged, then disappeared again into the landscape as we drew closer.

Henry's shoulder pressed against mine, and Ajax sprawled over our laps. Lucy sat across from us, her lips thin and her brow furrowed.

Last night I'd been furious at Buckland's betrayal, but my rage had been tempered somewhat in the hours since by Henry's soft hands and warm lips. Everything I knew had been flipped upside down. The man I loved like a father had betrayed me—and the man who once betrayed me now loved me.

I had mapped my life to Buckland's, and done so happily, because I believed—foolishly—that he cared about me. And maybe he had. Just not so much that he wouldn't use me.

That was the terrible irony of it all. I'd expected Henry to use me for his own aims. I had never expected it of Buckland.

The question I kept stumbling over was: *Why?* Why hadn't Buckland simply told me the truth, back in Lyme Regis? When I'd demanded a nomination, why hadn't Buckland just explained that it wouldn't be possible unless he was president? I would have understood. I would have trusted him.

But clearly, he didn't trust me.

Buckland must have feared that I would go elsewhere with Ajax—or with my loyalties. Maybe even to Henry instead, and Buckland couldn't risk that; he wanted the presidency too badly. Maybe as badly as I wanted that nomination. And when we made the arrangement, I hadn't understood how precarious Buckland's position really was. I hadn't known that his influence was waning, until Ajax and I had stanched the bleed in support. We lent strength to his cause, and hitched the Church behind, to boot. And still, he hadn't trusted me enough to tell the simple truth—and that, I think, was the poisoned tip of the arrow. The festering infection on top of the wound.

Up close, Glasswater Mill looked more like a fine estate than a factory. The flower beds were immaculate, and a fleet of gardeners was at work, digging near the hedges.

We wouldn't be long at the mill, Henry promised this morning while we were still abed. "Only long enough for me to grab a few papers, and then back to London," he'd said.

I'd flopped over, resting my chin on his chest. "Long enough for a tour, I hope."

I still had only the vaguest sense of the thing Henry called *the Loom*, and I was eager to see the mechanics at work. "How does the steam engine work? Is the reliquemical formulation the same as slickers use? And you say the subjects have to be in contact with the material?"

My rapid-fire questions made Henry chuckle, and he'd kissed me, and then we missed the inn's breakfast service.

Now I felt my chest flutter remembering what we'd been doing as our bacon went cold—as Henry helped me down from the coach. His smile deepened, as if he knew exactly what I was thinking.

Two men had come out to meet our coach, and Henry went to greet them. I hooked Ajax onto my shoulder, but before I could follow Henry, Lucy grabbed my hand.

"Mary"—her voice was soft—"are you certain about this?"

"Oh, yes, Henry wouldn't let us tour the mill if it were dangerous."

"No, are you certain about *him*. After everything before ... I am afraid Henry will only break your heart again. I ..." She shrugged; her mouth twisted. "I don't trust him, Mary."

I wished I could tell Lucy she was wrong. But she'd seen me shattered. She'd held me together. She had every right to doubt Henry Stanton.

Except she didn't have all the information. *Henry knows I can resurrect the dead. He's risked his own life—and career—to protect my secret. I trust him because he's earned it.*

I almost told her. But Henry was calling, waving us over, so I patted her hand. "It's different this time."

—⚬⚬—

The mill employees were a funny pair. One was young, with a rust-colored mustache and a charming smile. He introduced himself as Mr. Stewart, operations manager. The other was old and stooped, with a shock of white hair. He gave us only his name—"Farnsworth"—and Henry had to provide the title.

"Our chief science engineer." Henry clapped the old man's

shoulder. "He was my father's first employee, at Bridgewater. Father always said the mill would have failed if not for Farnsworth, and the same is certainly true for Glasswater." Mr. Farnsworth grimaced, but looked quietly pleased once we'd all turned away.

Mr. Stewart led us into a neat reception area. There was a steady, low vibration underfoot, and a repeating pattern of rhythmic whirring and grinding so that our guide had to raise his voice to be heard.

"I was delighted when Mr. Stanton sent word that you would like to see the facility. We've been operational for six months now, but I've had very few opportunities to practice my tour with anyone but poor Mr. Farnsworth," Stewart said.

A table had been laid with tea and warm biscuits, the tea rippling in its cups from the thrumming floor. Mr. Farnsworth snuck two of the biscuits to Ajax as we passed into the hall.

"Down that wing is a dormitory for workers. To our right, you'll find more offices, maintenance, and laboratory space, nothing much worth touring. Stairs just that way, up to the second level—we're wrapping up construction on the upstairs rooms—and, aha, here we go—through here"—he opened the door straight ahead with a flourish—"is the manufactory floor, and the first operational Glasswater Loom."

He had to raise his voice even further to be heard over the cacophony of sounds—grating and scraping, squelching and churning, clicking and grinding, and the *hiss, hiss, hiss* of steam powering it all.

I was hit by the sound first, and then the smell—oily and acrid—even as my eyes tried to make sense of the maze of pulleys and belts hanging from the ceiling, a net of crisscrossing thick black piping and clear glass tubes.

Ajax, on my shoulder, gave a high-pitched shriek and reared

back, clacking his beak and waving his head around, scraping my ear and cheek.

"Whoa, whoa, hey, hey. You're all right." I had to practically shout even to hear myself over the cacophony; no wonder Ajax was afraid, poor thing. I plucked him off my shoulder to cradle him to my chest. That usually helped him settle, but this time, he still struggled against me, flapping and whimpering. Poor fellow was terrified. "I'll take him back out to the coach. Just a moment."

But Mr. Farnsworth gestured. "Give him here. We'll just go and have some more nice biscuits, then, where it's quieter."

Farnsworth held him expertly, wisely offering another biscuit from his pocket as they made for the door.

With Ajax gone, I had nothing to do but marvel. The manufactory floor was one long open space, running the whole length of the building. One machine was half finished and still, but the one directly before us was a blur of motion and sound.

My first thought was of an octopus. At the center of the Loom was a glass bell jar, about three feet tall. Its lower half was filled with a black, viscous liquid. The substance had the telltale iridescent shimmer of reliq-serum. It roiled and popped in the jar, and the top half was opaque with steam and condensation. That had to be where they put fossils. The jar was overturned in a raised open vat of more of the same. The serum flowed outward from the vat via seven glass-tube "arms," passing through wrapped copper coils and then a metal shunt, through which it entered each pod.

Lucy gasped. "Are those..."

The pods were a rounded teardrop shape, chalk-white in color, but lacquered smooth as glass. I thought they looked a bit like scooped-out hard-boiled eggs. And reclining in each pod, chest-deep in serum as if lounging in a black-water bath, was a person.

None of them spoke, but they all turned their heads toward us. I might have expected curiosity—the owner of Glasswater was with us, after all—or maybe embarrassment—I gathered they were all naked under there—but each face shared a common weary blankness.

"As you can see," Stewart said, and led us closer, next to one of the seven pods, "the Loom is manned by seven subjects. The serum is activated by the physical contact with the body, just as a conventional reliq would be. Steam power is used to circulate the serum between the pods and back to the central charging station, there at the center."

His hand traced the path in the air, winding in and out and between the pods—more like a wheel, then, rather than an octopus.

I tried not to stare at the woman in the pod closest to us, but it was difficult not to. She was missing several teeth, and her face was deeply wrinkled, though I doubted she was out of her forties. Purpled, sunken bags hung under her eyes. Whatever she was outside of this place, or whoever she'd been before, her life was not a gentle one.

Now that I was looking closer, I saw several thin silver filaments emerging from below the black water, and another two that were embedded just under the woman's chin, in her neck. There was a web of silver cords, I realized, running between the pods. Conical copper beads zipped on defined paths, shuttling back and forth.

"Oh," I said, a little breathlessly. "It's blood, isn't it? You're linking them by blood, filtering it through all of their bodies . . . that's what compounds the magic? The serum, then, is treating them all as one being . . . is that how it works?"

I was speaking quickly now, walking along the machine and

examining the channels and tubes pumping blood and serum. I grinned, and Henry grinned back.

"Now that I see it—now that I understand, it's so *obvious*! How did no one think of it before?"

Henry laughed. "Well, they did think of it. The surgeon Al-Zahrawi theorized it would work all the way back in the first century. But it took the invention of steam power to make the transfer feasible."

"But that means there must be something about magic that requires oxygenation for storage and usability, doesn't it? Blood and breath. I wonder—" I stopped with a grimace. "Lucy?"

Mr. Stewart and I realized at the same moment that Lucy was not awed, as I was, by the scientific marvel of the Loom and the implications for magical theory.

No. She was *upset*.

Lucy had stepped past us all to grip the edge of the woman's pod. "Are you—does it—is this—oh my God."

Lucy covered her mouth, and her eyes went wide.

Stewart went to her side. "Miss Murray, I can assure you that the subjects are quite comfortable, there is no risk or danger involved, and they are compensated very handsomely for their participation, and, additionally, receive three complimentary meals per shift."

I put a hand on her back. "Luce, she's fine, they're all fine, see?"

The old woman turned her head. Her long hair trailed in thick, serum-coated tendrils over her shoulders. She blinked a few times, her eyes focusing, and then she chuckled.

"It's sweet of you to worry, dear, but it really isn't so bad. We're not even here, really," she said, and then straightened her neck as her eyes unfocused again.

I turned to Henry. "What does she mean?"

"They dream," he said softly, at the same time Stewart said, "Exposure to reliquemical serum is reported to have a hallucinogenic effect on its users; the same experience has been extensively studied by reliquemists, who describe it as a brief but pleasant euphoria."

"See?" continued Mr. Stewart. "No harm done. Look, have you seen this mechanism here, with those shuttles running back and forth along the wire? It's ingenious. Mr. Stanton, can you explain for us—"

"No harm done?" The white of Lucy's eyes flashed, and her cheeks flushed. "This is *barbaric*. And if you can't see that," she snarled at Henry and me, "then you're both more lost than I imagined."

"Lucy, come now, that isn't fair!"

But she was already slamming the door. Henry and I exchanged a bewildered look.

"Ahem. Erm." Stewart cleared his throat. "Well, Miss Anning, if you have any further questions, I'd be more than happy to answer them."

Chapter 45

I FOUND LUCY OUT FRONT, ON A DECORATIVE BENCH BY A BED of white roses. She didn't look up when I sat beside her.

I folded my hands in my lap and inhaled. The air smelled of fresh-turned dirt, sweet and loamy.

"When Henry stopped writing, all those years ago," I said softly, and swallowed, "I was terrified. Not because of Henry—I was *furious* with him—but I was afraid because of you."

Lucy did look at me then, her lips pressed tight.

"I was terrified I would lose you, too. You were so strong, and brave, and kind. I'd never met anyone like you before. I didn't even know there were other girls like you—like me—and it was, well, Luce, it isn't an exaggeration to say that meeting you was like finding the other half of my soul. I've made a lot of discoveries on that beach. But you were—you are—the best thing I've ever found."

I was blinking quickly now, trying my damnedest not to cry.

Lucy didn't say anything, but she grabbed my hand, lacing our fingers tightly together.

"You have been my sister—my heart, Luce—for so long, that sometimes it's easy to forget those hearts beat to different songs."

Lucy never bothered to hide her tears. They tracked down her cheeks, dripping from her jaw. She let them fall to her lap.

"It's horrific, Mary. What they're doing to those people is wrong. Why can't you see that? Are you just blinded because it's Henry?"

I started to speak, then stopped. I owed her a real, thoughtful answer.

Was she right? Was I blinded by love?

I did love him, but I wasn't starry-eyed about it. I didn't know what the future held—I could just as easily imagine us married in a year as estranged once again.

So it wasn't love that tinged my thoughts of the mill, but I did wonder if it might be, well, *need*.

I'd broken with Buckland. My only chance of nomination now was Henry. And if I turned on him? If I told him Lucy was right, and the Loom was an abomination? What then? I might lose that chance, too.

The idea of the Loom wasn't *pleasant*. I certainly saw her point there. Passing blood through a chain of bodies to mingle it was the kind of idea that had to make your skin crawl a bit.

But I'd seen the manifold reliqs at work. The power they could harness. The world was about to change forever, and the Society would be at the center of it, reaping the riches and the acclaim. And I would be with them. With the manifold reliqs, we would carve great beasts from the cliffs, and pull minerals from the deep, and map the whole of the Earth, and all the other things geomagicians dreamed of doing. I could taste it—we stood now on the edge of the unknown, with this new lamp in our hands, and I was desperate to see what we would find. What we would learn. So as distasteful as the methodology might be, that did not, for me, outweigh the quiver of excitement in my chest.

"It's progress, Luce," I said at last. "Sometimes progress is messy. Sometimes it's awful. But would their lives be any better if they were doing something else instead? Laboring in a field, or in a bed, or behind a real loom in a textile manufactory, working their fingers to the bone?"

"Yes," she said ferociously.

I dropped my voice. "Why? So they can end up selling their magic in the slicks anyway? Aren't those the same type of people the Prometheans want to help by raising the reliq-rates? And all for what, one one-hundredth of what they'll earn today? It's a good deal for them, Luce. Better than they'd get in the slicks."

"Well, maybe that's the problem!" She winced as if she'd let something slip, but it took me a moment to understand.

"You're afraid that when the Looms start to spread, the reform efforts will die," I said slowly.

Lucy exhaled, looking out into the distance. "I've wondered from the beginning if it was wise to pin our hopes on a national rate increase. As I told Edgar, that's just giving tacit approval to the whole system.

"*Libertas Magicae*," she said fiercely. "Freedom of Magic. That's the ultimate goal. Or I thought it was." She shook her head sadly. "But Edgar and Henry and that horrible machine will set us back fifty years, at least, if these things spread, with the wages Henry's offering."

I tried to think carefully about what I wanted to say next. I'd wondered it before, but had never been brave enough to ask.

"Lucy?"

She met my eyes this time.

"Why do you care?" I wet my lips and hurried on. "I mean, no one likes to sell their magic. It feels awful. It's shameful. But for most of us, selling magic is just one more unpleasant reality in a life full of them."

Lucy blinked at me, stunned.

"You've never had to sell magic, Luce. You've never even used a reliq. So why does it matter to you what other people do?"

I watched her brow knit tighter and tighter as I spoke, and then suddenly smooth. "You really don't know."

"Know what?"

She exhaled. "It was you, Mary. At least for Edgar and me—and for Henry, too, I'd wager—you were the first person we knew—and loved—who sold their magic in the slicks."

Red shame washed over me. So this was what Elizabeth meant.

"We were young, not blind," Lucy said. "We watched you sneak to the slicks after dark. We saw the hollows in your cheeks. The shadows under your eyes. We saw what it cost, to sell your magic."

She's fighting most of all for you! Always for you! Elizabeth had said. My mouth was dry. I could hardly bear the sympathy in her eyes. "You're saying I was, what, your—your charity inspiration? Have you pitied me all this time, then? Poor little Mary. Pathetic little Mary—"

"It wasn't like that," Lucy insisted. "You're right that I've never used a reliq. I've never been anything but a witch." Her lip trembled. "My father taught me to fear my own magic. To despise it. It wasn't until I met you that I understood what a gift my power was. My own magic, always at my fingertips. Wholly and utterly *mine*." She clasped a fist over her breast, and then let it fall. Her voice softened.

"If you were free," she said, "and you saw others in chains, wouldn't you want them to be free, too? To own your magic—to truly claim it, and know that it is yours, and no one else's—well, that's something I wish everyone could experience. And without trading reliqs for coin, we'd come closer. Your own magic, for your own life. One person, one reliq. It would be better. Don't you think that's worth fighting for?"

I didn't answer. I wished she hadn't asked. She never had before. And my stomach sank, because it was a line drawn in the sand, and we both knew it. We could never go back.

"It's not my fight." My voice was barely audible.

Lucy closed her eyes. Her lip twitched, and her nostrils flared. "Then," she said, slipping her hand from mine as she stood, "I suppose you've made your choice."

"Don't do this, Luce. We don't have to agree on this to be friends, do we? And what about Edgar? He supports the Loom, too." My voice cracked. "Please don't do this."

Lucy wiped her eye with a sleeve. "I'll try to convince him."

"And when that fails?"

"I don't know." She jerked her chin toward the mill. "But to stare evil in the face and swear it's not what it seems? I'd do almost anything for you, Mary, and for Edgar. But I won't do that."

I shut my eyes, willing this to be a nightmare. But not even in my worst dreams had I imagined that my closest friend, the sister of my heart, would end our friendship over a *machine*.

"Don't worry about me. I'll make my own way back to London. Oh, and Mary?" The gravel crunched underfoot as she turned back one last time. "Good luck with the election. I'll be rooting for you. Always."

Part of me wanted to call out. To run after her and beg her forgiveness. I wanted to swear I would condemn the mill, and promise to help her tear down all the slicks in England. But none of it would be true. And Lucy would know, because she knew me too well.

Instead I watched my dearest friend walk down the road into town, and tears rolled slowly down my cheeks.

Chapter 46

Henry and I had been back in London for two weeks, and the skirmishes were growing more deadly by the day.

We'd heard rumors, on the journey home, of the tension in the city. The Prometheans had—as I'd expected—launched their blockade during our time in Kirtlington. Every night brought a new bloody clash between protestors and lawmen. If either side had once assumed the conflict would be over swiftly, they knew better by now.

The wealthy neighborhoods—Henry's, and Buckland's, and around Palmanaeus House—were patrolled by constables and soldiers, with any *suspicious* types quickly detained for questioning.

But even those of us inside the safe bubble of wealth had ears to hear, and eyes to see: the shattering of glass, the firing of muskets, occasional smoke rising against an orange sky.

LIBERTAS MAGICAE! declared the posters slapped on every lamppost and pub door and garden wall. RISE AND RESIST; DON'T

SELL YOUR RELIQ, read some. Or PAY OUR WORTH, OR PAY THE PRICE. The fliers went up almost as quickly as they were pulled down and tossed into the streets to be trampled into the cobblestones.

Had Lucy written the slogans? Designed the posters? They had her voice. Her fiery style. Where was she now? I'd thought—hoped, I suppose—that she would make contact before today, at least.

Because today was *the* day. The Society's annual meeting. The day I would stand or fall as a geomagician.

Henry, sitting on the coach bench beside me, laced our fingers together.

"Don't look so worried, darling. Have faith. In both of us."

I scowled. "I was trying my best *not* to think of it."

Henry had invited me to stay with him when we returned from Kirtlington. But I hadn't wanted to risk our reputations so close to the election, so I'd taken a room in a boardinghouse not far away.

I'd seen Buckland once or twice in the halls of Palmanaeus since his return, but I turned and walked away whenever he tried to speak with me. Soon it was common knowledge that Buckland and I had fallen out, and that I was fully allied with Henry now. The rumors gave wildly conflicting, half-true reasons—sex, money, revenge, betrayal—but in the end, it didn't shift our calculations for the presidential election.

Henry kissed the top of my head.

"Well, we have done what we can," he said. "The rest we must leave to fate."

It was true. Henry had spent most of his waking hours shoring up his support, hosting "impromptu" discussions and lavish lunches. He promised committee seats and research funding, and introductions to members of Parliament. And he shook so many hands, his palms started to itch.

It was masterful, really, and based on our preliminary count, we were fairly confident he would win the presidency.

There would be sixty-two voting members of the Society; Charles Lyell was still on expedition in Switzerland, and Leopold Duncan was consulting in Vienna. Henry had thirty votes verbally guaranteed, and we guessed at twenty-six promised to Buckland. That left six geomagicians of whose loyalties we were still uncertain.

Then Mantell and Goldsmild came to my office together one afternoon after returning to London. They'd seen my outburst at Kirtlington. They knew what I sought.

"We're with you, Mary," Goldsmild said, when we sat together on the couch. His eyes glittered, and his voice was thick with emotion. "And if you need us to vote for Stanton, we'll do that, too, if it helps your cause."

Mantell chuckled. "Besides, my wife would kill me if I voted against the first woman geomagician."

I embraced them both, overwhelmed with gratitude. That was two votes we'd assumed locked in for Buckland—but *I* had won them over.

Still, we couldn't spread word too widely, or we risked it getting back to Davies, who would do his own lobbying to counteract ours. Henry feared he might even decline to retire at all, if he learned of the plan to nominate me.

I tried to distract myself. I studied the crowd through the coach window, the harried women in aprons and bonnets, with babies or loaves of bread in their arms. Men with hats and coats and scowls. Hawkers with popping sausages and gloves and shoes. It looked like any normal day, at first glance. But on second, there was a sour tension in the air—in sidelong glances and sharply turned cheeks. And I lost count of how many wore the black armbands around their upper arms after I hit twenty-five.

Three constables in crisp, clean uniforms were pressing through the crowd. I couldn't hear the exchange over the sounds of the street, but I watched one of the officers shove an arm-banded man against the wall of the bakery. He spat in the constable's face, and one of the other lawmen threw a punch. Our coach rolled past, and I had to crane my neck as the tension burst into a brawl, shouts and shoving and other bodies rushing in to join.

The coachman must have seen, too, because the horses picked up their pace, and soon we were too far away to see.

I sat back in my seat, chewing my thumbnail. So much for distraction.

I counted and then recounted likely votes in my head. Henry and I hoped that the vote for my nomination would fall out along the same lines we expected for the presidency. But we couldn't swear by it. There was no way to campaign for votes without giving away the game.

Which meant Henry and I had no real sense of who would back me, and who would balk, once my name came up. We were going in blind.

I'd imagined my nomination to the Geomagical Society of London in a thousand different daydreams over the last fifteen years. But I'd had no idea what Palmanaeus House looked like, or how to picture the hall in which geomagicians gathered for their annual meetings. Sometimes I pictured it like a grand opera house; other times, like the cozy interior of the parish church. In some of these fantasies, I stood on a stage before the crowd, and in others, I was in the center of an arena.

But in every fantasy, I was there, standing in the room, basking in the applause as the geomagicians welcomed me into their ranks.

The reality was far different.

"Unfortunately, you won't be permitted inside the auditorium," Henry had explained when he snuck me into the wings.

Instead I stared into the swaying black curtains that separated me from the stage. I paced back and forth behind the folds of rippling velvet, my nerves so charged, I thought I might combust.

On the other side, President Davies was delivering an overly long, obnoxious speech.

"I am extremely proud of what we have accomplished during my tenure as president. My authorization to investigate the reports of the awakened pterodactyl has yielded unprecedented leaps and bounds in our scientific study."

I rolled my eyes at the loud applause that followed. Davies couldn't even bother to say my name. Would they clap that loudly for my nomination?

"And under my leadership, we invested Society resources in the Glasswater Mill, successfully developing the first manifold reliqs in history."

More applause. I couldn't help noticing that these accomplishments were due to the two men vying to replace him. Both far greater men than he would ever be.

The self-congratulating went on for a while longer, and then, finally, Davies announced his retirement from the presidency, and there was a thunderous round of applause that went on much too long.

Things moved quickly after that. The secretary cleared his throat and called for nominations for the next president of the Geomagical Society. Conybeare—I recognized his voice—nominated Buckland. And Thomas Reed stood for Henry.

More applause. On the other side of this damn curtain, Buckland would be walking up to the podium to accept the nomination and give a brief speech.

I couldn't stand it. I darted off the stage and ran, full speed, skirts raised, down the halls. There was no one to see me. They were all in the auditorium. I took the side stairs two at a time, then stood outside the back doors of the gallery, panting to catch my breath.

I opened the door with agonizing slowness; the last thing I needed was sixty heads looking back to see what that creak was.

"... the world is full of doubt," Buckland was saying. The gallery was empty, thank God, so I closed the door and pressed myself against the wall.

"So many now look around and see change on the horizon, and they fear, and they are led by fear to doubt. To question the goodness and promise of God. Doubt is at the root of all that we see churning around us now: the violence, and anger, and resentment.

"But in the face of an unknown future, we, the Geomagical Society of London"—his voice rang out, and even through my anger, I felt it stirring some noble urge in my chest—"we can unveil the past. And in looking to the past—to proof of God's promise, and His wisdom, and His miracles..." His eye caught mine and lingered for a heartbeat. I held my breath. Regret and admiration and love and anger spun through me. And then his gaze passed on.

"... I pray that we can offer hope."

He bowed his head and then returned to his seat amidst the applause. He didn't look up at me again.

Clearly, I was not well hidden here on the balcony. Henry clocked me as soon as he took the podium; I could tell by the twitch in his cheek.

My hands were a sweaty mess, no matter how many times I wiped them on my skirts.

"Hope," Henry said. He cast his knowing smile around the auditorium, the kind that always made my knees a little weak.

"Our friend Mr. Buckland calls for hope. And I do, too. But where Mr. Buckland finds hope in the past—in the old ways, and old beliefs—I would urge us, instead, to embrace the future. To find hope in what we can do—what *geomagic* can do.

"The age of machines is upon us, my friends. Of steam. But the world will need minerals, and metal. We can map them. We can find them. We can pull them free of the earth.

"The people clamor for reform. You've heard them. You see them, marching even now in the streets. And we have the answer. With the manifold reliqs of the Glasswater Mill, we can raise the standard of living tenfold—build clean, wholesome tenements in moments, and yield a thousand times the harvest. We can do that. We have *the future* in our hands, gentlemen."

He gripped the podium, knuckles white. "Mr. Buckland would pull us back to the past. Tie us to the old ways." Henry was being very careful not to say *the Church*. But the allusion was clear to anyone who understood the difference between the two men.

"I don't want to take us back to the past, like my colleague does. No. Rather, let this be the Age of the Geomagician."

The applause was deafening. Half the crowd leapt to their feet. I suspected even some of Buckland's allies had risen for Henry, but it was hard to tell from the back; they all looked the same in their top hats and coats.

Chapter 47

HENRY, IN THE END, WAS THE VICTOR.

The split was wider than we'd anticipated, even. Thirty-nine to twenty-three.

Buckland's shoulders slumped, though he quickly set them back and shook Henry's hand sportingly.

I hardly had time for it to sink in before Henry was reclaiming the podium, as president of the Geomagical Society of London. My heart started to race again as Henry thanked them for their confidence, and promised to lead well.

Then he smiled, and his gaze swept to mine.

"Now, before we proceed further, I have another order of business. Miss Anning? Would you join me on the stage?"

My stomach flipped. This hadn't been part of the plan. Henry told me to stay backstage and out of sight for the vote. But now everyone was turning to look. I didn't have much of a choice.

I ducked back the way I'd come and hurried down the stairs. I took a deep breath. And then I walked into the auditorium.

There was a central aisle with a red-and-gold carpet leading to the stage. I kept my head high as I walked through the whispers and craning necks toward Henry. This must be what it felt like to be a bride on her wedding day: the thrill and fear and the thundering of your heart with every step, walking into the future.

Henry met me at the stairs to the stage.

"Change of plan," he whispered as he offered a hand.

I carefully avoided looking at Buckland in his front-row seat. Former President Davies was looking around disapprovingly and muttering, and I saw others frowning, too. But there were also smiles among the crowd.

I could hardly hear over the rushing in my ears as Henry directed the flustered Society secretary to retrieve the bylaws from the archives with haste.

"But, sir, she isn't a member—technically, she shouldn't even be in the same room as—"

"Collect them quickly, please. Or I'll choose a secretary who will," Henry said quietly. The man scampered off through the wings.

"Gentlemen," Henry said, "before we proceed to other business, it is time we right a great wrong. You know Miss Anning. You know what she has done for this Society, and for our cause. Every tongue in England speaks of geomagic now, when they hardly knew the word before.

"Because of Mary, we have a living pterodactyl to study. My God! It is a miracle—and let us not forget how miraculous simply because you hear the beast's call echo through our halls every morning. Rather, let that remind us how miraculous it is, indeed, that we might be grateful anew each day."

He looked toward me, his eyes shining, and I nearly burst with pride.

"We are all of us, each one, in her debt, and I can think of only one way to repay that debt, and to honor her contributions to our field."

The secretary reappeared at the edge of the stage, black velvet rippling behind him.

Henry waved him forward, and the moment he was visible, it was like a wave rushed through the crowd.

"You can't. He can't, can he?"

"What are you doing, Stanton?"

"Well, I say she deserves it."

"But she's a *woman*!"

The secretary held out a long, thin box to Henry. Henry touched the lid, and its lock sprang open. A scroll unfurled like a long yellow tongue, down to his feet. *Bylaws of the Geomagical Society of London*, it read, in an elaborate filigreed script.

He cleared his throat, ignoring the shouts and calls from the crowd. "With the power vested in me as president of the Geomagical Society of London, I hereby amend section two of the bylaws of the Society. Henceforth, relating to qualifications for nomination and admission, let the amendment read: *An exception shall be made for the nomination of Mistress Mary Anning of Lyme Regis, in recognition of her exceptional contributions to the field of geomagical studies.*"

As he spoke, the words wrote themselves on the scroll in a matching elaborate flourish. And when he'd finished, he nodded, and the scroll rolled itself up and locked tight.

At least I finally understood why only the president—and the president alone—could amend the bylaws.

What followed was an uproar.

"Gentlemen, gentlemen, please," Henry said calmly, as the secretary tried to bang his gavel over the shouts.

"All I have done now is amend the bylaws. The decision

whether to admit Miss Anning remains in your hands. And hear this clearly now."

The crowd quieted as Henry's voice dropped, as if they didn't want to miss what he said next.

"If it is not the will of this body that Miss Anning be a geomagician, well, I will resign immediately, and your next chosen president can undo my actions. Now—"

"I nominate Mary Elizabeth Anning"—William Buckland was standing, his fist across his heart—"of Lyme Regis, for membership in the Geomagical Society of London, with all rights and privileges hereof."

―⁓⁓⁓―

There was no secret ballot. That meant I had to stand there, trembling hands clasped tightly behind my back, as the secretary took the roll. He called upon each geomagician in turn to cast his vote, and my fingers turned numb with the strength of my grip as he neared the end of the alphabet.

The vote would be close. Very close. Too close.

Conybeare voted against me. We'd expected that. Davies, too, by rights as an ordinary fellow, cast his vote with the *nay*s, his face mottled purple with fury.

I won Samuel Enys, James Gilbert, and Adam Harrelson, all Buckland loyalists, but I lost Thomas Reed and Anton Purser, who'd voted with Henry for the presidency.

Mantell and Goldsmild both offered generous words with their votes of *aye* that made me blush with gratitude.

"A genius the likes of whom we are lucky to walk among, and never will again, I think," Goldsmild said, which made my face so hot, I thought I'd faint.

But then Edward Phillips had to be removed from the auditorium when his name was called. He'd leapt onto his chair and tried to throw a cane at my head, shouting that I was a Jezebel, and probably a sorceress, too.

"She's bewitched you! She's bewitched you all, you fools, with her womanly ways!" he cried. I was a little offended, frankly; we'd once had a very nice conversation about glacial formations in the Alps.

"I'm terribly sorry about this," his friend Richard Browning mumbled, as he caught Phillips under the armpits and dragged him back to the doors, heels kicking. Browning had voted against me, but at least he hadn't thrown anything. The bar was getting low indeed.

"You let a woman in and you damn us all," Phillips screamed, as the doors banged shut.

Jonas Finch rose next, into the awkward silence. "For what it's worth, I don't think you're a Jezebel, Miss Anning," he said, twisting his hands. My heart sank. "But I don't think a woman is fit to be a geomagician, either. Nay." He sat quickly.

I'd started to worry by this point, and after a few more names were called, all *nay*s, I began to lose hope.

Any hope I had left withered in my hand when Matthew Turner shook his head. "Nay," he whispered. He couldn't look me in the eye.

And that was it. My tiny, quivering lead was gone. The tally now stood evenly at thirty to thirty.

There was no way I could win. Only two geomagicians had yet to vote: Augustus Ward and Thomas Whaley.

I suddenly regretted, with every inch and fiber and hair of my being, that I'd ever told Thomas Whaley that his bezoar was actually petrified feces.

I held my breath as Ward rose in his seat, his face tense. He was one of Henry's allies, but he didn't look at Henry now. He looked down at his palms instead. Not a good sign. Not a good sign at all.

It was almost funny, really.

Would it have changed, if they knew the truth? What if these men knew that two streets over, Henry Stanton's townhouse was filled with living, breathing, swimming Jurassic creatures, raised by my own hand?

Would the vote have fallen out differently? Or would more have cast their votes in my favor? Or would more have called me sorceress and summoned the Inquisitors?

The worst of it, I think, was that even without Ajax—without any magic or witchery at all—I *deserved* to join these men.

I was more than qualified. I'd read nearly every book on geomagic; I'd studied every paper published here and abroad. I knew all the discoveries, all the finds, all the players. Even if I'd never found Ajax, never reanimated a damn thing, I was qualified. And everyone here knew it.

But it wasn't enough. It still wasn't enough, because nothing would ever be.

I was a woman.

I felt a smile cracking, and had to work to wipe my face blank. It really was hilarious.

"I abstain," said Ward.

My first instinct was to look at Henry, and his was to look back at me. Our eyes met, a shared spark of hope.

But too brief. The secretary called on Mr. Thomas Whaley, and I closed my eyes, luxuriating in the black for a moment, imagining I could erase all of this. Wishing I could go back to the day in Lucy's cottage when I'd insisted on coming to London. When

I'd foolishly declared I could win them over, if only I had the chance.

Buckland had known. All those times he told me to be patient. To wait. To work slowly and thoughtfully. He'd known it would come to this—to a public humiliation. But I just had to push, didn't I? Well, now I was reaping the harvest of that pride, all right.

Whaley stood. His eyes were hard. "I don't think it's any secret that I don't particularly care for you, Miss Anning."

He stared straight at me, as if I were the only person in the room. I wanted to melt right into the stage.

"But you're a damn fine scholar, and fossil hunter, and theoretician. I vote aye."

The rest was a blur. Henry shook my hand, pumping my arm with delight, and then I was shaking other hands, grinning and laughing, and men were thumping me on the back, and each other, and even the ones who'd voted against me were smiling and offering congratulations—well, some did—because I was one of them now. I was a geomagician at last.

Buckland caught my eye, through the crowd, as he made for the back doors. He nodded, once, and I felt it all. All the years he'd taught me, helped me, fought with me. Cared for me.

I have to go to him, I thought, urgently, wildly, and I started to push through the crowd, craning my neck to try and catch his eye again.

But by the time I broke through, stumbling to the edge of the stage, Buckland was gone.

Chapter
48

THAT NIGHT, I LAY CURLED IN THE CROOK OF HENRY'S ARM as he snored. I'd had every intention of going back to my little room at the boardinghouse, with my stiff pink sheets and the dirty mirror, and I would, tomorrow. But tonight was a celebration, and I wanted to celebrate with the man I loved, rumors be damned.

The sheer canopy around the four-poster bed frame danced with the summer wind. We'd flung open the balcony doors to let the moonlight in, and the sounds of the crickets and owls came with it.

I was happy. The ache in my spine and the tension in my neck were gone. I felt like I could breathe freely, for the first time in a long time. This was what happy felt like.

By rights I should have drifted off hours ago, to wander blissfully through dreams.

Except every time I started to fall asleep, I thought of Lucy, and then I thought of Buckland. Or I thought of Buckland, and then of Lucy. Either order, either way, their faces appeared in my mind's eye and dashed away the cobwebs.

I slipped out of bed, studying Henry for a moment. His lashes were long and dark. His face was smooth in sleep, lips parted.

I kissed his eyebrow and then slipped on one of the dressing gowns we'd tossed on the floor earlier.

On the terrace, I crossed my arms on the rail and met the moon's coy smile over the hedges and black trees.

I *was* happy. I couldn't lie about that, not even to myself. I was a geomagician. Of course I was happy. But without my friends to share this, it was a lonely sort of happiness.

Henry was lovely. But he'd been absent from my life for fifteen years. It was Lucy and Buckland who were with me then. They had walked with me through failures, and celebrated my successes, and, in Lucy's case, listened to me talk about ichthyosaurs long after her genuine interest had waned.

In all those years, I'd never imagined I would find myself in Henry Stanton's bed after I was elected a geomagician. I'd imagined that after my election, Buckland would hug me, maybe lift me off my feet and spin me round like a child. I would laugh and act flustered, and he would grow serious, those bushy eyebrows merging, and say, *I'm so proud of you, Mary.* It was silly. Foolish, really.

But I knew what Lucy would do. Would've done. She would have squealed and squeezed me so tight I couldn't breathe, pinning my arms to my sides. *I knew you could. I knew it.*

A thick tear landed on my cheekbone and tracked down, falling like a raindrop onto the flagstone far below.

"You should talk to him," Henry said softly.

"Gah!" I jumped, batting his arm. "I thought you were asleep."

He caught my hand and spun me, so that my back pressed against his chest, and wrapped both our arms across my waist.

"Like I could sleep through all that dramatic sighing."

"I was doing nothing of the sort."

"Of course not." Henry chuckled and kissed the top of my ear, sending a pleasant shiver down my neck.

He turned me around and laced his hands with mine. "I mean it, though. You ought to talk to Buckland."

I laughed as I pressed the back of my hand to his forehead. "Are you ill? Shall I call for the physiomagician?"

Henry shrugged a little sheepishly. "Feuding seems a bit juvenile, now that I've won the presidency. You were elected. And he *did* nominate you. Maybe it's time for all of us to move on."

I responded with a noncommittal grunt.

"Well, you know best." He kissed my brow, and went back to the bed. I stared awhile longer at the moon, my pride and regret at war, and then climbed in beside Henry and fell asleep at last.

"What do you want? Father isn't here, if you're looking to scold him some more." Elizabeth Buckland stood in her doorway, arms folded and glaring.

"Oh—I'm sorry I bothered you, then."

My formal initiation was this afternoon at one o'clock; I would just have to try to find a private moment at Palmanaeus.

"Wait." Elizabeth exhaled as I started down the steps.

I turned, and yes, waited.

"I want to show you something."

Warily, I followed Elizabeth down the hall until she disappeared into Buckland's office.

I paused at the threshold. It felt too much like stepping into

Buckland's private sanctum. I hadn't been invited here. But Elizabeth gestured impatiently.

"Come on, then."

She navigated around the mess of papers and books to open the glass doors of a cabinet. But her face was a hard scowl.

"What is all this?" I asked, studying the rows of mounted trilobites and ammonites and belemnites, carefully labeled in Buckland's tiny script.

"We call this his Mary cabinet," Elizabeth said.

"His—what?"

She pulled open one of the drawers. It was filled with letters.

"Why ... these are ..."

"All from you. Yes. He saved every one, I think."

Elizabeth met my eye, and her glare was hard. I thought at first she must be showing me all this to try and help us reconcile—*See, he has loved you all along.* I traced my own handwriting, my heart aching. That was how it touched me, at least, and I wanted to run and find him right this second, and beg his forgiveness.

But Elizabeth's face was cold iron. "How could you? How could you do that to him?"

Ah. It wasn't an attempt at reunion. She wanted me to feel guilt. I closed the drawer with a bang. "Your father lied to me. If he lov—*cared*—for me so much, why would he do that?"

She scoffed. "Would you have backed him if he told you the truth? If he told you what he planned for the bylaws?"

"What plans?"

Her mouth fell open. "You must be joking." She laughed, a harsh grating sound. How on earth did Lucy stand it? "You don't even know what you've done."

"Then tell me."

"Father was going to amend the bylaws for—for all women."

She wouldn't meet my eyes, and I realized she was trying not to cry.

I stood very still, my hands hovering, and trembling.

If he had told me his true plan, I would have begged him to reconsider. If he'd changed the bylaws so drastically just before my own nomination? I would have lost. I had no doubt.

I was under no illusions. Probably half the men who'd voted for me did so because it *was* only me. One woman threatened little enough. With Henry's carefully tailored amendment, they weren't making some kind of statement about the intellectual capabilities of women—a statement they surely wouldn't support.

Very likely, I would have lost. And it would have been worth it, to Buckland; I would have been a sacrifice, for the future of his daughters.

For Elizabeth.

And I couldn't even say he was wrong. I would have wanted my own father to make that trade.

"If that's true, then . . ." I cleared my throat and licked my lips, but my mouth was still dry. "Then he was right not to tell me."

Elizabeth looked up sharply, her face slowly losing its sheen of anger. "Let me get you some tea."

I stared for a long time at the cabinet, trying to unknot the thick braid of sorrow and anger that hung around my neck, and thinking of Charlotte Murchison, and Marged Davies, and Ann Mantell. They had asked me to teach them, and I'd refused. It would hurt my reputation, I thought.

But I'd been jealous, too.

Because the shameful truth, a sick thing rotting in the pit of my stomach, was that I thought I was the only woman who deserved to be a geomagician. I had fought through tragedy and poverty and a lack of education to carve a name for myself in a field of men—and, yes—yes, *fine*, I had believed it made me worthier than other women.

I sat heavily on the couch and stared at the wall.

Now that I'd pulled the dark thing up and raised it to the light, I could see all of its slimy, stinking flaws. I wasn't any worthier. I was smart, and I had worked hard, but I was also *lucky*.

It was luck that I was born in Lyme Regis, where fossils were as common as stone. It was luck my father had learned and taught me to search for them. Luck that I'd survived the lightning strike, and luck that brought me to Buckland. Luck that brought me to Henry, who shared his books with me. Luck that I was the one who found Ajax, and the one who could wake him.

Or, not luck. *God Himself has blessed you*, my father told me, long ago. The gratitude welled, hot and fast, and I pressed my hands to my face, overcome with emotion.

"Mary?" Elizabeth frowned from the doorway. "Are you all right?"

I nodded, struggling to speak. Elizabeth came and sat next to me.

"I'm sorry," I said thickly. I shook my head. "All I ever wanted was to be a geomagician. All I cared about was getting in. About kicking down the damned door to the Society."

Elizabeth frowned.

"But I realize now that I've locked it shut behind me. And I swear to you, Elizabeth,"—I touched her hand, tentatively—"I will help pry it open again."

We drank our tea in an uneasy silence.

"Mary." Elizabeth said my name very softly.

"Hmm?"

Elizabeth fiddled with the handle of her cup. "Have you spoken with Lucy lately?"

I tried not to look guilty as I shook my head. No need to let Elizabeth know all that had happened between us.

Elizabeth had spoken lightly, and I might have attributed the fidgeting to her crush, but there was an almost fearful energy to her movements that felt more serious.

"Why do you ask?" I set my own cup down on its saucer.

"She came by, yesterday, while Father was at the Society," Elizabeth said. Her eyes darted to the doorway. "She wanted . . ."

I leaned forward, now anxious myself. "What is it, Elizabeth? What are you not saying?"

"I think she's planning something. Something dangerous. I don't want her to get hurt." Her eyes were huge, wet with tears. "Can you talk her out of it?"

"What is it she's planning?"

"I don't know. She wouldn't say. She said it would be dangerous for me to know. But she wanted me to search Father's study for some kind of . . . blueprints? Drawings, she said. She said . . . she kept saying she had to destroy it."

My heart stuttered, as I understood.

Lucy was going after the Loom.

Chapter 49

I couldn't let her do it. Not just for the sake of the mill, or Henry. But for Lucy's sake, too. There was no way she wouldn't be caught.

I chewed my nails as Henry's coach carried us to Palmanaeus. He caught my eye and looked up from the book in his lap.

"Nervous about initiation?"

I managed a weak smile.

"Don't worry," Henry said. "You read the bylaws and sign your name, promising to keep the Society's secrets, to protect its interests and work on behalf of the Crown, blah, blah. But overall, I think you'll find initiation to be an . . . interesting experience."

I nodded, distracted. I could tell Henry Lucy's plan. He would simply increase security at the mill. He would never trust Lucy again, but at least she wouldn't rot in a cell the rest of her life. And that was the best scenario.

Henry closed his book, resting it across his knee. "Come up to my office when it's over," he said. "I've been thinking." He tapped his fingers over the embossed title: *Geomagical Faults and Thrusts of England.* "And there's an experiment I'd like us to attempt. If you're amenable."

"Your office after initiation," I said. "Understood."

Worst case, Lucy would be shot or killed with one of the very manifold reliqs they were manufacturing at Glasswater.

And what if I told Henry, and he went straight to the home secretary? I could beg him not to. But what if he didn't listen? It wasn't hard to imagine his fury if he learned of her plans.

I couldn't risk it. I would have to convince Lucy myself.

"You're late." Conybeare sniffed.

"Sorry. The roads were crowded."

He sniffed again. "Those black-bands? Prometheans? Ah. I understand, then. Menace, all of them. Well. Come along."

I waved goodbye to Henry and hurried to follow Conybeare as he strode down the hall.

Conybeare was master of fellows, responsible for inducting and training any new members. My chest fluttered. New members like me.

"Is Buckland here?" I asked, trying to catch up. Conybeare was surprisingly quick for an old man. "I need to speak with him."

"After. Initiation is a private affair. Here we are, then." Conybeare stopped in front of a narrow, unmarked door just inside the library. I don't think I'd ever even noticed it before—or if I had, I'd just assumed it was storage.

Conybeare unlocked the door. I followed him. It was empty except for some kind of podium in the center of the room. Then Conybeare lit the reliq-lamp and shut the door behind us. The walls swallowed both light and sound; the lamp's light struggled to penetrate the darkness.

I could hear my own breathing, too loudly, and I had the unsettling sense that the room had expanded beyond these four walls, and was tempted to reach out and try to touch one, just to assure myself they were there.

Only, what if they weren't?

"Come, Geomagician," Conybeare said, and I gasped, as the sound seemed to come from deep in my ear, inside my skull. But I thrilled, too. *Geomagician.*

The struggling light lit his chin and little more as he took the box from the podium—I recognized it now as the bylaws—and tucked it under his arm. Still holding out the lantern, he walked away.

I was frozen. He should have hit the wall in two steps. But Conybeare was still walking, the swaying lantern light growing dimmer with every heartbeat. I broke out of my stupor and followed, nearly dizzy with excitement.

Henry made it sound like initiation would be a quick signing—maybe a certificate to hang on the wall. Something prosaic like that. A secret, endless tunnel was much more fun.

We walked through the eerie black. I'd thought the cave in Kirtlington was silent and dark, but in comparison, that was riotously full of sound and light. I couldn't even hear my own footsteps or the sound of my breath. The darkness gobbled everything except the tiny pinprick of light from Conybeare's lantern.

We didn't walk long. Two minutes, maybe three. It felt eternal.

I knew we were through—whatever this was—when I began to hear my own exhalations. Short, anxious breaths. And moments after that, Conybeare's lantern light bloomed like a slow sunrise, the glow spreading warmly as it should have all along.

We were standing in a winery's cellar. Or maybe a distillery's. Large wooden barrels lined the rough-hewn stone, and stacks of crates and porcelain amphoras leaned against the back wall.

Before us, in the center of the chamber, was a table laid with a white cloth.

"Is this her?"

The hair on my neck rose; the voice had come from behind me. Had he been in the tunnel, following behind us in the dark?

But there was no passageway when I turned to look. Only more of the same—stone and barrels, and the most handsome man I'd ever seen.

The man had golden-blond hair and a neat, close-cropped beard—unfashionable, but somehow incredibly becoming. His eyes were a piercing green, and his jaw was strong and sharp.

Conybeare smiled slowly at my expression, and my stomach dropped.

Conybeare had never liked me, but I'd never been afraid of him before. Even when he turned me in to the Inquisitors, I hadn't taken it personally. He was a grumpy, fusty old man who didn't care much for women.

But had he led me here to kill me?

He couldn't. Right? Henry would know—they would all know—I was due to be initiated; the finger would land right on Conybeare. Was that enough to stop him?

"Mr. Conybeare," I said, backing up until the lip of a barrel pressed into my hipbone, "please don't."

Conybeare huffed. "Always with the dramatics. Miss Anning, please meet Sir Oswald Burgess, Her Majesty's Chief Reliquemical Scientist."

"Pleasure to meet you at last, Miss Anning." Mr. Burgess held out a hand. The nails were scrubbed pink and clean, but yes—there was a shadow of black on the cuticles.

Silly, silly girl. This must be the initiation. Maybe I was about to learn the scientific formula for reliquary serum. That made much more sense—yes. To serve the Society and protect its secrets, Henry had said. And what secret could be greater than this?

I shook his hand with obvious glee.

He laughed. "After you, please." He gestured to the white-clothed table.

The first reliquemists were priests who left the Church when reliquary enchantment became a secular function, during the formation of the Church of England. Those eucharistic roots were on full display now, as Mr. Burgess solemnly slid off the top white cloth to reveal seven engraved pewter bowls.

I leaned forward in excitement. Oozing black bitumen in one, and glittering chips of silver in another. Blocks of something yellow—ah, beeswax! Oil, and then a saltlike powder. "Is that alum?"

Mr. Burgess nodded approvingly.

One of the pewter bowls was empty, and I couldn't tell what the last held. Some kind of brownish powder, a little like cinnamon. But I didn't smell cinnamon.

"And that one?"

The two men exchanged a look. They were afraid to say.

"That's not ground-up fossils, is it?" I asked sharply. "Because that would be a terrible waste of good fossils."

"Heavens, no," Conybeare said quickly.

"It's bone," Burgess said, almost as fast. "Unconsecrated."

They shared a look again as I absorbed this.

Not fossil, then, but the bones of the poor dead souls who were banned from the Church graveyards for any number of sins.

Ah. Well. Yes. I could see, very well, why the reliquary formula was a secret. Not just for proprietary purposes, then, but because there would probably be riots across the country if the truth were out.

From the tension in the two men, I imagined this was the part where some new geomagical initiates reacted rather negatively to the revelation that our magic—our whole world, really—was powered by the bones of the dead.

I had no such qualms. What did the dead care? They were dead.

"I see. And the last bowl?"

Burgess smiled, and Conybeare's eyes widened for a split second. With surprise? Relief? Distrust?

Burgess reached into his coat pocket and brought out a knife.

Really, I'd expected it, after the Loom. I nodded, before I could lose my nerve, and Burgess gave it to me handle first.

"It only needs a little. Just prick your fingertip." He shook his head, chuckling. "That last fellow slashed his whole palm. We had to throw out the tablecloths."

Blood was always so much redder than I expected. It welled and swelled on my fingertip, then burst from its own bubble and dripped into the pewter bowl, sliding down the wall to pool on the bottom.

I wasn't paying attention to Conybeare, but just as I started to stick my finger in my mouth, he caught my wrist.

"Sign first."

He'd unrolled the bylaws, all the way to the bottom. It was a list of names, in bright red ink.

"It will make a mess," I protested. The other names were neat, clearly written with quill. I wasn't going to add a bloody scrawl; that would be embarrassing.

"It won't."

I hesitated, but when Burgess nodded, I set my finger to the paper and began to write my name.

Conybeare hadn't been lying. My scrawl was a clean replication of my signature, just below Gideon Mantell's.

"Per Her Majesty's Charter of the Geomagical Society of London," Conybeare said, "you are bound and bonded, as Geomagician, to faithful service of the Crown and the Realm; Her secrets are yours to keep, and Her purpose yours to obey."

The sensation of something thick coated first the finger with which I'd signed, and then my hand, and then my whole arm, as if I'd dipped them into wax. The feeling faded after a moment, sinking into my skin. My heart pounded. These were powerful enchantments indeed. But it was done now. I was really and truly a geomagician.

Conybeare stepped back, and Burgess began scooping and chipping from the other ingredients, settling them into the bowl with my bit of blood. I tried to pay attention to the measurements.

But when Burgess finished, there were still chunks of beeswax and silver. It didn't look anything like the viscous, oozing serum I'd expected. It looked more like bread dough.

Conybeare drew a deep breath. He was nervous. There was something else, then. Another ingredient? Or heat, maybe?

"Now," Conybeare said. He wasn't looking at me. "There are words that must be said." His hands twitched at his sides. "Words to set the enchantment."

I didn't understand. Words? That didn't make any sense. What kind of—

There was a hitch between my ribs. A tug, pulling me toward understanding.

"Sorcery," I breathed.

Chapter 50

No, not breathed; I couldn't breathe. Could hardly think. I'd faced excommunication and execution once on the charge of Sorcery. I didn't wish to face it again.

"This is a trick." I backed up, shaking my head. I hit the barrels. "A trap. You didn't succeed before, so you're trying again. I won't. I am not a sorcerer. I am a faithful Christian."

"Of course you are," Burgess said. "And so are we."

I didn't understand. It had to be a trick. Except Conybeare had the bylaws. And Burgess had the hands of a reliquemist. None of this made sense.

"I know it's a lot to take in," Burgess said. "I felt similarly when I learned the truth. I'm sure Mr. Conybeare did as well."

Conybeare nodded. He'd lost that anxious look finally. There was a sadness, almost, in his eyes instead.

"It took the archbishop himself to convince me. Buckland and me. That was back at Society's founding, before we started bringing fellows here to see it for themselves."

If he was telling the truth—*if*—then I could understand why Conybeare was master of fellows. He was widely known as the most devout of the geomagicians. If he said it wasn't sinful—that it was, in fact, demanded, by the Church and Crown both ...

"But sorcery is forbidden," I said, still shaking my head. "It is evil. The Bible is clear!"

"It isn't evil," Burgess said. His green eyes were gentle. "But it can be used, too easily, in the service of evil."

"And that's exactly why the practice, and knowledge, is so carefully regulated. The truth is too dangerous."

"But the reliquemists know," I said slowly. "And geomagicians. Who else?" I asked.

"Some of the clergy. Not your average parish priest, mind. But the bishops."

"And Royal Academy of Science fellows," Conybeare added.

"Oh, yes. And Bank of England leadership."

"Some of the military, too. Generals and such."

"Parliament, I assume?" I asked.

"If it's relevant."

I was dizzy. All this time. All this time, this secret world of sorcery, of forbidden magic, hidden away—going on under our feet. No. Going on over our heads.

I had been friends with Lucy too long not to think of it like that. The elite—and men, almost all of them—casting their spells in the dark, probably laughing at all the rest of us.

Except I *was* one of them now. The elites. And I had vowed already to protect this secret, with my own blood. I didn't have to like it. I'm sure no one liked it—but what was the other option?

I could refuse. Demand to leave at once. But I certainly wouldn't be able to stay a geomagician. And what good would that even do? I couldn't tell anyone what I'd learned. I wasn't stupid. If I spilled this secret, my own lifeblood would follow. I wasn't going to destabilize all of England just to die for it.

And if you did decide to run, there isn't even a door. The realization chilled my veins. If I refused them now, this place could very well be my tomb.

I had been quiet a long time. Long enough that they knew I wasn't going to throw a fit.

"It's your blood," Burgess said. "You have to do the honors."

I trembled as he had me dip my right hand into the pewter bowl.

"*Od commemahe do pereje,*" Burgess spoke slowly, and I repeated the unfamiliar words in a thin, quavering voice. "*Salabarotza kynutzire.*" The scent of copper filled the air as I finished the spell, and the waxy sensation ran down my neck and spine.

The materials in the bowl swirled around my fingers, the solid pieces melting to liquid, and it was pleasantly warm. The smell was oily and acrid, gentled by beeswax. I pulled out my hand at Burgess's instruction. My fingers were coated from the knuckle down, the sticky black clinging to my nails.

Burgess noticed my staring and handed me one of the white cloths. "It takes many times to stain, I promise."

I scrubbed and scrubbed, until my fingers ached and turned pink under the black. But the sensation of the slick black tar lingered long after I was wiped clean.

I climbed the stairs to Henry's office in a daze.

Sorcery. Reliquemical serum was made with sorcery.

The very notion still made my thoughts stutter and freeze.

I'd been taught to fear sorcery practically from the cradle. Sorcery, according to my childhood lessons—and reinforced by every theomagical book I'd read in the years since—was sinful because it tapped the language of creation. Using sorcery was akin to using the breath of life itself, a theft, in essence, of God's own power.

Except Conybeare and Burgess said sorcery wasn't evil at all. *Dangerous,* they'd called it, but not evil. Not sinful. That was rather well supported by the fact that apparently Church and Crown both knew, and approved. And always had.

I thought, then, of Edgar Murray. When we were children, he'd been convinced there were secret magics. Some magic more powerful than reliqs. Magic that could have saved his mother.

We'd humored him, reading his books and listening to his theories. But he'd been right. There was another magic. Secret arts, indeed.

His father had been a peer. Had he known? Had he let it slip, somehow, and set the young Edgar searching for the secret?

I had to assume Edgar knew the truth now, as a member of Parliament. I could picture my old friend easily: the grin of triumph spreading across his face as he realized the truth he'd always sought.

But not Lucy. Something angry churned in my chest, a reflexive defense of my friend. There was no way she knew. Because if Lucy Murray knew that reliquemical serum was made with sorcery? It would be the golden sword she'd searched for all her life: a blade sharp enough to slice through the heart of the reliq system and destroy it forever.

How many of the common folk would use reliqs if they learned they were sorcery-forged? Some would shrug and accept it with ease. But many would recoil in horror at the very idea, anathema to their faith. And where would they go? Straight to the Prometheans.

I groaned aloud. Once again, I found myself caught between Lucy and the Society.

But I was almost to Henry's office now. At least I could talk to him. He knew the secret. He could help me sort through these complicated feelings. He'd probably point me toward some obscure literature on the subject of sorcery that would set my mind at ease.

I slowed as I neared the cracked door to his office, because there were voices coming from inside. I didn't want to interrupt; Henry had only just become president, after all. This could be important Society business. I leaned against the wall to wait.

"... Six more dead last night. Innocent buyers, just trying to conduct their business in the slicks." I couldn't place the voice, but it was vaguely familiar.

"The chaos cannot go on unchecked." That was Buckland.

"And it won't," said the voice I didn't know. "The home secretary has been very pleased with the batch you provided on a trial basis. Not to mention, he was rather persuaded by your ... er, demonstration during the attack on Parliament. How exactly did you do it, Stanton?"

"Well, I didn't truly mean to kill them," Henry said. "Only to make them stop. But the manifold reliq was more powerful than I'd expected. Apparently, it stopped their hearts altogether."

"Well, it was effective nonetheless."

I pressed my back to the wall, the wind suddenly knocked out of me.

I recognized the other voice now. Lord Knackbull. They were speaking of what had happened in Parliament, when Henry had thrown down his reliq.

Henry had killed those two men. With a manifold reliq.

I hadn't put it together before. Granted, I had just been shot.

And, later, I'd simply assumed the soldiers shot them. It was only when I heard Henry just now that I even remembered the flash of white in the moments after I was shot.

I moved as close to the cracked door as I dared and peered through. Henry was facing away from the door, but I'd been right: Lord Knackbull stood across from him, flanked by Buckland and Davies.

There were ways to kill with magic. With enough reliqs at hand, you could enchant something to become very heavy and watch it fall on your enemy's head, or launch a knife through the air. I admittedly hadn't spent much time thinking of ways to magically kill a person, but most any method would involve many, many reliqs.

And even with all the reliqs in the world, you couldn't simply will a man dead with magic.

Except, apparently, Henry's manifold reliqs made it possible—simple, even—to reach into a man's body and stop his heart.

He'd told me how powerful the manifold reliqs were. Again and again. Seventy times more powerful than a usual reliq. And after my healing, I finally understood what that meant in practice, rather than theory. But this revelation showed the other side of that power.

"...the Society normally provisions our fossil finds directly through the minister of finance for distribution to the Reliquemical Guild. But of course we would be glad to deal directly with the home secretary, given the current state of emergency," Henry was saying smoothly.

Buckland jumped in. "I can assure you, our only aim as a Geomagical Society is to quell the violence in our streets. These are troubled times in which we find ourselves."

Knackbull nodded. They all did.

"They are indeed. I think it's clear these damned Prometheans must be stopped. I, for one, would feel more confident in my little granddaughter's safety if more of these manifolds were at our disposal.

"Our initial trial supply was for twenty-three manifold reliqs, I do believe?"

"Correct," Henry said.

"And those have already been distributed. How many more can you have ready within the week, Stanton?"

Henry puffed his lips. "Unfortunately, the Glasswater Mill is limited at current capacity to the production of one manifold reliq per day. But," he added brightly, "with additional guaranteed funding, I can start the second Loom and double production. And within three months we will finish construction on two more Looms."

"I see," Knackbull said. "I will pass this to the home secretary at once. I can't speak for Peel, of course, but I know he is deeply concerned about the state of the city, and eager for solutions. I don't see that we'll have any problems authorizing the funds.

"Well, gentlemen, I must be getting back home. My knees begin to ache. But this has been a pleasure. And I look forward to continuing this partnership with the Geomagical Society. Perhaps some good will come out of all this mess, after all." Knackbull shook their hands in turn.

I pulled back from the crack in the door, pressing my body flat against the wall.

They were going to sell manifold reliqs to the government.

No—they already *had*. Twenty-three. Twenty-three manifold reliqs in the hands of the constables.

I shivered, my hand unconsciously going to my chest. Where one of those reliqs had healed what should have killed me.

Lucy. *Lucy.* I should tell Lucy. She needed to warn her people.

If the constables or military—even only twenty-three of them—were armed with manifold reliqs, there would be a bloodbath next time they came into conflict with the Promethean protestors.

My stomach twisted. To warn Lucy would be to betray the Society. If all went well, the Society would earn a tidy profit from this business.

A profit that would turn around to me in the form of a fellowship stipend, now that I was elected. I wasn't proud of the thought, but it was there nonetheless.

And—an uncomfortable thought crept in—what if the Society men were *right*?

Perhaps I couldn't trust my own judgment on the matter. My own thoughts were clouded by Lucy's involvement, and my trust in her. But Lucy was only one person, and the Promethean movement was much, much larger than her. And she herself was the one who explained that there were other movements, too. Other groups more radical than hers.

Knackbull said six people were killed last night while trying to do business in the slicks. I'd been unconscious for those first riots, but I could certainly feel the tension in the air now. People were afraid. Maybe it really would be best for the government to have the reliqs if it helped quell this rising violence.

Think. I had to think it through.

I realized, too slowly, that now their business was concluded, and the men would be coming for the door. I scrambled back, nearly running to Ajax's room.

Chapter 51

I never had any secrets before leaving Lyme Regis. Now I carried too many. The human brain wasn't meant to hold so many secrets. All my thoughts felt like wool on a spindle, spun and pulled and stretched almost to breaking.

I unlatched Ajax's cage. The pterodactyl clambered across my crossed legs cheerfully as I stared into the distance.

"What do I do?" I whispered, stroking his head. "What *should* I do, Ajax?"

"There you are. I was looking for you." Henry was in the doorway, hands in his pockets.

His smile slipped off. "Mary?" He rushed to me. "Darling, what happened?"

"You said there would be secrets," I said flatly. "I thought it was a joke."

"Ah. Initiation." He relaxed and tried to take my hand. I pulled it away. "I wanted to tell you the truth. But the bylaws bind you. You physically can't speak of it with anyone who isn't also bound."

I stroked Ajax's cheek. He leaned into my hand, hooting softly.

"I came to your office just now, like you wanted. I saw Lord Knackbull was there."

"Oh, yes," he said eagerly. "We've negotiated a sale of some of the manifold reliqs to the home secretary."

Henry wasn't even trying to hide it. He was pleased. Proud. And he thought I would be, too. He frowned, realizing that I wasn't.

"People are going to get hurt," I said. "Killed. People who just want something better. For themselves. For their families."

"Of course. Of course they do. And as long as they remain peaceful, no one's going to get hurt."

"But it's like you've handed the government a loaded rifle—of course they'll fire it," I countered.

Henry narrowed his eyes. "The manifold reliqs are just a backup measure, in case things get out of hand."

"With weapons like that, they *will* get out of hand."

"Come. You're sounding like Lucy."

"Good," I said fiercely.

He scoffed, and a lock of dark hair swung over his brow. He pushed it back mindlessly, just as he used to do as a boy. The gesture still made me ache. But everything felt wrong.

Henry exhaled. "I suppose I'm surprised. I thought you'd be happy."

"Happy? How could I be happy?"

He snorted. "You're the most calculating person I know, Mary; surely you can see the benefit for the Society. A contract with the home office means we can increase production on the other Looms immediately, with guaranteed buyers. It's a huge influx of capital, and a great boon to our reputation. The payout for fellows won't be bad, either." He smiled.

I winced to hear my own thoughts reflected back at me.

I could still feel the slick of the reliquemical serum on my hands. Between my fingers. Secrets. Secrets and lies and blasphemy, and all to serve—*what?* Ambition. Wealth. Renown.

I suppose it's too easy to forget the exact curve of your mouth, or the precise shade of your eyes, when you've gone awhile without a looking glass.

It's only when someone holds it up for you, says, *Here—here you are. This is how I see you,* that you see it clearly.

I swallowed and set my jaw. And then I lied to Henry.

"You're right, of course," I said, and wrapped myself in his arms.

I knew it might be the last time. I was fairly certain it would be. I inhaled the smell of him, drinking it in. I kissed him, trying to memorize the feel of his mouth.

Ajax screeched with jealousy and raced back over, trying to climb my shoulders. Henry and I broke apart, but I kissed him once more, ignoring the pterodactyl's angry cries, and wished I could see another way.

I'd become used to riding in coaches. I'd forgotten how to navigate a crowd.

"Watch where you're going."

"My apologies," I said, and ducked my head. The man—tattered shirt, sun-speckled skin, black-banded arm—spat at my feet.

The tension was even sharper here on the ground. It felt like the air before a storm, heavy and darkening.

There were black armbands nearly everywhere I looked. The ranks of the sympathetic had grown faster than I'd realized. Or maybe I hadn't been paying attention. I'd been so focused on my own fate, and the Society, maybe I just hadn't noticed. I picked up my pace.

I'd expected the crowd to thin as I traveled closer to Westminster, but it grew larger, new bodies joining from every alleyway, like streams feeding a river. The number of constables increased, too. They moved in packs of three or four, casting dark, wary glances around as they carved through the streets.

A sense of dread started to form in the back of my throat as I passed with the throng through a garden square, muddy boots trampling the flowers.

There were no children.

I stopped short, the river splitting around me as if I were a rock in the waterway, black-bands all around. Where were the children?

Someone pushed me. I stumbled, caught my footing, and let myself be carried along. Skirmishes broke out on the fringes. My heart fluttered in my throat.

This was bad. Very bad.

I felt as if I stood on the beach, watching a wave begin to form in the distance. The tight sense of dread as it began to gather, and grow, and rise.

The golden tips of Westminster broke above the rooftop gables, and I cut away from the crowd, forcing my way through, running full speed down the empty street toward Edgar's house.

I took the steps two at a time and rapped loudly on the door, then turned at the sound of laughter.

A group of young men ran down the street toward me, a streaming black banner raised aloft. One launched a rock from mid-stride. It smashed through a window three houses down.

A boy with a beaked nose stopped just before Edgar's house.

"I suggest you get inside, ma'am," he called up to me. "It's dangerous to be outside just now."

"Especially for magic-poachers like you," snarled his friend. The one who'd thrown the rock. The beak-nosed boy put an arm out.

"Leave her be," he said, and the rock-thrower scowled, but they ran on without another look my way.

The door opened, and I fell backward.

The butler frowned in disapproval. Edgar pushed past him.

"Mary." Edgar looked shocked as he offered me a hand. "I'm sorry; I was up on the rooftop watching. There's quite a crowd gathering. What are you doing here?"

"I'm looking for Lucy. Have you seen her?"

But of course she wasn't here. She would be in the thick of it. Exactly in the place that would be most at risk if the manifold reliqs were used.

Edgar shook his head. "No. I haven't seen her since—" He squinted at the sound of distant shouts. "Mary, I think you ought to come inside."

"I have to go," I shouted over my shoulder, already darting away. "I have to help Lucy."

Chapter 52

I HAD NEVER BEEN TO WAR, BUT I'D READ ACCOUNTS OF COMbat. The haze of smoke and fear, the sounds of pain and fury, the meeting of metal and flesh.

I could imagine it now, as I struggled toward the square. It wasn't war, but there were soldiers nonetheless, with their bayonets level, advancing on the crowd. This certainly *felt* like war.

"Clear the area immediately. Clear the area immediately. On order of Her Majesty, clear the area, or we will be forced to take defensive action." The voice was on repeat, reliq-enchanted to be heard for a mile square.

The black-bands were singing, trying to drown it out.

In the center of the crowd was a platform made of several stacked, overturned carts.

Lucy stood atop it.

Her gold hair was loose, wild around her shoulders. She'd enchanted her voice, too. I could hear her, clear and warm, over the song and the orders both.

A row of constables and red-coated soldiers eyed the crowd

warily, as if they expected violence at any moment. But Lucy ignored them.

"They are few," she was saying, her eyes sweeping the crowd, "but we are many. The only power they have over us is what power we give them. Revoke that power. Reclaim it. It is yours. Your magic is *yours*, my friends!" She threw up her arms, and I could see the power of her conviction spreading, moving through the crowd. Heads nodding. Arms rising. I felt it stirring, even in my own chest, against my fear.

"They will say that we have nothing with which to bargain. But I tell you, you have *everything*. Do not let—hey! Hey! Leave her alone!"

A fight had broken out in front of Lucy's makeshift stage. A man in a tattered black coat grabbed a bayonet. Shouts rose. I was shoved from behind as the crowd surged forward. A gunshot went off, like a crack of thunder, and then the world exploded.

The earth bucked, the very ground under our feet rolling like a ship at sea. The rumbling roar that followed was guttural and terrible, and I thought of titans and gods, risen from Hades, and then the building on the far side of the square simply collapsed, like an old man whose knees have given out. It crumbled in a way I hadn't known buildings could, and a fog of dust swallowed us all, and everything was screams, and limbs, and blood.

I crawled over the wounded. They moaned and reached, tearing at my sleeves. They cried, and bled, and I prayed for them, I did. But I had to reach Lucy.

One of the red-coated officers stood stricken, face blank with shock.

I shook him by the shoulders. "Those manifold reliqs. I know you have them. Use them. They can heal."

He only stared. He had a long cut under his cheekbone, a waterfall of blood.

I slapped him on the other side. He blinked, startled, and focused.

"Heal them," I commanded, and waded on. The dust was clearing, and in its wake was horror—but also people cautiously rising to their feet, and then kneeling to wrap tourniquets and stanch wounds. I pressed on to Lucy.

She had tumbled between two of the carts, her leg caught in a wheel-spoke, her foot turned wrong.

Her body was limp and loose, blood-soaked strands of hair across closed lids.

I was too late.

"Lucy! Oh, God. No." I brushed the hair from her brow, and cradled her head. Tears streamed down my face, falling onto her matted-red hair. "*No, no, no, no, no.*"

Her lids fluttered. I gasped and shouted for help.

The officer helped me turn the cart. An old woman with silver braids worked Lucy's leg free. A thin man with tattered shoes tore his sleeve and wrapped it around her head. It soaked through at once.

"The manifold reliq," I demanded to the officer. "You can heal her."

He shook his head. "It's empty. I managed six or seven of the most grievously wounded, but ..." He gestured helplessly at the scores of the wounded around us. "I'm sorry."

"No," I said, gritting my teeth. "You did the right thing. Here. Help me carry her."

The man cradled Lucy in his arms, her head falling against his chest.

I didn't bother knocking this time. I kicked the damn door in, shouting.

Edgar raced down the stairs, freezing when he saw his sister in the officer's arms.

"She needs help." I burst into tears again.

I paced so long outside Lucy's room, I think I wore a pattern into the tile. I had no real idea what was going on outside this house; for all I knew, there could be more collapsed buildings and violence across the city. But I couldn't worry about any of that until I knew Lucy was safe.

"Mary?"

I spun at Edgar's voice. My shoulders unknotted. He was smiling.

"She's all right. She's awake."

I shoved past him into the bedroom. Lucy was still in her bloodied, dusty clothes. There was a neater, clean bandage on her head, but her hair was still matted red. She was the most beautiful sight I'd ever seen.

I sat in the chair by her bed and took her hand.

"Oh, Luce. I thought you were dead," I whispered.

"Well, now you know how it feels," she said drolly.

Edgar chuckled, folding his arms. "You know, I never had to play nursemaid so often before you two came to town."

"I don't even know what happened," Lucy said. "One minute I was talking, and then I think there was an argument, and the next . . ." She frowned.

"It was a manifold reliq. They used it like—like a cannonball, almost."

I looked at Edgar. He needed to know this, too. He could help.

"The Geomagical Society sold a trial batch to the home secretary's office, for the military to use against the black-bands. They plan to sell more. You have to stop it, Edgar. It isn't right. That kind of power . . . it's too dangerous."

Edgar was frowning. "You know this for certain?"

"Henry confirmed it," I said, and his frown deepened. "He thought I'd be pleased."

Lucy squeezed my hand and looked sharply at her brother. "You see? I told you. Nothing good can come of that cursed Loom. Nothing good at all."

Edgar exhaled, running a hand through his hair. "I am not too proud to admit you may be right."

"Tell us what happened, Mary," Lucy said. She tried to sit up a bit more, then winced in pain and settled back.

"Well, this morning I was initiated as a Society member, and I learned—"

I choked. Henry hadn't been lying. I was bound. Lucy's eyes were wide with alarm.

"I can't tell you," I croaked. "I'm forbidden. But let's just say, I learned how much they keep from us." I was surprised at the fury in my voice. "The powerful, I mean. The secrets that they hold. Isn't that right, Edgar?"

He nodded slowly. "It's true."

We were silent, Lucy looking between us, as if she might be able to read the truth there.

"So, following initiation," Edgar said, after a long moment, "you went to speak with Henry?"

I nodded. "That's when I overheard about the manifold reliqs being sold to the government. When Henry explained, I made him think I supported the plan. But . . ." I felt cold, remembering the way the earth had exploded underfoot.

"But?" Lucy asked softly.

I gripped her hands. It was time. There would be no going back after this. Not to the Society. Maybe not to Henry. My heart thumped against my chest, sorrow at odds with my conviction. But this was right. I was sure of it.

I leaned forward.

"I want to help you, Luce. I want to help you stop the Loom."

A long silence followed. Lucy studied my face. "You're sure?"

"After what happened today . . . the damage those manifold reliqs can do . . . yes, I'm sure." I exhaled, then quickly added, "Now, before you get any ideas, I'm not going to help you sabotage the machinery or anything like that. Not that you were planning such a thing."

Edgar raised a brow as Lucy flushed.

"But I'll help you campaign against it. Or try to persuade Henry to close it down himself. Or, Edgar, you helped finance the thing in the first place, right? What if you pull your funding?"

He shook his head. "I was an early investor, it's true, but there are plenty others now, and many more eager to take my place if I backed out."

"Then we'll do something else. We will figure it out," I said. "But I want to help. However I can."

"And what about Henry?" Lucy asked. "If he doesn't come around?"

"I don't know," I said miserably. "But there's something else I need to tell you, too. About Henry." I swallowed. "About me."

"You can tell us anything, Mary," Edgar said, with a steadying hand on my shoulder.

And I did. I told the Murrays the truth about Ajax. About the other reanimations. The tanks of ancient creatures currently at Henry's house. I even shared Henry's theory of magic, that I was some kind of witch with a special affinity for fossils. About Buckland's flood-hibernation theory. About how it was all a lie.

Lucy's eyes went wider and wider, her lips tighter and tighter as I continued.

"I . . . see," she said, once I finished.

Edgar watched me intently; I could practically see the wheels turning in his mind. "Who else knows about this resurrection power?"

I shook my head. "No one but Henry. Which is why, well . . ."

"Right." Edgar nodded. "If we try to stop his operations at Glasswater—"

"—and Henry decides to fight back—" Lucy continued.

"Then he can simply hand me over to the Inquisitors, with all the proof to damn me," I said, only to be met with a dreadfully discouraging silence.

※

I was still worrying at the problem when Edgar reappeared with tea, insisting it would help to keep our spirits up as we strategized.

Would Henry really turn me in to the Inquisitors? He claimed to love me. But he'd claimed the same before, and had chosen ambition nonetheless. I needed to be realistic, even if it hurt: I had to assume he might do the same again if we challenged his Loom.

Edgar brought the tray to the bed and laid it over Lucy's lap, fussing with the teapot.

"I'm not an invalid," she said, shooing him away. "I can pour it myself."

Edgar took his cup and saucer and walked to the bay window. "It looks like things have calmed down out there," he said, peering onto the street below.

I drank my own tea gladly, the heat coating my throat and settling my nerves.

Edgar sighed, still looking out the window. "It's really a shame our Henry is such a damned liar."

I snorted, but Edgar continued. "Only two days ago, he insisted you weren't yet ready."

"Mary?" Lucy's voice was thin, and her hand trembled on the quilt.

"Edgar, come quickly, she's gone ice cold," I said, and gasped as I caught her fingers.

Edgar didn't turn; he was a dark silhouette against the sunlit glass. "You weren't ready to accept your powers, Henry said. You needed more time. We had to be patient. The experiment would have to wait until you were ready to see the truth. To embrace it."

Nothing he said was making sense, and Lucy's lashes were fluttering shut. Her hand went limp in mine.

"I mean it, Edgar, Lucy needs help," I tried to say, but the words came out slurred.

Edgar finally turned and cocked his head. "But all this time, you already knew you were a witch. Because he'd told you! Even resurrecting things in secret." He chuckled. "The absolute gall."

I was slipping. Fighting against the weight of my eyelids.

My head flopped against the chairback, the muscles in my neck gone slack.

Edgar strode over, his voice gentle. "Don't fight it, Mary. It's going to be okay. It's just a sedative." He patted my cheek. "I'll see you on the other side."

Chapter 53

If only I'd come awake slowly, I could have taken in my surroundings. Maybe prepared some kind of plan, or tactic.

But instead, I woke with a gasp, swallowing air so loudly that Edgar noticed at once. I took stock of my surroundings as Edgar came closer. Lucy was beside me, propped against the same cool stone wall. Her chin slumped to her chest, but she was breathing steadily, and her lashes fluttered.

"Lucy," I said, and bumped her shoulder with mine. "Luce, wake up, wake up, wake *up*."

We were somewhere . . . large. A cavernous space with smooth gray walls.

I heard a familiar squawk and strained my neck; Ajax's aviary was set on the floor, close to where Edgar had been standing.

And there was—*oh*—there was a Loom in the center. Only this one didn't have a glass bell jar at its heart. The seven arms of the Loom fed into a vat of the black-tar serum, and lying in the vat were bones. Enormous bones. *Humongous* bones. The fossilized skeleton of a creature so large, my brain struggled to make sense of the scale. The thigh bone alone had to be nearly three feet long.

"Megalosaurus," I breathed, a shiver down my spine. The great lizard-creature Buckland hypothesized in 1824 based only upon the sawlike teeth. But Buckland never found a complete skeleton. Not like this one.

Edgar crouched before me. "Incredible, isn't it?" he said, as if we were having a nice chat in the library, and he hadn't drugged and kidnapped me. "Henry built the mill around the monster."

At least I knew where we were now.

Edgar offered me a hand. I didn't take it, though I wobbled a bit as I stood.

"I know you're scared, Mary, and confused," he said. "But please, just give me a chance to explain."

But I wasn't listening. Because I'd noticed that the pods around this Loom weren't empty.

Seven people were propped in the pods, bobbing naked in the serum. Some of their eyes were closed, but others displayed wide and vacant gazes.

I recognized one: the old woman from my last visit to the Glasswater Mill. There was also a young man with pale-yellow hair, and a middle-aged woman with a port-wine stain across her shoulder. A dark-skinned man with black curls; a skinny girl, hardly twenty. A man with deep lines on his brow, and two old men. Brothers, I thought. They shared the same nose.

"Are they—" I couldn't finish.

"Not dead. Only drugged. They all consented, I swear," Edgar said quickly, as if that would change things.

There were a thousand questions I wanted to ask. I started with the one that seemed most pressing.

"And what of us? Are you planning to kill us?" I tried to sound brave. Defiant, even. But the words came out thin and wavering.

"What? Of course not!" Edgar scoffed. "But I knew you would never come willingly, and I needed everyone together so I could explain everything, and—"

"WHERE IS SHE?"

The door burst open.

"*Henry*," I choked, as he swept across the room, his gray eyes a wild storm as he crushed me against his chest.

"Mary," he exhaled, breathing shakily, his face buried in my hair. Then he pulled back, holding my elbows. "Are you all right?"

I nodded, and he cupped my cheek, searching my face.

Then Henry turned to Edgar, his brow knotted in fury. "And *you*. What were you thinking? This was *not* what we agreed."

I caught my breath, and my wits, and wrenched free of Henry's arms. I remembered, suddenly, what Edgar said about Henry before the tea took effect. *You weren't ready to accept your powers, Henry said.* The two were partners in this, whatever it was.

I thought I'd been prepared for Henry's inevitable betrayal. But apparently not, because I felt now as if I'd been shot once again in the heart, the pain was so deep and fierce.

"Don't touch me," I snarled, and Henry stepped back in shock. "What do you mean, 'this was not what we agreed'? To what exactly *did* you agree?"

"Mary, please," Henry said, his face anguished. "Let us explain."

I was tempted to declare that no explanation would help their cause or dull my fury. But in truth, I *did* want an explanation.

"Fine," I said, glaring at them both. "Then explain."

Edgar and Henry exchanged a glance.

"I suppose we ought to start at the beginning," Edgar said. "Because it begins with you, Mary. You, and my mother."

Chapter 54

Edgar Murray watched his mother die.

"I was there, when she slipped away at last," Edgar said now, and still-fresh pain flashed over his face. "It was a mercy, really. The tumor had hollowed her. Devoured her from the inside out.

"And my father—he sighed as he rose from her bedside, and said, 'Now we can only pray that your sister proves stronger than her mother.'

"That was the first time I wished I was the witch, and not Lucy," Edgar said, shaking his head. "Of course, it was because I wished to protect her—to save her from what I knew was to come. What did come, after. The cruelty at our father's hands.

"But I suspect it was the first time I really understood that magic was *power*. My father was a powerful man, in every way that counts. Land, money, influence. Guns, and swords, men at his beck and call, and a backhand like a shovel. And he was terrified—petrified—of his ten-year-old daughter."

"And what does that have to do with me?"

Henry picked up the thread. "Well, after you reanimated the trilobite, I told Edgar about it. I didn't know what to do. I was afraid it was some kind of black sorcery. And Edgar was always reading those books about magic...." He shrugged.

After the trilobite. That was when Henry had pulled away from me. I'd always attributed that awkward period to the new, emerging desire between us. But apparently, he and Edgar had been scheming together, even then.

"I knew it wasn't sorcery," Edgar said. "I'd been studying theories of magic for years at that point. But it took Henry and me the whole rest of summer to work it out."

"Work out what, exactly?" I managed to choke.

"We knew you weren't a witch like Lucy, at least. You were like my mother."

I caught my breath, my gaze darting to Lucy, but she was still asleep.

"My mother wasn't always a witch, you know. It came on her late in life. There was a great hailstorm. It tore the roof off the manor's south wing. The roof was long repaired by the time I was born, but I remember the servants talking about how wild a storm it was." Edgar shook his head. "I wonder how long she managed to hide her powers, after that."

My mouth fell open as I spun to Henry. "But this is your theory, isn't it? About how witchery begins."

"My theory," Edgar interjected. "Mother could grow an oak from an acorn in half a day. But why couldn't she mend our clothes, or warm the tea as Lucy could? Why *couldn't* she save herself, once the illness began?"

His voice cracked, but he cleared his throat. "For purposes of taxonomy, we might say flora-witch now, but back then, Henry and I thought of her as a green-witch. I'm still fond of the title. Mother would have liked it."

I refused to be distracted by his grief. I crossed my arms. "I'm very sorry about your mother, Edgar, but what does any of that have to do with—" I gestured at the Loom.

"You're right," he said. "I'll get on with it. Henry and I didn't know, back then, how it all fit together. You had a gift, and my mother had a gift, and we knew there was a connection."

He laughed. "At first we actually thought it must be weather, in particular, that bestowed witchery powers. Yours from the lightning, my mother's from the hailstorm. Henry's map eventually disproved that hypothesis. You've seen the map, I assume?"

I remembered thinking Henry must have been working on it for years. Apparently I had no idea how accurate that was.

"Eventually, of course, we realized witchery could be caused by any number of natural disasters, but that was our starting theory."

I looked between the two of them, boys I'd loved and men I felt like I didn't know at all. "But—but why did you even care? Why does it even matter?"

Edgar cocked his head, like he couldn't understand my question. "I told you, Mary. All we want is a better world. The same thing Lucy wants. Isn't that what you want, too?"

I almost laughed. A better world? Elizabeth Buckland's criticism from Kirtlington rang in my ears.

Now I understood. Henry, and Lucy, and Edgar had loved me. All three assumed I must be serving some higher purpose—freedom, or change, or truth, or even pure knowledge.

But it was Elizabeth Buckland who, in her jealousy, had seen me best of all. *And what have you gained for others?*

Nothing. That was the answer. Everything I'd done, I had done for Mary Anning.

"Don't you understand? We want to give power to the powerless," Henry was saying. His voice had a desperate, pleading edge. *He does love me*, I thought, and hated that it mattered. At least that hadn't been a lie. Maybe I wished it had been.

"We poured all of our resources into the mill," Edgar said, looking at the ceiling. "We were so sure that the manifold reliqs would be the key to everything. But they weren't enough. Even the largest couldn't provide enough magic for our purposes. We were stuck."

"And then Buckland got your letter," Henry said hoarsely. "I began this work because of you, Mary. And then—all these years later—there you were again. It was like a sign from God."

His eyes were dark and pleading, and Edgar nodded sadly, and I wanted to launch myself at them both, shrieking and scratching. I'd like to claw Henry's damnable, beautiful eyes right out.

But I couldn't launch myself at him like an angry cat. I could only stare.

"And with a pterodactyl on your shoulder." Henry laughed, and I ached. "The moment I saw Ajax, I *knew*."

I caught my breath. "What does Ajax have to do with any of this?"

"Henry and I never understood how witches like you or Mother *worked*," Edgar said. "Why did you need reliqs for some things, and not for others?"

"Ajax was the answer," Henry said. "Because *he's* a reliquary, Mary. Everything you resurrect becomes a reliq. And you draw from those reliqs when you use your power. That's . . . I'm so sorry, darling . . . that's why so many of them died."

"No. No." I shook my head. Shook it again. "No. That doesn't make sense. Living things can't be reliqs. That's impossible." I shook my head wildly now, as if I could shake out the fear that they might be telling the truth.

"Yes, they can," Edgar said gently. "Even Lucy, and witches like her. We believe that she uses herself as a reliq, storing and drawing on her own life force—her spirit, maybe—to work her magic. She never needs a reliq, because she *is* one. Others, like you, with an affinity, turn things into reliqs when they work them. Water, or earth, or plants, or metal, or thread, or, yes, living creatures."

My chest hitched with dread. What he described sounded awfully, dangerously, like the old witch stories of vampyrism.

"I had a theory," Henry said quietly, "that your living reliqs were more powerful than others. Because they function like Lucy; they're not simply storing life force. They're generating it, too. Multiplying it.

"Well, I tested the theory. I brought one of your reanimated little sea snails here, and put it in the Loom. I ran the procedure and—" Henry blew out, lips puffing, eyes wide. "Mary, it was powerful enough to flatten a county."

Edgar nodded eagerly. "Not just seventy times more powerful. The living manifold reliq's was more like *seven thousand* times the standard. Just holding the thing, I felt like a god."

His gaze drifted past my shoulder to settle on the wires and tubes and bubbling black of the Loom, the dark bones at its center, and I shivered, gooseflesh rising on my arms as I understood.

They wanted to make that monster a manifold reliq.

The experiment. I whirled to Henry. "Is this what you wanted to discuss after initiation? Turning that creature into a living manifold reliq?"

Henry nodded slowly, but he was looking past me to Edgar.

"But *why?*" I pressed. "What do you want to *do* with it? With that kind of power . . ."

"The bones aren't the true experiment." Edgar smiled softly. "I am."

Chapter 55

"WHAT DO YOU MEAN, *YOU*?"

Edgar's lips twitched. "Isn't it obvious? I plan to become a witch."

I stared.

"Thanks to Henry's research, we have strong evidence to support our hypothesis," Edgar said briskly, "that witchery is a by-product of natural phenomena. But we've never been able to test it properly."

"You want to use that," I said slowly, nodding toward the megalosaurus skeleton, "to, what? Create a natural disaster?"

"Exactly," Henry said. "Ed and I believe we will finally be able to generate a sufficient power with a living manifold reliq."

"To what—birth a volcano? Trigger a tsunami?" I scoffed.

Henry smirked. "We thought we'd start smaller. With a classic."

"A good old-fashioned lightning strike," Edgar said. He cleared his throat. "Lucy, dear, I know you're awake. How much did you hear?"

I yelped in surprise as Lucy flinched.

She sighed and straightened. "Most of it, I think. You were talking about Mother when I woke."

Edgar drawled, "Oh, don't bother with magic. I'm sure you've already realized the sedative numbs your power. Just a precaution."

Henry's eyebrows shot up, but I don't think Edgar noticed.

Lucy stood, and we clung to each other, squeezing tightly. Her hair was still matted and red around the bandage, but she was breathing steadily, and her eyes were alert.

"The boys have gone mad," I whispered.

"I can hear you, you know," Edgar said crossly. "You're a very loud whisperer, Mary. And mad or not, I very much hope you'll both join my cause, once you understand what's at stake."

"You drugged us!" I said indignantly. "Why would we ever help you?"

"Because when this works, and the world is remade, we're going to need to be united. That's why I wanted the four of us to be all together."

"Ed," Henry began slowly, "wait. What exactly are you saying?"

"I'm saying that a window of opportunity has been opened, my friend. Thanks to Lucy, and her Prometheans. But also thanks to you and your Society. There are manifold reliqs in play now, and the Prometheans are ready to strike. London is destabilized. Teetering on the edge of chaos. We can't miss the window."

Henry inched closer to me, his hand fumbling for mine. Despite my anger, I clasped it, even as dread swelled in my chest.

"I suppose I am saying"—Edgar pursed his lips—"that the plan has changed."

"Mary," Henry said slowly, pressing a thumb into my palm. "*Run*."

But I was too slow. We all were.

Henry barreled toward Edgar, who sighed and muttered something that sounded like, "*Alalare lusdi.*"

My feet were suddenly leaden, so heavy I couldn't lift a toe. I cried out, flailing and nearly pitching forward.

"*Sorcery,*" I breathed. It was a stupid thing to say, but I said it nonetheless.

Henry shouted in fury as Edgar dodged his straining arms.

"Really, Henry, you're overreacting." Edgar *tsk*ed. "If I want to change things—*really* change things, forever, for good—this is the only way. This is how I make reliqs irrelevant. How I render the slicks unnecessary. Give power to the powerless. You do see that, don't you? Luce? Surely you, at least, can understand."

"I . . ." Lucy wouldn't meet my eye. "How would you do it?" Her voice was a whisper.

"Lucy, no!" I gasped. "You can't possibly support this madness!"

"Earthquake," Edgar said eagerly. "I've done the analysis. Earthquakes have the highest witch conversion rate with the lowest casualties."

I laughed. I didn't know what else to do. All of this was so surreal, so absurd. "What's that? Hundreds? *Thousands?*"

"Stop this, Ed," Henry said sharply. "You've gone too far already. This isn't what we planned!"

"You're right. This is what *I* planned." Edgar's eyes were hard as he wagged a finger. "You are a competent scholar and a fine industrialist, but we both know you've never been a visionary. Too easily distracted." He looked pointedly at me.

"You bastard," Henry spat. Every trace of his usual control had vanished, and his face was raw with pain. "Do you know what they say about you, Ed? Awkward. Arrogant. Odd. It's only his father's money and title that bought his career, they whisper. And every time, I came to your defense. *He's brilliant,* I've always said. *You just don't understand.*" Henry gave a choking laugh.

"I didn't need your pity," Edgar snarled, then collected himself, drawing up straight. "And as much as I truly want your support, Henry—yours, too, dear sister—the only one I really *need* is Mary. So, Mary? What do you say?" He held out a hand.

"Don't. Don't *touch* me." My lip curled back. I squared my shoulders. Now was the time to be brave. To be the woman my friends had always imagined me to be, and not the one I was. "I'll never help you raise that beast. You'll have to kill me first."

Edgar sighed. He looked over his shoulder. "I was afraid you'd say that. Mr. Farnsworth? Can you bring in our other guests, please?"

The door opened, and the old man shuffled inside, pushing a bound and gagged pair before him. *Buckland and Elizabeth.*

"I sent word that you were in dire need," Edgar said. "And, nobly but predictably, your friends rushed to your aid."

"Oh, God—Farnsworth, you're better than this," Henry called urgently. "Let them go."

Farnsworth ignored him. He pushed William Buckland to his knees before us. Buckland's eyes were wide with terror, or perhaps fury. But Elizabeth Buckland wept openly, the sound muffled by the strip of cloth between her teeth.

"*Elizabeth.*" Lucy's voice was raw. "Edgar—please. Please, no. Let them go."

"That's up to Mary now," Edgar said solemnly, as he loosened Buckland's gag.

"Don't do it," Buckland gasped, when the gag fell around his neck. "Mary, you can't."

Edgar unsheathed a knife, his face grim, and held it under Buckland's throat—close, but not so close that Buckland could reach it if he decided to be a martyr.

Horror thrummed through my veins, rushing to my heart. My ribs felt too tight.

"You wouldn't," I breathed.

"I would," Edgar said.

My teeth chattered and clacked. Edgar was a good man—or he had been, once. Would it be enough? Could I risk Buckland's life on it?

"It's up to you, Mary," Edgar said softly. "You know your part."

I swallowed. I could try to play along. Maybe then I could at least stall for time; try to give Lucy and Henry a chance to come up with a plan.

"Look, even if I wanted to help you, I can't resurrect something so large," I said quickly. "I tried to resurrect an ichthyosaur, and that failed miserably."

"Ah," Edgar said. "Except that would have been at Henry's house, isn't that right? And Ajax would have been at Palmanaeus."

Edgar nodded toward Mr. Farnsworth, who picked up Ajax's cage and brought it to me.

"If my theory is correct, then you don't have to be touching your living reliqs to use them. But you have to be close. You'll need to be near Ajax, in particular, for large workings. See, when you resurrected him, you made Ajax—"

"Oh. He's a familiar," Lucy whispered.

―──∽◉∽──―

I wish I could be certain that the flutter under my breastbone was dread. I wish I were sure that it was terror, and horror, and not some thin measure of excitement, as I walked toward the megalosaurus with Edgar at my heels.

Edgar flipped a switch along the control panel, and the steam engine began to turn with a whir.

"Now we begin," Edgar said. Serum bubbled and roiled around the gray bones.

Whatever I was going to do, I had to do it *now*. Only, now that the moment had come, I couldn't think of anything. I'd planned to distract Edgar, somehow. Maybe give Lucy time to do ... something. But now my mind cleared of everything but marvel and awe at the megalosaurus.

Its long jaw—the size of my leg; its teeth—as long as my finger; its legs—like tree trunks. Its skull, the great hollow holes like enormous black eyes. It would have been a carnivore.

A predator. A monster.

The kind of beast the others fled, whose every step shook the earth. I thought of the power in those limbs, the sheer strength in that jaw, hunting, tearing, ripping. I could see it, roving the fern-covered hills, trampling bracken under its three-toed feet. I could—

Edgar grasped my wrist and slammed it onto the skull of the megalosaurus. I gasped. Ajax screeched.

I understood now what I was doing, as I reached for the pterodactyl instinctively and drew magic from him in spirals of warm gold. I didn't mean to.

The wheel-like gear, suspended in parallel above the serum vat, began to turn with a mechanical whir. Blood and serum raced along the glass and copper tubes strung between the seven white pods and looped back through the central dangling hook at the center of the wheel. Some other mechanism kicked in, and metal chains rose slowly from the vat, dripping black serum over the great skeleton as they pulled taut in a net of linked steel.

Below these layers of coils and gears and chains, in the pit of black tar, the bones of the megalosaurus moved together. Joints popped into sockets, enormous vertebrae arranging themselves in a neat curve. Tendons and veins coiled like vines on a trellis, knitting over and between the bones.

The metal chains stretched over the back of a long, rising neck, and the soft tissue followed, then the green-gray flesh, and the megalosaurus tried to stand. *Buckland always theorized it was a quadruped, but I think it's actually bipedal.*

That's how I realized my brain was in shock. The creature, pinned under the straining net of metal, opened his jaw and roared.

Lucy slammed into Edgar, taking him to the ground.

"You absolute idiot," she hissed, as she pinned him with an arm to the throat. "Mother would be *ashamed*."

Henry wrested the knife from Farnsworth, who fell against the wall. He cut Buckland and Elizabeth free.

And the megalosaurus writhed against its chains. It gnashed its great teeth. It roared, and it was like a tiger's—deep and shuddering in a way that pulled every hair on my arms to stand.

The nostrils were huge black pits at the end of a massive jaw, and the sharp teeth below curved like blades.

Those were teeth designed to rip at flesh. To tear at muscle. Saliva strung between them like spiderwebs, drops raining from its jaw as it gnashed in fury. I'd known, in theory, that megalosaurus was an enormous creature, but my brain could hardly comprehend the reality; if it rose up on those curved back legs, the beast would be at least twice my height.

The people in the pods should have been screaming as the monster woke. They should have been pulling the tubes and wires from their flesh and running for their lives. But the faces around the Loom were still vacant. Maybe it was for the best they were drugged; I could imagine at least a few would have suffered heart attacks if they were conscious.

"This is *for* Mother," Edgar choked out.

I hesitated, trying to decide what to do. Whom to help.

I ran to the pods, to one of the old men, wincing as my arms plunged into the sticky, viscous serum. I ripped the needles from his veins and left the tubes floating atop the black liquid. The wheel overhead stuttered.

I ran to the next pod and did the same, then a third. The machine hitched and whirred as it slowed.

I grinned in triumph.

Crack. One of the chains snapped. The great tail whipped around, narrowly missing my head as I ducked.

The beast thrashed and roared. It was still crouched, held low by the chains, but they were bulging, straining now. It shook its head and struck out with the fingerlike claws of its short front limbs, toward the wrestling Murrays. If those claws caught flesh, Edgar and Lucy would be torn in half.

"Mary!" Henry was in my ear, grabbing my shoulders. Another chain snapped, and the tail whipped again.

Mr. Farnsworth, now wobbling at Henry's heel, wasn't so lucky this time. He was caught in the midsection by the swing, tossed hard against a metal stand anchoring the pods. He slumped to the ground, blood pooling immediately from his temple.

"No!" Henry shouted, but I had no pity to spare for Mr. Farnsworth. I snatched up Ajax's cage and dashed aside as a clawed arm swept through the chains.

Lucy cried out, and I spun back to the Murrays. Edgar had escaped Lucy's hold and was scrambling toward the megalosaurus.

"Mary! The beast is breaking free!" Buckland shouted, grasping my elbow.

It was true. Chains snapped across the creature's straining neck and spine. Black serum poured over the edges of the vat in shining waves as it thrashed.

"Those people in the pods," Elizabeth exclaimed. "We have to get them out before it crushes them!"

"You do that, then," I snapped. "I'll stop Edgar. Buckland— with me?"

"Always," he said, and we ran together toward the megalosaurus as it rose and roared.

Chapter 56

THE BEAST'S HEAD CRASHED THROUGH THE SPOKES OF THE wheel overhead. Shattered glass and metal, blood and black serum, rained down as the monster shook its head, gnashing enormous white teeth. It stood on two thick hind legs, its long spine pitched forward. Two shorter forearms, armed with long claws, were the perfect height to swipe a man's head clean off.

Cold terror swept over me, numbing thoughts and limbs both.

"Ajax!" Henry called, ducking as he ran to avoid the slashing forearms. "Use Ajax!"

His voice broke through my fear. Of course. Ajax was a powerful reliq, Edgar said.

I reached out toward Ajax, and the golden warmth flooded my senses, so much power I thought it would burn out through my skin. I gathered it all, and I sent it out toward the megalosaurus's left hind leg. *Break,* I willed.

A crack of bone, and the megalosarus roared, stumbling. But it didn't fall.

The beast tried to turn, enraged and snarling, held back only by the remaining chains.

"Ed, no!" Lucy screamed, as Edgar stumbled between the pods, through the broken tubes and coils, and across the shining black pool of spilled serum. He hoisted himself into the raised vat, near the animal's hind leg.

Edgar slammed his hand against the back ankle of the beast and closed his eyes, muttering something I couldn't make out.

The megalosaurus went suddenly still, and a terrible silence filled the cavernous room. Bile rose in my throat as the creature's eyes went dead and black.

Edgar smiled, sweeping his gaze to meet my eye, continuing to Henry's, and finally settling on his sister's.

"*Libertas Magicae*," he whispered, and the ground began to shake.

I dove out of the way as a seam appeared in the earth, running down the center of the factory. Racing due south, for London. Glass and copper and iron rattled, and the wheel overhead swung precariously. The ground rippled, and I was thrown to my knees.

"Edgar! Edgar, stop!" I shouted.

That's when I saw Buckland, sliding behind the flank of the megalosaurus and climbing into the knee-deep vat of serum. His face was grim, his fists balled.

I caught my breath. *No.* No. Buckland was a scholar, not a fighter. His paunch bounced when he laughed, and his hair was gray and thinning. He was going to get himself killed. Edgar ignored it all. He was focused on the crack in the earth. On pushing it south. Toward London.

But Henry saw Buckland and understood. He ran toward the two men, swaying against the bucking earth.

The motion finally alerted Edgar to Buckland, wading

through the black liquid. The professor lunged. Edgar swung out with his free hand, the other clasped tight to the megalosaurus's ankle.

"Stop, Edgar!" Lucy screamed, as she tried to catch her balance. "Please!"

A crack arched and branched across the plaster ceiling. Buckland slammed into Edgar, and a support beam above broke loose. It fell with a sickening crash, just missing Elizabeth and the unconscious man she was dragging toward the door by his ankles.

With another blow, Buckland knocked Edgar off-balance, and he lost hold of the creature's flesh.

I screamed. Now free of Edgar's spell, the monster roared and reared up. There were hardly any chains now, and those were snapping by the second. The remaining ones strained. The links disconnecting. Metal flying.

The wheel above, dangling overhead, groaned as its holding beam snapped at last. The spinning heart of the Loom fell in a shower of plaster and wood, metal and glass, cracking across the megalosaurus's back. The great lizard bellowed. Edgar looked up. Buckland cried out. I screamed.

The wheel struck. The two men tumbled together in a tangle of wheel spokes and limbs, over the edge of the black tar pit. And neither rose.

I couldn't pause. Edgar was either unconscious or dead, but the earth still trembled. A metal hook had carved a deep gash in the flank of the megalosaurus, and it was raging and wild.

"Mary! No!" Henry said.

"Help them," I said, and shook him off, gesturing toward the crumpled forms of Edgar and Buckland.

I clambered into the vat, dodging raking claws and rattling chains. The black liquid was a knee-deep sludge.

I reached for the megalosaurus. My hands roved over pebbled gray-green skin. I drew its magic into my core as I would a reliq's.

And with that power—like an endless, endless sea, lapping at my thoughts—I could see the land above and around us, as if I were a bird in flight. I could see the Glasswater Mill, a red mark in the green, and then the River Thames, running to London, and the crack in the earth tracing parallel, rushing and racing, splitting the ground in two.

Stop now, I told it softly. *That's far enough,* and I swear I felt the earth sigh.

I came back to the room, still brimming with gold and power. Edgar was right. This must be how God felt. Too full of power to doubt.

I looked around at the chaos, breathing hard.

Maybe Edgar wasn't completely crazy. It would be good to have more witches. To have magic freed from reliqs and serums and slickers. No earthquake, though—surely all I had to do was wish it. Will it. And it would be so, like any old, conventional magic. A little prayer. I would just—

"Mary. Mary?" Lucy was there now, looking up at me. "I think Buckland is—" She sobbed, and I released the power, and shrank back to myself. My own small self again.

Lucy knelt at their side, her finger on Buckland's pulse. Elizabeth wept softly, holding her father's hand.

The megalosaurus turned its long neck to look back at me, its beady amber eyes curious and confused. I walked forward and put a hand on its broken leg, as far up as I could reach.

"Sleep well," I managed to croak out, and then I ran as the bones tumbled down.

Lucy tried to wipe the faces clean, but the sticky serum clung to every wrinkle.

I should have waited. I should have waited—I could have used the megalosaurus as a reliq to heal Buckland. Stupid, stupid, *stupid.*

I crouched next to Buckland and Edgar. Blood pooled around their heads, but I couldn't tell whose it was. I looked at Lucy.

"Buckland's," she whispered.

"And Edgar?"

"Only unconscious." Her voice was thick. "But I have no power for Buckland. The tea is still blocking my magic."

I looked around. "Where is Henry?"

"Gone."

It hurt more than I expected. But I had no time for heartbreak.

"I'm sorry," Elizabeth said, when I looked at her hopefully. "That horrible man took our reliqs when he tied us up."

So, they had no magic, either. Except—

"Oh, God. Ajax!"

I raced to his cage, through the torn earth and field of bones. The aviary had fallen on its side, and Ajax was curled up, limp. I dashed away tears as I took him out, holding him to my breast.

Henry had said I'd used up the other living reliqs—that was why they died. I sobbed and stroked him, and he purred, weakly, shifting against my chest.

I'd pulled too much of Ajax when I'd woken the megalosaurus. I'd done this. I'd used him. And I would use him again.

My heart shattered as I stroked down Ajax's spine. I sobbed harder as I carried him back, dread and sorrow thick in my throat.

Elizabeth knelt at her father's side, murmuring comforting

words. I felt like I was going to die, my heart ached so much. Buckland was alive, but barely. I only knew because Lucy had her fingers on his pulse. The professor looked a corpse, otherwise.

"I'm so sorry," I said, and I kissed Ajax's beak. He slowly swung his head to look at me. "I'm so sorry, so, so sorry. I love you so much. I love you."

I couldn't stop sobbing. But what choice did I have? I couldn't let Buckland die. Even if it meant—

I couldn't stomach the thought. I closed my eyes, and I reached for Ajax.

"Here."

My eyes snapped open. Henry crouched in front of me. He opened my palm, and I closed my fingers around a trilobite.

"It will be enough for both of them."

I nodded, chin wobbling, and dashed away my tears.

Heal them, please, I willed, and I prayed.

Chapter 57

I'M NOT SURE ONE EVER GETS USED TO SITTING ACROSS FROM the archbishop of Canterbury. Maybe even worse, Chief Inquisitor Bishop Price sat beside him.

The archbishop's face was solemn, and I could read little but weariness as I told my tale. And the truth this time: that I'd resurrected Ajax through some sort of witchery, likely granted to me by the lightning strike in my infancy. That I could—*had*—done the same to other fossilized creatures.

"I . . . see," the archbishop said when I finished. He looked at Buckland, seated beside me. "So all your bold talk of hibernation, and divine cycles of resurrection . . ."

"I was hasty," said Buckland. "And too proud by far." His soft voice cracked. "If I had truly listened to Mary—or given Henry Stanton's theory of species change the consideration it deserved—"

"We would have hanged Miss Anning that same night," Bishop Price said, in the kindest voice I'd ever heard him use. "Professor Buckland, if you'd come to us with a girl who could raise fossils, nothing could have saved her, whether she passed the inquisition or not." He looked at me with so much pity, I thought I might weep.

I swallowed. And to think I'd almost convinced myself that it wouldn't have been so bad to tell the truth.

"And now?" I managed, in a weak voice.

The archbishop leaned back, exhaling and rubbing at his brow. He was quiet for a long, long time.

"Now, having examined the evidence you provided, I am sufficiently convinced that witchery such as yours is a natural condition. A blessing, even."

I bowed my head; it sounded like a benediction.

Henry Stanton had vanished after I healed Buckland and Ajax. He hadn't been seen since.

But I still had the key to his house. I'd taken the research—maps and books and pages of notes on witches and natural catastrophes—and provided it to the archbishop.

That wasn't the only thing we'd handed over, though. Edgar was currently convalescing in the heresy suite, under zealous Inquisitor watch.

"And yet, it must be secret," Price said.

"For now, at least," the archbishop added soothingly, before Buckland or I could object. "Until such time as we can determine more about the dangers of the witchery you've uncovered."

"You mean until you determine whether other witches can use living beings as reliqs," I said.

"Yes," the archbishop said reluctantly.

It was the first thing Buckland and I realized when we formed this plan.

What if there truly were witches who could resurrect people, as I did the fossils? And, more terrifying, could those revived humans also be used as reliqs?

Exactly as the old legends about witches claimed. *Vampyrism de l'âme.* The stealing of souls for magic.

"It would throw us right back to the witch hunts," Bishop Price said sharply. "And I have vowed: never again. The Inquisitors are better than that."

The archbishop nodded. "If it got out, we would have a schism. Or worse, a civil war. Even if we managed to avoid all that—and I do not think we would, given the precarious state of things already."

People were already calling it the Black Morning. Reports were that twelve people had died in the citywide clashes between military and protestors. Blood still stained the streets, and the wind still smelled of ash when it blew from the east.

But then, in the midst of the violence, the earth itself had trembled in fury. A divine warning, it was said. An unsteady peace lingered. But it wouldn't last forever.

The archbishop and Price were right. If we sowed suspicion of necromancy, of the resurrected dead? Of witches using living reliqs? It would be like pouring gunpowder on flame.

I weighed all these truths against the lie—a lie of omission, still a lie—and the cost of the truth was more death than I was prepared to accept. Was this always how it felt, to hold the world's secrets? It made my shoulders ache.

Buckland caught my eye. It was time. Still, I hesitated. I'm only human. Of course I hesitated.

It had been my idea, but that didn't make it any less awful to say aloud. To make it real.

"That's why it has to be a hoax," I said softly. "Ajax. That's the only way forward that I can see. We will say he was a toucan—or maybe a puffin—that I altered with glue and paint. It will be believable enough."

The archbishop straightened, his eyes widening. "Maybe to the crowds who saw him from afar. But what about your own Society members? They will know better." He turned to Buckland. "And would they believe you were deceived? They'll know it wasn't a hoax."

"The Society fellows can keep a secret," Buckland said meaningfully, "if it serves Her Majesty's purpose."

They would be bound to, in fact, if it was written into the bylaws. And Buckland had been elected president now, in Henry's mysterious absence; he could see it done.

"Hen—Mr. Stanton and Viscount Merlton worked out that Ajax served as a reliq easily enough. Others will, too," I said softly.

My friends—Mantell and Goldsmild—they would know the truth, at least. They would know I had not deceived them. I took solace in that. But they would never be able to defend me. To tell the truth. The sorcery would hold their tongues if they tried.

The archbishop's gaze sharpened. "Be that as it may. Your reputations will be ruined. All the good work we've done together. Tarnished. This will injure the Church, too."

I bit my lip, but Bishop Price shook his head. "And yet, I cannot see another way, Your Grace."

"Perhaps it is for the best," Buckland said quietly. His hands were folded neatly, and he was looking at the stained-glass window. Christ, bent with his cross on his shoulder. "I thought that if I drew the lines neatly enough between the Bible and geomagic, it could erase all doubt. But I have stretched the truth to do so, and those lines have blurred.

"Perhaps at some point we must let people decide what to believe, and trust they are wise enough to hold two things at once and find truth where they will."

The archbishop frowned. "I don't like it."

"None of us do," I muttered, and at least that made him laugh. The laughter turned into a sigh, and then I knew. He had agreed.

"I will have to give you both a very public chastising. Are you prepared for that, Miss Anning? Are you, Buckland? You will be stripped of your chaplaincy, and your post at Oxford, too."

His face paled, but he nodded. "I am prepared."

Buckland would have to step down from the presidency, after it was done. We would both resign from the Society.

Even if the Society knew or suspected that Ajax hadn't been a hoax, the rest of the world's geomagicians wouldn't understand why the propagators of said hoax were still members in good standing of the Geomagical Society of London. They would start asking questions. No. For this plan to work, we had to be completely, utterly disgraced.

"There is one condition," I said, clearing my throat.

Buckland spun. He knew very well we hadn't discussed any conditions.

The archbishop raised his brow. I swallowed.

"Whether you approve of their methods or not, the Prometheans have a point. I would urge you, Your Grace, to hear them out. Meet with their leaders, at least. Because the reliq system is cruel, and unfair." I took a deep breath. "Trust me. I have sold magic myself, in desperate times."

Bishop Price made a small sound of surprise. I wondered when either of these great churchmen had last spoken with someone who'd traded magic in the slicks.

"I certainly don't have the answers," I continued. "Higher rates, or reform, or destroying the system altogether. But what I do know, I know from the Proverbs, as my father taught me: *'Whoever oppresses the poor shows contempt for their Maker, but whoever is kind to the needy honors God,'*" I quoted meaningfully.

I was shaking when I finished. Who was I to recite scripture at the archbishop?

But he looked thoughtful. "I confess your words strike at my heart, Miss Anning. I agree to your terms. I will meet with their leaders."

I managed to untangle my tongue to thank him, and we rose from our seats, the business concluded. The archbishop shook my hand, and then put his other hand over both of ours.

"I doubt we will see each other again, Miss Anning, but please know . . ." He smiled, sadly, kindly, and I felt again that old pang of loss for my father, who had smiled like that, too. "You will be in my prayers, always." He patted my hand, and then he turned to Buckland. "Come, my old friend. Let us have one more drink before I defrock you."

I wasn't sure if I was supposed to follow them, but Bishop Price lingered. "The martyr's path is a noble one, but lonely," he murmured.

I stayed quiet, politely looking where he did, at the stained glass.

"The Inquisitors will be on high alert for signs of this fossil-magic, or bone-magic," he continued. "If we do hear of any, perhaps you might be willing to consult on such a case?"

I looked at the Inquisitor, startled, but pleased.

"I would be glad to consult," I said quickly. I had resigned myself to ignorance when I handed over Henry's research; the mysteries of witchery and natural magic would be unraveled by others, I'd assumed.

But I was still a scientist. And Lord knows, I couldn't resist an unanswered question.

"Please do contact me if any such case arises. I would be very pleased to consult on the matter."

Chapter 58

I TRIED ONE LAST TIME TO CONVINCE BUCKLAND TO LET ME take the fall alone. We were standing on his doorstep, and the coach was waiting. Ajax was already stashed in his birdcage.

There was nothing left for me in London. I'd set the fossils at Henry's back to stone, and Buckland helped me return each to their drawers and cabinets. I only cried a little.

I looked around anxiously, up and down the street. Lucy was late. But my ship was set to leave within the hour, and I couldn't linger any longer.

I hugged Catherine and the girls. I held Elizabeth extra tightly.

"Thank you," I choked thickly, into her ear. She looked concerned I'd lost my mind, but I just shrugged.

And then they slipped inside to give me a moment of privacy with Buckland.

"Think of your girls," I said, blinking quickly. "They don't deserve this. When you go to Palmanaeus House tomorrow, tell them it was me. Only me. Or blame Henry. Lord knows, he's not around to say otherwise."

He shook his head. His chin wobbled. "You know why that won't work, Mary."

"But—"

"Hush," he said, and he took my face between his hands. "Hush, now."

I exhaled. "What will you do next?"

"My penance." Buckland's chest rose and fell with a sigh. "I'm afraid we'll have to admit that Henry Stanton may have been on the right track regarding the nature of species change. Or at least," he muttered, "he was more correct that I."

I chuckled, but it turned to a quiet sob. I squeezed my eyes shut and felt Buckland's lips on my forehead, the scratch of his gray stubble.

"I would never presume I could take the place of your father," he said hoarsely, "but I hope that you know I think of you as one of my daughters, my dear. And you will always have a home here, with us. If you want it."

I flung myself against his chest.

"Damn you, Buckland," I sobbed. "Now I'm crying."

"And I love you, too, Mary."

The coach was already rolling, horses walking at a quick clip toward the river, when I heard Lucy calling.

"Mary!"

"Stop, please!" I called to the driver as I flung open the door.

Lucy clambered up, breathing hard. She took and squeezed my hand.

"You can go on," she called out, and the coach lurched forward. Then to me, she said, "I'm sorry I'm late. The London council received a summons from the archbishop, if you can believe it.

To discuss our grievances. It's a good thing, Mary. I think he might really listen to us."

I smiled. "That's great, Luce."

Her chest rose and fell quickly. Sorrow, or maybe regret, flickered over her face.

"And Edgar... do you know..."

"The archbishop said he's healing well," I said gently. "But he couldn't say what would happen next."

Edgar's sorcery should have earned a death sentence. But he was a viscount, with powerful allies. Lucy and I both hoped he might dodge the executioner's blade. Whatever his crimes, he was still our Ed.

Lucy blinked quickly, then glanced down and shook her head. "I'm sorry again. That I can't come home with you."

It was my turn to squeeze her hand. "Hush. We both know you belong here. You have work to do, still."

Her eyes were warm but liquid. "But are you sure you'll be okay?"

"No," I said honestly. London was rolling by, out the window. I was eager to see the last of it, I realized. I was eager to be home. In the salt air and the whipping wind, with the cliffs at my back. "But I will be."

Maybe the good people of Lyme Regis had heard about a pterodactyl. Maybe they heard it was all revealed to be a hoax, concocted with some Oxford don. Maybe a few—one, maybe two, or three, or more—even noted it coincided with my absence from town. But if they knew, it didn't change a thing.

I closed Anning's Fossil Depot. It would only draw attention; locals might not care about the goings-on in London, but tourists hunting fossils were exactly the type who might remember my name.

Once, I would have killed for that. Now, I only wanted to be forgotten.

―――∽◎∽―――

Buckland had quietly arranged for me to receive the fellows' stipend, and the archbishop made provisions as well.

I rented a small house above the cliffs. One bedroom and a large fireplace. Lucy had the right idea, I decided: a clean, quiet house of your own, far from town. A place to think, and sometimes cry.

I spent a few nights curled up on the small, rickety bed, stroking Ajax's chest, the wind battering the windows.

I knew what I had to do. I just didn't want to do it.

―――∽◎∽―――

I went at sunrise, when I was sure the beach would be empty. Ajax hopped behind me, curious, then went happily into my satchel while I climbed up to the cave mouth.

He ran ahead, cawing cheerfully. I wiped my tears before crawling after him.

He was waiting at the end of the tunnel. The stone of the floor was loose and churned where I'd turned it up to get out his mother's skeleton.

He'll be alone, I thought. My lip quivered.

I patted the spot beside me, and Ajax loped over obediently.

"You're a good boy," I whispered. "You're the best pterodactyl that there ever was." I kissed his head, and then his stupid, colorful, toothy beak, and he watched me with curious golden eyes.

"Thank you," I said, my chest shaking now with silent sobs. "I will never forget you."

I stretched out my hand, and Ajax pressed his head right into my palm, the way he always did when he wanted to be scratched. I closed my eyes.

Chapter 59

My head ached from crying. The sky was gray. Dark. A storm was rolling in. I could taste it in the air off the sea.

I stopped outside my house.

Henry Stanton was standing on my doorstep.

"Hello, Mary."

"I assumed you'd vanished forever." I folded my arms. I hated him. I loved him. I wanted to kiss him. I wanted to throttle him. Damn, damned, damnable Henry Stanton. "Did us all a favor, I thought."

Ajax fluttered down to land on my shoulder. I glared at Henry defiantly.

"You kept him," he said, and I knew he was trying to hide a smile.

"I don't know what you're talking about," I said flatly. "This is a puffin."

"Of course." The wind caught his coat, and it swirled around his legs.

"Why are you here?" I glared. "Oh, wait. It doesn't matter what you say, I know now that everything you say is a lie. All that talk about truth-telling, while you manipulated me. Used me. Planned it for *fifteen years*, isn't that right?" I snorted.

"I'm not here to seek your forgiveness, Mary," he said. "You're right. I lied, and I used you. I know I don't deserve that absolution after the things I've done. But I'm here because I—well, I found these when I searched Edgar's house."

He reached into the satchel and pulled out a stack of letters, bound in blue ribbon.

I took them, despite myself. My fingers trembled, running over faded handwriting. Mine. Henry's.

"The letters," I breathed.

"I always wondered why you stopped writing," he said. "I sent you so many. I begged you to answer. I didn't even care if you wanted to break our engagement, I wrote; I only wanted to know that you were well. And yet. Nothing. Eventually, I had to accept that you'd changed your mind."

"Edgar," I whispered. I pulled the bundle of letters to my chest unconsciously. "But why?"

Henry's gray eyes flashed fury. "I suspect he considered you a distraction. From our work together."

He had written. Henry had written. All those years, I thought he'd abandoned me, and he thought the same. My torn heart mended, just a little.

I didn't know if I should forgive him. He'd lied so many times. Lied, and lied, and lied.

But he had written.

"This doesn't change anything," I said abruptly. "You can't come inside."

"Of course. One other thing, and I'll be on my way." He pulled a large lacquered box from his satchel. Nestled in purple velvet was a pterodactyl skull. Fangs jutted out of both the top and bottom of the beak, the longest of which was the size of my smallest finger.

"Charles Lyell had this sent to you at Palmanaeus House," Henry exclaimed. "Lyell couldn't convince the collector, a Bavarian geomagician, to sell the original specimen, but he agreed to have a cast made to compare with Ajax."

I practically quivered with excitement as Henry handed me the box. The skull was of similar size to Ajax's, but the fangs were significantly longer, and the way they interlocked reminded me of a bear trap. I couldn't wait to measure the eye sockets. They looked larger than Ajax's, too.

"Well." Henry dipped his head. "That was all I wanted—"

"You can come back tomorrow," I blurted out, clutching the box to my chest. "If you'd like. Though you're still on stoop privileges."

Henry's grin was like the sun. "Then I'll see you tomorrow."

―――⁂―――

Later, I sat down at my desk and inked my quill to start the letter I'd been putting off.

Dear Mrs. Davies, Mrs. Mantell, and Mrs. Murchison,

You once asked if I would teach you. I declined, at the time, for reasons that would shame me now.

I am hoping you can forgive that offense and consider my proposal. Not that I teach you, but rather, that perhaps we might learn from one another.

In that spirit, I must humbly admit that Mrs. Davies's the-

ory about plesiosaur ambush hunting patterns may have some merit—

Ajax fluttered his wings and knocked over my pot of ink. I swore and chased him off, muttering under my breath as the ink spread quickly across my paper. I sighed. I would just have to start again.

The Geomagician Duology will conclude in book two,

The PALEOMANCER

Acknowledgments

A megalosaurus-sized thank you to my agent, Melanie Figueroa, and my editors, Tricia Narwani and Sam Bradbury, for the enthusiasm, insight, and guidance. I couldn't imagine a better publishing team.

And to every reader who took a chance on this book: thank you. May your phone always stay charged and your coffee never spill.

My endless gratitude to all the talented folks who've turned my Word document into a real book: Sara Bereta, Lydia Blagden, Marcelle Iten Busto, Lily Capewell, Keith Clayton, Richard Elman, Maya Fenter, Regina Flath, Paul Gilbert, Alice Gomer, Kirsten Greenwood, Ashleigh Heaton, Scott Heim, Tori Henson, Beccy Jones, Rachel Kennedy, Alex Larned, Julie Leung, Issie Levin, Aarushi Menon, Feranmi Ojutiku, Kay Popple, Barbora Sabolova, Scott Shannon, Sabrina Shen, Ayesha Shibli, Robert Siek, Armando Veve, Sophie Wingrove, and so many others. Thank you to Heather Baror for finding this story homes around the world, and to Stacy Jenson, Gabrielle Greenstein, and everyone at Root Literary.

This book exists because of the family and friends who read my other projects (now locked in my hard drive) and said, keep going. Dad, who read Tolkien and Lewis to me and sparked this dream. Mom, whose faith—and faith in me—is a lighthouse. Thank you, Meg and Caroline: from playing pretend to writing books, I'm unbelievably grateful you're my teammates. To my girls: thank you for sharing Mama with the laptop.

My Davidson & DC crew: Camila, Caroline, Emily, Leslie, and Morgan. I love you guys so much.

My author friends: Kalie Cassidy, Roselyn Clarke, Annika Cosgrove, Dani Cessna, Rob Hart, Carly Jonathan, Jennifer Knox, Lisa Majeska, and A.J. Van Belle. I can't believe I'm lucky enough to know such genius writers.

My dear book club friends, On the Rise Artisan Breads, Phoenix Coffee, Rising Star Coffee, and my spectacular in-laws, Mark and Kathy: thanks for making Cleveland such a great place to live and write.

To my husband, Stephen, who has always believed in me. Thank you for helping me build a life with space and time to write, and dream. I love you. And thanks be to God—who I firmly believe appreciates a good theomagical debate—for His grace.

About the Author

Jennifer Mandula lives in Cleveland, Ohio, with her husband, three daughters, and a neurotic corgi. She first learned of the historical Mary Anning while studying for her master's in education at the University of Oxford. In her spare time, she visits local bakeries and plans her next escape to the beach. *The Geomagician* is her debut novel.

jennifermandula.com
jennifermandula.substack.com
Instagram: @jennifermandula

About the Type

This book was set in Caslon, a typeface first designed in 1722 by William Caslon (1692–1766). Its widespread use by most English printers in the early eighteenth century soon supplanted the Dutch typefaces that had formerly prevailed. The roman is considered a "workhorse" typeface due to its pleasant, open appearance, while the italic is exceedingly decorative.